THE QUESTION

by

ZENA WYNN

© 2016

A Real Love Enterprises Publication

The Question
ISBN-13: 978-1537042176
ISBN-10: 1537042173

Copyright © July 2016 by Zena Wynn
Cover art: Shirley Burnett
Original copyright 2009 by Zena Wynn
eBook ISBN-13: 978-1-60659-174-1
First Edition – July, 2009
Second Edition – August 2016

This book is a work of fiction and any resemblance to persons, living or dead, or places, events or locales is purely coincidental. The characters are productions of the authors' imagination and used fictitiously.

Content Warning: This book contains sexually explicit scenes and adult language and may be considered offensive to some readers. Please store your files wisely, where they cannot be accessed by under-aged readers.

Printed in the United States of America

Dedication

The Bible is an awesome book full of rich, vibrant history, and real, wonderful people; a source of great inspiration. A special thanks to Bishop TD Jakes for making the story of Abraham, Sarah, and Hagar come alive in a way that I'll never forget.

Chapter One

"Will you have my baby?"

Gail Henderson abruptly began to loudly choke on her iced tea. All around her conversations ceased as they became the center of attention. As she coughed and wheezed with tears streaming down her eyes, she squinted at her best friend. Crystal Jabbar sat, calm as you please, as though she hadn't just dropped what amounted to a nuclear bomb into the conversation.

They were seated at a table in Golden Corral, sharing lunch after a hectic morning of Christmas shopping. The holiday was only a few weeks away. The place was packed as usual. The other diners slowly turned their attention to their own tables when Gail glared. Since no one had offered their assistance, she knew they were just being nosey.

"I've given this a lot of thought. You know I can't have children. If you had one for me, I would have the best of both worlds—a child created by the man I love more than anything and my best friend, who is like a sister to me," her friend continued.

Crystal had been pregnant several times. Each one had ended in miscarriage, the last almost taking her life. Afterwards her husband, Rashid, put his foot down. No more pregnancies. Crystal told Gail he'd threatened to get a vasectomy before allowing her to risk her life again in another pregnancy attempt, and she'd reluctantly complied with his decree. Gail thought Crystal had resigned herself to her barren state, but apparently not.

"What do you mean, have a baby for you?" she cautiously asked, blotting the tears from her eyes and face.

Crystal leaned forward in her chair, her gaze intent. "I want you to be my surrogate. I've been looking into it. Rashid would be its father, and we'd use your eggs. Once the baby was born, I'd adopt it, making me its legal mother and as my best friend, you'd naturally be its godmother."

Gail pushed back a few inches from the table, unconsciously trying to place more distance between them. "Isn't this kind of drastic? I thought you were considering adoption," she asked a bit desperately.

Crystal frowned. "I did, but that's not for me. I want a child of my own. At the very least, I want a child fathered by Rashid. You know how important family is to him. Do you really think he'd be satisfied with an adopted child?"

Rashid Al Jabbar was an Arab-American and his behavior was strongly influenced by the male-dominated culture in which he grew up. Because of his heritage, family and children meant a great deal to him. "Crystal, you know that's not fair to Rashid. He loves you. If you wanted to adopt, he would go along with it just because it made you happy."

A brilliant smile lit Crystal's face. "Yes, he does love me, doesn't he? That's why I want this so much. I need to give him the child he so desperately desires. Hopefully, it will be a son to carry on his family name." Crystal reached out and gripped Gail's hand. "Gail, please. You're my best friend in the world. There's no one else I would trust to do this for me."

Gail pulled her hand free and motioned between the two of them. "Crystal, look at us. We look nothing alike. Don't you at least want someone who is similar in appearance to you?"

Crystal was a short, curvy, natural blonde with pretty brown eyes. Gail was tall and slender with skin the color of nutmeg. Not only did they not resemble each other, they were from two different ethnic groups.

5

Crystal was Caucasian while Gail was African-American.

Her friend airily waved her hand. "Pshh. You know I don't care about things like that. Besides, who would know? Rashid is almost as dark as you." It was true. Rashid had the dark, olive-brown complexion of a Middle Eastern man.

Gail could feel herself caving. It's not that she didn't want to help her friend. She just had a bad feeling about it, and over the years, she'd learned to trust her instincts. She took in Crystal's pleading expression. "Have you discussed this with Rashid?" It was a last ditch effort to avoid the inevitable. She'd never been able to say no to Crystal, and Crystal knew it.

Crystal leaned forward again, determination showing in her eyes. "He'll agree. Don't worry. How could he not? This is a win-win situation."

Win-win for whom? Gail wondered. Then she sighed, knowing Crystal was right about Rashid. Crystal had him wrapped around her little pinky. "I'm not saying yes, but I'm not saying no. Let me look into it. Do a little research. This is too big of a decision to make on the spur of the moment."

Crystal squealed, causing the other diners to turn and stare—again. She got up from her seat and ran around to hug Gail. "Thank you, thank you, thank you."

Gail returned her hug but inwardly a feeling of dread grew. She was going to say yes. She always did but she sensed this time, the results would be disastrous.

◆ ◆ ◆ ◆ ◆

As promised, Gail spent the next few weeks researching Artificial Insemination and surrogate mothers. She had a much better understanding of what she'd be getting herself into if she proved crazy enough to agree to Crystal's scheme.

The problem was she and Crystal had a long history together. It went all the way back to junior high school when they'd first met in Mr. Peterson's third period gym class. They'd clicked, despite their obvious differences.

Gail had been the serious, studious one. The straight A student who always had a book in her hands and sat in the corner reading. She'd been on the debate team and the student council, and had even spent time working on the student newspaper.

Crystal had been a social butterfly who'd coasted through life on her looks and charm. She'd been a cheerleader and had won prom queen two years straight in high school. She'd studied and kept her grades just high enough to prevent being placed on academic suspension.

Being so different, they should have never become friends. Yet those very differences are what held them together. Gail had caused Crystal to be more serious, and Crystal had help Gail be more lighthearted. Somehow they'd maintained their close friendship, despite attending two different colleges, several hours away from each other. It was happenstance that they'd both ended up relocating to the same city after graduation. Crystal had married first, having met Rashid in college. Gail had met and married Jason a couple of years later. The two couples had interacted frequently, mainly due to the close friendship of the women.

Crystal rejoiced with her when Gail had discovered she was pregnant, and cried with her three years later when she'd lost both her husband and their son, Marcus, in a fatal car accident. That had been two years ago. She and Crystal had supported each other through every crisis, sharing the laughter and the tears.

Crystal had always been there for Gail in her time of need. How could she do any less for Crystal now?

◆◆◆◆◆

Gail traveled home to Alabama to spend Christmas with her parents, still no closer to a decision. The holidays were always rough. She couldn't help thinking about Jason and Marcus, and what Christmas morning would have been like if they were still alive. Having family around helped her get through the season without depression overwhelming her.

Christmas day was boisterous as usual. All of her brothers managed to make it home with their wives, the last one arriving early that morning just in time to exchange gifts. Later in the evening when everyone had finally left, her father pulled her into his study. "So, you want to tell me what's bothering you, baby girl? You've been mighty quiet all day."

She debated for all of a second the wisdom of saying anything, but her father had always been her confidant. "Crystal asked me to be a surrogate for her and Rashid, using my eggs."

"Well, now…" Her father settled his large, burly frame into his leather recliner and stroked his chin. "That's quite a favor to be asking. Which way you leaning?"

Gail settled on the floor next to him and laid her head on his knee. He immediately began stroking her hair. "I don't know. I feel for her, Dad, wanting a child so desperately, but I'm not sure this is the way. My gut tells me doing this would be a terrible mistake."

"But…?"

"We've been friends for so long. She's always been there for me. Can I honestly deny her?" Gail looked up at him.

8

Her father brushed her bangs off her forehead. "True, you two go way back, but sometimes, you have to trust your instincts and look out for number one. You've already lost one child. Can you handle losing two?"

"But this baby wouldn't really be mine," she protested, not knowing whom she tried to convince—her father or herself.

He arched one single eyebrow. "Blood will tell. It will grow in your body and have your DNA. And what about your mother and I? You weren't the only one affected by the loss of Marcus. He was our first, and only, grandchild. Now you're considering giving away another?"

She hadn't factored her parents' feelings into her decision. Gail thought for a minute and bit her lower lip. "So you're saying I shouldn't do this?"

"I'm saying it takes a strong woman to give away her own flesh and blood. Maybe your love for Crystal will carry you through. I don't know, but think very carefully before committing to do this. Some decisions, once made, can't be undone."

His words stayed with her a long time.

◆ ◆ ◆ ◆ ◆

The first of the year arrived and Gail knew she had to make up her mind. A month had passed, and it really wasn't fair to Crystal to put it off any longer. So, having made her decision, she invited Crystal and Rashid over to her apartment for dinner. For food, she'd gone with the basics—steak, baked potatoes, and salad, knowing from experience neither Rashid nor Crystal ate pork.

When they arrived, she opened the door and invited them in. Crystal searched her face anxiously, trying to see if the answer to her question was imprinted there. Gail kept her expression as impassive as possible.

9

Though she had decided, there were still questions to be asked and details to be worked out. Crystal floated past in a floral chiffon dress that emphasized her femininity. Rashid looked as debonair as ever in a pair of black dress slacks and black dress shirt.

After a quick glance at his face, Gail looked away from him and focused her attention on Crystal. Though she'd known the man for almost ten years now, something about him still made her uncomfortable. She was considered tall for a female, standing five-nine in her stocking feet, but Rashid towered over her by a good six inches. He was starkly handsome with features that were rugged, harsh even, bringing to mind desert sheiks and tales of Arabian Nights. His hair was the blue-black of the deepest, darkest black, thick with a glossy sheen evident even with his short cut.

"Come in. You want to eat first and then talk, or talk and then eat?" Gail left the choice up to them.

"Oh, talk definitely. What you're cooking smells heavenly, but I won't be able to eat a bite until I know," Crystal said decisively.

Rashid, as usual, said nothing, willing to go along with whatever pleased his wife.

Gail led them into the living room and sat in the recliner while motioning them to the couch. After they were all seated, she turned to Rashid. "I've given it a lot of thought, but I have a few questions to ask before finalizing my decision."

Crystal sat rigid on the edge of her seat, hands fisted on her lap. Rashid was a bit more relaxed, but just as intent in his focus on Gail. "What would you like to know?"

"The first thing I need to know is, are you in total agreement with this plan? Is this something you really want to do? Because once we start, there will be no going back." She linked her fingers together and lowered her

10

hands onto her lap in an effort not to betray her nervousness.

Rashid gave her question the serious thought it deserved. "I have reservations, naturally, but I've given it careful consideration. If you two ladies are willing, I'll go along. I know Crystal has her heart set on this course of action."

"You know what's involved? All the testing that needs to be done to both of us and the legalities to be ironed out?" Gail wanted to be absolutely sure he knew what he was getting into.

"Yes, I've researched everything and spoken to both my lawyers and personal physician. I know what's involved. Do you?" He continued to watch her closely.

Gail nodded. "As much as I can without having actually gone through the experience myself. Crystal, are you sure this is what you want to do? A child is serious business. You can't change your mind midstream and decide you made a mistake once I'm pregnant. This is going to have a tremendous impact upon all of our lives."

Crystal nodded emphatically. "Yes, I know what I want. I've given it a lot of thought and research. I won't change my mind."

Gail heaved a big sigh and swiped her bangs out of her eyes. She prayed she was doing the right thing. Crystal could be flighty at times, but she seemed to genuinely have considered all of the ramifications and still wanted to proceed. "If you are sure, then I'll do it."

Crystal bounded off the couch and rushed over to Gail, pulled her out of the seat, and hugged her tight. Then she began dancing around, so excited she couldn't contain herself. "I'm gonna have a baby. I'm gonna have a baby," she sang. Her happiness was contagious.

Gail couldn't help but smile at her antics despite her personal misgivings. She happened to glance at Rashid to see what his reaction was to all this. He was

11

looking directly at her, not his wife, and the expression on his face sent a frisson of nerves tingling down her spine. Feeling like a specimen under a microscope, she quickly returned her attention to her friend.

When Crystal calmed down, they went into the dining room to eat. The meal was a lighthearted affair with the food being well received. As they were leaving, Rashid told her he would make all the arrangements and call her when it was time to meet with the lawyer. She agreed and closed the door behind them as they left, feeling like she'd just made the biggest mistake of her life.

♦ ♦ ♦ ♦ ♦

While Rashid listened with half an ear to his wife's ramblings about her plans for the baby, his thoughts centered on Gail. Though she'd agreed to Crystal's request, he sensed she had as many reservations as he about the whole deal. It was nothing he could put his finger on, just a feeling no good would come of this.

He'd resigned himself to being childless. He loved Crystal and hated seeing how her desire to make a family with him ate away at her. He'd agreed with this plan because he wanted to see her happy again. After the last miscarriage, she had sunk into a depression from which she'd never fully recovered. He knew she felt defective, as though she was less of a woman because she couldn't bear him the children they so desired.

Watching her almost bleed out had killed any wish he had lurking in his heart for a child birthed with his DNA. His wife was more important to him than any baby she could ever produce, but she didn't seem to understand. Hence, this plan of hers.

He had nothing against Gail. She was a good woman who had been through a lot. Her husband,

Jason, had been a good friend, and Rashid still mourned his loss. He had made it a point to keep an eye out for Gail's wellbeing, just as he knew Jason would have done for him had their situation been reversed. He knew his wife well. She wasn't the most sensitive of beings. It would be up to him to make sure Gail didn't get hurt and was well taken care of during this process. She'd been through enough.

◆◆◆◆◆

After their meeting, things proceeded rather quickly. They met with the lawyer and the terms of the agreement shocked Gail so much she almost backed out. In addition to covering all legal and medical fees, which she expected, Rashid would pay all of her living expenses for the duration of her pregnancy, and the eight week recovery period after the delivery. Plus, he'd promised to invest an amount equal to her yearly salary into her stock portfolio, which his firm handled.

"It's too much," she argued. "Is this even legal?"

"These are my terms," Rashid said, refusing to budge.

Sensing Gail was ready to withdraw from their agreement, Crystal stood suddenly, reached down, grabbed Gail by the arm and pulled her from the room. As soon as the office door closed behind them, she pleaded, "Gail, please don't make a big deal out of this. Accept Rashid's offer. It's the least we can to recompense you for what you're willing to do for us, and it's not like we can't afford it."

"It's not what you and I discussed," Gail said.

"I know, but take it anyway."

Gail scowled. "Fine, I'll agree. You'd better be glad I love you," she muttered as she spun on one heel and stalked back inside the lawyer's office.

"Thank you, thank you, thank you," Crystal sang, trotting along behind her.

Though she'd given in, it still rankled. In none of their discussions had compensation been mentioned and if they had, she would have never agreed to it. Once the contract was signed, they'd gone from the lawyer's to Dr. Hagan's office for the first round of exams. Dr. Hagan was the specialist Rashid's personal doctor had recommended. A copy of her medical records had already been transferred. If everything checked out, the next step would be the monitoring of her body to determine her fertile period.

Two months later, she was back in Dr. Hagan's office with Crystal by her side, being inseminated. It was amazing how fast things could go when you had enough money to grease the wheels. Crystal was more nervous than she, gripping her hand as though Gail were in labor rather than hopefully being impregnated.

Amazingly enough, either she was extremely fertile or Rashid's sperm was potent, because his seed took root the first time. Two weeks later, they were having a celebratory dinner to the welcome news that nine months from now, Crystal and Rashid would be the proud parents of a brand new infant.

June—two months later

Gail awakened to the sound of raised voices. She was in the emergency room of Baptist Medical Hospital after having passed out at work. Rashid yanked back the curtain and strode to the bedside. She looked at him groggily. "Rashid, what are you doing here?"

He came to a stop by the bed and put his hands on the rail, gripping it tightly. "Where else would I be when the safety of my child is threatened?"

Gail grimaced and tried to sit up.

"Be still," he commanded and used the remote to raise the head of the bed.

She studied his stern features before glancing away. "It was nothing. There was no need for you to come rushing down here. I simply fainted at work, and they overreacted. Before I could stop them, they'd called Rescue."

She worked as a paralegal for a major law firm. The last thing they wanted was to be named in a lawsuit. Being given no choice, Gail had reluctantly allowed herself to be carted off to the emergency room to be checked out. If she had known they were going to call Rashid, she'd have put up more of a fight.

"That's not what the doctor said. Dr. Hagan says you're dehydrated and you're not eating enough. You've lost too much weight and are far weaker than you need to be." He eyed her steadily, his gaze daring her to deny it.

Ratfink doctor! Of course, Dr. Hagan knew on which side his bread was buttered, since Rashid was the one paying his outrageous fees. She should have known the doctor would call him. She glanced behind him. "Where is Crystal?" Maybe she'd be more reasonable.

"Waiting for me to bring you to the house."

At that, her attention snapped to his face. "I'm not going to the beach. I'm headed home to my apartment when I leave here."

He crossed his arms over his chest and glared down at her. "You either come with me so we can take care of you, or you'll stay here in the hospital, doctor's orders. Now which will it be?"

Gail stared at Rashid in horror. She didn't want to stay with them. This whole situation was awkward enough. "Why can't I go home?" She was startled to hear a whine in her voice.

He planted his hands on the rail and leaned forward. "You can't go home alone because according to what you told Dr. Hagan, you haven't been eating."

"It's not my fault I can't keep anything down. Blame this child of yours." Gail placed her hand over her stomach.

Rashid's eyes followed the motion of her hand, staring at her stomach for a few moments before returning his gaze to her face. She was shocked to see the blatant possessiveness in his expression before he blanked it out. "I am blaming my child for this. That is why you are coming with me. I have a list of foods and beverages you should be able to tolerate, as well as your prescription for the anti-nausea medicine Dr. Hagan recommended. By the time we get to the house, Crystal will have everything prepared. We will care for you and see that you don't overdo it. For the next two weeks, you are restricted to bedrest."

"Two weeks?" she echoed. "What about my job?"

"What about it? You're no good to them the way you are, and you definitely don't need the money. Don't you think your welfare and the health of this child are more important than your job?" he said sternly.

Gail knew he was right but things were changing too fast. She was trying to hold on to what was familiar with both hands; afraid if she didn't she'd be swept away. When she'd agreed to be Crystal's surrogate, she'd forgotten the complete disruption pregnancy caused in a woman's life. She was only two months along and already she was sick of all the hormonal changes this baby was taking her body through. Maybe she shouldn't have been so quick to reject the psychological counseling offered by Rashid's legal staff before she'd signed the agreement.

"You're right," she finally told him. "I'm just trying to keep my life as normal as possible. Things just aren't happening the way I imagined. Your house is fine, for now. We'll need to stop by my place so I can pack enough clothes to tide me over. I have enough leave time to cover the next two weeks." Actually, she had enough paid leave time to take off the next six months.

Rashid gazed at Gail, silently acknowledging normal had gone out the door the minute he'd received the call from the doctor an hour ago. He hadn't known how much he wanted this child until he'd feared losing it. This emergency phone call had reminded him too much of the ones he'd received concerning Crystal. He sat silently listening while Dr. Hagan came in with final instructions, then left when the doctor did so Gail could dress.

He wanted this baby. It shamed him to admit just how much he wanted it. He'd thought he could be satisfied with just the love of his wife, but now that his embryo was growing under the heart of another woman, he realized just how much he had deceived himself. Crystal had been right. Not about being less of a woman because she couldn't give birth, but correct when she said he wanted a son. One to continue his family name. He would be happy with a daughter, if that's what God chose to bless him with, but in his deepest heart, he wanted a son. A house full of them.

He looked at the woman who had made all of this possible as she stepped from behind the curtain, and felt gratitude well up within his heart. She was going beyond the norms of friendship in doing this for them. For her to be willing to bear a child for someone else, especially knowing how devastating the loss of her own son had been for her, was beyond extraordinary.

He'd never really given much thought to his wife's friend. At first, Gail had come with the territory—a kind of 'love me, love my friend' package he'd accepted when he married Crystal. Then he'd met Jason and by virtue of familiarity, the men became good friends. At that

17

point, Gail had simply been Jason's wife. As men do from time to time, they'd spoken of their wives and families and he'd known Gail was a good wife. Jason never had anything but good to say about her as a wife and as a mother. Other than Crystal, Rashid really couldn't have picked a better or more honorable woman to be the mother of his child if he tried.

This had to be difficult for Gail. Her routine, her very life was being disrupted by this pregnancy. She was basically giving up a year of her life to make their dream come true. Money couldn't compensate for this kind of love. He was going to do everything within his power to see she was well taken care of.

It was the least he could do.

Chapter Two

Rashid drove Gail to her apartment so she could pack. While waiting, he checked out the contents of her refrigerator. There wasn't much inside—some fruit and a few containers of yogurt. He knew it wasn't from lack of money. Gail worked because she chose to do so, not because she needed the income. It was something to do with the time on her hands. Jason, while not as financially well off as he, had nevertheless been quite comfortable and had made ample provision for his family in the event of his demise. Gail had benefited from two separate life insurance policies, the proceeds from the house she'd sold, and Jason's business, which she'd also put on the market. No, she didn't lack for cash.

There was no food in the house because she hadn't been able to keep anything down. This pregnancy was affecting Gail's appetite, which in his opinion, had never been healthy to begin with. Rashid could see he was going to have to keep a closer eye on her. He had assumed, since she had been through this before, that she could handle things on her own with minimal assistance from him, other than the financial kind. After his talk with Dr. Hagan, he could see he'd been mistaken.

He would have to speak to Crystal to make sure she understood how vital it was they gave to Gail all the emotional support she needed. Though Gail was her friend, Crystal's mind was focused on the end result, not the process necessary to achieve it. His wife had tunnel vision when she wanted something, and he didn't believe she'd allowed herself to consider or even realize the magnitude of the sacrifice required of Gail to provide them with a child, when she herself was gaining nothing but potential heartache from the deal.

He looked up as Gail walked out of her room, wheeling her suitcase behind her. From the size of it, she hadn't packed much, but then you didn't need a lot of clothes when you were supposed to be resting.

"We need to go by the office and pick up my car," she said distractedly. From the motion of her hands, she was mentally tallying the things she'd packed to make sure she had everything.

"That won't be necessary. I will drive you to the house."

At his words, her attention focused completely on him as her eyes examined him with laser-like sharpness. "I need to go by the office and pick up my car," she slowly repeated. "You can take me or I can catch a cab. Either way, I'm not leaving my car at the office."

Rashid opened his mouth then stopped, catching his words before they escaped. He had to be careful. This woman was not his wife. He had no authority over her in any capacity, even though she carried his child. Crystal would have never questioned his decision, but then, Gail wasn't Crystal. He nodded. "As you wish."

She studied him for a moment more before digging into her purse for her keys. Once she had them in hand, she headed for the door, only to stop suddenly and turn back. "I need to forward my calls to my cell phone." Task completed, she readied herself to exit only to stop as another item popped into her mind.

Rashid didn't rush her. He knew this was difficult for her. Her home was her sanctuary, and they were forcing her to leave it on such short notice. Finally, she was ready. He took the suitcase from her and escorted her down to his car. A short while later, she was pulling out of her employer's parking lot with him following close behind.

He pulled out his cell phone as it rang. A quick glance at the caller ID revealed it was Crystal. "We'll be there shortly. She wanted to stop and collect her car," he answered, knowing what her question was going to be before she asked.

"Oh, I was wondering what was taking so long. That's good. Gail would hate being here without any transportation. She's very independent."

"So I'm beginning to see. The only reason she agreed to stay with us is because the doctor threatened to keep her in the hospital," he stated with a grimace.

"I can't wait until she gets here. This is going to be so much fun."

Rashid frowned. His wife acted as though this were some teenage sleepover. "Sweetling, she's under doctor's orders to stay in bed," he reminded.

"Rashid, Gail isn't sick. She just needs to eat. I know her. She won't be able to stay in bed all day. I'll make sure she gets plenty of rest, and we'll still have fun. You'll see."

Rashid didn't comment. He wasn't pleased with his wife's attitude. Having miscarried several times herself, he thought she'd be more conscious of the risks.

At his continued silence, Crystal said, "Honey, trust me. I want this baby as much as you. I won't let her overdo it, but she won't be happy if we treat her like an invalid. Gail is not me. She's strong. She knows her body and its limitations. Everything will be fine. I'll see you when you get home."

"All right." He disconnected the call, still deeply disturbed. He'd have to monitor the situation closely. His only consolation was that Crystal's work as an interior decorator sometimes required her putting in long hours. She would be gone for much of the day, giving Gail an opportunity to rest, and he would be home at night to ensure she didn't overdo it. This baby was too important for them to take chances with its wellbeing.

◆◆◆◆◆

Gail drove towards Crystal and Rashid's home, wondering how much this was going to emotionally cost her. She was pregnant with her best friend's child, and would now be living in their home for the next two weeks. This whole situation was wrong, any way you looked at it.

Because of this pregnancy, she was being dragged deeper and deeper into their lives. Somehow, she'd thought she would become pregnant, she and Crystal would hang out as they'd always done, and in nine months she'd hand over a bouncing baby to the happy parents. That would be the end of it. It's the impression she'd gained from the material she'd read on surrogates. Of course, in none of those cases did the surrogate happen to be best friends with the couple. Still, she thought their friendship would make things easier for her. It's wasn't.

She hadn't been prepared for the emotional toil this pregnancy was taking. Memories of her pregnancy with Marcus and the way Jason had pampered her rose when least expected. Add those sad but wonderful memories to the hormonal fluctuations she experienced, and Gail frequently found herself in the midst of crying jags and a grief stricken depression the likes of which she hadn't experienced since the early days of her loss.

In addition, in all the time she'd known Crystal, the two of them had never actually spent time living under the same roof. Somehow, Gail had instinctively known if they had ever tried to cohabitate, their friendship wouldn't survive. Now their relationship was going to be put to the test, and at the worst possible time.

Maybe she was being silly, seeing problems where there weren't any. Still, she couldn't help thinking about the cardinal rules her mom had taught her about girlfriends and relationships. One: You never vented or complained about your man to your friends while you were angry with him, because when you calmed down, they were still upset with him on your behalf. Make too many complaints and they would take an active disliking to him and become vocal in their encouragement for you to end the relationship. Two: You never bragged about your man because some heifer you thought was your friend would see the good thing you have and try to steal him from you. Third and final: You never, ever allowed any of your single, non-committed friends to live under the same roof with you and your man, or spend a lot of time with the two of you. Some women could be trusted but most couldn't. No sense asking for trouble.

It was true while Jason lived, the two couples had spent a lot of time together. Now that he was gone, Gail spent most of her time with just Crystal, never forgetting her friend had a husband and responsibilities. Rarely were the three of them together like the other night at her apartment.

Gail cleared her mind of gloomy thoughts as she pulled into the circular drive in front of Crystal's home. She was here now. Her only alternative was to remain at the hospital and she couldn't see herself doing that. Gail pasted a smile on her face as she exited the car.

Crystal came rushing out of the door and down the steps, a big welcoming grin on her face. "I hate to say 'I told you so,' but I did. I told you if you didn't start eating the doctor was going to sic Rashid on you."

"Yes, you did. Looks like I'm your patient for the next two weeks."

Her friend planted her hands on her hips, an annoyed look on her face. "Patient? Spft. You're not a

23

patient. Get a little food in you, a little rest and you'll be good as new. In the meantime, we can have lots of fun, starting right now. I hope you brought your swimsuit with you because today's a perfect day to lounge by the pool. Miguel will take your bags to your room, and Carmelita's preparing lunch. Go get changed and I'll meet you on the patio in fifteen minutes. You're in the main guest suite."

Gail heaved a silent sigh of relief. The room she referred to doubled as a cabana and had its own separate entrance off the patio. It was loosely connected to the house by the kitchen and was a good distance from the master bedroom. She would be close enough to be considered under their roof and keep Rashid and Dr. Hagan happy, but not so close she intruded on her friend's privacy.

She followed Miguel to her room and unpacked her bathing suit, a modest one piece. With the heat index in the high 80s, today was the perfect day to lie by the pool. Maybe being off work for the next two weeks wouldn't be too bad. She could sure use the rest. During this stage of her pregnancy, she got sleepy at the oddest moments. Gail grabbed a towel, opened the door, and walked out to the poolside.

Carmelita was already there setting up lunch.

"Looks good, Carmelita, as always." Gail stooped down to give the much shorter housekeeper/cook a kiss on the cheek.

Carmelita smiled her appreciation. "We're going to take good care of you, Ms. Gail. You and the *niño*. Feed you lots of food. Ms. Crystal, she say she hire this nutritionist but I tell her, Ms. Gail just need some of my cooking and she be fine."

Gail sat at the table and allowed Carmelita to serve her, knowing she needed to eat. However, her stomach already rebelled at the thought of food. In front of her, Carmelita set a glass of tea. "You drink this first.

24

It will settle your stomach. Then you nibble on the food I give you. *Sí*?"

"Okay, Carmelita. You're the boss." Gail picked up the tea and took a small sip. The soothing taste of peppermint filled her mouth. "It's peppermint. Mmm."

Carmelita nodded. "*Sí*. Peppermint with honey. Very good for the stomach. Calms it so you can eat."

"Thank you, I'm feeling better already."

She smiled broadly. "Remember, nibble and sip. When you've had enough, stop, and *el niño* will be satisfied."

"Yes, ma'am." Gail saluted her, laughing when Carmelita popped her with her apron before returning to the kitchen.

Looking at the spread before her, Gail decided to start with fruit. The cantaloupe looked very appealing to her today. She forked a piece and put it on her plate. As she bit into it, she almost moaned in pleasure as the sweet juices flooded her mouth and rolled down her cheek. Disregarding the other items on the table, she attacked the melon, gorging herself, piece by piece, until it was all gone.

It was only as she lay the last rind on her plate that she became aware of Rashid's presence. Gail flushed uncomfortably as she wiped her hands and mouth, uncomfortably aware of the picture she must make. "How long have you been standing there?"

"Long enough to know we must be sure to keep a supply of melons on hand for your enjoyment. I've never seen anyone eat their food with such gusto," Rashid said with a gleam of amusement in his eyes as he came closer and seated himself at the table.

Whatever reply Gail would have made was lost as Crystal breezed onto the patio, her body barely covered in a skimpy, red bikini, the white cover up flapping behind her. "Oh, good," she called out gaily, "food's already on the table."

25

She ran her hand along Rashid's shoulders as she passed him and took a seat next to him. While she filled her plate with salad, Crystal kept up a steady stream of chatter, regaling Gail and Rashid with tales of the client's home she was currently decorating and designer horror stories of clients she'd served in the past.

Lunch passed swiftly and soon, Crystal and Gail were lounging by the pool, relaxing in the ocean breeze. Rashid had returned to the office. There was a lull in the conversation. Then Crystal turned to Gail, looking as serious as Gail had ever seen her. "I really appreciate you doing this for me. I know this is taking more effort than you thought it would. I can't thank you enough."

"You're welcome. What are friends for? Yes, it's harder than I thought it would be. I wasn't sick like this with Marcus. I just breezed through that pregnancy. I thought this one would be the same." Gail ignored the now familiar pang at the thought of the child she'd lost.

"Well, whatever the case, you're strong. Stronger than I am. You can handle it. We just need to find food you can keep down," Crystal said encouragingly.

"Crystal, you're not weak. It's not your fault you've miscarried. Please don't blame yourself. You know doctors don't know everything. Just because they can't determine the source of the problem doesn't mean that it's you."

"My head knows that but my heart says otherwise. Do you know one of the specialists I went to actually suggested the problem was that Rashid and I were incompatible? That something about our combined chemistry was the reason I couldn't carry a baby to full-term?"

Gail scowled. "I've never heard of that, unless he was talking about that RH factor stuff. You know, where the mother has a positive blood type and the babies are negative? I've heard it can cause miscarriages if the doctor doesn't catch it in time."

26

"I don't think that's what he was talking about. Anyway, it doesn't matter. You know after the last miscarriage, Rashid put his foot down. No more pregnancies for me. I failed him," Crystal stated dejectedly. Her eyes shimmered with the glint of tears.

Gail turned fully on her lounger to face Crystal. "You did not fail him! How can you say that? It's obvious to anyone with eyes that Rashid loves you for more than your ability to give him a child. Why do you keep putting yourself down like this? Like you're somehow less of a woman because you haven't been able to carry a child to term? Having a baby is not what makes you a woman. You've got a good man who loves you, a wonderful home, a great marriage, and the job of your dreams. Most of all, you're a wonderful person. Your womanhood is not defined by your ability to procreate. You need to get that out of your head. What does your counselor say?"

Because of her depression, Crystal's doctor had recommended counseling to help her adjust to all of the loss she'd faced.

"I don't know. I stopped going. He was a quack. How is a man going to understand my desire to have a child?" Crystal asked scornfully.

Gail shrugged one shoulder, hating to see her friend like this. "Maybe he couldn't, but why don't you find another counselor, a woman? Or maybe a support group of women who do understand because they're going through the same thing?"

"The last thing I want to do is be with a bunch of loser women crying into their cups about not being able to have children. I'm fine. You're absolutely right. I have a lot to be grateful for, and I'm not going to let this one little failing become more important to me than all the good in my life. Rashid is a good man, a great husband, and I'm an awesome interior decorator. Soon, I'll be a wonderful mommy, thanks to my generous friend," she told Gail with a smile.

Gail returned Crystal's smile but inside, she was concerned. She really wished Crystal would seek out a support group. Crystal wasn't adjusting as well as she thought she was, but Gail kept her fears to herself. She couldn't make Crystal get the help she so obviously needed. All she could do is continue to be there for her.

◆ ◆ ◆ ◆ ◆

The two weeks passed by swiftly, and before Gail knew it, it was time to return to the doctor. Crystal had an important meeting with her client so Rashid accompanied her. Dr. Hagan wasn't doing a full pelvic exam on this visit. This one was just to determine if she was to be allowed off bed rest and could return to work.

It felt strange, sitting in the waiting room with Rashid. She noticed some of the other women in the waiting room sliding envious glances her way. Gail wanted to announce, 'He's not mine. I'm just a friend,' but didn't because really, it wasn't any of their business.

Still, she supposed she could understand their envy. Rashid was an attractive man and an extremely courteous one as well. He carried his power and wealth around him like an aura. You just knew he was someone important as soon as he stepped into the room.

They called her name at the door, and Rashid clasped her elbow to help her to stand before escorting her to the back. He stood by her side while her vitals were taken. Then followed as she was directed by the nurse not to the office as she expected, but to an examination room.

"Excuse me. I thought this was just a follow up from the hospital?" Gail was uncomfortably aware of Rashid's presence. There was no way she was undressing with him around.

The nurse smiled reassuringly. "It is. Dr. Hagan wants to check the baby's heartbeat. You don't have to disrobe. Just sit on the table, and he'll be in shortly."

Gail nodded in agreement, glad she'd worn loose-fitting trousers and a top rather than the dress she'd started to wear. When Rashid had requested to come with her, she hadn't given any thought to how much intimacy they would be forced into with his presence.

A few minutes later, Dr. Hagan breezed into the office. "How's my favorite patient today?"

Gail rolled her eyes. "I'm good. I'm eating. Can I go home now?"

He clucked his tongue at her. "Answer a few questions for me first, then I'll answer yours."

A few questions turned into a barrage, some of which were directed to her, others aimed at Rashid. She was amazed at the accuracy of the answers Rashid gave, even the questions directed to her he answered when she hesitated. Rashid had to have been monitoring her very closely to know these things. She wasn't sure how she felt about that.

"Gail, lay back. I want to listen to the baby. Rashid, would you like to hear your child?"

"Yes," he answered, his posture showing just how interested he was as he watched the proceedings.

The nurse pushed the waistband of Gail's pants down below her still flat stomach and tucked a towel in them, overlapping the outside to protect the material. Then she lifted her shirt until it gathered under her breast, out of the way of the warm gel the doctor squeezed onto her belly.

Dr. Hagan placed the monitor on her stomach and rolled it around. The strong, rhythmic beat of the baby's heartbeat filled the room. Overcome by emotion, Rashid reached out and gripped Gail's hand tightly.

"Nice, strong heartbeat. The baby is fine. Now, for its momma," Dr. Hagan said as he put the monitor away. The nurse wiped her stomach clean and readjusted her clothing. When she stepped out of the way, Rashid helped Gail to sit up.

"So, what's the verdict? Can I come off bed rest? Is it all right for me to return to work?" she asked anxiously.

Rashid stood by her side, saying nothing while they waited for the doctor to answer. Dr. Hagan took a seat and motioned for Rashid to do the same. Once he was seated, Dr. Hagan directed his attention to Gail. "I know you want to return to work, but I'm still concerned about your weight. You've lost too much. In the last two weeks you've gained a pound, which is good. But since you've been pregnant, you've lost twenty, far more than is safe for you to lose and be healthy. I'm keeping you on bed rest until you gain at least five more pounds. I'd really like to see you gain ten." He waited expectedly.

Gail's response wasn't long in coming. "But I can go home, right? I want to go home. I want to be in my own apartment, in my own bed. I can stay off work another couple of weeks. That's no problem. Just let me go home."

Dr. Hagan shared a look with Rashid before answering. "I think it would be better if you remain in the Jabbar's home, at least until your next visit. You're already showing signs of improvement just in the short time you've been there."

When Gail opened her mouth to argue, he said firmly, "Doctor's orders. You live alone. At home, you would be tempted to overdo. At least with Rashid, I know you're being properly cared for." Dr. Hagan paused, allowing Gail the opportunity to respond. When she remained quiet, he continued. "You're scheduled to come back and see me in four weeks. We'll re-evaluate the situation at that time."

When she still had no response, Rashid stood. "Thank you, Dr. Hagan. I'll make sure that Gail is taken care of. We'll see you in four weeks." Rashid shook Dr. Hagan's hand.

"See the receptionist on your way out," he said and left the room.

As soon as the door closed, Rashid turned to Gail and watched her. When the silence became too much, she glared at him and snapped, "What?"

"Is it such a trial, living in our home?" he asked quietly.

Gail took a deep breath and turned her face away until she could compose herself. His calmness made her feel like an unreasonable shrew. "Rashid, I get that this is your child, and you have a vested interest in its development, but your child is in my body. And my body wants to be in its own home, surrounded by its own things, sleeping in its own bed," she finished softly.

"Come." Rashid held his hand out to her. "This is better discussed somewhere else. I'm sure they have need of this room."

She didn't want his assistance getting off the exam table, but to refuse would be churlish. Gail took his hand and allowed Rashid to help her down. She waited while he opened the door for her and then walked through, very aware of his presence at her back.

After a quick stop by the receptionist desk, they headed out the door. A few minutes later, Gail watched as Rashid crossed in front of the Mercedes after seating her inside. He slid smoothly into the car and started the engine. "Where would you like to eat? We can talk over lunch."

"It doesn't matter to me." She closed her eyes and leaned her head against the headrest.

"We'll go to my club," he said decisively as he spun out of the parking garage. "It's not too far from here and we can speak privately."

"Fine," Gail answered and remained quiet for the rest of the drive. She was bitterly disappointed. The only way she'd been able to manage being away from home was by telling herself it was only for two weeks. She could handle two weeks. Two weeks was a vacation. Something she hadn't had in a long time.

Now Dr. Hagan was talking another month. A month of her living in someone else's home, away from familiar surroundings and familiar things, like the pictures of her family. Gail couldn't do it. She wouldn't do it.

It was too much to ask of anyone.

Chapter Three

When they arrived at the club, Rashid told the Maître D they needed privacy to discuss sensitive business. He took one look at Gail's tense face and escorted them to a private alcove in the dining facility.

Rashid kept Gail waiting while they went through the tedious procedure of ordering their lunch. "We'll talk after we've eaten," he informed her as he handed his menu to their server.

After the server left the table, Gail asked, "Why can't we talk now?"

"I don't want any interruptions."

She narrowed her eyes at him. "Just be aware nothing you say will alter my desire to go home."

Rashid allowed her challenge to pass. Their food was delivered in record time. Rashid ate heartily while Gail nibbled on the fruit salad she'd ordered. Too soon, he laid his utensils down and set his plate to the side. "If you are finished playing with your food, I should like us to begin."

Gail pointed her fork at him. "If you want this to be a rational discussion between two adults, you'd better watch the condescending remarks. Keep speaking to me as though I was a child, and I'll retaliate as one would."

Rashid spread his hands in a conciliatory gesture. "You are right. I apologize. That remark was uncalled for."

Gail pushed her plate to the side and sat back, disgusted because Rashid was right. She had been playing with her food. Her stomach was too tight for her to be able to enjoy it. She was more subdued when she responded. "What did you want to discuss?" She was more than ready to get this conversation over with.

"I would like for you to live with us until you deliver the baby—"

"No."

He arched one eyebrow. "You did not allow me to finish. As the child's father, I would like to watch its development through every stage, right through its delivery."

Gail sighed and rubbed her forehead wearily. "Rashid, I know you want to be an active participant. That's why I allowed you to accompany me today. I am willing to be reasonable and accommodating up to a point. Moving in with you and Crystal is an action I'm not willing to take. I understand this is your child, but as I stated before, your child is in my body and I have a life, a home. I'm already sacrificing a year of my life to do this for you. Don't ask of me more than I can give."

Rashid placed his forearms on the table and leaned forward intently. "When you signed the contract, you agreed to do whatever was in the best interest of the child. I feel, and I'm sure Dr. Hagan and my attorneys will agree, that you staying with me where you can be adequately monitored and cared for is in the baby's best interest."

She dropped her hand and stared at him while fury built. "Are you threatening me?" she hissed at him, outraged that he would do such a thing after all she was doing for them.

"No, simply informing you of the measures I'm willing to take to be a part of this pregnancy." Rashid's tone was utterly implacable.

"Bastard." She shoved her chair away from the table, snatched up her purse, and stalked off, anger apparent in every inch of her bearing.

Rashid's low voice carried to her. "Gail, come back and let's finish discussing this."

"Screw you and your discussion," she called back loudly over her shoulder as she weaved through the other diners on her way to the exit. "Bastard! How dare he threaten me? He wouldn't be having a child if it weren't for me," she mumbled under her breath.

She reached the lobby and lengthened her stride, the exit in sight. She'd catch a cab back to her place and Rashid and his demands could just go to hell.

"Gail, wait!"

Almost there, she thought. Her hands were reaching for the door when she was pulled up short. Rashid snaked an arm around her waist, lifted her off her feet, and stepped off to the side of the entryway. Gail immediately struggled for her freedom. "Let me go!"

"Not until you hear me out," Rashid demanded as he set her down, spun her around by the forearm, and locked his arm around her waist. He pulled her tight against his body, restricting her ability to move. They glared at each other, a contest to see whose will was stronger.

"Mr. Jabbar. Ms. Henderson. Is there a problem?" The concerned voice of the club manager interrupted the stare down they were engaged in.

"We're fine. Ms. Henderson has just received some distressing business news," Rashid informed the man.

"Ah, perhaps you would consider moving somewhere a little more private to finish your conversation," the manager discreetly suggested.

Rashid finally turned away from Gail to address the manager directly. "We shall be but a minute more. If I see that the discussion will extend longer, I will, of course, seek your assistance in locating a place more suitable."

"Very good, sir." He nodded to the both of them before walking away.

Gail stood very still, and prayed for strength. Rashid's arm was an iron bar against her back and every inch of her body, from chest to thigh, was moulded against his. The interruption by the manager had

35

allowed her space to become aware of the riot going on inside. She was grateful for the padded bra she wore that disguised her traitorous nipples, which were responding to Rashid's nearness.

Of all the rotten times for her body to come alive. This couldn't be happening to her. Not now and not with Rashid, her best friend's husband. She turned her face away from him, hoping he wouldn't see the confusion and reluctant desire she felt. It must surely be reflected on her face. God must have heard her prayer for Rashid loosened his hold, allowing her to take a small step back and put some space between them.

"Gail, I'm sorry."

She almost turned to look at him to see how sincere he was. At the last moment, she realized what she was hiding and gazed at his nose instead of meeting his eyes.

"I should not have threatened you, but please, put yourself in my position. I've already lost five children to miscarriage. This child is my final hope. I want to be a part of every minute, and I fear the same thing happening to this one as has happened to the others. I know it is an imposition, but please consider it. This may be the only child I'll ever have."

Well, spit. Now that he put it in those terms, not to do as he asked would make her seem churlish. Gail took a deep breath and met Rashid's gaze. "Maybe we can come to a compromise that will give you the contact you need, and me the space I require. I know you're worried and want to be involved, but please, put yourself in my position. I need to maintain a bit of distance, a bit of separateness, or I'm never going to be able to turn over this child to you when it is time. I can't get so involved in your lives that I forget I have a life of my own."

Rashid gazed deeply into her eyes, as though trying to gauge the depth of her sincerity. He released her and took a couple of steps back, turned away, and gazed at the ceiling. Gail watched his shoulders rise and fall as he took a couple of deep breaths.

She allowed him time to compose himself. She needed time herself. Her mind still reeled with shock at her body's reaction to him. By the time he turned to her, she was outwardly composed.

"What are you willing to do? I do not want to be responsible for creating a stressful situation. It is not good for the child."

Of course, everything is about the child, she thought snidely before she caught herself. Then she was horrified by her reaction. Of course, his concern was for his child. It would be terrible if it weren't. "Let's just wait and see what Dr. Hagan says when I return in four weeks. I'll stay with you until then, and in the meantime, we'll both see if we can come up with a compromise that meets both of our needs. I'm willing to allow you to come with me to all of my checkups, along with Crystal."

Rashid nodded his head in acknowledgement and acceptance of her terms. He motioned with his hand toward the exit. "Shall we go?"

"If I'm going to be in your home for the next four weeks, I need to stop by my place and pick up more things," Gail said, preceding him out the door.

"Bring whatever you need to make yourself feel at home."

◆◆◆◆◆

Later that night, Crystal went to Gail's room. "Rashid told me what Dr. Hagan said. I know you hate being away from your home, but I'd be lying if I said I'm sorry. I enjoy having you here."

"I like being with you, too, but I'd rather be in my own apartment," Gail said as Crystal seated herself on the bed.

"Well, eat as much as you can, pack on the weight, and Dr. Hagan should allow you to return. Are you still bothered by nausea or is the medicine helping?"

Gail sighed and admitted, "I don't know if it's the medicine or the tea Carmelita gives me. I still don't have much of an appetite, even though I'm able to keep my food down now."

"Maybe you should do like they say in the baby books and eat more frequently. It's supposed to be healthier, eating smaller meals throughout the day rather than trying to eat three main meals." She looked Gail up and down. "Besides, Dr. Hagan was right about one thing, you need to gain weight. You're looking skeletal."

"Gee, thanks." Gail rolled her eyes.

"No offense, honey, but you look terrible. There are dark rings under your eyes, and I can see your collar bones. You get any smaller and they're going to put you in the hospital on a feeding tube." Crystal knew she was laying it on a little thick, but Gail really did look horrible, by anyone's standard.

"I'm not that bad," Gail told her. "But I will try to eat more. Dr. Hagan says I need to gain at least five pounds over the next four weeks before he'll release me from bed rest. Maybe I can drink some of those nutritional drinks they give elderly people who need to gain weight. You know, like Ensure or something."

Crystal smiled. "That's a good idea. I'll have Carmelita pick a few up from the grocery store. We can't have you getting sick because you're not getting enough nutrients."

They were quiet for a while. Crystal watched as Gail arranged her personal belongings in the room, making the space her own. She'd brought her CD player, pictures of Jason and Marcus and the rest of her family, and a few books.

"I can have Rashid get you a television," she offered, hoping to cheer her friend.

"That's okay. I don't watch it that much. I brought my laptop. If I spend time doing anything, it will be playing around on-line."

"Well, there's that and the pool. You're welcome to spend as much time in it as you desire. There's a large screen TV and an extensive movie library in the family room. Go in there anytime you like. As Carmelita would say, 'Mi casa es su casa.' You don't have to spend all of your time in this room, like you have for the last two weeks," she reminded.

"I don't want to intrude. You and Rashid need your privacy. Besides, I've been so tired, I spent most of that time sleeping. I hate to admit it, but I really did need the rest." Gail gave a rueful grin.

Crystal smiled. "Well, now you have another four weeks to do nothing but eat and relax. Think of it as an extended vacation. You don't have to cook, clean, or do anything you don't want. Catch up on your reading. You're always saying you don't have enough time to do things. Now you do."

"Yeah, that's true."

Crystal eased into the reason for her visit. "Rashid told me he wants you to stay with us until the baby is born."

Gail's expression turned guarded. "He mentioned something to that effect."

"Are you considering it?" Crystal plucked at the bedspread while waiting for her friend to answer.

"I don't know, Crystal. It seems an awful lot to ask."

Careful not to push too hard, she said, "I know, but it would mean so much to him, to us. He'd get to see the baby grow, and it would ease his fears. He's always blamed himself for my miscarriages, wondering if there was something he could have done to prevent it. He hasn't said anything, but I know he really wants this child. It freaked him out when Dr. Hagan called and said you were in the emergency room. I'm sure it brought back memories of all the phone calls he'd gotten about me over the years."

Gail's hands fisted at her sides. "Crystal, you don't know what you're asking. I've just decided it's time I do something about this limbo I'm living in. It's time to let go of the past and start living again."

Diverted from her mission, Crystal's eyebrows shot up. "Really? You're interested in getting married again?"

"No. Jason is my husband. I could never replace him." Gail twisted the wedding band she still wore on her finger. "But I think I'm ready for male companionship. Maybe it's time I started accepting some of the invitations I've been turning down."

Since she'd been encouraging Gail for the last six months to get into the dating ring again, Crystal could only agree. "If you're ready to start dating again, you'll definitely need your privacy. I'm sure you wouldn't be comfortable inviting a man to spend the night here. "

Gail scowled. "I didn't say I was ready for sex, just that I was thinking it was time I start dating again."

She smirked at Gail, inwardly laughing at her naiveté. "Believe me, nowadays, the two go hand in hand. Besides, you're a grown woman and you have needs. If you want to indulge in a little hanky-panky, then I say good for you. Jason is the one who died. You are still very much alive."

"I know, but it's only recently that I've felt like living."

Somber now, Crystal said, "Grief is hard to deal with. It grabs you in a chokehold and refuses to let go. I've grieved the loss of every one of my babies." She paused a moment to blink back tears. "I can only imagine the pain you must have felt, losing both the love of your life and the child you created together at the same time. That's why I say you're strong. You've survived something that would crush lesser women."

"I'm no stronger than the average woman. I mean, my God, look at you. Do you know how much courage it takes to lose one baby and keep trying? And you've lost five. Besides, I couldn't crawl into the grave with them. I had no choice but to keep living. I just took one day at a time. It's all I could handle. But now? Maybe it's time to start looking towards the future and making plans rather than going through the motions of this day by day existence."

The two women shared a moment of complete understanding. Then Crystal said, "Well, you're helping me to make my dream come true. When you allow yourself to dream again, maybe I can help you achieve yours."

"I'll hold you to that."

Crystal stood and straightened her pants. "It's time I go to bed before Rashid sends out a search party. Some of us still have to go to work in the morning." She laughed as she dodged the pillow Gail threw at her. "Goodnight," she sang as she walked out the door.

"Goodnight. See you tomorrow," Gail called out, just before the door shut.

◆ ◆ ◆ ◆ ◆

Crystal entered the bedroom to find Rashid already in bed, waiting for her. "Did you speak with her?" he asked tensely.

"I did." She pushed the door closed and began to undress.

"And?"

"Now we wait. I know Gail. She has a soft heart. She'll probably do as we ask, but not if we badger her." She paused and shook her head. "I can't believe you threatened her."

"I admit, it was ill-advised of me to do so."

"Yeah, well, fortunately for you, you have me to fix things for you when you screw up." Crystal went into the bathroom and washed the makeup off her face.

"So what do we do now?" he asked when she returned.

"We wait."

Rashid made an impatient sound. "For how long?"

"For as long as it takes. Gail will think about it and see the sense in it. In the meantime, we make her as comfortable as possible and hope it's enough." Crystal could tell Rashid wasn't satisfied with her answer, but Gail was her friend. Crystal knew her best. If she said they needed to be patient and wait, then that's what he'd do. Crystal slid into bed naked and reached for him. He welcomed her into his arms with a kiss. She stroked his body, silently inviting him to do more than kiss her goodnight.

They kissed and touched each other, building the passion between them until Rashid rolled Crystal beneath him. Then he reached into the bedside drawer and pulled out a condom.

"We don't need that, baby."

He tore open the package and sat back on his heels, sheathing his penis with the protective covering. "We've discussed this. I'll not take any chances on getting you pregnant."

She pushed up to her elbows. "But I'm on the pill. I hate the way latex feels. I want to feel you in me, skin to skin."

"So do I, but it's not a risk I'm willing to take. I love you too much to take chances with your life."

Rashid moved to cover her again, but she pushed him off her.

"I'm not interested anymore," she said and rolled onto her side away from him.

"Because I'm not willing to come to you unprotected, you're calling a halt to everything?" She glanced over her shoulder. Rashid gazed at her with an expression of disbelief.

"I don't need your protection. I'm on the pill and you know it. You're just being difficult," she snapped angrily.

"No, I'm concerned for your safety, or have you forgotten your last pregnancy, the one that almost took your life, was conceived while you were on the pill?"

Why was he always throwing that in her face? "It was a fluke. It won't happen again."

"Indeed it won't, for I will make sure of it." Rashid flopped back onto his side of the bed before jerking to his feet. He stalked into the bathroom to dispose of the condom.

Crystal noticed he was no longer aroused when he came to bed. He lay on his side and turned his back towards her. She tentatively laid a hand on his shoulder, wanting to make amends. He shrugged it away.

"Rashid, I'm sorry. Don't be angry." She hated when he was angry with her.

"Forget it. Let's just get some sleep," he said shortly.

Crystal snuggled down beside him. She knew he had every right to be furious with her, more than he knew. She'd orchestrated her last pregnancy, so sure this time the result would be different. Instead, she'd almost died. Rashid had never accused her of becoming pregnant deliberately. As far as she knew, he still thought it an accident, but he would take no more chances.

Before, she had been able to convince him to leave the birth control up to her. Now he was taking matters into his own hands. This wouldn't do. Despite what she'd promised, she had every intention of trying again.

She'd heard stories of infertile couples suddenly being able to conceive once adoption proceedings had been initiated. Surrogacy was close to adoption. Crystal was certain if she got pregnant just one more time, she'd be able to carry the baby to term, but first, she had to get Rashid to lose the protection he insisted on.

Crystal lay in bed plotting her next move. She had to have a child of her own. She just had to.

Chapter Four

Gail sat on the floor, observing Rashid through the sheer curtains of the French doors leading from her room to the pool. Over the last three weeks, it had become a habit of hers to watch him power through the water as he did his early morning exercise.

This explained why his shoulders were so broad and why the rest of him was so lean. Rashid had a swimmer's physique, and she got a vicarious thrill out of watching him while he was unaware. Something about the power of his movements, the way the early morning light shined on his rippling, glistening muscles, fascinated her. She knew she should look away. Ogling her best friend's husband was wrong, but it was such a harmless way to pass the time and the hormones rushing through her body were wreaking havoc with her senses. Frankly, she was horny.

A sad smile crossed her face as she remembered her first pregnancy...

So aroused she couldn't wait for evening, she surprised Jason by coming to his office.

"Baby, what's wrong?" he asked when he looked up and saw her standing in the doorway.

"I need you." She reached behind her and locked the door, then lifted her skirt and removed her panties, letting them drop to the carpet.

Jason pressed a button on his desk. "Sarah, send all my calls to voicemail and go to lunch."

"Yes, sir," his secretary said with a hint of laughter in her voice.

His eyes gleamed as she strode toward him with her sexiest walk, rubbing her distended nipples through her shirt and bra. By the time she rounded the desk and stood before him, his pants were around his ankles and he was hard as a rock. Gail hiked her skirt to her waist and straddled his lap. He moaned when she reached between them and grasped his erection, lining it with her opening. As she sank down, he lunged up.

She rode him hard, having spent the entire morning thinking about this, despite having awakened Jason for an intense lovemaking session before they both left for work. It didn't take long for her to orgasm. She collapsed against his chest, breathing hard. Jason gripped her hips and thrust into her, rushing toward his own release.

Once his breathing calmed, he laughingly stated, "If I'd known being pregnant would turn you into a nymphomaniac, we'd have done this much sooner. I should keep you barefoot and pregnant, just so I can reap the benefits."

Gail pushed the memory away. This time, there was no loving husband to relieve the sexual tension in her body. Being cooped up, she had to get her jollies wherever she could. In another week, she'd return to the doctor. She had gained weight these last three weeks, exceeding the requisite five pounds by three. Dr. Hagan should be very pleased with her progress. He definitely wouldn't have any reason to keep her on bed rest, and that meant that she could go home.

While she couldn't deny that being waited on hand and foot was very appealing, it didn't compare to being in her own apartment. Despite how welcome Crystal and Rashid had endeavored to make her feel, she could never forget she was a guest in their home.

Gail couldn't wait to get back to work—back to the real world. She felt hemmed in, caged. She needed to get out, and she needed to get laid. She didn't know if it was the pregnancy or what, but her body had come to life with a vengeance.

When Jason died, everything sexual within her had died with him. Or so she had believed, but it had only been hibernating, frozen into a deep sleep by her grief. Now she was thawing, her body and emotions coming alive.

Just because she wasn't interested in being married again didn't mean she couldn't enjoy having a man in her life and in her bed. She would take her time, because while she wasn't interested in happily ever after, neither was she cut out for one-night stands. What she wanted was a 'friend with benefits' type relationship. Nothing too serious. Nothing that would threaten her heart. Just someone she enjoyed spending time with who wouldn't mind adding a little sex to the mix occasionally. That wasn't too much to ask, was it?

Rashid climbed out of the pool and dried off, his body barely covered in a small piece of black cloth masquerading as a bathing suit. He kept himself in good shape. Jason had been like that. She smiled with the memory. No matter how busy he'd been, Jason had always made time to exercise and keep in shape. He'd said a toned body made for a sharp mind. Apparently, he and Rashid had that in common.

Rashid draped the towel around his neck and walked off.

Gail sighed. Show's over. She got off the floor and climbed back into bed. For one more week, there was nothing to do and no place to go, and her only motivation for getting out of bed just went into the house. It was going to be another long, boring day.

◆◆◆◆◆

Today was the day. Gail was so excited she couldn't stand it. Rashid wanted to drive her to the

47

doctor's office, but she had refused. She was driving and after her appointment, treating herself to a day out on the town.

First she would go to the spa for a facial, a pedicure, manicure, and a massage. Then she'd eat a decadent lunch, loaded with calories. Finally, she'd top off the day with shopping. Something she hadn't done in ages. But she couldn't do any of those things until Dr. Hagan released her.

Crystal and Rashid joined her in the waiting room. When the nurse, a different one than before, called for her to come back, all three of them stood. The nurse's eyebrows rose. "Will both of you be accompanying Ms. Henderson?"

"Yes," Gail answered for them. "Is that a problem?"

Professionalism firmly in place, the nurse said, "No, it's not. I was just surprised. Come this way so I can get your vitals."

Crystal and Rashid stood by and watched as Gail was weighed and her blood pressure was taken. Then she had to go pee in the cup. Oh joy!

Rashid stood outside the exam room while she undressed and put on the paper gown. Once she was covered and situated, Crystal called him inside. It was beyond awkward, sitting there, the next thing to naked with Rashid there in the room. Actually, she wasn't too comfortable with Crystal seeing her nude, but at least she was a girl. She had all the same body parts. Rashid was all male.

And the father of this child, her conscience reminded her.

Dr. Hagan came into the room and she focused her attention on him. Maybe he was aware of her tension, or he was just sensitive to the awkwardness of the situation, but he had Rashid sit where he could be a part of the procedure but not too up close and personal for her comfort. Dr. Hagan did the whole routine, including a full pelvic exam. Nothing like having a man with his whole hand up your unmentionables with spectators watching the show.

"Everything looks good. How's your appetite?" Dr. Hagan asked as he removed his gloves and let down the stir-ups.

"It's okay. I'm eating more frequently and eating smaller meals."

"Good. Any nausea?

"A little. Not that often. I'm having more heartburn than anything."

"Stay away from fried, greasy food. Eat lots of fruits and vegetables, and drink milk. The heartburn should go away."

"Milk gives me gas. I don't like milk." Gail couldn't help the frown on her face. Baby or no baby, she was not drinking milk.

Dr. Hagan arched an eyebrow. "What about yogurt? Do you like yogurt?"

"Yeah, it's okay. Kind of sweet."

"Eat lots of it. I don't care what kind. It's good for your digestive system and a good source of calcium. Eat it for the baby. If you don't get enough calcium, the baby will take it from your bones. We don't want that to happen."

"No, we don't. Okay, I'll eat more yogurt."

"Now, let's check on the baby. How would you two like to see your child?" Dr. Hagan asked Crystal and Rashid.

"Oh, could we? That would be wonderful," Crystal answered for both of them.

"Prepare her for an ultrasound," Dr. Hagan said to the nurse.

The nurse laid a towel over Gail's hips and another one over her chest, preserving her modesty and leaving her stomach bare. Her belly was just beginning to pooch out, something only noticeable when bare like it was now. Then she squeezed gel on Gail's belly.

Dr. Hagan moved the ultrasound machine closer to the bed and motioned for Rashid and Crystal to move forward. Crystal stood on Gail's right while Rashid stood behind her, near the head of the exam table.

Dr. Hagan placed the scanner on Gail's belly and the monitor came to life. "Well, lookie there. What do you know? Looks like you folks are getting two for the price of one."

"What are you talking about?" Gail asked confused. She was still trying to make sense of the images on the monitor, which was hard to do with Dr. Hagan rolling the scanner around like he was. The picture kept moving. A glance at Crystal and Rashid showed they were trying to do the same.

"What I'm saying is that we've got ourselves a set of twins." The rest of his words were drowned out by the buzzing in her ears. Twins? How had this happened? She hadn't taken any fertility drugs to increase ovulation. She and Crystal had decided to try insemination without it the first couple of times, with the drugs as a last resort. They'd been trying to prevent something like this from occurring.

While her mind was reeling, her eyes had been tracking Dr. Hagan as he explained to the stunned parents-to-be exactly what they were seeing on the monitor. Gail tuned in just in time to hear Dr. Hagan tell Rashid it was too soon to determine the sex of the babies but in another month or two, he should be able to tell.

Then he put down the scanner, removed his gloves, and took the printout from out of the machine and handed it to Crystal. "Here's your first baby picture. Take it, and you and Rashid go into my office and wait."

Once they were gone, he turned to Gail. "The nurse is going to help you clean up. Once you are dressed, come into my office and we'll discuss things."

"All right," Gail agreed, still partially dazed. Two babies weren't actually a problem, she reminded herself. Rashid had covered multiple births in the contract. She'd never thought it would happen, and couldn't help but hope Crystal could handle it. Being a mother to one newborn was tough enough. Now they were talking about two.

Oh well, not her problem. At least, she couldn't let it be her problem. That way laid disaster. Gail couldn't allow herself to be concerned about the quality of care these babies received outside of the womb. Her job was to be an incubator. Incubators had no feelings. She couldn't afford to have any either. That was one of the things the online surrogate support group she'd joined stressed.

Gail dressed and joined the others. Rashid rose from his chair, allowing her to be seated. Dr. Hagan came in behind Gail and sat behind his desk. "I'm pleased with the weight you've gained and the development of the babies. Actually, the extreme nausea you experienced in the beginning was a good sign. It means you had a good amount of the pregnancy hormones flooding your system. There is no danger of miscarriage."

Gail inwardly groaned. Sure, it was a good thing because he wasn't the one going through it.

"I still want you to take it easy. Take care of yourself. A healthy mother means healthy babies. I'm releasing you to return to work, but I don't want you working more than thirty hours per week. If you feel yourself getting tired, rest." At his words, she wanted to jump up and down with joy, but restrained herself.

Dr. Hagan played with his pen before continuing. "Keep eating like you have been. Soon you'll find yourself eating more as your body's demand for calories increases. I want you to get some form of low-impact, aerobic exercise daily, preferably walking or swimming. It will help with the delivery. They have yoga classes specifically designed for expectant mothers. You may want to check it out. Does anyone have any questions for me?"

"Is she really okay to be released on her own?" Rashid asked.

Gail's eyes narrowed, and she glanced at Rashid in warning. He'd better not bring up the issue of her living with them again. However, Rashid's attention was focused on Dr. Hagan and didn't notice.

"Yes, she should be fine. Gail has entered her second trimester. Her appetite and energy levels should increase and her system balance out. We'll review the situation again when she enters the third. She'll find herself tiring easier, have more difficulty getting around, and premature delivery will be more of a concern, but that's another two to three months from now," Dr. Hagan told him.

Gail could tell from the expression on Rashid's face he was hoping for a different answer. She looked at Crystal to see what her reaction was to all of this. Her expression was surprisingly neutral.

"Any more questions?" Dr. Hagan asked the group. When everyone responded in the negative, he told Gail, "See you back in four weeks." He stood and excused himself from the room.

"Well," Crystal said, "that was certainly exciting. Now that you have your freedom back, what do you plan to do?"

"I'm going to the spa to get the full treatment. Then, I'm going shopping. My clothing's getting a little tight in the waist. Another couple of weeks and I won't be able to fasten them at all."

At her words, Rashid went into his wallet and pulled out a black credit card with an American Express logo on it. He held it out to Gail.

"What's this for?" she asked, making no attempt to take it. The Centurion Black card from American Express was so exclusive you couldn't even apply for it. AmEx issued it by special invitation only. There was no way she was touching it.

"You stated a need for more clothing. According to our agreement, we are responsible for supplying all of your pregnancy related needs." He motioned for her to take the card.

"I can't use your credit card, Rashid. I'm not your wife. They'll think I stole it." Gail tried to push it away.

Rashid took her hand, pried it open when she tried to resist, and placed the card inside, closing her fingers around it. "It's not my card. I opened an account in your name to cover all of your expenses. Charge whatever you need against it—food, clothing, rent, etc— and the bills will come to me."

Crystal snatched the card out of Gail's slack hand. "You got her a Black American Express? Don't you think that's a bit much? I don't even have one of these." She flipped it right side up to reveal Gail's name etched on the card.

"Crystal's right. I appreciate the sentiment, but I can't accept it."

"It's not sentiment. It's a legal obligation and gratitude to the mother of my children," Rashid said as he took the card from Crystal and handed it back to Gail.

Crystal sucked in a sharp breath.

Gail could hardly believe her ears. "Rashid, I'm not the mother of your children. Crystal is. I'm just the incubator."

"Yes, yes," he said dismissively. "Is this not what I mean? Regardless of how you term it, through your

53

generosity our dream of children is being realized. It is the least that we can do."

Gail looked worriedly at Crystal, her concern over the card forgotten.

"Take the card, Gail. He's right. We are responsible for your expenses while you're pregnant. After all, you're giving us the use of your body and your time. The least that we can do is make sure it doesn't cost you anything financially."

"Are you sure?" Gail hesitated. Crystal was saying all the right words but something about it didn't ring true.

"I'm positive." This time, Crystal smiled. "If I didn't have a meeting today with a new client, I would be going with you to help you spend Rashid's money."

The smile is what convinced Gail. It was sincere. "Okay, if you're really sure."

"I am. Are you coming back to the house tonight?" Crystal asked as she stood and collected her purse off the floor.

"Maybe not tonight. I've been away from home for too long."

"Okay, call me when you get in and tell me about your day. I've got to go." Crystal gave Gail a fierce hug.

"I will."

"I'll see you at home," Crystal told her husband. She walked out the door, leaving Gail and Rashid to trail behind. Rashid waited while Gail set up her next appointment and input the date and time into his iPhone.

He escorted Gail to her car and waited until she was settled inside. Before she could close the door, he asked, "Have you given any more thought to my request?"

Truthfully, she hadn't but looking into his earnest face, she couldn't tell him that so she made herself really think about it now. "In addition to going with me to my doctor appointments, short of living with you guys, what is the minimal amount of contact you can accept?"

Hands resting on the door, he stared down at her. "I will accept whatever amount of contact with us you are comfortable giving."

"Well, how about this for starters? Dr. Hagan wants me to get daily exercise. You have a pool. Why don't I come over in the evenings to swim and let Carmelita feed me? That way you can see for yourself how I'm doing, and I won't feel like I'm intruding on your and Crystal's privacy."

"And later on, as your time draws near?"

"Let's just get through this. We'll re-evaluate things when that time comes, okay?"

He gave a short nod. "This is an acceptable compromise."

"Okay, now you need to go make nice with your wife." Gail gave him serious eyes so he knew she meant business.

"What do you mean?" From the look on his face, the man didn't have a clue.

"I mean, it was rather insensitive of you to refer to me as the mother of your children when your wife has been trying to give you some for years," Gail told him sternly.

He frowned, his expression one of confusion. "Are you not the mother of these children? Is it not your eggs and your body giving them life?"

"That's not the point. Yes, if you want to be literal about it, I am the mother of your children, but...emotionally and in every way that counts, Crystal will be their mother." And he'd better not forget it.

"You're telling me nothing I don't already know."

"You may know it, but your words said otherwise. You really hurt Crystal. You need to go and make it right. Yes, I'm making it possible for you to have children, but none of this would be happening if Crystal hadn't come up with the idea and approached me with it. Maybe some of that appreciation you've been showering on me should be directed to your wife."

He appeared startled, as though the idea had never crossed his mind. "You are right. I owe my wife a huge debt of gratitude. Thank you for bringing it to my attention."

"You're welcome. Now, please excuse me. Your credit card is burning a hole in my wallet, just begging to be used," Gail said with an impish grin.

Rashid didn't return her smile, but stated seriously, "I meant what I said. Charge all of your expenses today to me. You deserve this treat."

"Hey, it's your dime. If that's what you want, I'll be more than happy to comply." She gave him a two-finger salute and motioned for him to move back. With one hand, she started the motor while with the other, she closed the door. With a quick wave, she backed out of the parking space and left Rashid standing there.

◆◆◆◆◆

Later the same evening, Gail entered her apartment loaded down with shopping bags, ready to drop. She'd had a blast and was sorry to see the day end. Because she hadn't had the foresight to call ahead, she had to skip her spa day. Her day had been much too precious to waste time sitting in their waiting room, hoping for an opening.

She'd left, gone to the mall, and shopped to her heart's content, buying things she could wear now and later as her pregnancy advanced. She also indulged in body sprays and scented lotion sets from her favorite store, Bath and Body Works. And, oh, the shoes! She loved shoes. With Marcus, her feet had grown a half size. This time, she was prepared. Gail purchased several pairs of shoes, a half size larger than she normally wore, to go with the outfits she purchased.

She'd rounded off the day of shopping with dinner and a movie. All in all, it had been a great day, and the night looked even better. Tonight, she'd get to sleep in her own bed. How wonderful.

Remembering her promise, she called Crystal.

"Hello?"

"Hey, why are you whispering?" Gail automatically lowered her voice. In the background, she could hear the low murmur of Rashid's voice, then a quickly stifled moan from Crystal.

"Can't talk now. Got to go," Crystal said breathlessly.

"I understand," Gail replied with a laugh, but Crystal was already gone. It looked like Rashid had taken her advice and made amends. Good for him.

Gail spent the rest of the evening catching up on mail, returning calls, and generally just reacquainting herself with her space.

Dang, it was good to be home.

◆ ◆ ◆ ◆ ◆

The next morning, her phone rang early. "Hello?"

"Good morning. I'm so excited. Guess what Rashid did?"

Gail sat up in bed and smiled. "If it's X-rated, I don't want to know."

"Umm, he did that too, but that's not what I'm talking about. Now guess."

"I don't know. Tell me." From the excitement in her voice, Gail knew Crystal was about to burst with her news.

"He bought me flowers and took me out for dinner. Best of all, he wants us to go away for the weekend on a mini-vacation. He said once the babies

57

arrive, we wouldn't have as much time for just the two of us. Isn't that sweet?"

"Yes, it is. A good idea too. He's right. Once you're a mommy, there will be a large demand on your time." Gail spoke from memory.

"I know. We've talked about hiring a full-time nanny to help, especially now we know there are two, but I'm not sure that's what I want. I think I want to stay home and be a full-time mother, at least while the babies are young. I can always go back to work once they are in school."

Gail remembered having the same conversation with Jason when she was pregnant with Marcus. "True. So, are you happy about the twins? I mean, I know it had to be a shock. I certainly was surprised."

"It hasn't sunk in yet. Probably won't until I'm holding them in my arms. What about you, Godmommy-to-be? Are you ready to have two godchildren?" Gail could hear the laughter in Crystal's voice.

"Sure. My job's easy. I show up for the Christening, buy presents, babysit every now and then, and listen to them gripe about what a bad mother you are and 'why can't mom be cool like you' when they're teenagers," Gail finished with a laugh.

"You have to go with me when I shop for baby furniture. I can't wait to get started. I'm thinking about white so it will match no matter what color scheme I use." Gail could tell Crystal's decorator genes were humming.

"Well, decorating is your specialty. I'm sure your kids will have the best designed room around."

"You know it. I have to go but when we get together, you've got to tell me how your day went yesterday."

"Will do. Bye," Gail said as she rolled over to put the phone back into the cradle.

"Bye, yourself. See you later."

Chapter Five

Monday morning, Gail returned to work, happy to be there. So glad in fact, she brought in an assortment of muffins and donuts for the whole office.

Greg Richmont, one of the firm's top divorce lawyers, came and sat on the edge of her desk. "Hey, Beautiful. It's about time you returned to work. I missed you."

Gail rolled her eyes. "Sure you did," she said with a smile.

"Oh, you wound me," he said, clutching his heart dramatically. "When are you going to put me out of my misery and go out with me?"

"Greg, if I ever said yes, you'd run in the other direction. I'll save both of us the trauma and keep saying no." She shook her head and laughed a little at the thought of his reaction were she to finally say yes, after his year of asking.

Greg was suddenly as serious as she had ever seen him. "Don't let the act fool you. If you ever said yes to me about anything, I'd do my damndest to make sure you'd never regret it."

Gail sat back in her seat in stunned surprise. In all the years she'd known him, she'd considered him to be a flirt, the original ladies' man. This was a side of Greg she'd never seen. "What did you have in mind?"

He straightened his relaxed posture, hands fisted by his side. "Don't toy with me, Gail. You have the ability to do serious damage to my heart."

She would have scoffed, but the look in his eyes caused her to swallow her words. He wasn't joking. "I'm not toying with you. I'm not saying I'm ready for a serious relationship, but I recently decided it was time for me to start dating."

"Let me see your hands," he demanded.

"What?"

"Your hands. Hold them out. Now."

Confused, she did as he commanded. He took hold of her right hand, on which her wedding band now resided. "You're serious." He toyed with the ring. "It's not off yet, but this is an improvement."

"What do you mean?" Gail fidgeted in her chair, uncomfortable with the attention he paid to her hand.

"I mean, I've been waiting a long time for a sign you were ready to move on. I don't know what brought about this change, but whatever it was, I'm grateful as hell. What are you doing tonight?" His gaze speared her where she sat, demanding a response.

Her mind blanked. "Tonight?"

His grip tightened on her hand, as though to prevent her from fleeing. "Yes, tonight. I'm not giving you a chance to change your mind."

"Uh, nothing, really." *Oh Lord, what have I started?*

"You are now. I'll pick you up at seven. Wear something nice," he tossed over his shoulder as he walked off, not giving her a chance to respond.

Gail spent the rest of the day feeling like she had fallen into an alternate reality. The harmless flirt she'd thought would be safe to test her rusty dating skills on was turning out to be a bit more dangerous than she imagined. In all the years Greg had flirted with her, she'd never once imagined he might be serious.

She knew Greg was sharp. He had to be to be as successful as he was, but he did a good job of hiding his commanding nature behind a flirty, playboy attitude. Tonight should be interesting.

Later that evening, when she was dressed and waiting for her date to arrive, Gail realized just how isolated she'd allowed herself to become. Never an outgoing person, after the death of Jason and Marcus, her circle of friends had slowly dwindled to one, Crystal. She severely felt the lack tonight, when nerves had her wanting to call someone for support. Normally she'd call Crystal, but she and Rashid were still away on their mini-vacation. She would just have to sweat it out, but Gail made herself a promise. She would renew what friendships she could and be more open to new acquaintances.

Before her nerves could wind too tight, the doorman buzzed. "Ms. Henderson, Mr. Richmont is here."

"Send him up, Paul."

"Yes, ma'am."

Gail wiped her sweaty palms on her dress, trying to calm her shaky nerves. She went to the mirror hanging in the entry foyer for one last check of her appearance. She had on one of her favorite dresses, an old standby, the classic black dress. Only hers had an empire waistline with a deep V-neck and flowing bell-shaped sleeves that emphasized her femininity. The dress stopped just above her knees, showcasing her long, shapely legs.

A knock sounded at the door, causing her to jump. Oh boy, she really needed to calm down. Smoothing her hands down her sides again, she took a deep breath and opened the door.

"Wow!" The word just slipped out. Her heart beat an uneven rhythm, and she was suddenly nervous for an entirely different set of reasons. Greg looked a little too good standing there, framed in the doorway. The man looked like he'd just stepped off the front page of GQ Magazine.

"Wow, yourself." His grin was devilishly sinful. She felt her face flush as his gaze traveled from her hair, gathered casually at the nape of her neck, down to her feet shod in her favorite, strappy high-heeled sandals. "Somehow, I always figured you to be a red toenail kind of girl."

The comment made Gail itch to hide her feet, the toenails of which were polished a deep burgundy. She wondered exactly what he meant by that comment, but was too chicken to ask. "Let me grab my purse, and I'll be ready to go."

"Take your time. The view is so lovely I find I'm in no rush to deprive myself of it, even temporarily."

Gail looked at him uncertainly.

"I'm making you nervous, aren't I?" Greg shifted subtly, betraying a hint of his own uneasiness.

She blinked and wondered how to respond. Finally, she decided honesty would be best. "A little. I haven't been on a date in nine years."

He tugged at the neckline of his shirt. "So am I."

"Why are you nervous?"

"I've waited a long time for this opportunity. I don't want to blow it. It might be the only chance I get," he said solemnly.

Gail looked into his earnest face and read his sincerity. Her nervousness shifted into concern—for him. She took his hand and pulled him inside, suddenly feeling much more in control. "I think, before we go anywhere, we need to talk."

"Damn, I haven't even got you out of the apartment and already I've messed up," he teased.

Gail laughed, glad to be back on a more comfortable footing with him. "Come in, silly."

Greg let her lead him over to the couch and pull him down beside her. He sprawled there, sexy in a pair of loose pleated black slacks and olive green collarless shirt that showed off his broad chest and deep tan. He placed an arm on the back of the couch and turned to face her, closing the gap between them.

"Yes?" he asked inquiringly, eyebrow raised for emphasis.

"I need to know what your expectations are," Gail said a little nervously, not sure how he would react.

"Are you asking me my intentions? Isn't it a little early in the relationship for this conversation?" he asked playfully.

She shook her head, all business now. "No, not intentions, expectations. What do you expect from me? I'm concerned you want more than I can give. I don't want to inadvertently hurt you."

Greg's playful manner dropped, and once again, she saw the serious man from this morning. "Why don't you tell me what you're looking for, then I'll answer your question."

Fair enough, Gail thought, although this wasn't what she planned. She took a deep breath before moving to mirror his position, arm on the back of the couch, turned to face him. She gave him a searching look before responding, reluctant to put into words the feelings of which she'd recently become aware. It would leave her too exposed. But, she realized, if she couldn't be open with him now about what she needed, there was no sense in this going any further, and she was strangely reluctant to call a halt to things. At least, not before she saw what could develop.

"I miss having a man in my life. I miss having a male point of view. I miss being a part of a twosome, a couple, and to be honest, even though I'm not sure I'm ready for it yet, I miss sex. Not the scratch an itch variety of one-night stands, but the comfortable sex that comes from knowing and caring for your lover and being cared for in return."

"You want a lover," he said bluntly.

Mentally, Gail shied away from putting a label on what wanted. "Maybe, eventually. But first, I want a friend." She searched his face for understanding, knowing she wasn't explaining herself well. It was hard to articulate what she wanted. Hard to explain the need she felt deep in her heart with every fiber of her being.

Greg reached out and cupped her check with his hand. Leaning forward, he kissed her slowly and lingeringly. Gail's eyes closed automatically as she sank into the heady sensation of being kissed for the first time in years. Oh so slowly, he drew back.

When her eyes opened and she was once again able to focus on his face, he said, "I'll be your friend, for now, but eventually, I'll be your lover. I've waited this long. I can wait until you're ready for more."

Unconsciously, Gail's tongue slowly slipped out to lick her lips, bringing his flavor into her mouth for a taste.

Heat flared in his eyes and his face hardened as his eyes followed the movement. "I'm trying to be good here, but you're making it difficult. If there's nothing else to discuss, we need to leave before I forget all of my good intentions."

He made a move to stand but stopped when Gail placed her hand on his thigh. She snatched it back when she felt the muscles stiffen beneath her hand, and he froze as though turned to stone. Her hand had been uncomfortably close to the bulge in his pants.

"Before we go," she said quickly, trying to distract her mind from the hard-on outlined by his pants, "there's something else you need to know about me."

He leaned forward and braced his hands on his knees. "Whatever it is, tell me quick. My control is hanging on by a thread."

She rushed into speech. "I'm about four months pregnant with twins. You should know because if we start dating, people are going to assume they're yours."

She fell back against the couch with a gasp as he loomed over her. "Who's the father?" he asked through clenched teeth. "Scratch that. Were you raped? 'Cause I know damned well you didn't go to his bed willingly, did you?"

"What! No! It's nothing like that. I agreed to be a surrogate mother for my best friend and her husband." Gail was shocked by his reaction.

Greg drew back with a frown. "Let me get this straight. Your friend asked you to be a surrogate for her knowing you'd already lost one child? Are you sure she's your friend?"

"Yes! Well, she can be a little flighty sometimes, but we've been friends since junior high. She's really been there for me through the years. Helping Crystal and Rashid have a child of their own is the least I could do after the way they supported me when I lost Jason and Marcus." Gail defended Crystal, even though in her heart of hearts, there was a part of her that agreed with his assessment.

"Un-huh, I'm sure you'd know better than I." He held his hand out and let it hover over her stomach. "May I?"

"Yeah, sure." She held still as he placed his hand on the small mound of her belly.

"You're not very large. Is this why you fainted at the office?" His hand measured the roundness of her stomach, massaging it lightly.

"Don't worry. I'll blow up soon enough. And yes, this was the reason for my fainting spell. I kept getting sick so I wasn't eating. The doctor put me on bed rest until I could keep my food down and regain some of the weight I lost."

"Speaking of food, let's go and get you fed. I don't want you sick again. You just got back to work. I couldn't handle another long absence." He stood to his feet and reached for her. Gail took the hand he extended and allowed him to help her to her feet. "You're sure you're all right now?"

Gail smiled reassuringly, not wanting him to worry. "I'm fine. Dr. Hagan said now that I'm in my second trimester, things should go much smoother."

"Well, I still think your friend's got a screw loose for asking you to do something like this, but if you need me for anything, just call and I'll come running. What's the deal with your friend anyway? Why can't she have her own kids or adopt like everyone else?" he asked as they walked out of the door.

"She's had several miscarriages," she said as they entered the elevator. "The doctors don't know what's causing them, but the last one almost killed her. Crystal really wants a child of her own but says she'll settle for one fathered by her husband. As for why she asked me, she doesn't trust anyone else. She'd rather the eggs come from me than some faceless stranger."

Greg cupped her elbow as he escorted her to his car. "So, does she go with you to the doctor? How involved are they in this process?"

"Very. I spent my time on bed rest in their home. Crystal's been to all of my appointments except one. We agreed she would be to all of them, as much as humanly possible, so she can feel connected to the babies even before they're born. Rashid recently started coming as well. The first one he attended was as a fill-in for Crystal. Now he's really intense and focused about the whole thing, wanting to be involved with every aspect of the pregnancy. It's annoying, but it's not like I can deny him. They're his children. I'm just the incubator," she said with a laugh.

Greg cast her a sideways glance. "Is that how you see yourself?"

"It's the only way I can afford to view myself. I have life growing in my womb, but I can't allow myself to become emotionally attached or think of them as mine."

"That's very wise of you. You're a strong woman. Not many women could do what you're doing, especially considering what you've been through."

Gail sighed. Greg sounded like Crystal. "It's not strength. It's an inability to say no to a close friend. I just hope this whole thing doesn't come crashing down on our heads," she said grimly.

"It's a delicate situation, that's for sure. Most surrogates aren't this closely involved with the adoptive parents, and they usually have families of their own to keep them from getting too attached. You have none of that. What happens if you decide not to give the child up?"

"I'm carrying twins," she reminded him. "And I don't see that happening. Legally, Rashid is already their father. The only portion remaining is for Crystal to complete the stepparent adoption after their birth. She's going to make a wonderful mother, and she's waited a long time to have a family of her own," Gail said firmly. Keeping these babies was not something she was emotionally equipped to do. It didn't even bear thinking about.

He opened the car door for her and stood there as she eased inside. Then he closed her inside and crossed around to the passenger side. He waited until they were on the road to speak again. "I know it's too late now, but put my mind at ease and assure me you had good legal representation," he said, his legal side peeking out.

"I'm a paralegal, remember? I know how not to get screwed by contracts. The terms were generously in my favor. Too generous, according to Florida law. I tried to get Rashid to dispense with the compensation but he wouldn't budge," Gail finished with a huff of remembered frustration.

They arrived at their destination, one of the expensive restaurants located near the Riverwalk downtown. Greg turned off the car then turned to Gail before getting out. "I know it's not my business and I'm not your man—not yet anyhow—but I would really like to take a look at the contract. I know they're your friends, but I'd like to see for myself that you haven't been taken advantage of."

"You may not be my man but you are my friend, and because of that, I'll let you review them. Just remember, I may only be a paralegal, but I have a law degree hanging on my living room wall at home," she reminded him with a laugh.

Greg exited the vehicle and came around to escort her from the car. Once they were seated at the table and had placed their drink order, he resumed the conversation. "That's one thing I don't understand. You have the degree. Hell, you passed the Bar. You could be practicing law. Why are you wasting your education and training?"

Gail leaned back in her chair and allowed her gaze to drift around the restaurant while she composed her answer. "I love the law. I always have. I love studying it, researching it, and surrounding myself with it. What I didn't like was being a lawyer. I don't have the heart for it, I guess. Let someone else play in the courtroom. That's not for me."

"You don't have to be a trial lawyer. There are plenty of areas where you could practice that don't include court. Why don't you try one of those?"

She shrugged one shoulder. "I considered corporate or family law. One was too time consuming and the other too heartbreaking. With the way folks are today, everything has the potential to end up before a judge, even probate. Being a paralegal allows me to work in the field I love without having to put in all the crazy hours you guys work. I come in, do what needs doing, and go home. My work stays at the office, and I'm a lot less stressed at the end of the day."

The waiter came and took their orders. Gail allowed Greg to order for both of them. When the waiter left, Greg picked up where they left off. "I see your point, but you'd make more money as a lawyer."

Gail threw back her head laughed. "Money isn't everything. Besides, with the hours you put in on a case, who's really making more? I have a job I'm happy with. That's important to me. All the money in the world wouldn't mean a thing if I hated what I was doing."

Greg leaned forward intently, forearms resting on the small table. "That's one thing I like about you. Most women look at me and see dollar signs. Not you. You're the first woman in a long time to make me work for a date. Most throw themselves at me at the slightest sign of interest on my part. "

Gail reached out a hand and touched his face briefly, causing his eyes to widen in surprise. "Are you sure it's your money they're attracted to? You're a very handsome man."

He was the very embodiment of tall, dark, and handsome. If Greg weren't a lawyer, he could make a killing modeling, with his tanned skin, black hair, and deep, dark eyes. His hair was too long to fit his conservative profession, and he wore it pulled back into a short, curly queue at the nape of his neck. In one ear, he wore a diamond stud, giving him a rakish look. He looked like the playboy he was, and she'd seen women fall over themselves trying to attract his attention.

He grasped her hand as she drew it back and held it in his own on the table. "It's nice to know you find me attractive. You brushed me off so many times I was beginning to think you were immune to my charms. Either that or I was the wrong color. Is that a problem for you?"

"You mean the fact you're white and I'm not?" He nodded. "No, not really. I've never dated outside of my race before, so this will be really different for me. But in this instance, that's a good thing. I won't be mentally comparing you to Jason at every turn." Jason had been African-American like herself with a dark complexion. She used to refer to him as her Hershey bar.

"The last thing I want is to be compared to another man, especially your sainted, deceased husband." Greg released her hand and sat back as the first course was served.

"Sainted?" she echoed sharply.

"You know what I mean. Your husband was a good man. Even if he wasn't, death tends to lessen people's memory of the bad, humanizing things of the deceased's nature. As a result, they remember only the good, elevating the deceased to a sainted status. There is no way I could compete. I'd always fall short."

Gail's mouth gaped as her fork hung in mid-air over her food. "You're right. I never thought of it that way. We're taught as children not to speak ill of the dead, whether they deserve it or not. I know plenty of women who won't date widowers for the reason you just cited. Although I'm a widow and in a better position to understand someone else's pain, I still would have to think twice about accepting an invitation from one," Gail was able to admit.

"Fortunately for you, accepting other men's invitations is not something you have to worry about." His look challenged her to disagree with his claim of exclusive rights to her company.

She let the challenge pass, not willing to make it an issue, especially not on a first date. She'd wait and see what happened when and if an invitation from another man presented itself. For the rest of the meal, they spoke of mundane things—happenings at the office, mutual acquaintances of which Gail discovered there were many, and general things men and women discussed when trying to establish a relationship apart from the office.

The evening was fun and relaxing. Greg was good company. When they finished their meal, they strolled along the Riverwalk, enjoying the breeze coming off the river. The city was pretty at night. They sat for a while at Friendship Fountain before deciding it was time to call it a night. Gail reminded him they both had to work the next morning, and it was getting late.

Greg took her home after extracting a promise that tonight wouldn't be their last night out together. At the door, he pulled her into his arms. "Just in case you're thinking of putting me into the buddy category..." His mouth swooped down and plundered hers in a kiss that left her breathless.

When he released her, she sagged against the door, needing its support for her suddenly weak knees. "Not a buddy. Got it," she agreed hoarsely.

Reaching past her, he opened her door and guided her gently inside. As he placed the keys in her hand, he whispered, "Goodnight," and closed the door behind him as he left.

Gail leaned against the door and drew in a shaky breath. Lord, she needed to get laid. For the first time in memory, she envied Crystal. No doubt about it, wherever she was, Rashid would make sure she got sexed—frequently.

Chapter Six

Crystal was ready to scream. She could feel it building on the inside but couldn't let it out. Rashid was ruining all of her plans. It wasn't fair.

He'd brought her to Paradise Island in the Bahamas. Their hotel was right on the beach, and the suite had an ocean view. For the last week, he'd done nothing but pamper her. Her every whim was satisfied and he'd spent an ungodly amount of money on her, taking her shopping and sightseeing.

As an Investment Banker, he'd been unable to totally escape work, but he'd kept the interruptions to a minimum. They'd made love constantly, over and over. Their vacation had turned into a second honeymoon.

With all that lovemaking, you'd think once, just once, Rashid would slip and forget to use a condom. He never did. Crystal did everything she could think of, going above and beyond in an effort to make him mindless with passion. She'd gone down on him so much her jaw was sore, and every time she thought she had him, thought that this time she'd finally got him to the point where all he could think of was getting inside of her, he still took the time to put on a condom.

She'd truly believed this vacation was a sign from God that this was her time—time to give life. How could she not? Rashid's offer of a mini-vacation coincided with her fertile period. Surely, somewhere over her three-day window she would conceive. Then she could present Rashid with the child he'd always wanted, and they wouldn't need Gail's.

Oh, they would make sure her children were provided for, of course. After all, Gail was her friend. She couldn't just dump twins on her. Besides, Gail would be happy to have a child to replace the one she'd lost, but none of this would happen if she couldn't get Rashid to lose the protection. She even tried hiding it from him. It hadn't worked. He absolutely refused to come inside of her unless he was sheathed in a condom.

If she heard him say, "It's for your protection. I don't want to lose you," one more time, she *would* scream. Never mind what Rashid would think.

God, haven't I suffered enough? Haven't I done enough penance for my mistakes? As usual, there was no response to her prayer, but then, she didn't expect one.

As a willful youth, she'd gotten pregnant. There'd been no way she'd mess up her life by having a child at an early age. She hadn't been scared of what her parents would think. She knew they would have supported her had she chosen to keep the baby, no matter what anyone else thought. She hadn't wanted it. At the time, she'd been too young and having too much fun to be tied down with a baby. Her whole life had been ahead of her, and she'd planned to live it unencumbered with unnecessary responsibilities.

Because she'd committed a terrible sin and murdered her unborn baby, God continued to punish her by denying her the one thing she wanted most in life. It was the only thing that made sense. The minister she'd spoken to after her first miscarriage had tried to convince her she was wrong. He'd said God wasn't vengeful and sometimes these things just happened, but she knew the truth. She was cursed. That's why the doctor's couldn't find a reason for the miscarriages. There was no medical reason.

After each miscarriage, her doctors had convinced Rashid to send her to a counselor to help her deal with her grief. Five different counselors and each one a quack. They'd all had the same diagnosis. They believed she'd sabotaged her pregnancies; killed her precious babies. Reciting the same mumbo-jumbo about the mind being stronger than the body, they'd said she'd willed herself to lose her babies because she wouldn't forgive herself for the abortion—an act her conscience mind couldn't deal with because of her strong religious upbringing. Guilt had surfaced in the form of miscarriages.

They knew nothing. She wasn't the one who needed to do the forgiving. She needed God's forgiveness. She needed absolution, and the proof he'd forgiven her would be when she delivered a healthy baby and presented it to Rashid.

Each time she'd discovered she was pregnant, she thought to herself, "This time, I've been forgiven and I'll give my husband a child." Each time, she'd been wrong. But next time... Next time would be different. She was willing to stake her life on it.

◆◆◆◆◆

The next morning at work passed quickly but quietly. Her unplanned absence had caused a backlog, and Gail dove in to help her fellow paralegals catch up. She'd seen neither hide nor hair of Greg, but before leaving last night he'd told her he would be busy all morning with depositions.

Just when her stomach reminded her it was time to take a break and eat, Greg appeared at her cubicle, seemingly from nowhere. "Let's go."

He reached into the drawer where she kept her purse and snagged it. Rolling her chair away from the desk, he lifted her out of her seat and had her walking towards the elevator before she could get her wits about her.

"Where are we going, and what's the rush?" she asked breathlessly, trying to keep up with his long-legged stride.

"Out of here. I need a break before I hurt someone," Greg muttered as he jabbed the down button on the elevator.

"It was that bad?" she asked softly. Divorce cases were messy business, even the high profile ones.

The doors to the elevator glided open. The car was empty. Greg pulled her inside and jabbed the lobby button. As soon as the doors closed, he wrapped Gail in his arms and kissed her hungrily.

"I'd rather think about this," he murmured when he lifted his head. "I missed you last night. I look forward to the night when you won't feel the need to send me home." He'd leaned in for another kiss when the doors opened and another passenger got on.

They both shifted to make room and remained quiet the rest of the way down. Gail was glad for the opportunity to catch her breath. She was going to have to make a decision and make it soon about whether or not she wanted Greg as a lover. Otherwise, he would simply overwhelm her defences and the choice would be out of her hands.

He was certainly attractive enough, and she enjoyed his company. At this point, she couldn't tell if she was sexually attracted to him or simply vulnerable to the attention he gave her because she'd gone without sex for so long. That's what she needed to determine before things got out of hand. The last thing she wanted to do was use the man and lead him on because she was horny, then dump him when someone better came along.

They spilled out into the lobby and headed for the door. "Where are we going?" she asked again.

"The café around the corner. They should have food you can eat, and we'll both get out of the office for a while." His hand was on the small of her back as he led her down the sidewalk.

In no time at all, they had their food and sat at a corner table. "How's your day going?"

"Busy." She told him some of the research she was involved in. He offered a few helpful tips and she made a mental note to look up the cases he'd referenced.

"What time do you get off?"

"Two o'clock." Her new schedule only allowed her to work six hours a day.

"What are your plans after work?"

"I'm going by the gym to walk on the treadmill for an hour. Then I need to go grocery shopping, since my cupboards are bare. After which, I'm headed home to cook dinner and relax." Home to my own apartment, she thought. Lovely.

"I have some files to go over tonight, but I wouldn't say no to a free meal and some entertainment if a certain somebody were feeling generous," he said with a boyish grin on his face.

Gail observed his grin for a moment, and then had to laugh when he waggled his eyebrows invitingly. "Would you like to come over to my place after work for dinner and a movie?"

"Why, I would love to. How nice of you to ask. I'll even bring the movie," he offered generously.

Greg looked at his watch and swore. "I have to get back. I have a client coming in about ten minutes. Are you finished?"

"Yes, I'm done with this. Ready to go whenever you are."

He took both their trays and threw their trash away. When he finished, Gail was by his side. They walked back to the office in silence. Before they went their separate ways, Greg bent down and kissed Gail on the cheek. "See you tonight."

Gail looked around cautiously, wondering if anyone had seen the uncharacteristic display of affection. No one seemed to have noticed. She sighed in relief and headed for her cubicle. She wasn't ready to go public with their relationship.

Much later that evening, Gail opened the door to a tired looking Greg. He was still in his business suit though the tie had loosened. A bulging briefcase hung from one arm and in his hand, he held a movie and a rose.

"Come in. You look tired. Are you just leaving the office?" Gail glanced at the clock on the mantle. It was a few minutes after seven.

"Yes. Some last minute business came up on one of the cases I'm working that had to be dealt with. It couldn't wait." He stooped and kissed her briefly on the mouth on his way in. "You look good enough to eat. What's for dinner? I'm starved." He handed her the movie and the rose.

"Thank you. I hope you like stir-fry because that's what we're eating. I have to stay away from greasy food and eat healthy. I foresee a lot of stir-fry in my future. It's quick, easy, and healthy." Gail led him into the living room.

"I'm all for quick and easy. Whatever you cook will be fine."

Motioning to the couch, she said, "Here, sit down and make yourself comfortable. You said earlier you had files you needed to go over."

"Yes, I did and I still do," he said grimly, indicating the briefcase in his hand.

"Well, there's the table. Feel free to spread out while I prepare dinner. Give me twenty minutes and the food should be ready."

"Thanks." He took off his jacket and tie, rolled up his sleeves, and loosened the top two buttons of his shirt. Pulling the coffee table closer to the couch, he spread out his paperwork and got down to business.

"Would you like something to drink?" Gail asked, her hostess skills coming to the forefront.

"I don't suppose you have any beer?" he asked, busy sorting papers.

"Nope, nothing alcoholic. I have soda, juice, or bottled water." Then she rattled off the variety of juices and sodas she had on hand.

"Just bring me a bottle of water. That would be great." His tone was distracted, his mind already focused on work.

Gail took a bottle of water out of the fridge and prepared a small tray of cheese and crackers to tide him over until dinner was done.

"Thanks," he said absently when she set the items within reach, but safely out of the way of his paperwork.

Back in the kitchen, she took her time with dinner preparations, knowing Greg would need longer than the twenty minutes she'd offered to review the mountain of files on her coffee table.

She bustled about the kitchen, humming under her breath as she worked. Having a man to cook for was nice, and she was woman enough to admit it. Cooking for one was lonely and many times she didn't make the effort. Food was to be shared and enjoyed, not simply eaten as a means of survival.

She sliced the veggies and set them to the side. The meat was cubed, marinated, and waiting. The wok was on the stove heating. Gail was talking to herself, reviewing what she'd done and what still needed doing when an arm snaked around her waist, pulling her back into a hard body. "Do you always talk to yourself when you cook?"

Gail shrieked and would have jumped a few inches off the ground if he hadn't been holding her.

"Did I frighten you?" he asked with a chuckle.

"No, I always go around jumping and screaming for no reason. Don't do that," she commanded and pinched him on the arm. "Make noise or something. It's not nice to sneak up on people."

"But you looked so cute, and I didn't want to intrude on your conversation with yourself. It would have been rude." He reached out and took a green pepper, dancing out of the way when she tried to slap his hand.

"Very funny. Har, har, har. Are you done going over your files? I thought you'd still be at it."

"I'm done for now. I'm tired of working and ready to play. Want to play with me? We can play doctor. You get to be the patient. Take off your clothes and let me examine you," he said with a leer.

"I'll pass, thanks." Judging the grease hot enough, she threw the meat into the wok, waving away the blanket of steam that arose. Once she deemed the meat done enough, she added the veggies.

"You did that like a pro. I'm impressed." Gail glanced over to find Greg watching her, an intent look on his face. "You like to cook?"

"Love to, but it's not much fun cooking for one," she confessed.

"You can cook for me anytime."

"How do you know I'm a good cook? You haven't even tasted this." She turned off the burner and moved the wok from the heat. "Hand me those plates, please."

He passed her the dishes, and she scooped up food for both of them. Greg took the plate and fork she handed him, and immediately took a bite of food.

"This is good." He nudged her out from in front of the stove and added more food to his plate.

"Help yourself," she said dryly. "Please, feel right at home."

He leaned down and kissed her lightly on the lips. "I'm going to ignore the sarcasm, because I know inside that feminist heart of yours, there's a southern belle tickled pink I like your food enough to get more," he smirked.

She laughed, knowing he was right. The complaint was for show.

"Would you think I was a heathen if I suggested eating in front of the TV while we watch the movie?"

"No, I would have suggested it myself, but didn't want you to think I was trying to rush you out of here." Gail grabbed her food and got a drink from the fridge, motioned for Greg to do the same, and headed for the living room.

Greg cleared the papers off the table and set his food down. Then he went and set up the movie and started it playing. They ate through the previews and by time the feature started, they were almost done eating.

The movie was one of those action packed thrillers that captured her attention from the very beginning and held it. She barely noticed Greg clearing the dishes from the table and taking them into the kitchen. He returned with bottles of water for both of them. She murmured irritably when he disturbed her viewing pleasure by repositioning both of their bodies. Greg reclined on one of the couch pillows and she lay between his legs, her upper body supported by his chest.

She was totally engrossed in the movie, so much so that she couldn't tell at what point she drifted off to sleep. Her body was being stroked from shoulder to hips, and she arched into the caress like a cat. "Jason," she sighed sleepily and the stroking stopped.

When she murmured a complaint and rubbed against the erection pressing against her stomach, it continued. Gail slowly surfaced from sleep to realize her head was pillowed on Greg's chest. At some time during the movie, she had rolled over and one of her legs was thrown casually across his. A glance at the TV showed the movie was over.

Embarrassed, she planted a hand on either side of his chest and tried to lift up. "I am so sorry I fell asleep on you. I must have been more tired than I realized."

Greg locked his hands together at the small of her back, keeping her from moving. "Don't be," he said huskily, right before he flipped her onto her side between him and the back of the couch.

He captured her mouth in a kiss that gave no quarter. It demanded and got a response. He ate at her mouth, displaying his considerable skill as a lover. While her sleepy mind tried to catch up with the onslaught, his hand delved under her top and released the clasp on her bra. Once free of the encumbrance, his hand quickly claimed its prize. He caressed, stroked, and plucked her nipples until her whole body shuddered with need.

When she arched and rubbed against him, frantic to put out the fire he'd created in her body, Greg pulled away. "My name is Greg, not Jason. Maybe this will help you remember whose arms you're lying in, hmm?"

Gail gazed blankly at him, her passion fogged mind not up to the task of deciphering his comment. Greg got up and gathered his coat and tie. "Bring the movie with you to work tomorrow, or I can just pick it up the next time I'm over. Don't bother seeing me out." He leaned down and kissed her lightly on the lips. "See you tomorrow. Get some rest."

Greg grabbed his briefcase and walked out of the door. She heard the click of the lock engaging behind him.

Gail lay on the couch, stunned and bewildered. She wanted to be mad that he'd deliberately aroused her when her guard was down and left her hanging, but something he said kept playing through her mind. Why had he mentioned Jason?

She could understand him being upset because she fell asleep. It was rude of her, but what had that last crack mean? She rose from the couch and straightened her clothes, then the rest of the place, her mind going over the events of the evening.

Finally, it came to her when she was lying in bed, half asleep. She thought she'd been dreaming, but

81

maybe she hadn't. Had she really called him Jason? Oh boy, no wonder he was ticked. No man liked being called by another man's name, for any reason. What he'd done had been cruel, but effective. Gail knew his touch now and wouldn't automatically assume the hands caressing her belonged to her dead husband.

Well, at least one question had been answered. She could definitely say it was Greg to whom she was attracted and not just the idea of having a man in her life and the personal attention he provided.

◆◆◆◆◆

The next morning, around ten, she called Mandy, Greg's secretary. "Is Greg with a client? I need to talk with him but don't want to disturb him if he's busy."

"No, he's free right now if you hurry. He has to leave in about twenty minutes for court."

"Thanks, Mandy. I'll be right up." Gail quickly rose and stopped briefly to let a co-worker know she'd be away from her desk for a few minutes.

When she entered Greg's office, Mandy told her to go right in and winked at her, leaving her to wonder if she knew about the recent change in her and Greg's relationship. She tapped on the door and walked in before he could grant her entrance.

Greg looked up with the phone attached to his ear, his expression showing irritation at the interruption. When he saw it was her, he said to whomever was on the phone, "Listen, let me call you back later. Someone just came into the office...um-hmm...all right, goodbye."

Gail rounded the desk and moved his paperwork to the side. Once it was clear, she sat on its edge, between his legs. "You know, I should be seriously pissed with you for getting me all stirred up and then leaving me hanging," she scolded, her legs kicking back and forth between them.

"Really?" He sat back in his chair and stretched his legs out on either side of hers. "Then why aren't you?"

"Because I have this vague memory of calling you Jason. Although I feel allowances should be made for the fact I was half asleep at the time and didn't know what I was saying, I can understand you're being a bit miffed at the time."

One eyebrow arched. "Is that so?" He captured her by the ankles, lifted and separated her legs, and tugged. She slid off the desk and into the chair with him, straddling his lap, her skirt indecently high.

He slid his hands up the back of her thighs. "Thigh highs. I like," he murmured approvingly.

She settled more securely on his lap and braced her arms on his chest. "Glad you approve." Gail lifted her chin and tilted her head, giving him easier access to the neck he nuzzled.

He removed his hands from beneath her skirt and held her by the waist. "I told you I'd be your friend until you were ready for more, but I've been treating you like we're already lovers. If you're feeling pressured, if I'm moving too fast, let me know. "

Gail leaned forward and kissed him, the first one she'd initiated. "I'm not ready to get naked with you, but I enjoy the attention and the affection you give me. I'll let you know if I begin to feel uncomfortable." In a way, she was glad he'd taken the initiative and forced her to accustom herself to his touch.

"Good, because the next time I have you in that position, I won't stop until we're both shaking and shuddering with satisfaction. Consider yourself warned." He pulled her closer until her damp heat nestled against his erection. With one hand cupping her head, he kissed her long and deep. "I have to be in court soon," he said between kisses. "If I don't leave in the next few minutes, Mandy will buzz to see what the holdup is." He possessed her mouth in another passionate kiss as his hands slid to cup her bottom and rub her gently against him.

Finally, Gail gathered her scattered wits and pushed him away. "I need to get back to my desk before they send out a search party." She climbed off his lap and stood, straightening her clothes.

Greg rose from his seat, crowding her against the desk. "It's going to be hell walking into court with this massive boner."

The "boner" in question pressed solidly against her stomach. "You've no one but yourself to blame." She tried to ease around him.

He caught her by the waist and brought her close for one final kiss. "There's no telling how long I'll be at court, and I need to come back to the office afterwards. I won't be able to see you tonight, or tomorrow night either. Why don't I take you out Friday? We can catch a movie or something?"

"Sounds good to me." Gail waited while he slipped on his suit jacket and straightened his tie. She brushed his hair back off his forehead. "Perfect," she proclaimed.

He picked up his briefcase with one hand and put the other at the small of her back. When they reached the door, he opened it and pulled it shut behind them. "Mandy, take messages. I'm not sure when I'll be back. Put anything that can't wait until tomorrow on my desk."

"Yes, sir." Mandy's gaze bounced between the two of them.

Gail resisted the urge to look down and see if her clothes were mussed and wished she had a mirror. This was one time she was glad she wasn't a makeup wearer. At least she didn't have to worry about smudged lipstick.

Greg kept his hand on her back as he escorted her out of the office and into the elevator. More than a courtesy, it felt like he'd staked his claim. When the elevator stopped at her floor, he said as she exited, "If I get the opportunity, I'll call you tonight."

Gail nodded to acknowledge she'd heard him as the doors slid shut and went back to her desk. Miraculously, nobody seemed to have missed her or inquired as to her whereabouts. She got back to work, happily anticipating the weekend to come.

Chapter Seven

A week later, Gail was relaxing at home when her phone rang. "Hello?"

"We're back," Crystal announce flatly.

"That must have been some trip. Four days turned into two weeks? That wasn't a mini-vacation. It was a second honeymoon," Gail teased.

"Yeah, I guess you could call it that."

Instantly concerned, she asked, "What's wrong? You just spent two weeks relaxing with your man. Why do you sound so depressed? Didn't you have fun?" If she'd just spent two weeks in the Bahamas, Gail would have been so mellow it would ooze out of her voice.

"Oh, the trip was great. He took me to Paradise Island, and it was beautiful. Anything I wanted to do, and any place I wanted to go, we did. You should see the stuff I bought. Oh, and I got you a souvenir."

Gail smiled. "Sounds wonderful. What's the problem?"

"It's Rashid. He's making me crazy. You're right. The trip was a second honeymoon. Everything would have been perfect if it weren't for those damned condoms," Crystal complained.

"Uh, did you say condoms?" Gail wasn't certain she'd heard correctly.

"Yes, condoms," Crystal confirmed bitterly. "I hate those things. Rashid knows I do, but still refuses to make love without one, like I'm going to give him a disease or something."

Squirming uncomfortably in her seat at the too personal topic, Gail hesitantly asked, "Have you discussed this with him? If you haven't, you should talk to him about how you feel." Crystal may be her best friend, but a couples' sex life was their private business. She didn't want to know what went on in their bedroom.

"I've told him I don't like the damned things, and we don't need them. He insists. Says he won't chance me getting pregnant again. It doesn't matter that I'm on the Pill."

"Other than that, you enjoyed your vacation, right?" Gail said, trying desperately to redirect the conversation. "I hope you got plenty of rest, because I'm sure your work piled up while you were gone."

Crystal sighed. "I have assistants, but some of my projects still got behind schedule. I'm going to have to work long hours to catch up. That's another reason I called. I may not make it to your next doctor's appointment. Will you be okay by yourself?"

"Yes, I'll be fine. It's probably going to be routine, and hopefully very short. You won't be missing anything," Gail assured her.

"I just wanted to make sure. We're supposed to be doing this together, and I promised to be there with you at all of the appointments," Crystal said, sounding worried.

"Hey, stuff happens. I understand completely. You just make sure your schedule is free when Dr. Hagan does the sonogram to tell you what you're having."

"I will. I wouldn't miss that for the world. Well, I better get off the phone. We just got back, and I have things to do. Before I go, is everything okay with you? Anything new in your life?"

"I'm fine. Things are quiet. I go to work and come home. However, I have made it a point to get out of the house more often and renew old acquaintances. Things of that nature. Nothing worth talking about." Gail wasn't ready to tell Crystal about Greg. The relationship was too new. Maybe in another month or so, if it lasted that long.

"All right then, why don't you come over for lunch tomorrow? We can catch up and I can show you the stuff I bought."

"Make that dinner and you've got yourself a deal." Gail planned to attend church with Greg in the morning and knew she wouldn't be free for lunch.

"Dinner's fine. Early or late?"

"Why don't I come over around four? We can eat at five and lounge around the pool or something."

"That's a good time. Okay, I'll see you tomorrow at four."

"Until then, take care and cheer up," Gail told her.

"You, too."

As Gail put the receiver back on the cradle, she shook her head. Her friend complained about the strangest things. Condoms, indeed.

On the other end of the line, a scowling Crystal hung up the phone. She turned to find Rashid standing a few feet away. How long had he been there and how much of her conversation had he heard?

"Was that Gail?" He pointed, indicating the phone.

"Yes. I called to let her know we were back."

"Is she well? Has she had any complications with her pregnancy?"

Crystal rolled her eyes. "She's fine. We were only gone for two weeks. She's coming over tomorrow evening for dinner so you can see for yourself. I've got to go. I have some running around to do, and I need to stop by the office to see how things are going. You want me to get you anything while I'm out?"

"No, I have need of nothing. Thank you. I may go by my office as well."

"Okay, if you do call and let me know what time to expect you home." She kissed him on the cheek, grabbed her keys and left, still wondering how long he'd been standing behind her.

◆◆◆◆◆

That evening, Crystal opened the door to a ragged, sweaty-looking Gail.

"What happened to you?" Crystal asked. She reached out and took the beach bag Gail toted.

"Too much sun," Gail whispered. "My head is killing me."

"Oh man, that sucks. Have you taken anything for it? You know you get migraines when you get overheated," Crystal reminded as she pulled Gail inside of the air-conditioned house.

When Gail pulled off her sunglasses, Crystal winced. From the look of those eyes, if Gail hadn't taken something for her headache, it might already be too late. They were narrowed against the light and filled with pain.

"Not yet. It wasn't this bad earlier. My air conditioner picked today of all days to go out in my car. It must be at least ninety-five degrees today. And of course, the traffic was stop and go the whole way here," Gail complained softly, as though the sound of her own voice hurt.

Crystal dragged Gail into the kitchen and pulled the pain reliever out of the cabinet. She passed the bottle to Gail and poured her a cool glass of water. Gail shook out three, popped them into her mouth, and added a large swallow of water. Then she pulled her hair out of the ponytail it was in, a sure sign of the pain she felt.

"Come into the family room and sit in the recliner. It's not as bright in there. I'll go upstairs and get the things I want to show you." Crystal waited until Gail had herself situated before walking off.

As she walked past the office, she stuck her head inside. "Rashid, Gail's here. She's in the family room trying to cool off and relax. If you go in there, try to be quiet. She's got a bad headache because she got overheated. The poor dear is prone to migraines. Hopefully the medicine I gave her will take effect in time."

Humming to herself, she went upstairs and gathered the items together. There were pictures and a video, things Rashid purchased for her, etc. Now where had she put the seashell she'd bought for Gail? She looked all over the room before remembering she'd stuck it on the shelf in the closet. Once she had it, she was ready.

As she neared the family room, she heard the quiet murmur of Rashid's voice. "You need to take better care of yourself than this. If the heat makes you sick, you should stay out of it. You are especially vulnerable to its effects right now."

"I know, Rashid, and usually I do but stuff happens. I had no control over the A/C in my car malfunctioning. It will be Wednesday before I can get it to the shop to have it fixed. Thank you, that feels good."

When Crystal entered the room, a damp kitchen towel rested on Gail's forehead and Rashid stood behind her chair giving her a neck massage.

"Your neck and shoulders are very tight. It's contributing to your headache, and why are you fixing the vehicle? You should purchase a new one. It's been tearing down more and more," Rashid said as he took the towel off her forehead, rung it out in the bowl next to him and replaced it, this time on her neck.

It did something funny to Crystal's stomach to see Rashid playing nursemaid to her friend. It was petty, she knew, but still, she didn't like it one bit. She pushed her negative feelings aside and joined the conversation. "I'm with Rashid on this one. I don't understand why you haven't bought a new one. It's not like you can't afford it."

"The stuff breaking down on my car is normal maintenance things that have worn down because of the mileage. It's expected. Besides, and I know you'll both think this is foolishly sentimental of me, but that car is the one Jason bought for me when the business first started doing well. It's the last piece of him I have. Thanks, Rashid. I feel much better now." Gail removed the towel from her neck and handed it to him.

He took the towel and the bowl and left the room. Gail looked at Crystal and told her, "You have a wonderful husband. You're very lucky. It's at times like these I miss Jason the most."

"Yes, I do," Crystal acknowledged, feeling guilty. How childish of her to begrudge Gail the little bit of comfort Rashid had given her, considering all Gail had lost. Rashid was hers. Every loving and caring ounce of him belonged to her. So he'd spent a few minutes helping her sick friend? She should be happy he was compassionate enough to do so, instead of jealous of the attention he'd paid someone else. "I'm glad you're feeling better. Now I can show you the pictures from my trip."

For the next hour, Gail laughed, ooh'd and ah'd over everything Crystal showed her. Then they joined Rashid in the dining room for dinner. Crystal served since Carmelita only worked half-days on weekends. The conversation was lively and fun and Crystal enjoyed herself immensely. When the time came, she was sorry to see Gail leave but realized she needed to rest.

As they cleared the table, Rashid commented, "She's really not that large to be four months pregnant with twins. Do you think it's normal? Are we sure everything's all right?"

"I'm sure everything is fine, but if you have any questions, she has an appointment next week. You can ask Dr. Hagan then." Once again, all of this concern over Gail was starting to annoy her.

"Do you think she'll purchase a new vehicle? Jason wouldn't want her holding onto that thing, not if it's starting to tear up. It was used when he bought it."

"I'm sure Gail will do whatever she deems best," Crystal said shortly.

"I'll talk to her. See if I can convince her to buy another one. She'll eventually need something larger and higher off the ground. As her pregnancy advances, she'll have difficulty getting in and out of her car, as low as it is," he finished thoughtfully.

"Well, if she doesn't, you can always buy her one," Crystal suggested sarcastically as she finished loading the dishwasher and turned it on. "I'm going up to take my shower. Are you coming?"

"I'll be in the office." She watched as he left the kitchen, his mind clearly on other matters.

◆◆◆◆◆

Friday, when Gail walked into the waiting room, she was startled to find Rashid waiting. After checking in to let them know she was here, she took a seat next to him. "Hi, I'm surprised to see you here. I thought you'd be busy like Crystal."

"I had my secretary put your appointment on my schedule so I wouldn't miss it."

"Oh, that was smart." Gail mentally scrambled for another topic of conversation. When she couldn't find one, she reached for one of the pregnancy related magazines on the table.

"You are feeling better? There's been no return of the headache?" he asked, his intent gaze studying her face.

"Yes, I'm fine now. I really don't get headaches that often any more. It took me by surprise." Gail really had no one but herself to blame. She knew she was prone to migraines and should have taken something when the headache first began, instead of trying to wish it away.

"And the car? Is it fixed?"

Inwardly she sighed. Of course he'd ask. "It will be in another couple of days. For now, I'm driving a rental. They had to replace the whole unit."

"Ms. Henderson!" the nurse called.

Gail stood, happy for the interruption.

The visit was routine right up until Dr. Hagan asked if they had any questions. Rashid had a whole list. He questioned if her stomach was too small, if the babies were growing properly, and if Gail ate and drank enough to facilitate their development. He reported the incident with her headache, which really pissed Gail off because then she had to listen to a ten-minute lecture from Dr. Hagan on the dangers of heat exposure.

By the time the visit ended, she seriously regretted granting Rashid permission to accompany her to all of her appointments. As they prepared to leave, Rashid asked Gail in front of Dr. Hagan, "Have you been getting your daily exercise?"

Both men waited expectantly for her answer.

Mentally, Gail cursed. "No," she admitted reluctantly. She'd done fine for a week or two, but between Greg and the job, she'd forgotten all about it.

That negative response earned her another lecture from Dr. Hagan on the benefits of exercise. Gail was ready to kick Rashid when it was all over with. The sooner she got away from him, the better.

She escaped as soon as she could and went to set up her next appointment. Then she had to relieve her bladder again. Gail hoped Rashid would be gone when she came out of the bathroom. No such luck.

Rashid escorted her to her rental. "Do not forget you promised to come over in the evenings, use the pool, and eat dinner with us. I know you couldn't while we were gone, but we have returned."

Darn it! When she'd made the promise, she didn't have a life. Now there was Greg, and the women whose friendships she had renewed. Did she really want to spend every evening with Crystal and Rashid? No, but a promise was a promise.

She sighed. "I did forget, but I'll make it a point to be there tomorrow."

"I will see you then." He moved out of the way so she could shut the car door.

Later that same night, she was telling Greg all about it as they shared a pizza. "I'm telling you, Greg, I wanted to hit the man. It's not like I haven't done this before."

"Give the man a break. He's lost...how many kids now? It's bound to make him a little paranoid."

"I know, I know. I'm really trying to be patient and understanding. Really, I am, but it's difficult. We're not married. We were never lovers. I'm just the woman who's carrying his children. It's awkward. Until they're born, to get close to them, he has to stay close to me." She rolled her neck to loosen the tension before continuing. "Rashid and I have never been friends, never had what you would call a close relationship. He's just my best friend's husband. Someone I'm familiar with but don't really know. Now we're being forced into close contact. It was supposed to be me and Crystal doing this. I never really gave much thought to Rashid's role in this whole thing. I just kind of assumed he would donate his sperm and then show up at the hospital to pick up his kids. Boy, was I wrong."

Gail sighed and took another bite of pizza. "I have to go to their house every evening, which was fine when I suggested it. It was a compromise to keep me from living with them. Now that I have you, I really don't want those kinds of demands on my time."

94

Both of his eyebrows shot up. "They wanted you to move in with them?"

"Yeah, well, mostly Rashid. Although I think Crystal agreed with him. My answer was no. I said for my own emotional stability, I had to maintain a certain degree of separateness from them. I couldn't do that if I lived with them. I'm giving up enough of my life as it is."

"What, exactly, did you tell him you would do?" Greg reached out and stole a pepperoni off her slice of pizza.

"I told him I would come by every day and use the pool for the daily exercise I'm supposed to be getting and let Carmelita feed me."

Greg's hand hovered over the pizza pie as he glanced at her. "Were those your exact words?"

"I'm pretty sure they are. Why?" Where was he going with this line of questioning?

"You want to keep your word but not have every evening tied up with them, correct?" he asked as he made his selection.

"That's the idea," she confirmed.

He pointed at her with his pizza slice. "Here's the solution. Go over to their house as soon as you leave from work and take your swim. Then allow Carmelita—that's her name, right?" At her nod, he continued. "Allow Carmelita to feed you. Afterwards, you head home. You didn't commit to a certain time, did you?"

"No, no time was mentioned."

"There you have it." He emphasized his point by taking a bite of pizza.

Gail gazed at him in admiration. "That was positively devious. Brilliant, genius even, but devious. You know that wasn't the intent of the agreement."

"No, but it is the letter of it," he said smugly.

Gail laughed. "Remind me to never argue with you."

Whatever he would have said in return was lost when the doorman buzzed. "Ms. Henderson?"

She rose from the table, crossed to the door, and pushed the call button. "Yes, Paul?"

"Mr. Al Jabbar is here to see you."

"Rashid! What's he doing here?" she asked Greg. Pressing the button again, she told the doorman, "Send him up."

"Very good, ma'am."

"I wonder what he wants," she said to Greg, completely puzzled by Rashid's presence at her apartment.

"We'll find out in a minute, or should I leave?" He stood and wiped his hand on a napkin.

Gail tried to wave him back into his chair. "No, don't go anywhere. I'm sure whatever business he wants to discuss won't take long."

"In that case, I'll take the rest of the pizza into the living room and get the movie ready."

"Okay."

A knock sounded at the door and Gail went to answer. "Rashid, come in. This is unexpected. Is everything all right? Where is Crystal?" Gail spoke rapidly, curious about his reasons for being here, and a bit unnerved and unsettled at the thought of him meeting Greg. Absurdly, Gail felt like she'd been caught cheating.

"Crystal is at home. Everything is fine. I did not mean to alarm you. I simply stopped by to drop off something for you."

Gail examined him curiously as both hands appeared to be empty. The clearing of a throat interrupted her inspection of Rashid. She snapped to attention as Greg walked into the foyer.

"Hi, I'm Greg Richmont. I don't mean to intrude, but honey, did you mean to keep him standing in the foyer all night? Or were you planning on letting him come further inside so he could have a seat?"

Rashid's posture stiffened at the sight of Greg and his eyes narrowed at the casual endearment, though he shook the hand Greg held out to him. Gail saw him take particular note of the casual yet possessive arm Greg laid across her shoulders.

"I'm sorry, Rashid. Please come into the living room." Gail was flustered, and she was sure it showed. It wasn't like her to be so rude.

"No, that is all right. I did not come to stay long. As stated before, I only stopped by to drop off something for you. My ride is waiting below." That being said, he removed a set of keys from his pocket and held them out to her.

She reached for them automatically, even as she asked, "Keys? What are these for?"

"The blue Santa Fe I leased for you. You may return your rental in the morning."

"You got me a car?" Her voice rose with each word. "Are you out of your mind?"

Greg squeezed her warningly. "Shh, let the man explain. I'm sure he has a good reason for doing what he did. "

Gail closed her mouth and forced herself to listen to Rashid's explanation.

Rashid slid his hands into his pants pocket and rocked a little on his heels. "It is not a purchase, but a lease. I wish for you to use it for the duration of your pregnancy. I know you have, as you say, a 'sentimental attachment' to your vehicle, but I am concerned for your safety. I would feel better if you had reliable transportation. In addition, as your pregnancy advances, you will have difficulty entering and exiting your car. The Santa Fe is higher and roomier, and it is an automatic. Please use this until the children are born. It can be returned to the dealership at that time."

When Gail looked as though she would argue, Greg voiced his opinion. "He's right and his request is reasonable. Your car isn't the most reliable of vehicles. I don't like the idea of you driving it myself. What if it breaks down on you somewhere? You do a lot of driving. Think about the babies. "

"What about Crystal? What does she think about this?" Gail wanted to argue against taking the vehicle, but they had a valid point. This wasn't about her pride or preferences. This was a safety issue, and it fell under the guidelines of the agreement she'd signed.

"It was her idea," Rashid informed them calmly.

"For the twins," Gail reluctantly agreed. She wondered why Crystal hadn't told her what they'd planned. On the other hand, Crystal probably knew Gail would have protested if she'd known what they had in mind. Much better to present her with a done deal.

"I must take my leave now as someone is waiting for me. We'll see you again tomorrow?" he asked, a reminder of their earlier conversation.

"Yes, I'll be there sometime tomorrow afternoon."

"Until then." Rashid reached out a hand to Greg again, and they shook. "Nice meeting you." Then he left.

"You're right. He's very intense," Greg said as they headed back into the living room. "Just imagine if you were married to him. He's very protective of these children."

Gail shuddered. "If he were my husband, his possessiveness would drive me crazy. I don't know how Crystal stands it."

◆◆◆◆◆

Rashid rode with the car salesman back to the dealership, his mind in turmoil. He didn't like the idea of Gail having a man in her life, not while pregnant with his children. It startled him to realize he felt possessive

98

of her when he had no right to be. Still, he'd wished he'd had the foresight to include a clause in their agreement that she remain celibate throughout the whole pregnancy, and not just during the time when she was being inseminated.

The two appeared very cozy together and had the closeness of lovers, or soon to be lovers. The man had possessively made his claim known. Rashid wondered why Crystal hadn't told him about this man in Gail's life. Undoubtedly she knew. Those two didn't keep secrets from each other.

When he arrived home, he found his wife in the study, looking at design books. "Why didn't you tell me Gail was seeing someone?"

She glanced up, forehead furrowed in confusion. "Seeing someone? You mean, like a man?"

"Yes, a man. Did you know she was involved with one?" he asked irritably.

Crystal frowned. "No, she hasn't said anything to me about it, though she did say she was ready to start dating again. How do you know she's seeing someone?"

"I saw them together. He's quite possessive, too. If they aren't lovers, they will be soon," he muttered in disgust, almost angry at the thought of it.

At this news, she set her book aside. "You saw them? Where?"

"He was at her apartment tonight. They were obviously spending the evening together." He yanked off his suit jacket and tie, and headed for the bedroom with Crystal following close behind.

"Her apartment? What were you doing at Gail's apartment?"

Rashid sat on the bed and removed his shoes. "I had the dealership follow me over there to drop off the vehicle."

"Vehicle?" Crystal's voice raised an octave. "What vehicle?"

"The one I leased for Gail to use for the remainder of her pregnancy. That car she insists on driving is not safe. So I provided another one. One that is."

"You bought her a car?" Crystal echoed in disbelief.

"No, I leased one. Did I not say so? It is like an extended rental," he explained, wondering what the problem was.

"I know what a lease is," Crystal snapped. "What I can't believe is that you got Gail a vehicle without discussing it with me first."

"It is for her use, yes, but it is in our name. Therefore it is not her vehicle. I don't understand your reaction. This was your idea," he reminded her. "I wouldn't have thought of it otherwise."

"My idea?" Crystal cried. "I didn't tell you to go out and lease a car for Gail."

"No, you suggested I buy her one. We both know she wouldn't have accepted had I done as you said. This is a good alternative."

"Rashid, I was being sarcastic. I didn't actually mean for you to go out and get her a vehicle to drive. What kind of car are we talking about?"

"A Hyundai Santa Fe. The safety ratings on it were outstanding, and its height will make getting in and out of the vehicle easier as her pregnancy advances. The roomy interior will also be good for her as her stomach increased in size. "

His wife threw up her hands. "I can't believe you did this. Unbelievable."

"How so? There is nothing I wouldn't do for the safety of our children," he said firmly.

"Safety of your children, you mean—yours and Gail's," she mumbled under her breath.

Rashid glanced at her, eyes narrowed in disbelief, certain he'd heard wrong. Dismissing the thought, his mind promptly went back to the issue concerning him most. "So, she has not spoken to you of this man she is seeing? You have no idea how long the relationship has been going on, or if they are lovers?"

"What's it to you?" Crystal asked sharply. "Why do you care what she does, or who she does it with?"

"While our children are in her womb, it matters very much to me what she does. Anything she does has an impact on their well-being."

The look she gave him was full of scorn. "Gail's not going to do anything to endanger the twins, and she deserves to have a life. I'm glad she's finally found someone. Jason is the one who died, not Gail, and she shouldn't have to spend the rest of her life living off the memory of their love. It was time for her to start living again. High time, if you ask me, and if she's found herself a lover, all the better."

"I wish she would have waited until after the children were born," he muttered as he stalked naked into the bathroom. The door shut behind him with a sharp click.

Selfish bastard, Crystal thought. Everything was about his precious babies. It should be me. Me pregnant. Me being fussed over and catered to. Me with the new vehicle and the black American Express card.

Crystal left the bedroom still furious about the vehicle Rashid had bought Gail without consulting her. She picked up the phone to call Gail, then thought better of it. Tomorrow would be soon enough.

She'd call and have Gail bring her new man over so she could meet him. As for the rest, Crystal hoped he spent the night screwing Gail's brains out, no matter what Rashid thought about it.

Chapter Eight

Early the next morning, Gail's phone rang, dragging her out of a deep sleep. She fought free of the covers and brought the phone to her mouth. "Lo?"

"Somebody's been keeping secrets." The female's voice was bright and cheerful, too cheerful for this early in the morning.

"Crystal?" God, what time was it? It couldn't be morning already.

"Wake up, sleepy head. I want to hear all about your mystery man," Crystal chortled.

"Who? Greg?" Gail sat up and pushed her hair out of her face. Her jawbone cracked as she yawned widely, still trying to wake.

"Is that his name? Rashid didn't say. Tell me about him. How long have you been seeing him? And why didn't you tell me? As your BFF, I've got to tell you I'm hurt."

Gail groaned. "See, this is why I didn't say anything. I knew you'd be like this. Nosy little heifer."

Crystal giggled. "Quit with the name calling and dish already."

Bowing to the inevitable, she said, "His name is Greg Richmont, and he's one of the lawyers in the firm where I work."

Crystal made a humming sound. "Greg... Isn't that the name of the guy you complained is always flirting with you?"

Trust Crystal to remember. "That was a long time ago, and I wasn't complaining. I was just telling you how big of a flirt he is."

"And if I remember correctly, didn't you say he was white?" Crystal's voice was accusing.

Geez, the woman had a memory like an elephant. "He's Caucasian. What of it?"

"Nothing. I'm just surprised. In all the time I've known you, you've never looked twice at a man who wasn't black."

She frowned. Crystal's comment made her sound racist. "That's not exactly true. I'm not against interracial dating. Greg is the only man who's shown any interest. Until recently, I never believed he was serious."

"What changed your mind?"

"When he asked me out, I threatened to call his bluff and say yes, thinking he would back off. He showed me a side I'd never seen of him. Turns out he's been waiting for me to take him seriously and give him a chance." Gail smiled at the memory.

"Ooo, sounds romantic. So, you do the dirty with him yet?"

"No, I haven't. Not that it's any of your business. We haven't been seeing each other long," Gail said a bit stiffly.

"Well, how long is long enough?" Crystal asked irritably. "You've been without sex for a long time. I thought you were horny? Here's your opportunity to get some."

"Crystal, it's not that simple, and you know it," Gail replied with some heat of her own. "It's only been a couple of weeks. I need to know him a lot longer before I could feel comfortable being sexually intimate with him. Besides, part of me feels like I'm cheating on Jason just by going out with Greg. Sex isn't a step I'm ready to take," she finished firmly.

"Gail, you have to let go of the past sometime. The only way you're going to get past feeling guilty about having sex with another man is to just do it."

"Crystal, my life is not a Nike commercial, and sex is more than something you do to get it out of the way." Gail didn't know why she bothered trying to explain. Until she lost a husband, Crystal would never understand. Besides, her sex life was really none of her friend's business.

Obviously sensing she'd crossed a line, Crystal backed off. "All right, all right. I'll let it go for now. When can I meet him?"

"I don't know. Like I said, he's a lawyer and his schedule is very busy." Gail wasn't ready to introduce Greg to her friends. She wanted to keep him to herself a little while longer.

"If the man has time to see you, he has time to meet your best friend. Come on. Give me a day. I won't leave you alone until you do," Crystal sang.

"You are such a pest!"

"I know," Crystal acknowledged cheerfully. "Don't you just love me?"

Gail couldn't help but laugh. "Okay. I'll check with Greg and see if he's free Friday night."

"You do that and bring him here for dinner. Tell him to bring his swimsuit and we can swim and grill out by the pool."

Gail sighed. "I should have known when Rashid showed up last night he would say something to you about Greg. Speaking of last night, while I appreciate the generous offer, I really wish y'all would have asked before leasing a car for me to use."

"I know how you feel about your car, Gail, but even you have to admit it's not in the best condition."

"Yeah, I know. It's starting to cost more to repair it than to buy a new one. Actually, at the rate I'm going, I'll have replaced everything in it soon and it will be new again—on the inside that is."

"Gail, really. Jason would be horrified if he knew you were driving that death trap simply because he bought it for you. It's a car, girl. Find some other way to remember him by," Crystal said admonishingly.

"It's not a death trap. It's just got a lot of miles on it," Gail said, defending her car. Then she admitted, "That's what Greg said, too. I know you're right. It's just hard. I've had that car for so long it's comfortable. I like it. I wouldn't know where to start looking for another one or what kind to buy."

Crystal was silent for a moment. "Drive the one we got for you and see how you like it. Give yourself a chance to get used to something different. By the time you deliver, maybe you'll have a better idea of what kind of car you want, and the idea of getting a new one won't seem so difficult."

"I'll do that. And, thank you for the Santa Fe. As mad as I was at the time, I knew just my pride was offended. Although I don't think my car is that bad, I would hate myself if something happened to these babies because of it that could have been avoided," Gail said solemnly.

"Don't worry about it. You made the right decision. You always do," Crystal said encouragingly.

Not always, Gail thought, and laid her hand on her rounding stomach.

◆ ◆ ◆ ◆ ◆

Dinner was a complete disaster. It started bad and continued downhill. When they arrived, it was evident from the tension between them that Crystal and Rashid had been arguing. Crystal was artificially cheerful with everyone but Rashid. With him, she was an iceberg.

Rashid was his usual quiet self. Although with Greg he seemed ultra-reserved, as though he had judged and found him lacking. He made no effort to be cordial and only spoke to Greg when politeness demanded he do so.

On the other hand, she couldn't shut Crystal up. She questioned Greg about everything. No topic was too personal. Gail was so embarrassed. Crystal also threw Jason's name into the conversation, seemingly every chance she got. She brought up memories of their times together that Greg would have no knowledge or any interest in, leaving him out of the conversation on many occasions.

As soon as she reasonably could, Gail got them out of there. As they drove away from the house, Gail apologized profusely. "Greg, I am so sorry. I swear, if I had any idea it would be this bad, I'd have never have agreed. I don't know what got into Crystal. I've never seen her so...so, I don't even know what to call it. And Rashid? He was almost rude. He's not the most talkative person I know, but I've never seen him so...well, almost unfriendly."

Greg reached out and captured the hand she gestured with. "Don't worry about it. It's no more than I expected. I'm the new man in your life. It's natural that comparisons would be made. Besides, it was easy to see they'd been fighting when we arrived. Do they do that a lot?"

"No, not normally. I mean, all couples have spats from time to time. Usually, it's Crystal flying off the handle about something or another. Rashid's pretty unflappable, very easy going. That's why his behavior tonight didn't make sense."

"That's cause you're not a man. It made perfect sense to me. I'm poaching in his territory, and he doesn't like it," Greg said reasonably.

"His territory? That's crazy. You just met Crystal tonight."

"Not Crystal. You, babe," he said with a laugh. "I'm talking about you."

"Oh, now I know you've lost it. I don't belong to Rashid. He has no reason to feel possessive of me."

"Sure he does. Two of them, right here." He rubbed their joined hands against her belly. "It's instinctive. You're carrying his children, therefore you…and the children, belong to him."

"That is the stupidest thing I've ever heard. Rashid and I don't have that kind of relationship, and never have. You must be mistaken." He had to be. If she and Rashid had ever been lovers, Greg's reasoning would make more sense.

"Think what you like, but I know what I'm talking about. Now your friend, Crystal? That's a different story. Has she always been jealous of you?"

Gail jerked her body around to face him completely. She wished he weren't driving so she could see his face. "What did you mean by that? Crystal's not jealous of me. She has no reason to be."

Greg cast a quick glance in her direction. "Honey, that woman's so jealous of you she positively oozes with it."

"What are you talking about? She just spent the evening singing my praises. I wished I'd known what to say to shut her up."

"Yeah, and she said all of that because she knew you'd be uncomfortable. Why do you think she kept mentioning Jason? She was trying to get to you and run me off at the same time. Most friends would have gone out of their way to avoid saying his name, just to put me at ease. I'm telling you, she knew what she was doing. Crystal's not as flighty as she acts."

Gail didn't know what to say. She didn't believe his assessment of the situation but she had to admit, neither Crystal nor Rashid had made a good impression tonight. It would be a long time before the four of them got together again, if ever.

◆◆◆◆◆

Gail floated in the pool and allowed her thoughts to drift, simply enjoying the peace and quiet. This was the best part of her day. The next place she moved into really needed to have a pool.

The last few weeks had been quiet. She hadn't seen much of Crystal or Rashid. Greg's suggestion had worked like a charm. Gail went to their house immediately after work. She exercised, let Carmelita feed her, and left. If she saw them at all, it was as she was leaving the subdivision and they were entering. Crystal believed Greg was keeping her too busy to come around.

Her stomach grew daily, as though the twins had decided it was time to make their presence known to the world. Her respectable "B" cup had swelled to an awe-inspiring "D." Greg was very much in favor of her new curves. She wore maternity clothes full-time now, as none of her regular clothing fit. Anyone who hadn't known she was pregnant before was aware of it now. As expected, it was the source of a lot of speculation in the office.

Many were aware she and Greg were an item, as he made no attempt to hide his interest in her. Rumor said it was his child she carried. Since no one was bold enough to ask her directly, Gail said nothing to set them straight. It wasn't their business, anyway.

Her thoughts, as usual, drifted to Greg. He was always on her mind. He would absolutely flip if he could see the bikini she wore. She grinned evilly at the thought. She was gleefully considering all the many ways he would try to coax her out of it when a muscle cramp hit without warning. She immediately doubled over in pain, sinking beneath the surface of the water.

Bubbles rose as she let out an involuntary gasp of pain. She grabbed her calf, trying to massage the tight muscle while she sank lower and lower into the pool. Just her bad luck she'd caught a cramp right when she was floating over the deep end. Gail forced herself to remain calm though she would soon run out of air and needed to swim to the surface to get more. However, she couldn't as long as the pain kept her muscles locked up.

Just when she was beginning to seriously worry, a pair of strong arms grabbed her from behind and pulled her to the surface. She broke through and sucked in a lung full of desperately needed air. Gail's body was turned, and she immediately reached out and clung to Rashid, her arms locked around his neck, holding onto him like a lifeline.

With a few powerful backstrokes, Rashid swam with her to the shallow end of the pool where the stairs were located. When Gail tried to release him and stand, her muscle spasmed and she cried out with pain. She would have gone under again if Rashid hadn't swung her up into his arms.

"What is it?" he asked sharply.

"Leg cramp," she got out between teeth clenched against the pain.

Rashid carried her out of the pool and set her down in one of the patio chairs. He knelt in front of her. "Which leg? Never mind."

He brushed her hands aside when a particularly vicious cramp had her hands shooting to cradle her calf, her left leg drawing up reflexively, close to her body. Rashid grabbed her ankle securely with his hand and began to firmly massage her calf muscle as he slowly forced her leg to straighten. Gail hissed in pain and tightly gripped the sides of the chair, her body arching as she instinctively struggled to get away. She wanted to knock his hands away from her leg but knew he was only doing what needed done.

While he worked the knotted muscle, he berated her. "It was beyond foolish for you to be in the pool alone. Do you not know even the most basic rules of swimming safety? What if I had not decided to come

109

home early? Do you think I wish to come home and discover my wife's dearest friend and my unborn children dead in my pool?"

Gail let Rashid's words wash over her. She knew it was the fear talking, manifesting itself as anger. She was a little shaky herself at the close call.

Crystal came in just as the last of the cramp left her leg. "Gail, when I saw your car in the driveway, I thought I'd find you still back here by the pool. What on earth is going on?" she asked suspiciously. "Rashid, why are you all wet?"

Rashid still had on his suit, obviously having stopped only long enough to take off his shoes and jacket. He was drenched from head-to-toe, with water still streaming off him. "Leg cramp," he told Crystal tersely. "I came home to find our friend here in the process of drowning."

"Drowning?" Crystal echoed, her eyes shooting to Gail for confirmation.

"It hit me while I was floating in the pool," Gail confirmed.

"Alone," Rashid muttered angrily. "In the deep end."

Ignoring him, Gail continued. "I was trying to work it out when Rashid so gallantly rescued me."

"Stretch out your leg. See if it's gone," Rashid instructed.

Gail extended her leg and flexed her foot. "It's a little sore, but I think it's leftover tenderness from the cramp. I'll know for sure when I put weight on it."

"Stand and let's see." Rashid moved back and gave her room, but remained on his knees.

Gail stood and drew in a sharp breath.

"There is pain? Where?" He was looking at her leg, feeling the muscle to see where it was knotted.

110

"No, my leg's fine. It's the babies. They're moving." Gail was awed. She'd felt flutters before but this was actual movement.

Rashid's gaze shot to her belly. "Where?"

"Quick, give me your hand." He held it out, and she placed it on her stomach. "There. No, wait. Right here." She adjusted his hand.

"Do you feel it? It's not very strong." Gail kept her hand over his, pressing it firmly against her mound. She found herself holding her breath, as though that would allow him to feel them better.

They both startled when one of the babies made a strong kick, right against the place where Rashid's hand was resting. Gail laughed as Rashid looked at her in astonishment. "Did you feel that?" he asked excitedly.

"Yeah, I did," Gail said dryly, but was grinning when she said it.

His reaction was so cute. She looked to Crystal to share the moment, only to discover she was gone. Gail wondered briefly where she'd disappeared to but was distracted by Rashid. He asked a ton of questions. How did it feel? How often did it occur? Did it hurt? The whole while, he kept his hand on her belly, waiting for it to happen again. The incident in the pool had been forgotten.

Gail ended up staying for dinner. As they were eating, Rashid told Crystal about the experience in vivid detail. Crystal made all the appropriate responses but seemed a little distant. Watching her, Gail felt a moment's unease. Greg's words from a few weeks ago came to her. *How long has Crystal been jealous of you?* She shrugged them off. Crystal was probably tired from work or she could have simply had a bad day.

When the meal was over, Gail excused herself. "Don't forget about my appointment next week. You'll get to find out the sex of your children. I'm so excited for you."

"We'll be there," Rashid assured her as he walked her to the door. He escorted her all the way to her vehicle and stood there until she was comfortably strapped inside. With a final wave, Gail pulled away from the house, Crystal's cool behavior forgotten.

◆◆◆◆◆

Crystal waited until the last minute to show up at Dr. Hagan's office. She wouldn't have come at all but knew there would be too many questions to answer had she given this appointment a miss. She walked into the waiting room just as the nurse called Gail's name. Had she been in a better mood, the look of relief on Gail's face would have amused her.

"There you are. I was starting to worry," Gail told her.

"Just running a little late," Crystal assured her as she watched Rashid help Gail stand.

To Crystal, Gail appeared to be huge. She looked like she'd hid a beach ball under her shirt, and there were still three more months to go. They all paraded to the back. Rashid was visibly excited, if you knew the signs. This visit today was all he had talked about last night and again this morning until Crystal had to bite her tongue to keep from hollering, "Shut up already about those damned babies."

She watched in silence while they set up for the sonogram. When Dr. Hagan was ready, he called them closer and pointed to the screen. "As I told you before, Gail is carrying twins. See this line right here? That means there are two different amniotic sacks, which means fertilization of two eggs. What we have here is a set of fraternal twins, not identical. Now let's see if we can see tell what sex the embryos are."

Rashid stepped closer to the bed, eyes glued to the screen. Crystal made room by moving further away.

Now that she was here, she couldn't help but be curious. After all, there was still the nursery to decorate and baby items to purchase.

"I'd say this one right here is a boy. Now let's see if the other one will cooperate," Dr. Hagan said.

Crystal watched the screen intently as she waited for the doctor's verdict. How he could tell what anything was on the monitor was beyond her.

"I'm not a hundred percent sure since the baby's in an awkward position, but it looks like we've got ourselves a mixed set—a girl and a boy."

Rashid whooped, caught Crystal up in a bear hug, and spun her around. "A son and a daughter. We are truly blessed by God." Then he leaned down and kissed Gail lightly on the cheek. "Thank you for doing this for us."

Dr. Hagan interrupted the celebration. "If you are going to take childbirth classes, now is the time to do so. I don't know who's going into the delivery room with Gail, but it's recommended you be trained on what to expect."

"Crystal is going to be my coach," Gail informed the doctor.

"I would like to be there as well," Rashid said to Gail.

Gail looked at Crystal, her eyes asking a question.

"You might as well let him be in there with us. Otherwise, he'll drive the doctors and nurses crazy and get himself kicked out of the maternity ward."

Crystal had been serious, but Gail laughed as though she'd told a joke. "All right, you can be in the delivery room, Rashid."

Rashid nodded his head. "And I shall take the classes with you as well. I, too, would like to know what to expect and how to be of assistance to you."

"That's an excellent idea. Why don't the three of you go together? It will be a bonding experience. They even teach you how to care for your newborn once you bring them home from the hospital, very valuable information for new parents. I would take advantage of it. It will cut down on panicked calls to the pediatrician," Dr. Hagan suggested mildly.

Crystal decided then and there she would not be attending birthing classes. She was not sitting in a room full of pregnant women learning how to give birth if she wasn't one of them. Rashid could be Gail's partner. It was his children after all. If anyone needed to know what to do, it was he.

She tuned out the rest of what Dr. Hagan said, but interrupted long enough to tell the group she needed to return to work. As Crystal left the building, she thought of the tender expression on Rashid's face when he'd given Gail the kiss and was sorry she'd ever suggested this surrogacy business.

◆◆◆◆◆

After the sonogram, Crystal pushed harder than ever for Rashid to make love to her without protection.

"Crystal, I'm doing this for you."

"I know, but I don't like them. I don't like the way they feel. I prefer to feel you skin to skin. Besides, it's not like we need them. You know I'm on the Pill," she whined.

"We do need them. It is the only way I can guarantee you won't get pregnant. While not one hundred percent foolproof, between these condoms and the Pill, I know you will be safe," he said firmly.

Planting her hands on her hips, Crystal delivered her ultimatum, confident Rashid would give in to her demands. "I don't want to be safe. I want to feel you, not latex when you're in me. I've told you it's unnecessary. If you insist on continuing to use them after knowing how I feel about it, then we just won't be having sex."

His face impassive, Rashid studied her until she began to feel like a piece of scum. It was all she could do not to squirm. "If you feel this strongly about it, I will make an appointment with a specialist and schedule a vasectomy. It's a simple procedure. With the twins, we'll have one child of each sex. There will be no need for more children."

"No," Crystal protested, horrified. "That's not necessary. I don't want you doing anything drastic. "

Rashid exploded. "Then for God's sake, Crystal, what is it you wish for me to do? You complain to all who would listen about the protection I use for your safety. You whine and make threats to me, withhold your body more than you share it, and when I come up with a viable solution to meet both of our needs, you reject it. What do you want from me? Let's hear it in plain English, for I tire of these games."

Crystal dropped her aggressive pose and took a step back, suddenly afraid. Rashid was well and truly angry, and she was at a loss. He'd put her on the spot with his demand, and she couldn't confess her real agenda.

When she continued to stand silently with tears rolling down her face, Rashid heaved a big sigh. "I'm tired of this. Tomorrow, I will call the doctor and make the appointment. By the end of the week, it will be done."

His tone and facial expression told her Rashid's decision was final. There would be no persuading him otherwise. Crystal burst into angry tears and left the room. Nothing was turning out as planned. This was all Gail's fault. If she weren't pregnant with twins, none of this would be happening.

Chapter Nine

Halfway through her third trimester, Gail's face, hands, and ankles swelled. Instead of the graceful stride she'd once had, she lumbered like a big, brown bear, and felt like a beached whale. The only time she felt like her old self is when she was in the pool.

After her near drowning incident, Rashid switched to working at home in the afternoons so he could be there to monitor her while she swam. He usually brought his laptop out onto the pool deck and conducted business with clients, one eye on the computer, and the other on her. When she had enough of the pool, he joined her as she ate, many times sharing the meal with her.

As she'd been warned to expect, Gail hadn't seen or heard from Crystal. She recalled their last conversation.

"You won't see much of me these next few weeks. I'll be working long hours to finish my projects ahead of schedule. I want to be free to stay home with the children when they are born," Crystal said.

"You're abandoning me? Now, when we're almost at the finish line?" Gail said.

Crystal held out a hand in appeal. "Gail, I'm sorry. Don't be angry with me. I know what I promised, but all the work I'm doing now is for the children. Besides, you have Rashid. Isn't one of us really all you need? Right now, as the babies' father, I feel it's more important Rashid be there."

Crystal's words hadn't lessened her anger, but what could she say?

So Rashid accompanied Gail to all of her doctor's appointments, which, as her due date drew near, were many. It was Rashid who partnered with her as her coach during the childbirth classes. Without Crystal there as a buffer, Gail got to know Rashid as a person, and they became good friends. She discovered he had a fascinating mind and was a financial genius. She understood now why Jason had gone to Rashid whenever he needed financial advice.

Underneath his reserved air was a very sharp wit. Contrary to Crystal's claim, Gail discovered Rashid did have a sense of humor, albeit a dry one that gently poked fun at things. Many times, if you weren't paying close attention, much of his humor would float right over your head. In his own way, once he opened up, Rashid was a lot of fun to be around. She could see why Crystal married him.

While she was at work Thursday, Rashid called. "Do not go to the house after work. I will not be there to monitor you. Urgent business matters have arisen, and I do not know how long I shall be. Promise me you will not swim alone."

"I promise. I learned my lesson. I don't want a repeat of last time."

"What will you do in my absence?" She could hear the concern in his voice.

"Don't worry, Rashid. I have plenty to do to keep me occupied. I'm getting so big that everything takes twice as long to accomplish, and I'm falling behind. "

"I offered to hire you domestic help. I even requested your return to our home so we can assist you," he reminded her.

Gail rolled her eyes at the mini lecture, sorry she'd mention it. "I know, and I appreciate the offer. I wasn't complaining. Simply explaining that the hours I normally spend at your house can be put to use today catching up on the things that have fallen behind, like laundry and household chores."

"If you still would like to take your swim, I can call when I get home and you can come over then," he generously offered.

"That's all right. I haven't been getting enough sleep. When I leave work, I'm going to turn off the phones, lie down, and take a nap. Then I'll do my chores."

In the background, Gail could hear the murmur of men's voices. "I have to go. They're waiting for me. I will see you tomorrow, then. Take care and be sure to rest," Rashid instructed.

"Yes, yes," Gail agreed hurriedly. "Go! They're waiting for you," she reminded him and hung up the phone. Rashid, she'd recently discovered, was a worrywart.

Greg stopped by her cubicle shortly before she was scheduled to leave. "Headed for the pool?"

"Not today. Rashid has to stay in the office." Greg, aware of the incident in the pool, was in perfect agreement with Rashid that she not swim alone.

"Does this mean you're free tonight?" His expression was hopeful. Although their relationship was still going strong, they hadn't seen as much of each other as they'd liked to because of his busy schedule.

"I'll be home, but I really need to rest. It's getting harder and harder to sleep comfortably at night. I'm going home to take a nap and then catch up on my housework."

"If you're having trouble sleeping, I know something we can do that's guaranteed to relax you into a good night's sleep." As he spoke, he discreetly adjusted his pants, drawing her attention to his crotch.

Flirtatiously, Gail slowly licked her lips and winked. "I'm sure you do, and one day, I'll take you up on that offer."

By tactic agreement, they'd kept their sexual relationship on the level of heavy petting, deciding to

118

wait until after she delivered to become lovers. To Gail, it didn't feel right contemplating sex with one man while carrying the babies of another. As for Greg, he'd stated that when they did finally make love, he wanted her focus to be totally on him.

"Are we still on for tomorrow?"

"Yes, just don't come by too early. I may want to sleep in," she warned him.

"That's fine." He helped her stand and walked with her to the elevator. "Go home and get some rest. You look tired."

She leaned into his strength, and he wrapped an arm around her waist. "I will. The phones will be off, so don't try to call."

"I won't. I'll just see you in the morning." Greg tilted up her chin, making sure he had her complete attention. "If you need anything, you call me."

"Will do," Gail told him as the elevator doors opened.

"Go on. I'll take the stairs."

Gail allowed the doors to close and headed home.

◆ ◆ ◆ ◆ ◆

After rising from her nap, Gail put up her Christmas tree, finished cleaning and decorating her apartment for the holidays, and now stood debating whether to shower before heading back to bed. The water might cause her to lose this lovely sense of drowsiness she felt, and she did not want another sleepless night. Deciding to skip the shower, she was heading for her bedroom when someone pounded on the door.

Must be one of the neighbors, Gail thought, as she headed to answer its urgent summons. A glance out the peephole showed a wild looking Rashid standing at the door. In her rush, she fumbled the locks. Soon as she got it open, she had to jump to the side to keep from being run over.

"Where is she? And why do you not answer your phones? I've been calling for hours," he demanded.

"Where is who? And I told you the phones would be off while I slept. I must have forgotten to turn them back on." She waddled slowly behind Rashid as he stalked further into the apartment.

"Where is my wife? I know you know where she is. She tells you everything." He turned to face her, his hands on his hips and a forbidding expression on his face.

Both her eyebrows rose in automatic response to her surprise. "Crystal? I haven't actually seen or talked to her since Thanksgiving Day. Every time I call, she's busy. She isn't home from work yet?" If that was the case, no wonder Rashid was upset. It was almost midnight. As far as she knew, Crystal never worked this late.

At her words, Rashid burst out in a string of curses that caused Gail to flinch. For the first time, Gail realized Rashid wasn't just upset, he was pissed. "Rashid! Rashid! Calm down and tell me what's going on." Though based on his reaction, Gail wasn't really sure she wanted to know.

"She's gone."

"What do you mean, gone?" Gail asked sharply.

"Departed, left, vanished. Packed a bag, withdrew money from the bank, and left. No note. No word of where she was going or when she would be returning," he said shortly as he paced back and forth. He reminded her of a caged tiger at the zoo.

At his words, Gail felt a little faint and sat abruptly to keep from falling. "She can't be gone, Rashid. You must be mistaken. Crystal wouldn't leave you. Where would she go? Are you sure she didn't say anything? Maybe she had to go out of town unexpectedly and forgot to tell you," Gail said a bit desperately. "Check with Carmelita. She would know."

Rashid shook his head sharply. "She gave Carmelita the day off. Called her yesterday and told her not to come in."

"Have you called her cell phone? There has to be a reasonable explanation for all of this. I can't believe she would leave, not with the babies' arrival so close."

"I did that first. Her cell phone is off. She left it at the house, along with her house keys and credit cards." The look he shot her said he was not an imbecile. He'd already done all she suggested.

Gail latched on desperately to what he said. "Well, there you have it. Something must be wrong. Crystal would never leave her credit cards, not willingly. Call the police. She must have been kidnapped."

Rashid came, sat on the couch, and grabbed her hands. "I called the police when I discovered her car in the garage. It was my first thought too, that something happened. She is gone, Gail. Believe it. There is no sign of foul play. No reason for the police to believe this was anything other than voluntary on her part."

Gail snatched her hands from Rashid and pushed at him. "Well, don't just sit there. Go find her and bring her back. This is your wife we're talking about. Whatever problems you two are having, get over them already! The twins will be here in a few weeks."

The more upset Gail became, the calmer and more resolved Rashid seemed to be in contrast. "Calm yourself. You are too close to your time to be getting this upset. I have called the security company we deal with to make some discreet inquires. Other than you and her coworkers, she had no friends of which I'm aware."

"What about work? Crystal loves her job. She wouldn't just up and leave it." None of this made sense. Crystal could be flighty at times, but this was off the charts.

Rashid stood and paced again. "She told her assistants the babies were born premature, and she would not be returning to work. Her projects are all completed so her presence would not have been missed."

"I don't understand. Why would she do something like this? Why leave now, when my due date is so close? Oh God, the twins. What are you going to do?" Gail was starting to get angry. If she could get to Crystal right now, she'd shake her until she couldn't see straight. How dare she do something selfish like this?

Rashid came and knelt at her feet, placing his hands against her stomach as though he needed to feel close to his children. "I don't know what was on her mind. I do know that she was unhappy, and nothing I did seemed to please her."

"Maybe she just left to get her head together," Gail suggested softly, placing her hands on top of his. "Maybe she just needed time alone to think and once she's had it, she'll be back."

"Perhaps, but in the meantime, I will not allow my children to suffer for her foolishness. I need you, Gail." He looked her straight in the eye. "Our children need you. If Crystal has not returned by the time they are born, I need you to help me care for them."

Gail felt the shock of his statement right down to her toes. She pushed his hands away and leaned back in her seat in an instinctive effort to distance herself from his request. "Rashid, you don't know what you're asking of me." Her voice was shaky.

"I do know. I have given it careful consideration. I know it will be difficult for you, but my children need someone to care for them. I want that someone to be you."

"Then hire a nanny. I am not their caretaker. I'm the Godmother, remember?" Gail shook her head back and forth. She couldn't do what he asked. She wouldn't do what he asked.

"And does not the Godmother step in to help with the raising of the child if one or both parents are unable to do so? Is this not one of their duties?" He grabbed her hands when she tried shoving him away so she could stand.

"This is different and you know it. You can't ask me to care for them, to risk becoming emotionally attached to them, and then step aside when Crystal returns." She struggled fruitlessly to free herself.

"Be still before you hurt yourself," he commanded sharply. "It is doubtful Crystal will return. If she does, we will deal with it when the issue arises. "

Gail quit struggling and sat there breathing heavy, tired from her efforts. "What happened to the nanny you were going to hire?"

"A nanny cannot provide the love and attention these children need. The love you, their birth mother, can give to them. Of course, I will hire someone to assist, but what they need is you. One mother has already abandoned them. Will you do the same? Think on it, please. Perhaps it will be as you say. Crystal will return and all will be well. There is still time for decisions to be made." He got to his feet, forestalling any argument she would make. "I must go. You have much to think about and it is very late. You need your rest."

Gail pushed off the couch and struggled onto her feet, trailing behind him to the door. "Seriously, Rashid, find Crystal and bring her home. She's probably feeling overwhelmed with the coming of the children. Maybe this is just a desperate bid for your attention, and she needs for you to prove how important she is to you by coming after her."

Rashid looked as though he disagreed but held his peace. Her heart ached for him as he left, even as she cursed Crystal and called her all kinds of a fool. What was she thinking, jeopardizing her marriage like this? Rashid was a good man, a wonderful husband, and an excellent provider. Crystal may have just messed up the best thing she had going for her in her life.

◆◆◆◆◆

Gail slept through the morning and into the afternoon. She'd just started her day when Greg arrived. He kissed her as he came through the door. "You were supposed to rest yesterday, but you still look tired. Rough night?"

She pushed the door closed and leaned wearily against it. "You could call it that. Rashid came over late last night looking for Crystal. She's gone. Packed a bag and left. I still can't believe it. My mind's been racing all night, trying to figure out where she could be and what's going on in her mind."

Greg whistled soundlessly. "Rashid must be livid. Has he spoken with her?"

Shaking her head, Gail pushed off the door and waddled into the living room. "He has no way to contact her. She didn't take her cell phone with her. Neither did she take her car. Foolish woman even left her credit cards behind. No one knows where she is. She didn't even leave a note explaining why she'd left."

"She probably called a cab. If she left her cell phone, credit cards, and car, it sounds like she doesn't want to be found. Is Rashid hiring someone to track her?"

Gail sighed heavily and lowered herself onto the couch. "I really don't know. I advised him to but will he do it? You should have seen him last night. He was furious, but it was a cold, deep anger. Truthfully, right now, I don't know if he wants to see her again. I can't say I blame him. At first, he thought something had happened to her. It wasn't until he contacted the police that he realized she'd left him. I'm still having a hard time believing she did something like this, especially now, with the babies' arrival so close."

Greg dropped down beside her on the couch. "That's probably why she left."

Gail looked at him blankly, and then shook her head. "Maybe the lack of sleep is affecting my ability to comprehend, but that made no sense to me."

Greg studied her for a moment, obviously weighing the words he wanted to say.

She frowned. "Stop debating and just say it."

Coming to a decision, he said, "I want you to listen and hear me out. No interruptions, even though you won't agree with what I'm saying."

"How do you know I'm going to disagree?" He arched an eyebrow at her until she flushed. "Sorry. I interrupted."

"I know you'll disagree because Crystal is your friend, and you're very loyal to her. You're also too close to the situation to see clearly, and completely biased in her favor. I don't know her so I can be more objective." Greg paused for a minute, probably waiting for her to comment. She kept silent since so far she agreed with everything he'd said. "Crystal's greatest desire is to have a baby, right?"

Gail nodded.

"How do you think she feels, seeing you grow larger every day with the babies she can't have? Seeing the attention, the preferential treatment, her husband gives you because the children in your womb belong to him?"

"That's crazy. Rashid's not doing anything that wasn't outlined in the contract we signed," Gail burst out, unable to help herself. "Besides, this whole thing was Crystal's idea."

"Yes, it was. That's part of the problem. She's jealous and angry, and has no one but herself to blame because she set this whole thing in motion. She can't call

125

it off because Rashid has already bonded with his children. Didn't you say she'd been missing doctor's appointments lately?"

"Yes. She hasn't been to one since we discovered their sex," Gail admitted.

"Has she been to any of the childbirth classes?"

"No, she's been working long hours, trying to clear up her projects before they arrive." Gail was glad to be able to give him a reasonable explanation for Crystal's absence at the classes.

Greg arched an eyebrow. "Has she really been working, or was it just an excuse to distance herself from the whole process?"

Gail opened her mouth to answer, thought about it for a moment, and then closed her mouth, words unsaid.

"Has she decorated the nursery? Bought any baby clothes? Has she spoken of any plans or preparations she's making for when they come home from the hospital, other than the work she claims she's doing?"

Gail felt like a witness on the stand for the defense being cross-examined by the prosecution. "No," she whispered, truly shaken by this unsettling view of the friend she thought she knew so well.

He settled more comfortably on the couch, with one knee on the cushion and his arm thrown casually across the back. "Crystal's disassociated herself. She probably doesn't even view them as hers, since they're not coming from her body, but yours and Rashid's. I see it all the time in couples that come to me for a divorce. A couple adopts a baby, and only one of them is able to bond with the child. I've even run across a few surrogacy cases where the parent not genetically connected to the child feels left out and is unable to bond with the baby, even though both parties initiated the process. They thought they would both love the child, but when it came right down to it, one of them just couldn't connect."

Gail didn't like what she was hearing but couldn't argue. It was too logical and his analysis of the situation seemed to fit. "So you don't think she's just gone off for a while to get her head together? You believe this separation is permanent?"

"It doesn't matter what I think. What you need to be concerned about is what happens now? Rashid's focus is going to be on his children, now more than ever. Don't be surprised if he asks you to step in and help out with them now that Crystal is gone," Greg warned grimly.

Gail's eyes slid uncomfortably away from his, her mind on Rashid's words from last night.

Greg jumped up off of the couch. "Son of a bitch, he's already done it, hasn't he? Asked you to help him with the infants when they are born?" He stood over her with his hands on his hips.

"He mentioned it, yes. I am the babies' Godmother. It's one of the responsibilities of the position," she said defensively.

"Godparents step in and raise the children if both parents are dead. Crystal isn't dead. She went AWOL. Rashid is perfectly capable of raising the twins on his own. He has money and resources a lot of men don't. Let him hire a nanny. Hell, hire two, one for each child. He can afford it. He doesn't need your help."

Gail leaned her head against the back of the couch and closed her eyes. "That's what I told him. That he didn't need me and what he asked was too much."

"Well, stick to your guns. Remember, you're just the incubator. Once these babies are born, your job is done." He sat back down and tugged her into his arms. With a sigh, she curled into him. "Honey, I know they're your friends, but don't you get caught up in their drama. Rashid may be angry now, but when Crystal returns, he'll take her back and you'll be left out in the cold. Don't allow yourself to be used as a substitute mother for these little ones. Yes, he may need you now, but what about later? Don't get involved. You do and you'll have nothing but a lifetime of heartache to show for it later."

He lifted her face to his. "When this pregnancy ends, our time officially begins. I want you. You know that. More, I care for you. I want to see what develops between us once Crystal, Rashid, and these babies are no longer in the way." Greg lowered his mouth and kissed her deeply and hungrily, a physical reminder of what was in store for her once this surrogacy agreement was no longer an issue.

His words stayed with her the rest of the day. Gail knew Greg was right and even agreed with him to a certain extent. She couldn't let Rashid talk her into getting involved with the care of these children after they were born. That way laid madness.

Deep in her heart, she truly believed Crystal was indulging in a temper tantrum—a bid for attention. When she calmed down and could reason again, she'd return. Gail didn't know what had gone on between Rashid and Crystal, but things had been tense for a while. She hadn't asked, not wanting to intrude upon their personal business.

Despite how bad things looked now, she knew Rashid really loved Crystal and would welcome her with open arms when she returned. Then where would she be? On the outside looking in, that's where. There was no way she could begin mothering these children and then step aside when Crystal returned. She had to turn them over to Rashid and stick to the original plan, no matter what.

Gail rubbed her stomach. They were active today. Maybe they felt the tension in the air. For their sakes, she hoped Crystal returned home soon. The babies needed their mother, and Rashid needed his wife.

Chapter Ten

The next few weeks passed in a blur of activity. Greg, damn his hide, had been right. Crystal had done absolutely nothing to prepare for the coming of the babies. Rashid didn't know what needed to be done, and there wasn't time for him to learn. The twins could literally come at any moment. She'd already dilated two centimeters. Since she had been through this before, Gail stepped in to help.

Each morning she went into the office for four hours. Afterwards, she headed straight to Rashid's house to direct the work on the nursery. Furniture was ordered and delivered. Clothing, diapers, and baby paraphernalia purchased, seemingly by the truckload. Rashid spared no expense. Nothing but the best for his children.

Gail loved the nursery. Rashid hired a mural artist to paint the room, and the results were outstanding. She'd created a glade in an enchanted forest. The ceiling was the sky, painted blue with lots of fluffy clouds. The walls were covered with flowers, shrubs, and trees with large branches, reaching towards the sky. Scattered here and there were fairies, pixies, and other woodland creatures hiding, waiting for discovery by curious small eyes. The carpet was the exact shade of a freshly mowed lawn.

Every day Rashid insisted she quit working and move into the house until the children were born. Both Greg and Rashid were acting like mother hens, monitoring her every move. That she was still going in to work every day worried and annoyed the both of them. They still didn't particularly care for each other but on this one subject they agreed.

Tuesday, Gail went to work feeling exceptionally tired and cranky. Sleep was elusive and had been for the last couple of nights. It was difficult to find a comfortable position to lie in, and the lack of rest showed. There were dark circles under her eyes and she knew she looked wrung out.

Her fingers had swollen so much that she'd removed her rings for fear of them getting stuck. One baby was sitting on her bladder, and the other one was kicking against her ribs. Dr. Hagan had her coming in every few days to check her progress and the position of the embryos, concerned one of them would turn breech.

She managed to put in two hours' worth of work, but it was a struggle. She wanted to get up from her desk and move. Sitting there was driving her crazy. She managed a tired smile for Greg when he stopped by her cubicle to check on her.

"Hey, Beautiful. Not ready to have those babies yet?"

"More than ready. I'll pay you good money to take them out of me," Gail told him, only halfway joking. She winced as a sharp pain shot through her back.

Greg noticed and immediately snapped to attention. "What's wrong?"

"My back hurts. It started last night. I must have moved wrong and twisted it or something." Gail reached awkwardly behind her and tried to rub the small of her back where the pain centered.

"Sure," he said skeptically. "Have you called your doctor?"

She scowled. "For what? It's just a backache. Pregnant women get them all of the time."

"Humor me and call him." He picked up the receiver on her desk and put it in her hand. She stared at the phone, and then at Greg, her mouth mulishly set.

"I'm not calling Dr. Hagan. He'll tell me to come in again. I was just there yesterday. I'm not going back again today."

"Call Dr. Hagan, or I'll call Rashid, tell him you're in labor and won't admit it. I'll also tell him you're stubbornly refusing to call the doctor," he threatened.

"You wouldn't dare. Besides, you don't know his number."

He took the receiver from her and dialed a number. Watching his fingers closely, she recognized Rashid's cell phone number. She reached out quickly and disconnected the call. "All right, I'll call Dr. Hagan. Jeesh, you're worse than Rashid. Just have to have your way, don't you?" she grumbled.

She dialed the office and when the receptionist came on the line, told her who she was and why she was calling. The receptionist placed her on hold to go get the nurse. While she was waiting, Gail gave Greg an evil look. "You know he's only going to tell me to come in so he can check me, then send me home and tell me to rest."

Gail held up her hand to forestall the comment he was going to make, her attention focusing on the phone as the nurse came on line. "Ms. Henderson? Becky said you were having pains in your back?"

"I'm sure it's nothing. I—" Gail gasped and hunched over as a wave of pain started in the small of her back and traveled outward until it encompassed her whole stomach. Sweat broke out on her forehead, and her hand clenched the phone so tight she was surprised the thing didn't break. The pain was so intense, it sucked the breath from her body. She could hear Greg and the nurse calling her name, but couldn't respond.

When it passed, she slumped against the desk, panting. Greg pried the phone from her hand. "This is Greg Richmont, a friend of Gail's. She's definitely in labor. I'm going to take her to the hospital now." He listened a little bit. "Understood, we're on our way."

Greg pushed the disconnect button and dialed another number. "Mandy, I'm going to be out of the office for the rest of the day. Cancel all of my appointments. Tell them an emergency came up...yes...all right. You know how to reach me if you have to."

He hung up the phone, reached down and grabbed Gail's purse before pulling her to her feet. "Up you go." As he escorted her out of her cubicle, he called to one of her coworkers that he was taking Gail to the hospital, which fortunately wasn't very far.

Gail was inundated with well wishes and congratulations from the women in her section. One of them ran ahead to call and hold the elevator. Gail thanked her as they walked inside. The next pain hit when they reached the parking garage and almost brought her to her knees. Greg caught her and held her steady as she tried to breathe through it. She'd forgotten how much having a baby hurt.

What the hell had she been thinking, agreeing to do something like this?

"We'll take your car. There's no way you'll fit in mine." He dug into her purse for her keys as she stood hunched over.

"Sure...take mine. Wouldn't want...my water...to break...in yours. Might ruin...that fine...upholstery," she panted, a nasty edge to her voice. A minute later she sighed as the contraction eased. Straightening, she said, "I'm sorry. That was uncalled for."

"It's the pain talking. Let's get you to the hospital." He placed an arm around her waist and half-carried her to her vehicle.

They reached Baptist Medical in record time. Gail was pre-admitted, so after answering a few basic questions, she was taken directly to the birthing suite.

Someone thought to call Rashid, something she realized only after he came rushing into the room. Immediately behind Rashid came the nurse.

"Ms. Henderson, let's get you out of those clothes and checked out." She held out a gown to Gail for her to change into. "Which one of you gentlemen is the father?"

"I am," Rashid said, stepping forward.

"All right, you can stay. Sir, you'll have to step out of the room—" The rest of what she said cut off as Gail entered the bathroom and closed the door.

It was difficult and slow going, but Gail managed to get changed before the next contraction hit. It came as she walked out of the bathroom. With a keening cry, she held onto the door and the frame with white knuckles as the pain swelled and then receded.

When she came back to her surroundings, Rashid was by her side supporting her with an arm around her waist. He helped her get onto the bed and settled as the nurse returned to the room.

"Well now, let's take a look and see what we've got," she said in that nauseatingly cheerful voice most medical professions seem to use with patients. Gail wanted to smack her. She pulled out the stirrups and had Gail place her legs in them. Then she checked her cervix to see how far she'd dilated.

"Seven centimeters. You're definitely in labor. You hang tight while I go inform your doctor."

Once it was determined this was the real thing, the room became a hive of activity. Rashid left the room to change and quickly returned wearing scrubs. While he was gone, Gail was hooked to various machines—one to monitor the babies, another to monitor her heartbeat, and one to track the contractions.

"Tell me again why we're doing this?" Gail questioned through gritted teeth as she rode the wave of another contraction.

133

"So that we can bring two beautiful new people into the world?" Rashid responded in a strained voice as he tried to pry his hand loose of the death grip she had upon it.

"There's got to be an easier way to do this," Gail complained as she slumped back against the bed.

Rashid shook his hand and flexed it a few times before taking her hand again in his own, the other one this time. "I am sorry that your pain is necessary to bring me such joy."

"Not your fault. You're not the one who knocked me up. Well...you are, but...you know what I mean. You keep holding my hand, and I won't be the only one feeling pain. I wish Crystal was here so I could wring her neck for talking me into this."

"As do I," Rashid agreed grimly. Something in his tone made her wonder which part of her statement he agreed with—wishing Crystal were here or wringing her neck.

The nurse returned and informed them that Dr. Hagan was on the way.

"Is there nothing you can give her for the pain?" Rashid demanded to know.

"She's so close there really wouldn't be any point. The only reason she hasn't delivered yet is because her water hasn't broken. We can try to give her an epidural, if she insists, but at this stage of labor, it's risky." The nurse's tone and expression conveyed her disapproval of that course of action.

"No," Gail said firmly. "No epidurals. Nobody's getting near my spine with a needle."

"Another option would be to attach an IV to her arm and give her something for the pain intravenously, but it might slow down the contractions." The nurse spoke to Rashid, but kept her attention on Gail.

"I'm fine, Rashid," Gail assured him, knowing he was the one who had to be convinced. "The medicine won't do anything but make me lightheaded in between contractions. I'd rather be aware and know what's going on. Oh God, another one's coming. I can feel it."

Gail squeezed Rashid's hand until the tips of his fingers turned white. He immediately went into coach mode. "Breathe, Gail. Breathe through the pain, just like we practiced."

"You...breathe...through...the...pain." If she'd had enough breath in her lungs, she would have cursed him.

Dr. Hagan breezed into the room and checked the monitors. "Well, young lady, are you ready to bring these little ones into the world?"

"Past ready," she growled, still in the grip of the contraction.

"Okay, folks. Let's get these babies born. Rashid, get up there and support Gail like they showed you in class."

The nurse helped Gail to sit up while Rashid climbed on the bed. He knelt behind her, supporting her back with his body. When he reached for her hands, she didn't hesitate, but quickly linked hands with him.

At the other end, Dr. Hagan grabbed a stool and rolled it to the end of the bed, a tray of instruments at his side. Through the facemask he said, "I need to break your water. You're fully dilated, so as soon as I'm done, your contractions will increase and you should feel the need to push."

There was a feeling of pressure, a popping sound, and then Gail felt a gush of fluid leave her body. "There, that's better. With the next contraction, I want you to bear down and push. Stop when I tell you to. Ready whenever you are."

Dr. Hagan's actions caused wave after wave of labor pains to crash over her body, coming back to back. Gail's world narrowed down to the overwhelming need to push, and the quiet murmur of Rashid's deep voice speaking encouragements directly into her ear. She closed her eyes, braced herself against Rashid's chest, and bore down hard until she heard Dr. Hagan commanding her to stop. She slumped weakly against Rashid, panting and gathering her strength for the next round.

"Look, there is the head," Rashid said in awe.

Gail heard a baby's cry, then Dr. Hagan telling her to push again. There was a release of the pressure on her body when the baby slid all of the way out into Dr. Hagan's waiting hands. He passed the infant to one of the nurses. She caught her breath as the urge to push hit her again. Her grip on Rashid's hand tightened in response.

"Just a second, Gail, and I'll be ready for you to push. Try to hold back for a few more seconds. Can you do that for me?" Dr. Hagan asked.

Gail nodded her head and gritted her teeth. She turned her head to the side and rested her forehead against Rashid's neck. She let his praises wash over her while her attention focused inwardly on controlling her body.

"All right, Gail. Let's bring this little one out so she can join her brother."

Gail pushed until she felt faint. She was relieved when Dr. Hagan said, "That's enough." He turned the baby and it slid right out into his hands.

While Dr. Hagan was cleaning and stitching Gail, one of the nurses approached the bed. "Would you like to see your son? He's a handsome fellow. Six pounds, three ounces, and nineteen inches long."

Rashid held out his hands. Since his arms remained wrapped around Gail, she instinctively reached out to help support the baby. Gail looked down and immediately fell in love. He was beautiful. He had her complexion and Rashid's wavy, black hair, giving him an exotic look. His face was all scrunched up against the lights, and he squirmed in their arms.

"Come on, handsome. Open up those eyes and let me see what color they are," she cajoled.

As if he recognized her voice, his eyes opened a crack and he peeked out. Black, like Rashid's. "He has your eyes."

"But his mouth, nose, and the shape of his face are yours," Rashid replied.

The nurse came and took the baby from them. "Sorry, but we need to take this little tyke down to the pediatric ward and have him checked out."

As she left with the first baby, another nurse came with the second one. "Would you and your wife like to see your daughter?" Gail barely heard her. Her arms were already reaching for the newborn.

As she brought the infant to her chest, she began to nuzzle. Gail laughed and turned to Rashid. "I think she's hungry."

Rashid had tears in his eyes as he looked down at the baby in her arms. He met Gail's gaze, his eyes full of emotion and kissed her lightly on the lips. "Thank you for my children."

Gail flushed and turned away, her heart heavy with the reminder that these precious newborns were not hers. Reluctantly, she handed the baby back to the waiting nurse and watched as she was taken from the room, a piece of her heart going with her.

One of the aides came over and helped Gail to sit up while Rashid eased from behind her. He went to confer with the doctor while Gail received instructions. The aide recommended she soak in the tub to ease the soreness, and helped her into the bathroom where she ran water in the Jacuzzi tub and poured some minerals in the water. "A sitz bath will help ease your discomfort. When you're ready, call and someone will help you out of the tub. While you're bathing, the linens on your bed will be changed and the room cleaned."

Gail nodded and took her case from the aide. She withdrew her nightgown and set it to the side within easy reach. When the aide left, Gail eased into the tub. The water felt so good. Tears came to her eyes as she thought about all Crystal was missing. She leaned her head back against the wall and let them come. She needed a good cry. When they finally stopped, she was exhausted but much calmer.

Her strength was rapidly giving out. She washed quickly in the cooling water and made a move to get out of the tub. She couldn't. There wasn't enough strength left in her arms to push up onto her feet. She called out for help. "I'm ready to get out."

The door cracked open and Rashid's voice inquired, "Do you need assistance?"

Gail drew the washcloth protectively against her chest, even though she was behind the door. "Could you call someone? I need help getting out of the tub."

"No need to disturb them when I am here. I will assist." He pushed the door open further and began to enter.

Gail squealed. "Wait! No! Don't come in," she protested and tried to sink down into the dubious protection of the mostly empty tub.

"I just watched you give birth to my children. Surely you are not concerned with my seeing you in the bath?" His tone was disbelieving. Rashid ignored her protests and came into the bathroom.

Finding a towel, he approached the tub. "Arms up." He held the towel out in preparation of wrapping her in it.

Gail had her legs drawn up to her body, trying to hide her nakedness and wouldn't move.

"Come, this is foolishness. I do not want you catching chill."

I can't sit here all day, she thought, and the water is getting cold. She looked over Rashid's shoulder, unable to look him in the face, and raised her arms.

In a tremendous display of strength, he hauled her to a standing position, wrapped the towel around her body, and lifted her out of the tub. When she was steady on her feet, he turned to leave. "If you need anything else, call out."

When hell freezes over, she thought to herself. It's not like she expected the sight of her nude body to drive him into a lust-induced frenzy, but she could count on one hand the number of people who had seen her naked. She never intended for Rashid to be counted among them.

Gail managed to dry off and put on her robe and gown without any further problems. She left the bathroom and went back into the room, ready to lie down. Rashid stretched out in the recliner, flipping channels on the TV.

He looked up when she entered the room. "Lie down before you fall down. They will arrive soon with dinner."

Gail slowly eased her body onto the bed. As she settled, she heard a cry and looked for its source. Both incubators were in the room. "Rashid, why are the twins in here instead of the nursery?" Where they belong, she finished in her mind.

"The nurses are short staffed. It was requested the babies remain in here with us." He crossed over to the crying infant and picked it up before it could disturb its sibling.

She'd just bet the nurses were short-staffed. It seemed mighty convenient to her. "What do you mean by 'us'?" She watched him while she adjusted the bed to a more comfortable position.

"Us. You and I. I am here and will remain as much as possible to see to the care of you and the children."

Gail closed her eyes, too tired to argue with him. She needed to be at full strength to deal with Rashid and right now, he had her at a disadvantage. Instead of calming, the baby seemed to become more agitated. She opened her eyes, curious. "Rashid, what are you doing to that child?"

"I am attempting to calm him." He was walking around, gently bouncing the baby in his arms.

She knew she was going to hate herself later, but the crying bothered her. "Bring the baby to me." Rashid handed him over with relief. The baby's eyes were closed tight, his face red. Gail unwrapped the blanket and checked the diaper. As soon as his hands were free, his fist shot to his mouth and he began to suck.

"Oh poor thing, you're hungry. Rashid, see if they brought any bottles."

He didn't move. "Can't you breastfeed?"

Gail gave him a look of disbelief. "No, I can't breastfeed. I have no intention of nursing these infants, and even if I wanted to, my milk hasn't come in yet. Now see if they left us some bottles before this little one finds a way to eat his fist."

Rashid went to the correct drawer and pulled out a bottle and a nipple, displaying his knowledge of their presence. He put the nipple on the bottle and placed it in her hand. "Breastfeeding is best for an infant. The mother's immunity is passed through the breast milk to the child until the infant's immune system is strong enough to defend itself." He sounded like he was quoting from a manual. Knowing Rashid, he probably was. He'd read enough of them.

Gail ignored him as she fed the baby. Breastfeeding was not in the agreement so he could just get over himself. "Have you decided upon names?"

"My daughter shall be called Jamilah Melek Al Jabbar. It means 'beautiful angel.'"

"And your son? What name have you decided on for him?"

"I'm considering Ahkeem Jamal Al Jabbar."

"Does that name have meaning as well?"

"It means handsome ruler," he said with pride.

"Those are beautiful names, Rashid. So, handsome, what do you think of the names your daddy picked out?" The baby, intent on its bottle, didn't even look at her.

Rashid watched her very carefully. She had no doubt he was memorizing her actions so he could repeat them when the time came. When the baby began pushing the milk out of his mouth, she removed the bottle. Lifting little Jamal to her shoulder, she began a combination patting/rubbing motion until she heard him burp.

"Rashid, bring me a diaper and see if they left any wipes." Once he handed her the requested items, she changed the baby and swaddled him again.

"Why do you wrap the baby so tightly?"

"It's called swaddling. It comforts them. Makes them feel like they're still in the womb. You can put him back in his incubator now. He should sleep. I've shown you what to do. Next time, it's your turn."

"You're friend Greg stopped by to see you while you were in the bath. He asked me to pass the message he would see you tomorrow. Some business came up that needed his attention."

Wondering why Rashid hadn't given her the message earlier, she let it go without question when dinner arrived. They ate in silence. When she finished eating, Gail could barely keep her eyes opened.

Rashid moved the tray from in front of her. "Rest. You've done enough for today. Do you need anything?"

"Another blanket. I'm a little cold."

Rashid found one and spread it over her. "Sleep. If you need anything, I'll be here."

♦♦♦♦♦

Gail awakened from her doze, late the next morning, to the sound of someone tapping on the door. "Come in," she called out groggily.

Greg came through the door, a vase full of red roses in his hand. "Morning, Beautiful. How's my lady doing today?"

"How lovely." She eagerly reached for the flowers. "I'm doing better. Still tired and sore. I'll be glad when they let me out of here so I can actually get some sleep. I've forgotten what a full night of sleep feels like." She brought one of the roses to her nose.

Watching her, he asked, "Don't I get a thank you kiss?"

"Put these over there, then come and get your kiss. A dozen roses deserve a great kiss," she concluded.

Greg placed the vase on the table she indicated and came to claim his thank you. Gail wrapped her arms around his neck and kissed him deeply, making sure to give him plenty of tongue action.

"Mmm, very nice and look," he gently squeezed her waist, "no belly coming between us."

"The belly's gone but these are still here." She cupped her breasts.

Greg covered her hands with his. She slid hers out of the way, leaving him holding her flesh alone. With his thumbs, he gently rubbed the distended nipples. "Can we keep these? They're nice."

She laughed and pushed his hand away. What he was doing felt too good and her body was in no condition to do what it wanted.

He sat on the side of the bed facing her. "How are you feeling, seriously? No complications from the birth?"

"So far, so good. Keep your fingers crossed. If none pop up, I get to go home tomorrow." Gail crossed both fingers and sent up a quick prayer.

He arched one eyebrow and tilted his head to the side. "But you won't really be going home, will you? Remember, it was arranged for you to stay with Crystal and Rashid while you recovered from the birth," he reminded her.

Face dropping in disappointment, she asked, "You don't think he'll hold me to that portion of the agreement now that Crystal is gone, do you? How would it look for his wife's best friend to be living with him, not even a month after his wife left?"

"Honey, Rashid doesn't strike me as the kind of man who worries about people's opinion. Unless he says otherwise, I think you should stick to the agreement. Go, let yourself be taken care of until you get your strength back. It's not like you can return to work, and you know you'll go crazy sitting around the house for six weeks doing nothing."

"As usual, you're right," she acknowledged.

"Glad you realize it. Now, I want to talk to you about something. I would have waited until you left the hospital, but this can't wait."

"What is it? Is something wrong?" she worried.

"No, it's good news. Great news. A headhunter approached me from another law firm. They've seen my work and want to hire me. If things work out, in another two years I may be considered for partnership. This is the offer on the table." He named a figure that caused Gail's mouth to drop open.

"Are you going to take it?"

Greg grinned. "I'd be crazy not to. I've checked them out, and this would be a good career move for me."

Gail didn't doubt it. It was the dream of most lawyers to reach partner. There was no hope of that

143

happening where he was now. "Then go for it. I'm so happy for you. This is wonderful."

"I'm glad you think so." He took her hand and held it firmly. "The job's in California."

At his words, her heart sank.

"Gail, I've thought seriously about this and I want you to come with me. I've checked and with your credentials, you can get a job with any firm out there. I can't promise you a wedding ring. I've seen too much to believe in happily ever after, but I can promise you fidelity. Live with me. I don't know if this is love, but I've never felt for any woman the feelings I have for you. I'm seriously thinking of trying the rings, the church, and 'til death do us part' bit. No other woman has ever tempted me so."

Gail leaned back against her pillows, speechless. He was serious. "This is so sudden. You're talking a major move. How long do I have to decide?"

"I'm flying out Monday for a meeting with the partners. I'll officially let them know my decision at that time. They have a big case that just came to them they want me to handle. They're going to help me find housing until I can get something more permanent. By the end of the month, I plan to be moved."

"Three weeks! I won't be released from the doctor for another six." Her head reeled with the suddenness of his announcement.

His gaze stared intently into hers. "I know, and I've taken that into consideration. Come join me when the doctor releases you. You don't have to return to work right away. You can come, find us a home, and get settled before looking for employment. Whatever you choose for us will be fine with me. I want you to be happy in our home."

Her free hand flopped around helplessly as she tried to gather her thoughts. "Greg, we've only been together a few of months. That's not very long. Are you sure you're ready for something like this? Are you sure we're ready for this level of commitment?"

"Yes, I'm very sure. Maybe it was not being able to have sex that did it, but I know you. Really know you, and I like what I know about you. I can't wait to discover more. How about you? Do you have any feelings for me at all?" Gail could tell her answer was very important to him.

She cupped the side of his face. "You know I do. I can't put a name on them yet, but what I feel is very strong."

"There's one more thing you should know before making your decision." The look on his face caused her heart to stutter. "It's only fair to warn you I've made the decision to never have kids. I was the victim of divorce, and I see what divorce does to the families that come to me. I'm never putting my kids through it. Since there's no guarantee a relationship will last, no matter however much we might want it to, I prefer not to bring children into an uncertain situation. And please, understand, this is non-negotiable. I won't change my mind later."

"I understand." And she did. She'd decide how she felt about his revelation later when it had time to sink in.

"Good. I'm glad to hear it. I know this isn't the best time to lay this on you, but I couldn't wait. I'm really hoping that in spite of all I've said, you'll make the decision to come with me. I know I've given you a lot to think about, and you're still tired. I'm going to leave and give you time to think. I doubt I'll make it by to see you tomorrow before you leave, but I'll call you from California."

She squeezed his hand. "You do that, if for no other reason than to let me know you made it there safely."

"Yes, ma'am." He leaned forward and kissed her goodbye. "Say yes," he whispered.

As he walked out of the door, Gail's mind went into overdrive. California. The west coast. As far from Florida as you can get and still be in the continental United States. It might as well be a foreign country. She would be away from everyone she knew. All of her family was on this coast. Everything would be new, different, and strange. Could she make this kind of a move with a man she'd been in a relationship with for such a short period of time?

And what about Greg? He wasn't promising marriage. However, after Jason, Gail knew a wedding ring didn't guarantee a lifetime of love and happiness. And here was the clincher, if she went with Greg, she would be giving up any hope she had of ever having another child of her own. Not that she was sure she wanted any after losing Marcus, but she still wanted to leave the option open.

While she was considering all of the potential ramifications of making such a move, the door opened and the hospital administrator came in. "Ms. Henderson. We need you to verify and sign the birth certificates."

She looked at the paperwork in the woman's hand and frowned in confusion. "But I'm not the babies' mother. I'm the surrogate."

"I understand, but legally, we have to have the birth mother's name on the certificates. Mr. Al Jabbar's lawyers will petition the court to have your name officially removed and the intended parent's names added at a later date."

"Oh, if you're sure I should be signing these…"

The woman held out the paperwork and a pen. "Very sure."

Gail reached for the forms and added her signature. She vaguely remembered the lawyer mentioning something about this when she signed the agreement. Rashid must have given the officials the twins' names. "You'll have to have Rashid verify the spelling of the names."

"I'll be sure to do that," she said and then left the room.

Chapter Eleven

Rashid stood outside the door of Gail's room, hesitant to enter. He was not looking forward to the coming conversation. He took a deep breath, squared his shoulders, and entered. Gail was dozing in the recliner in front of the television. She looked so peaceful he was loath to wake her.

He took the other chair in the room and positioned it near the recliner. Then he reached up and turned off the television. As he sat, he called her name softly. "Gail."

She stirred a bit before her eyes opened. Then she smiled. "You're back. I must have drifted off."

Rashid didn't return her smile. "We need to talk."

Gail's smile disappeared and her expression became as serious as his. "That doesn't sound good. What's wrong? Has Crystal been found? She's not dead is she?"

"No, none of that. I owe you an apology."

Any lingering traces of sleep cleared from her eyes as Gail tensed in the recliner. "What did you do?"

"It's what I've been doing that I need to apologize for. I misjudged you. I didn't believe you about Crystal. Despite what you said and how you reacted, I thought you knew where she was and was covering for her."

She gaped at him. "Why would you think that?"

"You've been friends with her for such a long time; much longer than I've been her husband. Your loyalty lies with Crystal. I knew if you believed she had just cause, you'd hide Crystal from the devil himself."

Gail sat quietly. Rashid wished he could read her better. He really wanted to know what she was thinking. Finally, after what seemed an eternity, she spoke. "And now?"

He spread his hands wide. "Now I know you don't know where she is and had nothing to do with her disappearance."

She studied him intently. "You seem very certain of yourself. Do I even want to know what changed your mind?"

Rashid allowed his gaze to drift away from hers. This was the difficult part. There was no excuse for what he'd done. It was a gross invasion of privacy. "I hired a private detective to find Crystal and told him my suspicions. He reported to me today. He was able to track her until she reached Vegas. After that, he lost the trail. No one knows where she is. She hasn't contacted any of her relatives or acquaintances, including you. It's as though she vanished off of the face of the earth."

Gail looked puzzled. "She went to Vegas? But, she doesn't have any family there. As far as I know, she doesn't know anyone, either. How could she just vanish? She has to have a place to live, some means of supporting herself. How far can she get without her credit cards? She must have used her ID for something. Crystal has very expensive taste. She couldn't have gotten far, using only cash."

"Crystal cleaned out her personal savings, maxed out her credit cards, and emptied the joint account. She could easily have fifty thousand in cash. I don't know how much was in her savings. I do know she didn't get more than a thousand from the joint account." He kept the balance in their joint account low. Crystal had proven early in their marriage her inability to handle the family finances. Now, Rashid paid all of the bills and gave his wife an allowance that, in addition to any money she earned, was hers to spend. He didn't know how many credit cards she had but knew there were a lot. His name wasn't on any of them, so he didn't concern himself. They were Crystal's and she was responsible for paying the balance on them.

"Fifty thousand sounds like a lot of money, but to someone like Crystal who spends money like it's water, it won't last her long. Eventually she'll run out, apply for credit or employment and you should be able to find her."

They were both silent with their own thoughts, then Gail looked at him with narrowed eyes. "I know Crystal hasn't tried to contact me, but how does the detective know?"

Rashid forced himself to hold her gaze. "He monitored your calls and your mail."

Gail's mouth dropped open and for a few blessed seconds, she seemed incapable of speech. Then she blasted him. "You tapped my phone? Are you crazy?"

Inwardly he flinched at the anger in her tone, knowing he deserved every bit of it. "Yes, and I'm sorry, but I had to be sure. You were so insistent that I find her and in your belief this was just something she was doing to get attention. I figured it was a ploy of Crystal's to get her way, and you were involved. It's why I said the things I did. I figured if I put enough pressure on you to help with the twins, you would in turn pressure Crystal to give up this foolishness and return home. I had difficulty believing she would do something of this nature—deliberately leave me and our children, right when she was needed the most. I truly believed she was playing games and would return once she had made her point. Now, I have no choice but to accept this was her intent all along. By her actions, Crystal has proven she no longer wishes to be a part of this marriage, nor does she intend to be a mother to our children." His voice was tight with the pain and anger he felt because of his wife's betrayal.

Gail reached out and laid her hand over his, which was clenched into a fist on his thigh. "If I knew

150

where she was, I would tell you. I'm just as amazed as you. I never would have believed, not in a million years, Crystal would be capable of something like this. As her friend, I'm unbelievably hurt. She talked me into this then she just up and left. I can't begin to imagine the pain you must be feeling right now. What you did was wrong—a serious invasion of my privacy and illegal as hell—but I understand. In your position, I might have done the same. The question is, what happens now?"

Rashid sighed and turned his hand over so he held hers. "My marriage, obviously, is over. I need to focus on the children. Because I believed this situation to be temporary, I made no attempt to find a caretaker for them. With the hours I work, and the frequent traveling I do, I need a nanny—someone reliable that will live-in. I've made arrangements to work from home for the time being, but I don't have a lot of time to find someone. My children are too important to me to trust their care to just anyone."

Gail nibbled on her lower lip, before saying hesitantly, "If you'd like, I can help you with the search. It will be six weeks before I can return to work. According to our original agreement, I was to spend that time with you and Crystal. If that's still the plan, while I'm there I can help you conduct interviews and give you my opinion of the candidates, for what it's worth. I realize that the twins belong to you, and you have the final say in any decision made."

Overcome by her generosity, Rashid covered her hand with his free one so her hand was sandwiched between the two. "Our arrangement still stands. I want you to stay at the house so you can fully recover. And thank you. Your help will be greatly appreciated. I need all I can get. Never underestimate the value of your opinion where the children are concerned. One thing I said before holds true. As the twin's birth mother, you are the only mother they have. Crystal may have initiated the process, but it is you who have given them life. By leaving, she proved her unsuitability to be their mother."

He paused to swallow the lump in his throat. "I know you didn't start this with the intention of being a mother again, but I ask that you would consider the needs of the children—our children. Help me raise them. I ask for their sakes and mine. Our children deserve two parents who love them. They could have no better mother than you, and I say this with all sincerity. You were a great mother to Marcus, and I have no doubt you will be the same with the twins, if you'd allow yourself to do so." The twins would be fortunate to have Gail as a mother. He was sure they could come to an agreement regarding their parenting.

Gail slid her hand from his and gripped them over her stomach, an uncomfortable look on her face. "There's something you should know. Greg has asked me to move to California with him, and I'm seriously considering it."

"He asked you to marry him?" Rashid's stomach rebelled at the thought of Gail married to Greg.

"No, he wants me to live with him."

He frowned. "He wishes you to be his mistress? And you are considering it?"

"No! Who uses terms like that anymore? We would be living together, sharing a life. Greg's not sure he wants to marry anyone—he doesn't believe in it after all of the divorces he's handled—but if he did, it would be me. After Jason, I'm not sure I'm ready to risk my heart in another marriage. This seems like a reasonable alternative."

He shook his head, unable to believe what he heard. "You would be living together without the blessing of the church. What about your children? How will you explain your living arrangements to them?"

Her gaze slid from his and she plucked at the blanket. "Greg doesn't want any."

Rashid could do no more than stare. "You were born to be a mother. You would do this? Live with this man without the security of marriage, knowing he would never give you children? What would your parents say?" Rashid knew from Jason that Gail's parents were very traditional, as she herself was.

"I didn't say I was going to do it. I said I was seriously considering it. It's a lot to think about. I really care for Greg. I'm not ready for our relationship to end, but I'm not sure I'm willing to follow him to California, either. I like having a man in my life. As for children, losing Marcus hurt so much I almost lost my mind. I can't go through something like that again. Maybe not having more children would be a good thing."

"It's too late for that. You already have more, two of them, right down the hall in the nursery." He pointed in the nursery's direction.

Her gaze snapped to his and shot fire. "Those are not mine. They are yours, and Crystal's, wherever she might be," she denied vehemently.

"Who are you trying to convince? Me…or yourself? I see the way you look at them when you think no one is watching. You already love them, just as much as you loved Marcus. Do you think you can just walk away now that you've held them, and cared for them? If you do, you're not being honest with yourself." Rashid stopped talking as the nurses returned with the twins.

Let her think about what he'd said. He rose and went to greet them as Gail watched from the recliner.

◆◆◆◆◆

On Gail's second day out of the hospital, her milk came in. Her breasts were so engorged, they swelled until they were hard as rocks. Her nipples were tight and sensitive and everything hurt. She tried standing under the shower, hoping the hot water would cause the

153

milk to flow and ease the tension. The heat ran out of the water long before she saw any results.

For two days, she alternated between massaging her breasts and standing in a hot shower, and still the milk refused to flow. In desperation, when it was time for Jamal's next feeding, she brought him into her room and held him to her breast. Maybe his suckling would provide the relief she needed.

In textbook perfection, Jamal latched onto her nipple and began suckling his little heart out. After a few minutes, he released her and let out a loud, angry cry. He was hungry, and she wasn't releasing any milk. Gail wanted to cry with him. The baby's suckling had increased her pain instead of relieving it.

Gail hurt too much to care when Rashid stuck his head in the door. "What is wrong? Why is the baby screaming?"

"He's hungry. Take him and feed him."

Rashid crossed over to the bed to get Jamal, who was still beating and nuzzling, searching for the milk he could smell. "You were attempting to breastfeed?"

Gail handed the baby to Rashid, flinching when her arm brushed against the side of her areole. "It won't come out. For two days now, I've been trying to get the milk to flow. Nothing I do works. I'm scared they'll get infected if it doesn't come out soon."

"Stay right here. I'll be back in a minute." Rashid took the crying baby out of the room.

Gail gave up the fight to be strong and let the tears fall. Her breasts hurt so much. She couldn't sleep. The slightest bit of pressure on them was painful. She'd done everything she could think of, every recommendation made by the experts in the books, and still she hurt. She just wanted the pain to stop.

She was crying in earnest when Rashid returned to the room bearing an empty, plastic pan. Gail blew her nose and tried to stop the flow of tears while Rashid went into her bathroom. She heard the water turn on and wondered what he was doing. He came out of the bathroom with a pan of water so hot she could see the steam rising from it. On his arm were two small towels.

"What are you doing, and where is Jamal?"

"My son is with Carmelita. I'm going to get your milk to flow. Open your top and lay down." He placed the pan on the bedside table and dropped both towels in the water.

Gail did as instructed, past the point of modesty. If he could make the pain go away, she would do whatever he asked. He muttered some very distinct curses under his breath when he caught a good look at her red, swollen, irritated-looking breasts.

Rashid swirled the towel around in the water, then rung it out. "This may sting." He dropped the towel on one of her breasts. Gail hissed as the moist heat hit her sensitive skin. She gripped the covers, her back arching reflexively when he did the same to the other breast. He repeated the process over and over until the water cooled. Gail closed her eyes and endured.

"Sit up."

At his command, she opened her eyes. Rashid was standing over her with a bottle of olive oil in his hand. "What are you about to do?"

"Massage your breasts. See if I can get your milk to flow."

"I've already tried that. It didn't work." Gail sat up and leaned forward when he indicated, catching the towels in her hands. She gave them to Rashid and he tossed them back into the almost empty container.

Then he climbed onto the bed behind her, a reminder of their position in the delivery room. "My hands are larger and stronger than yours. You probably didn't apply enough pressure, or the angle was wrong."

Once he settled behind her, he liberally coated his hands in the oil and placed the container on the table. "Lean back against my chest."

When she was in position, he took both hands, slippery with oil and placed them at the base of her right breast. Firmly stroking, he glided his hand from the base to the nipple in a milking motion. He did it over and over, switching from one side to the other. "I know this is painful for you. I'm sorry, but it needs to be done."

Gail's nails dug into Rashid's denim covered muscular thighs. Her head was pressed against his chest, teeth clenched and eyes squeezed shut. "I know. Just do it. Don't worry about me," she forced herself to grit out.

"Of course I worry about you. I dislike seeing you in pain." They were silent while he continued his massage. When he stopped, Gail opened her eyes and relaxed her fingers.

"Do you trust me?"

Gail turned until they were almost nose-to-nose. "What kind of question is that, Rashid? Of course I trust you."

"There was one more thing Carmelita suggested I try if this didn't work."

"What?" His manner was making her nervous.

"Turn sideways." He helped adjust her body so she lay sideways. Both of her legs were across his thigh, her arm around his neck, and his arm supported her back. Rashid tilted Gail back and lowered his mouth to her breast. Taking as much of it as he could into his mouth, he began to draw strongly with Gail's nipple trapped between the roof of his mouth and his flattened tongue.

"Sweet mother of God!" she hoarsely cried out. Her hands came up and convulsively clutched his head, whether to push him away or to pull him closer, she couldn't decide. Under her hip she could feel Rashid's cock harden and lengthen. The knowledge this excited him too caused the muscles in her stomach to clench, and she bit back a moan.

He's Crystal's husband, she desperately reminded herself. *He's just trying to help. No lusting allowed.*

Against her will, her hands tightened in his scalp when he lifted his head. She smothered her sigh of relief when all he did was switch to the left side. Once again he suckled strongly. Gail could feel it in her womb. Each tug on her breast caused a corresponding one in her nether region. The sheer intensity of the pleasure of his suckling, combined with a small bite of pain, brought her to the edge of orgasm.

Please, please, please, don't let me come. It would be so embarrassing.

Just when she thought she couldn't take it anymore, that she was going to embarrass herself for sure, he stopped. Rashid hovered over her breast, his breath hot and moist on her nipple. Then he did something that completely destroyed her. He brought his thumb up and lightly stroked it across the tip of her nipple.

"Arrggh!" Gail's hips bucked as she exploded.

Rashid's gaze flew to hers. She saw shock give way to fierce satisfaction and something that looked suspiciously like barely suppressed lust on his face. Gail closed her eyes as embarrassment warred with the fulfillment racing through her body. Her response to him was so wrong.

Rashid eased her still shuddering body back onto the bed. "The milk is flowing now." He lightly stroked her nipple again, causing her body to jerk. Then he held up his thumb, displaying the drop of milk on its tip before bringing the digit to his mouth and licking it off. "Carmelita said once the milk was flowing, you needed to let the twins feed for a while before weaning them off, to allow the milk to dry up slowly. Otherwise, your breasts will engorge again."

Gail opened her eyes to find Rashid studying her breasts with hunger in his eyes. "All right, if she believes that would be best."

He glanced briefly at her face before returning his gaze to her chest. His head dipped towards her nipple. Then he seemed to catch himself. He hovered over her, his jaw tight as he appeared to war within himself. Finally, he snatched his head back, causing Gail's hands to fall away. "I'll go and get Jamilah. It should be time for her to eat." His voice was terse.

Rashid lifted her legs, placed them to the side, and got off the bed. At the door he paused, turned, and looked at Gail. The heat in his gaze reminded her that her shirt still gaped, and she clutched at the edges, pulling them together over her breasts. "After I bring you the baby, I'm going down to the pool to swim. I need to work off some energy." He turned and walked out the door before Gail could respond, not that she could think of anything to say.

◆◆◆◆◆

The theme song from "Animaniacs" blasted through the darkness, jerking Gail from a sound sleep. After glancing at the number displayed, she quickly swiped the screen and brought it to her ear.

"Hey, you! I was wondering when you'd call."

Greg's deep voice came through the phone. "Mmm, and I suppose it never occurred to you to call me?"

"Of course I thought about it, but with the time difference and not knowing your schedule, I didn't want to chance interrupting something important."

"Listen up because I'm only going to say this once. There's nothing more important to me than you. You call. I don't care if I'm in a meeting, taking a test, or asleep. If you need me, call. I'll drop what I'm doing. You're my number one priority."

Gail didn't know how to respond to his statement, so she tried to redirect the conversation. "How are things going?"

Greg was quiet just long enough to make her squirm. Then he sighed. "They're going well. I've met with all the partners and toured the firm to get a feel for how they operate. They have a nice set up. I told them about you and they're very interested. The turnover among paralegals is very high. Everyone here wants to be a lawyer or work independently. There's a job waiting for you when you arrive." Then he named a figure that made her head spin.

"Are you serious? They pay paralegals that much? That's almost twice what I make now, and even factoring the higher cost of living, it's still a lot of money." Gail was financially secure but even so, the offer was very attractive.

"They feel you're worth it. They pay more to reduce turnover. Everyone's hiring. The demand is so high you can basically name your price and they know it. So, have you thought any more about joining me?"

"Every day, whenever I get a moment to myself."

"What are you doing? You're supposed to be recovering, not working."

"I've been helping out with the twins. Rashid really thought Crystal would have returned by now so he didn't hire a nanny. He's going through applications now. In the meantime, we've all been pitching in."

It was silent on Greg's end before he quietly asked, "Are you sure that much contact with the twins is wise? I don't want you getting too attached to them. With Crystal not there, it's natural that Rashid would turn to you. Don't let him get too comfortable with your being there. It's only temporary."

"He knows. I told him I'm considering relocating to California with you."

Greg snorted. "I'm sure that went over well. What did he say?"

Gail hesitated then thought, why not? It was no secret. "He's not too happy with the idea."

"I'll bet."

"I don't think it has anything to do with the twins. It was the idea of us living together without the 'sanctity of marriage'—his words, not mine—that really upset him. He said if you really loved and respected me as a woman, you'd ask me to marry you, not just live with you." She and Rashid had discussed the issue several times since their initial conversation in the hospital.

"What business of it is his, anyway? His views are totally archaic."

"Rashid's just voicing what I was raised to believe. My parents would totally agree with him. "

"Does that mean you're not coming?"

"That's not what I'm saying. I'm just letting you know it's not an easy decision to make. All of my friends and family are here. This is a major deal. I would be totally dependent upon you since my support network would be on a different coast."

"Like I'll be totally dependent on you," he argued. "Just pretend I'm Jason. If he asked you to move, you wouldn't have hesitated, would you?"

"You're not Jason, so it doesn't matter," Gail said shortly.

"I see." His voice was flat, all emotion removed.

Oh hell, now she'd hurt his feelings. "I didn't mean that in a bad way. Jason and I were married and had been together for years. You and I have only been a couple for six months. I don't know if we're strong enough to survive such a big transition. It's just so far away from everything familiar. I'd have the same reservations and questions even if it were Jason asking me to make this move."

"So what you're saying is that if we were married, it would make everything easier for you? Is that what it's going to take to get you out here?"

Gail counted to ten before answering. She did not want to get into an argument with him about this. "Greg," she said softly, "I'm not pushing for marriage. I'm trying to explain to you what's going on in my head. This is a big deal and I'm scared. I want to be with you. Never doubt it. I just need more time. It's only been a few days since you sprung this on me. Give me a little longer to settle all the questions in my mind."

Greg heavily exhaled. "You're right. I'm just scared you'll say no. I mean, really, what am I offering you in terms of security? I'm not promising marriage. I flat out told you I won't be giving you kids. On top of it, I want you to move away from everyone you know and love. What woman would go for that?"

"Not everyone," she informed him quietly. It was the closest she'd come to saying she loved him.

"Really," he purred. "That's good to know."

"When are you coming home? I miss you."

"I miss you too. Probably another week here before I head back. I have plenty of leave time. I can stay another month and not make a dent in my time on the books."

Gail could well believe it. Greg was something of a workaholic. "I guess it's a good thing you're not here. Keeps me from doing things my body's not ready for."

"Is Rashid taking good care of my woman for me? Do I need to come have a talk with him?" he joked.

Gail's mind flashed back to earlier today when Rashid had "cared" for her breasts. She cleared her suddenly dry throat. "Yes, he's taking care of me. He and Carmelita monitor me carefully to make sure I'm not overdoing. Carmelita also makes sure I eat enough.

If I didn't have the twins to help with, I'd go a little crazy. There's nothing here to do except sleep and eat."

"That's all you need to be doing. Don't try to do too much too fast. Remember, you're still getting your strength back. I don't want you getting sick."

"Don't worry. Carmelita watches me like a hawk. If she even thinks I'm getting ready to do something I shouldn't, she scolds me," Gail said with a laugh.

"It's getting late on your end, and you need your rest. Take care of yourself and don't be afraid to call."

"You be careful out there and watch out for those hussies."

He laughed as she intended. "Yes, ma'am. Good night, love."

"Goodnight." Gail disconnected the call and laid there holding the phone. She'd never been one to sit up under her family, so why was she making such a big deal out of this? Could Greg be right? Was she holding out for a wedding ring? If they were marrying, would that make her decision any easier? It was definitely something to think about.

◆◆◆◆◆

The next few days were relatively quiet event wise, but her mind was in turmoil. She'd almost managed to convince herself the incident with Rashid never happened—almost, but not quite. If she could just attribute it to overly sensitive mammary glands, she wouldn't feel so bad. However, on the occasions when she and Greg had fooled around, not once had she orgasmed from having her breasts suckled. Nor had it ever occurred with Jason, even when she was pregnant with Marcus.

She blamed the episode on a host of contributing factors—breast engorgement, the hot towel treatment and massage followed by suckling on her already sex-deprived, hormone driven body. Yep, that's all it had been. Nothing more. There was no reason to feel guilty. It could have happened to anyone. With the issue firmly settled in her mind, Gail was finally able to drift off to sleep with a clear conscious. If her dreams featured a certain dark-skinned man of Arabic descent with a fascination with lactating breasts, well, that was beyond her control.

Several hours later, Gail's feet hit the floor and her body was moving towards the door before her brain understood what happened. At the entry of the nursery, she met up with a sleep rumpled, sexy looking Rashid, clad only in a pair of low-riding lounge pants. The shrill cry came again, jerking her to attention. She bypassed Rashid, who'd stopped to turn on the overhead light and headed straight for Jamilah's crib.

Jamilah was screaming at the top of her lungs. "Oh poor baby. Look at you. Rashid, bring me a towel."

Gail removed the infant's sleep shirt, which was saturated with the milk she'd thrown up. She tugged it off and set it to the side, then went to work on the diaper. Poor thing, she had it coming out both ends.

Rashid returned with a towel. "What's wrong with her? Why is she screaming?"

"She's sick. Go run water in my tub so I can clean her." While Rashid left to do her bidding, Gail cleaned Jamilah as much as possible with wipes before wrapping her in the towel.

When Rashid returned, she handed him the baby. "Start bathing her while I clean up the mess in here."

Rashid took one look at the crib and left with the screaming baby. Gail stripped the crib sheets from the bed, took them along with dirty nightclothes to the laundry room, and started the washer. When she returned, she sprayed the mattress with disinfectant and wiped it down before placing new sheets on it. Then she changed the bag in the diaper pail and took the full bag to dispose of it outside in the trashcan.

When she returned, Rashid had Jamilah on the changing table. "Come look at this."

Gail couldn't prevent the gasp that escaped when she saw her body. Jamilah covered in little red spots. They centered mostly around her mouth, on her face and neck. "That looks like a rash."

"Look at her stomach. It's so swollen it feels tight. Is that natural?"

"I don't think so. You'd better call the doctor." Gail dressed the crying baby in a fresh diaper and clean nightgown. Then she rocked her in the rocking chair, making soothing noises to calm her. She got scared when the crying turned to wheezing. Gail jumped up and rushed into Rashid's room with the baby.

"Rashid, she doesn't sound good. We need to take her to the hospital. Now!"

Rashid turned his attention from the phone, took one look at the baby, and hung up. "Get dressed. I'll meet you in the nursery."

Gail turned and ran to her room. After placing the baby in the center of her bed, she threw on the first clean thing she could find. A minute later, she had on her shoes and rushed with Jamilah into the nursery. Rashid already there, strapped Jamal into his car seat.

Gail placed Jamilah in her seat and packed the diaper bag while Rashid strapped her in. Rashid carried the babies down the stairs and into the garage, while Gail hurried behind. "We'll take yours," he called over his shoulder.

Gail stopped long enough to grab the key to the Santa Fe off the hook. She unlocked the doors and threw her things inside before helping with the car seats. Rashid pressed the remote to open the garage door, started the car, and drummed his fingers against the steering wheel impatiently while waiting for Gail to finish and get in the car.

As she closed her door, Rashid shoved the car into gear and as soon as her seatbelt clicked, he careened down the driveway and swerved onto the street.

"Rashid, slow down! It won't do the baby any good if you kill us all on the way to the hospital." Gail had to raise her voice to be heard over the noise. Jamal awoke and must have sensed something wrong, for he was crying. Between his crying and her wheezing, it was difficult to hear.

Rashid slowed the vehicle to a less heart-pounding pace, but still drove well above the legal limit. He accomplished a thirty-minute drive in less than fifteen, and came to a screeching halt in front of the Pediatric Emergency Room's entrance doors. He shoved the gear into park and opened his door.

Before he could step out of the car, Gail told him, "You take Jamilah while I park the car. I'll take Jamal with me."

"The car seat is too heavy for you to carry this soon after delivery," Rashid protested.

"I brought the pouch. I'll leave the car seat in the car."

Rashid opened his mouth to argue. "Rashid! We don't have time for this. Take Jamilah inside where it's warm. I'll be right behind you."

With a muttered curse, he got out, unbelted the car seat, and took the infant inside. Gail drove into the emergency room garage, parked the car, and followed with Jamal in her arms. He settled down when she held him and was soon on his way back to sleep. Rashid was already in the back when she entered the crowded waiting room.

She found a seat in a corner with a view of the television and settled down to wait. She adjusted Jamal to a more comfortable position and placed the baby bag between her feet on the floor. They were there for hours. Jamal went through two feedings and diaper changes before she was called to the back to join Rashid.

Rashid was the first person Gail saw when she pushed aside the curtain. "How is she? Have they said what's wrong?"

He rubbed his face wearily. "The doctor will return in a minute to tell us the test results. I had them get you so you could hear the diagnosis first hand."

"Thank you. I was so worried. Oh God, look at her. She's too small to be hooked up to so many tubes." One tube looked like an IV drip. The other was attached to her nose and must be helping her breathe. There were various patches attached to the baby connecting her to monitors, which continuously beeped.

Rashid put his arm around her. "She'll be fine. We got here in time. The doctor believes it was an allergic reaction. He's trying to determine the source."

She looked at him with tears in her eyes. "Being here again like this is my worst nightmare come to life."

"Don't cry. She's fine. "

He hugged her as close as he could with Jamal between them, and Gail leaned her head on his shoulder, needing the comfort. While Jason died instantly, Marcus had lingered for days after the accident in intensive care. Seeing Jamilah like this resurrected all of those painful memories.

The doctor entered the room. "Excuse me. Is this the mother?"

"Yes," Rashid said.

"Rashid mentioned you'd recently begun breastfeeding?"

"They're mostly bottle fed, but I have been supplementing it with breast milk. Jamilah, in particular. It's the only thing that seems to calm her."

"It's good that you did or that young lady might not be here today."

166

Rashid's grip on Gail's arm tightened until it was painful. "What are you saying?"

"She had a severe reaction to the formula which, although it's rare, sometimes occurs. I recommend you switch to breastfeeding exclusively, at least for the next six months. Let's give her digestive system a chance to develop. Is this your son?"

"Yes, this is Jamilah's brother."

He took the baby from Gail and examined him. "He seems to be okay but just to be safe, I'm changing his formula to soy based. If she's allergic to cow's enzymes, chances are he is as well. It just hasn't caught up with him yet."

"What about Jamilah? Is it safe to give her the formula?"

"Usually babies with milk allergies can drink the formula I'm prescribing. However, in some instances, they have an adverse reaction to it. Jamilah may be one of those babies, judging by the severity of her response. I recommend strictly breastfeeding for the first couple of months. After that, you can try integrating formula in with her breast milk—no more than an ounce at a time—to see how she handles it." He made a notation on the chart in his hands and looked up to be sure they understood his command. He waited until both Rashid and Gail nodded their agreement before continuing.

"Don't worry about not being able to keep up with the demand. Your body will produce as much milk as needed. In addition, there are herbs you can take to increase your supply that won't harm the children. A lot of my colleagues think women can't produce enough milk to handle the demand of two hungry infants. That's not true. If you watch what you eat and drink plenty of water, your body will adjust as the demand increases."

"Because of Jamilah's milk allergy, you," he motioned to Gail, "need to stay away from dairy products—no milk, milk products, or cheeses. Yogurt is

167

good and will give you the calcium your body needs. Also watch your caffeine intake. Remember, whatever you eat goes through you and into the baby. In two weeks, I want you to follow up with your pediatrician. Any questions?"

When they replied in the negative, he wrote something out on a pad and gave it to Rashid. "This is for the baby, in case she accidentally ingests milk and has another severe reaction." After leaving them with a few final instructions, the doctor left the cubicle.

Gail closed her eyes and turned her face into Rashid's chest when they began removing the tubes attached to Jamilah. She couldn't bear to watch, sure they were hurting her, but couldn't make herself leave. She needed to be there. Rashid held her and made sure Jamal wasn't smashed between them.

"Why don't you step outside until they're finished?" he murmured in her ear.

She shook her head, rubbing her forehead against his chest. She needed to see for herself that Jamilah was alive and well, even though her crying was breaking Gail's heart. She blinked back tears, determined not to cry with her. The last thing Rashid needed right now was two weeping females.

He rubbed her back soothingly. "They're almost finished. You're sure you won't step outside? I'll make sure nothing happens to her."

"I'm all right. I just can't bear to watch."

"Then you just stand here hiding your face against my shoulder while I watch over the proceedings."

Gail could hear the laughter in his voice. She thumped him on his back with her closed fist. "Don't laugh at me. I can't help it if I'm squeamish."

Rashid clucked his tongue. "I wouldn't dare laugh at you. I'm just happy to know you do have some feminine weaknesses. It allows me to be the big, strong male you turn to for support."

She raised her head to glare at him, only to find him smiling down at her. "You're teasing me," she accused.

"No, I'm distracting you. They're done with the baby."

Gail spun around to see for herself. Indeed, they were finished and were dressing Jamilah to leave the hospital.

"How long until we can leave? Should I go and get the car?"

"We already have your discharge papers. As soon as we finish here, you'll be free to leave. We'll only be another couple of minutes," the nurse stated.

"In that case, Jamal and I will get the car and bring it around to the exit," she told Rashid.

"Go ahead. We should be out shortly."

Gail was happy to leave. This place held too many bad memories for her. The need to breastfeed Jamilah was going to put a kink in Greg's plans for them. He wasn't going to be happy, but it couldn't be helped. If he fought against it, then he wasn't the man she thought he was.

This also meant she'd be living in Rashid's home for the next six months instead of weeks. However, she was willing to do anything necessary to keep Jamilah out of the hospital. She'd already lost one child. She wouldn't be responsible for losing another.

When they got home, Gail didn't want to let Jamilah out of her sight. She let Rashid put the twin to bed while she went and changed. As soon as he left the nursery, Gail crept in and held Jamilah in her arms.

She sat in the rocking chair and rocked the infant while she slept; her mind on Marcus's final moments.

She didn't know how long she'd been there when Rashid's voice came from the doorway. "Gail, she's fine. Lay her back in the crib and go get some sleep."

Gail clutched Jamilah a little closer. "Can't sleep. I keep remembering Marcus."

He crossed the room and stood next to where she sat. "Gail, you're so tired you're dozing in the chair. Come, give me the baby so I can put her back in the crib."

"I really don't want to be alone right now. Tonight brought back too many memories," she said as she reluctantly handed Rashid the baby.

He took Jamilah and laid her in the crib. When he finished, he took her hand, pulled her out of the rocker, and led her out of the nursery. "Let's go to bed. Tonight, you don't have to be alone. I was scared as well. I welcome the company."

He led her into her bedroom, over to the bed, and pushed down on her shoulders until she sat on the mattress. "Get in bed. I'll be back in a minute."

She climbed under the covers and waited, shutting down the part of her brain that questioned what she was doing. They both needed comforting, and tonight she wasn't going to deny either one of them out of a false sense of propriety. When Rashid reappeared in the doorway, she slid over to the other side of the bed, making room for him. He turned off the light and climbed into bed beside her.

Gail turned away from him and scooted back until she was in the center of the bed. She held still until she felt him curve his body around hers and settle against her back, his arm thrown casually across her waist. Then she released the breath she was holding. For tonight, they were two concerned parents who'd suffered a fright about their child. Tomorrow they'd return to normal.

Chapter Twelve

To Gail's fatigued mind, it felt like only a few minutes had passed when she heard a baby's demanding cry. She groaned and tried to make her tired muscles move.

"Stay here. I'll bring the baby to you."

She jumped, having forgotten Rashid slept beside her. He disentangled his legs from hers and went to get the infant. While he was gone, Gail used the bathroom and splashed water on her face, trying to become more alert.

When she came out of the bathroom, Rashid had a freshly diapered Jamilah on the bed playing with her. "Look, here's mommy now with your food."

"Rashid," she chided, "don't confuse her. I'm not her mommy."

As usual, he ignored her. "Mommy's going to feed the baby. Yes, she is," he cooed.

Gail sighed and sat on the bed, undoing the front catch on her bra. As she brought Jamilah to her breast, she told Rashid, "I need to go to the store. If I'm to continue breastfeeding, I'll need maternity bras, a breast pump, and cream. I also need tops that button in the front so I don't flash anyone when I'm feeding."

He lounged on the bed beside her, watching the proceedings with his usual intensity. "We can have Carmelita watch them while I take you shopping."

"I also need to go by my place and get more of my things."

His forehead puckered as he frowned. "Pack up all your belongings and bring them here. We need to discuss what to do with your apartment. There's no sense in it sitting empty over the next several months while you are here. Your lease expires at the end of the month. I suggest you pick out the things you want with you here, and I'll place the rest in storage."

Since his suggestion made sense, she didn't argue. "Our current living situation has been on my mind. While it makes more sense for me to live here and be closer to the twins, I'm concerned about what people will think. You're a respected businessman in the community. It doesn't look good, my living here with you a few short months after your wife left. People will believe I'm your mistress, the twins the result of our affair, and my pregnancy the reason Crystal left. That kind of talk could damage not only your reputation and mine, but your business as well. And what if Crystal returns? How will you explain my being here?" Gail looked at the baby in her arms. "With a breast pump, I could express the milk and bring it over." However, honesty forced her to admit, "But I'd rather be here feeding her just like this."

She reached behind her to adjust the pillows so she could lean against them.

"Let me help you." Rashid shifted so he rested against the headboard. Reaching out, he turned Gail so her back was against his chest, her arms supported by his. He rubbed his thumb against the baby's cheek while she fed. "Let people think what they want. Those who know me will know the truth. I couldn't care less about the others. As for Crystal, don't worry about it. If she ever surfaces, I'll handle her."

Gail glanced at him and quickly averted her gaze. She didn't like the expression on his face.

"If it's your reputation you're concerned with, there's an easy solution. I'll hire you to be the baby's wet nurse and nanny. If anyone questions your presence in my home, you can tell them the truth. Is this agreeable, or do you wish to return to your legal position?"

"I don't want to give it up forever, but I can take a break. We can give this a try for the next six months and see how it works. Most women stop breastfeeding around that time anyway because the little ones begin to grow teeth. It will also allow you more time to find a real nanny." She gazed down at the baby and a shank of hair fell forward, hiding the longing on her face. Jamilah was such a precious child. She was going to miss her, miss this when she was gone.

Rashid tucked her hair behind her ear and bent so he could see her expression, which Gail immediately wiped clean. "What about Greg? How will he react to all of this?"

She sighed. "He definitely won't be happy. He has a job lined up for me with his firm making good money." She told Rashid the amount of the salary offered.

"I can't match that but I can give you the thirty thousand I was going to pay the nanny."

"I don't like the idea of taking money to care for these sweethearts. It doesn't feel right, especially after the obscenely large settlement you gave me to have them." She was silent for a moment, thinking of all the ways her innocent presence here could hurt Rashid. "I'll take the position as nanny, but we have to do it right. I'll sign an employment contract and you'll add me to your payroll, just like any other employee. Also, Carmelita has a niece who's in college studying child development. Talk to her. She may be willing to live-in and help out part-time with the twins. The salary you pay her will help with college expenses, and assisting with the children will give her hands-on experience towards her degree. You can take ten of the thirty thousand you were going to pay me and give it to her instead."

"It's a deal, but I insist on continuing to cover your medical expenses."

"Works for me." Gail lifted the baby from her right breast, burped her, and switched sides. Right now, with the hospital scare so fresh in her mind, she was willing to do whatever it took, make any sacrifice necessary, to see that these children—Jamilah in particular—remained healthy and alive.

July—six months later...

"Gail, quit torturing that child and bring me my grandbaby."

Gail glanced over from her position in the pool. "Mom, I told you—"

"Yeah, yeah, yeah," her mother interrupted. "I know. They're not my grandchildren. You're just the nanny. They belong to Rashid. Yada, yada, yada. My blood's running through their veins, and that makes them mine. Now bring me my grandson."

Her mother, Martha, had been here visiting with her for the last two weeks. Gail lowered her voice and asked the splashing baby in her arms, "What do you say, Jamal? You ready to leave the pool and go play with the crazy lady?"

"I heard that. Don't you be teaching that child to disrespect his elders," her mother said.

"Yes, ma'am." Gail rolled her eyes at Jamal and he let loose with a string of baby gibberish. "So glad to see you understand," she told him as she waded to the side of the pool and handed her mother the baby.

Her mother hoisted him up above her head, causing him to laugh with glee, before carrying him to her seat. She took a towel and began to dry him while he squirmed on her lap. Jamal was an active child and rarely like sitting still. Gail took the opportunity of being child-free in the pool to swim a few laps.

"How's the hunt for a nanny going?" her mom asked when she paused for a breather.

175

"Mom, it's crazy. Who knew it was so hard to find someone reliable to care for your child?"

"Where have you been? If nannies were easy to find, everyone would have one."

"I'm beginning to see what you mean." Gail climbed out of the pool and water streamed down her long, lithe body, generously displayed in the blue bikini she wore. She walked over to the lounger next to her mother and dried off with the towel. Carmelita's niece had taken Jamilah inside for a diaper change and lunch, and would return shortly for Jamal.

"You should have seen some of the people we interviewed. The first lady showed absolutely no interest in the twins. All she wanted to know was how much did the job pay, how many days off did she get a week, and if the job provided benefits."

"Those are all important factors to know about any job."

"I agree, but when you go on and on about how much you love children—infants in particular—then never ask to see the children you'll be caring for, or ask any questions about them during the interview, what are we to think? Her words and actions didn't match." Gail shook her head in remembered disgust.

"What about the rest of them? Y'all have been looking for months. Surely, one of them looked promising."

Gail dropped the towel onto the small side table and plopped down into a chair. "Well, there were the women who were more interested in Rashid than the job. One made a pass at him right in front of me and Jamilah, who I was holding at the time. Then there was the woman who took one look at me and said she wouldn't work for 'my kind.'"

"You're kidding!" Her mother's eyes rounded in shock.

"No and it gets even better. When Rashid told her to leave, she accused him of being a terrorist and threatened to call immigration." She was getting angry again at the memory.

"What did he do?"

"Rashid didn't do anything. I covered the baby's ears and cussed her up one side and down the other before kicking her out of the house," Gail told her mother with fierce satisfaction.

Her mom arched an eyebrow at her tone, before saying sternly, "Gail, I know I raised you to be a lady at all times, but in this instance, I say 'good for you.' How dare she come into your home and speak to the two of you that way. What I'd like to know is why can't things continue the way they are now?"

"Mom, I have a life I'll eventually need to get back to. I can't live here indefinitely."

Her mother scowled at her over Jamal's head. "And why not? Having and raising children is one of the most important things a woman can do in this life. I didn't raise you to shirk your responsibilities."

Gail rolled her eyes. "I'm not shirking my responsibilities. How many times do I have to explain that these children belong to Rashid and Crystal? I was the surrogate. That means I can't claim them as my own, legally or otherwise."

"I hear your mouth talking but my eyes see something else. You love these babies as much as you ever loved Marcus, and don't try telling me differently." Her mom gazed at Jamal and asked in a tone reserved for babies, "Isn't that right, Jamal? Yes, you know it is," she cooed and nuzzled his neck.

Gail sighed tiredly. "Yes, I love them. How could I not? It doesn't change the fact that they aren't mine. Any day now Crystal could come walking through that door."

Her mom arched her eyebrows. "And what if she does? If she had wanted these little ones, she would never have left. You ask me, she forfeited her rights with both the twins and her husband when she walked out the door. And speaking of husbands, you got a good thing sitting right under your nose. You better snap him up before someone else does."

"I can't believe my own mother is encouraging me to chase after a married man. I ought to tell your pastor. Besides, I'm not interested in him that way, and even if I were, Rashid and I don't have that type of relationship." She couldn't believe what her mother was suggesting.

Her mother snorted.

Highly offended, Gail asked, "What's that supposed to mean?"

"Honey, you may be able to fool yourself and maybe Rashid, but I know better. You want that man, and he wants you. Don't have that type of relationship, humph," she mocked.

Gail stared at her mother in complete puzzlement. "I don't know what you're talking about. Rashid and I are friends. I'm also the temporary nanny and until recently, their wet nurse. There's nothing else between us."

Her mother made another sound of patent disbelief before she chuckled. "That's why you run to the phone every night when he calls."

"I do not!" Gail hotly denied.

"And," her mother continued, "that's why y'all have spent hours on the phone each night that I've been here during the time he's been gone."

"We're talking about the children." Gail couldn't believe this. Where was her mother getting this stuff?

Wide eyed, her mother said, "For two hours? Every night? Honey, these are babies we're talking about. Even if you told him everything they did from the time they woke in the morning till you put them to bed at night, it wouldn't take more than fifteen minutes. You want that man. Admit it to yourself, even if you won't admit it to me."

Gail looked at the baby in her mother's lap. "Mom, I have a man. A very nice man, remember? In case you've forgotten, his name is Greg and as soon as we get this childcare situation straightened out, I'll be joining him in California."

Her mother rolled her eyes, causing Gail to narrow hers in warning. She better not say anything disrespectful about Greg, she thought to herself. When Gail had taken him home to meet her parents, her mother was friendly but reserved. While she'd never come right out and said anything, Gail knew her mother wasn't too thrilled with Greg being white.

"Gail, I have nothing against Greg. From what little I've seen and from what you've told me, he seems like a good man, but I also happen to believe you're using him as an excuse to keep Rashid at an emotional distance. Not that I blame you. This whole situation is unusual. Here the two of you are, living together and parenting these babies. You're both young, healthy adults with physical needs. Things are bound to happen."

Gail closed her eyes and leaned her head back against her seat, suddenly tired. "Nothing's happened. I would never be the cause of anyone breaking their marriage vows."

"I know because I raised you right. But can you honestly tell me that if Rashid weren't married, things wouldn't be different between you two."

"Of course they would be different. For one, there wouldn't be any children. We probably wouldn't even know each other."

Her mom shook her head. "All right, I'll leave it alone. It's obvious you're not ready to deal with this yet so—"

"There's nothing to deal with," Gail argued.

"Excuse me, Ms. Gail, Senora Jones. Senor Rashid, he is on the phone for you. Senora Jones, I'll take the little one so he can join his sister."

"Thank you, Carmelita." Gail took the phone from her. As Carmelita left, she took Jamal, whom her mother had reluctantly handed over, with her. "Hi. This is a pleasant surprise." The irritation she felt towards her mother was instantly forgotten in the pleasure of his call.

"Are you enjoying your visit with your mother?"

"Mostly, although sometimes..." She left the rest unsaid and laughed.

"Enough said. What were you doing?"

"The twins just finished pool time, and now Angelina is fixing their mid-morning snack."

"How are they doing with the lessons? Any changes?"

"Your son is part fish. Jamilah hasn't decided if she likes being in that much water, but she didn't cry today when I dipped her beneath the surface."

"Tremendous progress."

Gail turned slightly to the side, trying to ignore her mother who watched every word as it left her mouth. "When are you coming home?"

Rashid sighed in her ear. "This business is taking longer than anticipated. It will be another two weeks minimum before I can return."

"Two weeks? That will make a whole month you've been gone. That's a long time to be away from the children."

"I know. If the trip weren't so long, I would have you and the twins join me. I miss them."

"They're changing so much. They may not know you when you return." She didn't know why she was pressing the issue. He'd already stated he'd come home if he could.

"It can't be helped. As soon as my business is completed, I'll be on the first flight back. The next trip I take, I'll bring the three of you with me."

"You know, you never told me where you are."

"When I return, we'll talk and I'll tell you everything. You're sure things are okay on your end? If necessary, I can come home, but then I would have to come back and start all over again." She could hear the frustration in his voice.

"Rashid, we're fine. Do what needs doing so you can return." She wanted him home, but not if he had to turn around and go back.

The phone beeped. "I've got to take this call. I'll talk to you later."

"Take care."

"You, too."

Gail laid the phone on the table and sat staring at it. Another two weeks, she thought dejectedly. He was supposed to have been back tomorrow.

"Is everything okay with Rashid? You seem upset."

"Hmm? Oh, yes. He's fine. Rashid isn't coming home tomorrow as planned. His business is taking longer than he thought."

"How much longer?"

"At least two weeks, maybe more. This is such a critical time in the babies' development. They're learning to recognize faces. They won't know him when he returns." And the thought of that upset her.

"They'll figure it out. What about you? Are you going to be okay with this delay?" Her mother's face showed her concern.

"I have Carmelita, Angelina, and Miguel to help with the children. I'll be fine."

"That's not what I was referring to, but I'll let it go. I'm supposed to leave Sunday, but I can stay longer if needed."

"And daddy will come and get you if you do. Go home. I can handle things here." Gail smiled to show she was all right with her mother leaving.

"You could always come home with me. Your father would be happy to see you and the twins."

"I can't remove Rashid's children from his home without his permission." She couldn't believe her mother had made the suggestion.

"They're yours too. You have just as much right to them as he does. The rest of the family would love to see them."

"Mom." Gail drawled the word out into two syllables. Then she sighed, tired of repeating herself. "Never mind." It was no use. Her mom had her mind made up and there was no swaying her. "We'll be fine."

◆◆◆◆◆

A little over three weeks later, Rashid returned to his sleeping household. He left his bags in the entryway and headed upstairs, needing to see his children after being gone for so long. Entering the nursery, he stood by their cribs, noting the changes that had taken place during his absence.

Both babies had grown. Jamilah had more hair on her head and her complexion was darkening. Jamal's features were evolving. He looked like a masculine version of Gail. Rashid kissed them both, being careful not to wake them. Gail said they routinely slept the night through. Yet another change during his absence.

He went to the next person on his list. Gail lay sprawled on her back, almost in the center of the bed.

The light from the hallway shined across the center of the mattress, leaving her face in the shadow. He sat on the edge, hesitant to wake her when she slept so deeply.

It amazed him how important Gail had become to him in such a short period of time. A year ago, she'd been his wife's best friend and had been welcome in his home on the basis of their relationship. Today, she was one of the most important people in his life. Not only was she a close friend and confidant, she was the mother of his children. They were friends, equals, and parenting partners.

Each evening he looked forward to sharing his day with her. He frequently found himself rushing home because he knew she was there. He could talk to her about anything. Best of all, she understood him. She laughed at his jokes. Not out of politeness like some, but because she got them.

As much as he'd loved Crystal, she'd never really understood him. His marriage with Crystal had revolved around her—her needs, her wants, and her happiness. Crystal hadn't been a selfish woman, but she had been high maintenance and a bit self-centered. She'd expected to be catered to, and he'd been happy to do so. These last few months with Gail had shown him there could be so much more to the male/female relationship than what he'd shared with his wife.

He and Gail had bonded over the last year. They'd really gotten to know each other during her pregnancy and become intimately acquainted during the delivery. The scare with Jamilah had only served to bring them closer. These last six months of living together had taken their friendship to a whole new level.

Rashid reached out and lightly caressed Gail's cheek. "Gail."

Her eyes slowly opened and then she smiled at him sleepily. "Rashid, you're home. When did you get in?"

"A few minutes ago."

"What time is it?" she asked around a yawn.

"A little after one."

She turned onto her side facing him and rested her cheek on her hand. "Mmm, you must be tired. How was your flight?"

"Long and tiring."

Gail reached out and touched his arm. "Go get some rest. You'll be here in the morning, won't you? You're not going into the office?"

"I don't plan to go anywhere." Wild horses couldn't pry him away from his family after so long an absence.

"I'm glad you're home. You were missed," she told him around another big yawn.

"Go back to sleep. The twins will have you up early. I just wanted you to know I was here." He held her hand briefly before laying it on the mattress.

"I'm glad you did. Things weren't the same with you gone," she murmured. Her eyes were already closing.

"I missed you, too," he whispered softly.

He wanted nothing more than to climb into bed beside her and curl up around her warmth. At this moment, his empty bed seemed cold and lonely. He leaned down and kissed her lightly on the lips.

Rashid left Gail's room and went to his own, so tired he was ready to drop. Underneath the tiredness was a sense of satisfaction. He'd accomplished what he set out to do. Now he could move forward with the rest of his plan.

◆◆◆◆◆

Gail lay on the floor of the nursery playing with the twins when she thought she heard Rashid moving around in his room.

"Hey you guys, Daddy's home. Let's go say hello to the sleepyhead." She picked up both children, walked down the hall to his bedroom, and nudged open the door with her foot. Rashid sat on the side of the bed and looked up as she entered. "I brought someone to see you," she told him.

A huge grin crossed his face and he held his hands out. Both babies clung to Gail when she tried to hand them over to him. Jamilah turned her face into Gail's chest and began to whine. Rashid looked like someone hit him.

"It's just a stage they're going through. They'll warm up to you soon. A month is a long time to them." Gail sat beside him and then fell onto her back, a game she often played with the twins. She would fall backwards, they would laugh, and clutch at any part of her they could reach. This time they clutched at her, keeping a wary eye on their father. "Rashid, lie beside me and get comfortable. Give them a chance to relax."

Rashid lay on his side and propped his head on his hand. "They've changed so much. They're a lot bigger, and their features are changing."

"Have they? I knew they were growing, but they look the same to me. I guess it's because I see them every day."

"Jamal looks like a miniature you; completely different from when he was born."

"Isn't it amazing? Jamilah still looks like you. She even has your hair." Gail cupped Jamilah's head, running her fingers through the coarse, silky strands which lay flat against her head with not a hint of curl.

As they lay there conversing, the babies gradually warmed to Rashid, allowing him to hold them as long as she stayed near. "You must have been really tired. You slept all day."

"Jet lag. I flew through several time zones. My body's trying to adjust."

185

"I know you miss them, but it's time for these little ones to go to bed. They get cranky if they get off schedule. When you're ready, dinner's on the stove." She stood, hoisted a child in each arm, and started out of the room.

"Eat with me?" he called, causing her to pause and glance over her shoulder.

"If you'd like. Let me get them settled first."

Rashid took Jamal from her and carried him into the room for her, then returned to his room to dress. When the babies were lying in their cribs, Gail turned on the intercom, turned off the light, and went downstairs.

Rashid was already in the kitchen warming his food. "I've missed Carmelita's cooking."

"It's so good, if I didn't swim every day, I'd be huge." She turned from the cabinet to find him studying her body. It should have made her self-conscious. Instead, curiosity compelled her to ask, "What are you thinking?"

"If I hadn't seen it with my own eyes, I'd never believe you gave birth to twins. You haven't gained a pound."

Gail laughed in disbelief. "You must be blind. I'm still carrying an extra ten pounds I haven't been able to get rid of, even though I swim daily."

Rashid arched one eyebrow. "If this is how you look with extra weight, you need to keep it."

Gail grinned, ridiculously pleased with the compliment but slightly embarrassed as well. She fixed her plate and stuck it in the microwave to warm. "Would you like something to drink? There's a pitcher of freshly squeezed lemonade in the fridge."

"Sounds good."

She poured them both a glass of lemonade and brought them to the table. The timer on the microwave went off and she got her food and sat down. They both dug in.

"Have you heard from Greg?"

"No, and I'm starting to worry. I've called both his cell and apartment. He's not answering nor has he returned my calls."

Rashid looked up from his food with a frown. "Try calling the office."

"I really hate to bother him at work. He gets so many phone calls as it is. He's never not returned my calls."

"When's the last time you spoke with him?"

"Almost a week now. He told me he was going to be busy and hard to reach, but I didn't expect this." She and Greg usually spoke every day, even if it was only for a few minutes. When they had more time, they used Facetime. It wasn't the same as being together, but they'd found a way to make it work.

"He still wants you to come out there, doesn't he? You don't think he finally lost patience with you, do you?"

That's what she was afraid of, though Greg had seemed to understand when she'd told him about Jamilah's milk allergy. He'd agreed with the child's health at stake, she needed to be here. However lately, she sensed a change in his attitude. "I don't know, Rashid. The twins are both weaned now. He knows the trouble we've been having finding a nanny, but I worry he's getting tired of the delays. We both thought I'd be with him by now."

Rashid set down his fork and leaned his forearms on the table. "I know we've gone round and round on this subject, but I still think you need to reconsider rearranging your whole life for a man unwilling to commit to you."

Gail withheld a sigh. "You're right. We have gone over this time and again. That's why we agreed to

187

disagree, remember? We're never going to see eye-to-eye."

His gaze drilled into hers. "What if you had another option?"

"What kind of option?" she asked warily.

"I want you to—" The doorbell rang, interrupting him.

Gail laid down her fork. "I wonder who that is? We don't get many visitors."

Rashid frowned, visibly annoyed with the interruption. "Probably a salesman. Ignore it. I have something important to discuss with you."

The doorbell rang again, longer this time, like they were leaning on the buzzer. Whoever was at the door was impatient. "We live in a gated community. It can't be a salesman." She left the table and went to the door, aware of a disgruntled Rashid trailing behind her.

Gail glanced through the glass pane at the side of the door and squealed excitedly. "Greg!"

She slung open the door and flung herself into Greg's open arms. He picked her up and spun her around in a circle before claiming her mouth in a hungry kiss. Gail lost herself in his embrace, matching his hunger and intensity until a dry voice intruded. "Unless you'd like to continue entertaining the neighbors, I suggest you step inside."

She pulled away from Greg with a breathless laugh. "Come in." Taking his arm, she tugged him across the threshold, and shut the door. "I was just talking about you. Oh my God! I can't believe you're here." She hugged him again, and then punched him on the arm. "That's for not returning my calls. I was so worried."

Greg used the hand she hit him with to pull her back into his arms. "I wanted to surprise you."

"Mission accomplished." Gail was pulling his head down for another kiss when a throat cleared behind her. She paused, a flush sweeping over her face as she glanced over her shoulder and saw Rashid still standing there. "Where are my manners? Greg, you remember Rashid, don't you?"

"How you doing, man?" Greg stepped forward, hand held out to Rashid while holding Gail close to him.

Rashid shook his hand. "Fine. Yourself?"

Greg smiled broadly and glanced down at Gail. "Great now that I've got my woman in my arms."

"I'll give you two some privacy."

"Thank you," she said to Rashid's retreating back. "Let's go in the den." She turned and pulled Greg by his tie into the small family room, and though it wasn't necessary, shut and locked the door behind them.

Greg dragged her to the couch and tugged until she straddled his lap, her gauzy skirt riding high on her thighs. "Now where were we?"

She wrapped her arms around his neck.

"Oh, yes. Now I remember." He swooped in for another breath-stealing kiss.

Gail moaned and gave herself to him whole-heartedly. She'd missed this. Missed him. When she was breathless and trembling with desire, he released her mouth and trailed kisses down her neck as his hands slid underneath her bikini bottoms to cup her butt. She arched against him, rubbing her wet crotch against the long length of his erection while she tried to catch her breath. "What are you doing here? I thought you were working an important case."

"I was. I came back to get my woman." He nudged the spaghetti strap of her tank aside and licked the tip of her exposed nipple.

Gail clutched his head to her, whimpering when he drew her breast into his mouth and suckled. She groaned in disappointment when he pulled back and blew on the taut peak, only to catch her breath when one of his fingers probed her wet sheath.

"I miss you and don't want to go another day without you. Marry me. Come to California with me as my wife."

"What?" She drew back in shock.

He tipped her back onto the couch and came down on top of her. "I said, marry me. Put me out of my misery. These last seven months have been hell without you. We survived six months of dating with no sex and another seven months of long distance without growing cold. If we handled this, we can handle anything. What do you say? Will you marry me?"

"Yes!" She didn't need to think twice. She kissed him deep and long. "You know I love you, right?"

"I think you've mentioned it a time or two," he murmured as he nuzzled her exposed breasts.

She wrapped her legs loosely around his thighs as she tunneled her hand between them to get at his straining erection. "I would have come to you without a marriage proposal. I just needed to get the twins settled first." Gail wanted it to be clear that she had not held out for a wedding ring.

He shifted and allowed her to stroke his cock through his pants. Greg rested his forehead against hers, eyes closed in pleasure as she alternately squeezed and rubbed in a manner she knew he enjoyed. "Your devotion to Rashid and his children is admirable, but I need you too," he hissed as his hips jerked violently. "Maybe Rashid would try harder to find someone if he didn't have you to depend upon."

She paused in her ministrations. "He really has been trying to find a nanny. I know you don't believe it, but it's true."

Greg snorted in disbelief. "A man seriously trying to hire someone to care for his children doesn't take off and leave town for over a month. Did he ever tell you where he was, or what important business matter required him being gone for so long?"

Gail frowned and removed her hand completely as she defended Rashid. "No, but I'm sure it was critical. He wouldn't have left otherwise."

"If you say so. I don't want to talk about him or the twins. I'm holding my soon-to-be wife in my arms that I haven't seen in months. There are more important matters on my mind." He glanced down at her bare breasts and licked his lips.

"Do tell?" She gave him her sexiest smile.

"Mmm-hmm." He nuzzled her neck, working his way to her ear. "How soon will you marry me? I hope you don't want a big wedding. I only have a week before I need to return, and I want you on the plane with me. We can stop in Vegas on the way back."

"A week! I don't know if I can be ready in a week." She frowned as her mind busily calculated all needing to be done to accomplish this feat.

He drew back to look at her. "What is there to do? Your stuff's already in storage. The few things you have here we can ship or put with the rest in storage. Hell, I don't care. Sell all of it and buy new when we get home. Make a fresh start of it all the way around."

"But what about the twins? I can't leave Rashid in the lurch," she protested, her conscience cringing at the thought of leaving before he had someone to replace her.

"Isn't Angelina on summer break? She and Carmelita can handle things until he finds someone else. It can't be that difficult. Are you telling me out of all the candidates you interviewed, none of them were suitable?" His eyebrow arched, daring her to disagree with him.

Gail thought about it, mentally reviewing all of the applicants that had come to the house. "There were a couple that weren't so bad," she grudgingly admitted.

"See! Problem solved." He cupped her cheeks. "We love each other. I think we've waited long enough to be together. Let's not wait any longer."

"You're right. I'll talk to Rashid."

"Thank you." He glanced at his watch. "It's getting late. I still need to check into a hotel."

Not wanting him to leave when he'd just arrived, she said, "I'm sure Rashid wouldn't mind you staying here. You can stay in the pool house."

Greg kissed her on the nose. "If I stay here, it will be in your bed, and I have too much respect for Rashid's values to do that. When we do finally make love, I want you all to myself. No babies crying or you wondering if anyone can hear you screaming." He kissed her again. This time a lingering one on her lips before slowly rolling off her onto the floor. As he gazed at her still sprawled on the couch, skirt around her waist and top below her breasts, he stated, "I'd better leave before I forget all my noble intentions."

Gail stood and straightened her clothing, conscious of Greg watching her every move with heated desire. When she was decent, he caught her by the waist and headed for the exit.

At the front door, he paused. "I have some errands to run tomorrow, but I'll come and get you for dinner."

Gail hugged him and laid her head on his chest. "You just got here. I hate to let you go."

"It won't be for long. I'll call you in the morning." He claimed one last kiss before leaving.

Gail stood at the door until he turned out of the driveway. When he was out of sight, she closed the door and turned to find Rashid standing there waiting. "Oh, I didn't hear you."

Rashid's gaze roamed over her face, no doubt taking in her kiss swollen lips and tousled hair "I need to speak with you. I heard Greg leaving and came out to finish our discussion."

Pressing a hand to her suddenly nervous stomach, she agreed. "Yes, we do need to talk. Did you finish eating?"

"While you were in the den."

Gail headed to the kitchen to clean up the mess she'd made. In an effort to delay giving her news, she asked, "What did you want to talk about? Is this about your trip?"

"In a way. Sit down, please." He motioned to the kitchen table.

"Okay." She left the sink and came to the table where they sat across from each other.

Rashid rested his forearms on its surface. "We've become good friend over the last year, wouldn't you say?"

She gave a one-shouldered shrug. "Sure."

"And we work well together, especially when it comes to the children. You're a good woman, and a wonderful mother. Someone I have a tremendous amount of respect for. I think we have the makings for a good marriage."

Gail's eyebrow shot up to her hairline. "Marriage," she echoed faintly.

His gaze pinned hers. "I know we're not in love with each other, but I think we have enough of a foundation to build a solid marriage. We both love the twins and want what's best for them. We're close friends, and we already know we can live together peacefully. I know this isn't the most romantic of proposals, but I'm asking you to marry me." Rashid leaned forward, his body visibly vibrating with tension as he waited for her to answer.

Gail's mouth dropped open and she stuttered, "But...but...you're already married."

"Not any longer. I went to Guam and filed for divorce. It was final two days ago."

"But how is that possible? You don't know where Crystal is. There's no way she could have agreed to this. Is the divorce even legal in the US?" Gail was totally blown away.

"Very legal. Guam is a US territory, so it's just like getting a divorce here in the States, only quicker. I filed on the grounds of abandonment. Divorces under those circumstances are harder to obtain, but you can do it if you have enough documentation. It just takes longer. That's why I had to stay so long."

Gail rubbed her forehead, feeling stress gather there. "I hate to see any marriage end in divorce. Are you certain you didn't act too hasty? Crystal hasn't even been gone a year." In Florida, the missing spouse had to be absent for a year before abandonment could be claimed as grounds for divorce.

Rashid scowled. "My marriage was over the day she walked out the door. Leaving me is the one thing she knew I wouldn't tolerate or forgive. Crystal knew what would happen when she left."

Privately, Gail wasn't so sure. Crystal had always been able to wrap Rashid around her thumb.

He reached out and placed his hand on top of her restless one lying on the table. "You didn't answer my question. I really believe we can make this work. You don't have to make a decision right this minute, but promise me you'll be thinking about it."

Guiltily, she withdrew from his touch and crossed her arms over her chest. "I'm sorry, Rashid. I can't. Greg asked me to marry him tonight, and I said yes. That's what I wanted to discuss with you. When he leaves next week, I'll be going with him."

Rashid sat back in his chair. "I see," he said quietly.

"A couple of the nanny's we interviewed weren't so bad, and Angelina is out of school on summer break. I'm sure she would be happy to work more hours.

Carmelita and Miguel can both help out with the children until you hire someone," she said, her words almost tripping over each other in her rush to get it out.

Rashid studied her face. "Are you sure this is what you want?"

Gail nodded solemnly. "I love him."

After a few tense, silent moments, he sighed. "Don't worry about the twins. I can hire someone from an agency until I find someone permanent. Congratulations on your pending nuptials. Greg's a lucky man. When's the wedding?"

Relieved Rashid was being so agreeable, she said, "He's pressed for time. I don't want another big wedding, so we're going to layover in Las Vegas and do the deed there."

One of his eyebrows rose in patent disbelief. "What is your family going to say? I'm sure they'll want to be there to witness it."

At the mention of her close knit family, Gail quickly squashed her qualms, hoping Rashid hadn't noticed her sudden sense of misgiving. "I'm sure they'll understand. If not, they'll get over it sooner or later. We've waited long enough. I don't want to wait any longer."

He pushed to his feet and came around the table. She rose to meet him, and he placed his hands on her shoulders. "I'm disappointed, but I wish you every happiness in the world."

"Thank you, Rashid." Touched because she knew he was sincere, Gail gave him a brief hug and then watched him turn and leave the kitchen.

For just a moment, she allowed herself to entertain the thought of what marriage to Rashid would be like. Goose bumps broke out on her skin at the thought of sharing a bed with him every night. With a shake of her head, she dislodged the disturbing image from her mind.

Her thoughts turned to Greg and her pending marriage. If she was leaving in a week, there was a lot to do. No time like the present to get started.

Chapter Thirteen

The next morning, Gail called her mother to tell her the happy news. "Mom, I'm getting married."

"Rashid proposed?" Her mother's excited voice came through the line. "Frank," she hollered, "Rashid proposed and Gail said yes."

"Mom! No! Wait! I'm not marrying Rashid. Where'd you get a crazy idea like that? I'm marrying Greg." Gail couldn't emphasize his name strongly enough. She could hear her father's strong voice in the background asking questions.

"Greg! Who is...? Oh, the guy you brought home for Thanksgiving. I thought he was in California. You're marrying him? But what about Rashid? What about your children?"

Gail wanted to scream. "Mom, for the last time, the twins aren't mine nor have they ever been. I signed a contract waiving my legal rights to them. Yes, it was my eggs but they were never meant to be my children. Why are you having such a hard time getting this through your head? You raised me to keep my word. Drilled it into me as a child. Well, I promised to have a baby for Rashid and Crystal. Her leaving doesn't change my end of the agreement. Enough already. The twins belong to Rashid. End of story." Gail took a deep breath in an attempt to calm down. This was the closest she'd ever come to yelling at her mother.

The other end of the line was silent for a long time. "Gail, I hear what you're saying, and I know that's what your head believes, but what about your heart? Is it in agreement? You are absolutely correct. Your father and I raised you to honor your word, no matter what. If everything had gone as intended, I would agree with you totally—Jamilah and Jamal belong to Rashid and Crystal. But it didn't. Crystal took off, leaving those children motherless. Now, if you can go off and leave those motherless babies to fend for themselves, you're not the woman I raised you to be. Those children need you, and so does Rashid."

Her mother paused to take a deep breath. "There's no way that you could have carried those darlings under your heart for nine months, cared for them another seven months, and not, in your heart of hearts, consider them yours. Every time you held them to your breasts and fed them, they should have stolen another piece of you. That's how it was for me with all of you. You're a grown woman and I can't tell you what to do, but I urge you to rethink. Think about the impact your decision will have on the lives around you, and I think you'll make the right decision."

"Mom," Gail said on a sigh, "I have thought about it. I've been thinking about it for the last seven months. My mind's made up. I love Greg and want to be with him. I'm going to marry him, and I want you and daddy to be there to witness it. It's not going to be anything fancy. We're stopping in Vegas for a few days and exchanging our vows there. I'll pay for you and daddy fly to out."

"If this is what you really want to do, then I wish you happiness. However, your father and I won't be there. I think you're making a big mistake, and I just can't bring myself to be there and watch it."

Stunned by her mother's response, pain and disappointment viciously stabbed Gail in the heart, and she drew in a shaky breath. "If that's how you feel…" Her eyes stung as tears made their presence known.

"It is."

"I've got to go. I have a lot to do. Talk to you later," she choked out, determined not to cry.

"Gail," she heard her mother calling as she pushed the end button, disconnecting the call. A few seconds later, the phone rang again. She looked at the display. Her mother. She laid the phone on the dresser—unanswered. Her mother had made her position perfectly clear. There was nothing more to say. Thank God she hadn't told her about Rashid's proposal.

Through the monitor, Gail heard the twins stirring and went in to check on them. Her mother just didn't understand. She had to leave. She'd already lost one child. Her heart couldn't take losing another.

Things with Rashid were so uncertain. She had no legal rights where the children were concerned. At any moment, they could be taken away and there was nothing she could do to stop it. That's why she'd been so careful to withhold a piece of her heart. Yes, she loved them, but she loved them the way she loved her nieces and nephews—as dearly beloved family members. That's how she made it through the pregnancy and the last seven months, and it was this mindset that was going to enable her to get on a plane and leave next week.

That night, at the restaurant with Greg after their food had been served, she told him about the conversation with her mother.

"Don't be mad with her. She doesn't want to lose contact with her biological grandchildren, and you are her best hope of having them in her life," he said.

Gail shook her head, refuting his words. "Rashid would let her keep in touch with the children."

Greg pointed his fork at her. "It's not the same. Without you here, she's dependent upon Rashid's goodwill and kind nature. There's no security in knowing that at any moment, the privilege could be snatched away from her and there is nothing she could do stop it."

She sighed, inwardly acknowledging the wisdom in his words. "You're probably right, but it still hurts. I want my parents there with me. This is my special day, our joyous occasion. Her disapproval and refusal to be there is ruining it."

"Would you like me to call and talk to her? Maybe she'll change her mind."

"Thank you but no. I'll be all right once I adjust to the idea of them not being there. The important thing is that we're finally going to be together."

Greg took a sip of his drink. "Did you talk to Rashid?"

"We talked last night." Gail pushed the food around on her plate while she gathered her words, trying to decide how much to say. Finally, she decided it would be best to tell Greg all of it. "I hesitate to tell you this, but I don't want there to be any secrets between us. You know that trip Rashid took? He was in Guam, getting a divorce. He filed on the grounds of abandonment. That's why he was gone for so long. Apparently, it takes longer if you don't have the other party's consent."

She paused to take a bite of her meal before revealing the rest.

Greg set his fork down and gave her his full attention. "The look on your face tells me there's more you're not saying."

She met his gaze. "He asked me to marry him— not for love or anything of that nature—but a marriage of convenience based on friendship, compatibility, and the children."

"What did you say?"

Gail tilted her head to the side and narrowed her eyes. "I told him you'd proposed, and I'd accepted. That I love you and will be leaving with you when you fly back at the end of the week."

She hadn't realized Greg was tensely awaiting her answer until the tension visibly left his body. "How did he react?"

"He wished me well and told me not to worry about the twins."

Greg was silent, obviously contemplating something. "If I hadn't proposed, would you have said yes?"

Her response was quick and instinctive. "No. In my mind, he's still my best friend's husband. Anyhow, I'd already made a commitment to you."

"And if you hadn't?" he stressed again.

Her response came slower this time. "I don't know. He made a pretty compelling argument. My pregnancy created a bond between us, allowing us to become close friends. Living together these last seven months only strengthened it. We're both committed to caring for Jamilah and Jamal to the best of our ability. Following his logic, we do have the basis for a good marriage."

He gave her his lawyer's face—cool and collected. "What about passion? Sex? You're a passionate woman. Would you really agree to a passionless marriage?"

Gail shifted uncomfortably in her seat. This wasn't something she wanted to discuss.

"Something happened between you, didn't it?" he asked suspiciously.

"Sorta, kind of. I don't know. You tell me." Then she told him about the incident with her breasts and her subsequent conclusions.

There was silence as he processed her words. "You're sure that's all it was? Hormones and a sequence of events? What if it's more?"

Gail shook her head. "It can't be more. He's Crystal's husband."

"Not anymore, he's not," Greg said grimly.

Feeling like she was being cross-examined, she asked, "Just what are you getting at?"

Greg reached across the table and captured her left hand, toying with the solitaire engagement ring he'd

201

placed on it earlier this evening. First he'd removed the wedding band from her right hand. His message was clear. She no longer needed reminders of the past. "All I'm saying is it would be perfectly natural for the two of you to be physically attracted to each other. You've been through a lot together. He's the father of your biological children. Your attraction to Rashid doesn't take away from your feelings for me. I'm secure enough in our love to handle your being attracted to another man. Just don't lie about it, to yourself or to me."

Gail searched deep inside and then finally said, "I'll admit there might be a slight attraction there, but it feels so sordid. It's just wrong to desire my best friend's husband."

"It's not sordid, and it isn't wrong. It's the circumstances of the past year that caused it to develop. Were you attracted to Rashid before all of this happened?"

"No," she replied vehemently.

He arched an eyebrow. "And if Crystal hadn't left, would you be attracted to him?"

This answer she didn't even have to think about. "We'd be closer because I really got to know him on his own merit during my pregnancy, but he would still be Crystal's husband, who also happened to be my friend."

Greg gave her hand a reassuring squeeze. "Then you have nothing to worry about. You've done nothing wrong. Nothing sordid. You lived in the man's home for the last seven months and did nothing to act on the desire you feel. Attraction is nothing more than the body's chemical response to another person. It's what you do about it that causes the problems."

Gail searched his face. She knew how he felt about infidelity, having to deal with so much of it in his business. "So, you're okay with this?"

A huge grin split his face. "Hell yeah. I got the girl. You may be physically attracted to him, but I have your heart and when we get to Vegas, we're going to set the sheets on fire."

Gail smiled in agreement. "I can hardly wait."

◆◆◆◆◆

"How are things going? Are you almost packed? You leave tomorrow."

Gail took another stack of clothing out of the drawer and placed them in the suitcase. "Rachel, things have been crazy. Who knew moving was so much work?"

"Like what? Your stuff's already in storage. What else is there?"

"Not all of it. I brought a lot of it here with me—knickknacks, memorabilia, and things of that nature. My computer desk, books, recliner, and movie and music collection—it's all here and needs to be boxed up. The desk and recliner, I put into storage. I also had to quit my job."

"I thought you quit that months ago?"

"No, I was on FMLA. I spent almost a whole day at the office filling out paperwork. Fortunately, I'd already brought home the items I had at my desk, or it would have taken even longer."

"Mom still refusing to come to Vegas?"

"Yes," she hissed, still mad about the whole situation. "Can you believe it?"

"Well, if it were me she was doing it to, yes I could, but you're the favored one. The baby girl in a family full of boys."

Gail rolled her eyes. "I am not the 'favored one.' You've been married to Frank Jr. too long. He's rubbing off on you. But still, what mother refuses to attend her only daughter's wedding?"

"Apparently yours."

"Don't remind me," Gail said on a groan.

"You know Frank and I would be there if we could."

"I know. Deb said the same. Tim has some big project going at work and can't leave. Mike's in Iraq, so that leaves him out. I'm a big girl. I can handle it."

"Be sure to take lots of pictures, and don't get one of those cheesy chapels. If you're going to do it, do it right."

Gail had to laugh. "Yes, ma'am."

"Now I don't mean to sound like Mom, but are you sure you're doing the right thing?"

Gail flopped down on top of the crowded bed. "Not you too. This wasn't an overnight decision. We've been planning this move for months."

"But that was before Rashid asked you to marry him. You could stay there. Be the twin's mother for real."

"No, I'd be their stepmother. There's no security in that."

"But you'd be married to Rashid. Wouldn't that make you their legal mother?"

"Not as long as Crystal's name is on the birth certificate. Rashid only wants to marry me because of the kids. What if he falls in love with someone else? What if Crystal returns and he decides our marriage was a mistake? I'd be right back in the same position I'm in now, only it would be a lot more painful."

"Couldn't you adopt them?"

"Adopt my own biological children. Hmmm, does that sound as weird to you as it does to me? I can only adopt them if Crystal gives up her legal rights. I don't see that happening any time soon. We don't even know where Crystal is to ask."

"I see what you mean. So you're really leaving? Who's watching the babies?"

204

"The agency sent over a nanny yesterday. I've been trying to teach her the twins' schedule in between all the other stuff I'm doing."

"Sounds like you have everything worked out. I won't keep you. I know you're under a deadline. Call me when you get to Vegas. Put me on speakerphone and let me hear the ceremony. Or maybe you can find a chapel with one of those computer thing-a-ma-jingies that lets us watch it live."

Gail fell on her back laughing. "They're called web cams. I'll see what I can do. Talk to you later."

"Bye."

◆◆◆◆◆

"Is this the last of it?" Greg asked as he took the bag from her hand.

"That one's going on the plane with us. You have the rest."

"I'm going out to the car. We have a little extra time, but don't take too long saying goodbye," he cautioned.

"I won't. Thank you."

Everyone had gathered in the foyer to see her off. Gail turned to Ms. Gooseby, the temporary nanny, who held Jamal. "I tried to write down everything I could think of. Ask Angelina or Carmelita if there's something I missed that you need to know. They're really sweet babies and you shouldn't have any problems."

She held her hands out for Jamal. Ms. Gooseby handed the boy over. "Little prince, you be good for your daddy. Don't let me get any bad reports or you won't get any really cool gifts from me."

He spouted a bunch of gibberish and grabbed her bottom lip. Gail gently bit his fingers, causing him to flash his semi-toothless grin. She kissed him and gave him back to the nanny. After smoothing her hand over

205

his silky head one last time, she turned to the next person waiting. "Angelina, take care of yourself and make sure you get that degree. I'm expecting great things out of you. I'll be checking."

"I will. Congratulations on your upcoming marriage. Be careful out there in California. Don't forget to keep in touch," Angelina said.

Jamilah launched herself out of Angelina's arms. Gail dropped her purse and caught her. "Hey, baby girl. You feel a little warm. Do you have another tooth coming in?"

Jamilah laid her head on Gail's chest and snuggled in. She gently stroked the back of her head and rocked her. "Give her some Tylenol. If this goes like before, she'll be cranky and her nose runny. Watch out for diarrhea."

She kissed her forehead and passed the baby back to Angelina. Jamilah immediately cried, reaching out to Gail. "I'll take her to the nursery and give her the medication before she eats." Angelina turned and carried her quickly away.

Gail watched them disappear, a tight feeling in her chest. When they were gone, she turned to the housekeeper. "Carmelita, I'm going to miss you. When I get settled, I'll be calling for some of your recipes."

Smiling, Carmelita wiped her hands on her ever present apron. "You do that, Ms. Gail. Keep your husband nice and fed. Is the way to a man's heart, no?"

Gail grinned. "I'll take your word for it." Carmelita has been married to the same man for over thirty years. She ought to know.

Everyone walked off, leaving Gail and Rashid facing each other alone in the entry foyer. Saying goodbye was so much harder than she'd expected. Gail willed the right words to come to her mouth. "You'll be fine with them. You're a good father. I knew you would be, that's why I agreed to do this. Take care of yourself and don't work so hard."

Rashid stood with his hands in his pockets, a somber expression on his face. "Be happy, Gail. Keep in touch. The children and I will miss you."

"I'm the god-mommy, remember? I expect lots of pictures and email updates on their progress. You'd better keep in touch as well. We're friends now. Friends keep in contact." She floundered awkwardly, trying to decide what to do. Finally, she held her hand out.

Rashid looked at it then used it to pull her into a bear hug. "Don't go. Stay," he whispered into her ear.

"I can't. I gave my word." She clutched him tightly.

Long moments later, he released her, setting her gently onto her feet. "If you change your mind, my offer still stands. You'll always have a home with me. Call when you get settled, and I'll bring the twins out for a visit."

"Thank you." Her gaze locked onto Rashid, she swooped her purse off the floor and took one step back, and then another. Finally she turned and strode the few remaining steps to the door where she stopped with her hand on the knob. She fought with herself, needing to open it and leave but unable to, not just yet.

Gail spun around and threw herself at Rashid. He caught her and brought her close, squeezing the air from her as he crushed her to him. She kissed him lightly on the cheek and jerked away. Without pausing, she rushed out the door to where Greg stood leaning against the car.

"Ready?" Greg asked, glancing behind her toward the house.

"Yes." Gail refused to look back. She knew Rashid stood in the open doorway. Could feel the weight of his stare on her back.

Greg opened the car door open for her.

"Thank you." She slid into the passenger seat, set her purse on the floor, and fastened her seatbelt.

As Greg walked around to his side of the car, Gail surreptitiously wiped the tears from her eyes. This was a happy occasion, darn it. She was getting married. She would not be sad.

On the drive to the airport, Greg kept up a steady stream of conversation. "After we land, there should be enough time for us to check into the hotel and head for the courthouse to get our license. We can pick up brochures from the various chapels and look them over while we're eating."

"Rachel said to get one that had a web cam so they could watch it live."

He glanced at her. "I don't know if they have that yet but if they do, I'm on it. Hell, let's get the whole package. I'm only doing this once. There should be one that does tux and gown rentals, photos, videotaping, as well as the actual ceremony."

Gail rested her hand on his muscled thigh. "Sounds good to me. My family will definitely be happy."

He folded his hand over hers. "We still need to pick out wedding rings. The hotel should have a decent selection. If don't see anything you like, we'll go elsewhere. "

She turned to him in surprise. "You're going to wear a ring?"

"Of course. I want everybody to know what a classy lady I belong to, and don't expect just a simple gold band from me. I plan on getting you a ring sparkly enough that they'll see you coming and know you're taken."

Gail smiled at the thought. "Just don't make it so big that I get mugged."

He sent a laughing glance in her direction as they stopped at a red light. "You are a strange woman. You should be demanding the biggest, most expensive ring I can buy."

She waved his comment away. "My tastes are simple. It's not the ring, but the meaning behind it that's important."

"So I can get rid of this and get you a cigar band instead and you'll be happy?" he asked, once more toying with the engagement ring on her hand.

"Hell no! You'd better represent." She glared at him.

Greg burst out laughing. "That's what I thought. *'It's the meaning behind it that's important*,'" he mimicked.

She shook her head at him. "You know what I meant. I don't expect you to go broke trying to buy me something expensive, but I do expect my ring to show the esteem you place on our relationship."

He brought their joined hands to his mouth and planted a kiss on hers. "I know, baby. I'm just teasing."

They turned in the rental car and checked their luggage. Greg took her hand and brought it to his mouth for another kiss, as they stood in the security line waiting for TSA to approve them to enter the terminal. "I can't tell you how happy I am you're with me."

Gail leaned into him, enjoying the feel of his strong, masculine body next to hers. "Me, too."

Once they made it past the security check point, he motioned to the eateries and asked, "You want to get a bite to eat?"

"Definitely." She'd been too excited to eat breakfast.

They chose one of the more interesting looking cafes to dine in. As they ate, Gail watched all of the people coming and going. The babies, in particular, caught her attention. They were everywhere. Some were crying. Many were sleeping. Some were in strollers, while others carried in their mother's arms. A few toddled slowly along under their parent's watchful gaze.

Her thoughts went to Jamilah. Had they given her medication? Was she still feverish? She hoped Ms. Gooseby was being patient with her. Jamilah got really fussy when she didn't feel well and wanted to be held, even while sleeping.

What about Jamal? If Jamilah was teething, it was certain he was, too. She forgot to tell Ms. Gooseby to check his ears. Jamal was prone to ear infections, but unless you checked, you wouldn't know because unlike Jamilah, Jamal rarely cried.

That got her to thinking. What else had she neglected to tell her? There were so many things she did automatically that she didn't even think about anymore. Gail just knew it needed doing. For instance, you couldn't leave the house unless Jamilah had her pacifier with her. Jamal only sucked his at night when he was sleepy. Jamilah got hot easily and would sweat all night if you dressed her in more than a t-shirt. Jamal was cold natured. He needed socks on his feet and his little cap on his head or he got sick.

She hoped Jamilah wasn't missing her too much. Of the two, Jamilah was more particular about who she let comfort her. Once, Gail had gone shopping for the day. When she'd returned home, the house was in an uproar. Jamilah was screaming and no one, not even Rashid, could calm her. As soon as Gail held her, she immediately quieted. Jamilah wouldn't let Gail put her down any that night. Gail had actually ended up sleeping with the baby on her chest.

Well, they would figure it out. The twins would eventually adjust to her not being there. With their short memories, they would soon forget her. She would become "godmommy," the woman who sent money on birthdays and Christmas. They won't know she'd been the one who had given them life. "Mommy," their real mother, would be the woman who had disappeared while they were young and had never been heard from again. Or even worse, the woman Rashid married to provide his children with a full-time mother.

As for herself, she'd have a new husband and a new job—plenty to keep herself busy. So what if she'd be missing their first steps? Who cared that she wouldn't know what their first words were? Or wouldn't be there to see them grow and change, or watch their emerging personalities develop? She'd have her life and the twins would have theirs. She'd still get to see them occasionally.

The food she ate turned sour on her stomach. Rashid said he'd bring the children for a visit, but would he really? He had good intentions but stuff happened every day. With the whole continent between them, it would be so easy losing touch. Between the three-hour time difference, and their busy lives, the things that held them together would slowly fade away.

A finger snapped directly in front of her face, causing her to jerk and flinch away. "Gail, you in there?"

"What?" She looked at him blankly for a minute before her mind cleared. "Oh, I'm sorry. My mind must have wondered. Did I miss something?"

Greg's mouth twisted in wry grin. "No, not really. I've only been speaking to you for the last hour."

Her mouth dropped open. "An hour? Couldn't be. We just sat down."

He tilted his head to the side and examined her curiously. "What were you thinking about?"

She made a vague gesture with her hand. "I was looking at all of the babies and toddlers. I didn't expect to see so many in the airport."

"Is that all?"

Gail shrugged. "Basically, why?"

"Because not only haven't you heard a word I said, you've been crying the whole time. What else is going on in there?" He took her hand in his.

She snorted and rolled her eyes. "I would know if I were crying. There's no reason for tears, unless they're tears of joy."

Greg reached out with his finger, gathered some of the moisture on her cheek, and showed it to her. Gail looked at it dumbly, and then brought her hand to her face, surprised when it came away wet. "I'm so sorry. I didn't realize. Geez, what a way to start our life together."

He scooted his chair even closer and placed one arm on the back of hers. She felt enfolded by him. "You can make it up to me by telling me what's going on in your head."

Reluctantly, she admitted, "I was thinking about the twins, wondering how they're getting along without me. I tried writing down everything I could think of that Ms. Gooseby needed to know. I'm realizing now that I'm not rushing, there was so much I left out."

"Honey, they'll be fine. They have Rashid, Angelina, and the housekeeper. Anything she needs to know, she can find out from them."

She pushed her half-eaten food from in front of her and shredded the napkin. "I know. It's just harder than I expected it to be. I could hear Jamilah crying for me as I ran out the door. I hope she's calmed by now. She's not comfortable with the nanny. Usually, I'm the only one who can calm her when she is upset." She worried over the thought, knowing there was nothing she could do.

"...do?"

Gail realized she'd drifted again. "What did you say?"

"*Delta Airlines, Flight 91, now boarding at Gate A3. First class.*"

"That's our flight." Gail placed their trash on the tray for disposal and reached down to get her purse and carryon.

Greg placed a hand on her arm, stopping her. "Go home, Gail. Go home to your babies."

Shocked, she stared at him. "What! Why...?"

"Hear me out. I know you love me. There's no doubt in my mind. But you also love them. What kind of man would I be to take you away from your children? You could marry me and maybe you would be happy, but part of you would always mourn their loss. If I could give you more children, it would be a different story, but I can't. I was sterilized several years ago. I said I didn't want any children, and I don't, but for you I would have made an exception. Rashid's offered you the opportunity to be their mother for real. Take it."

"You can't be serious." She placed her hand on his cheek and stared directly into his eyes. "Greg, I love you. I want a life with you. Yes, I love the twins. How could I not? But my life is with you now. I'm sad about leaving them—it's only natural—but I'll get over it. I don't need or want children of my own. I have you, and you're more than enough for me."

Greg gathered both her hands in his and brought them to his mouth, placing a kiss on her knuckles. "Sweetheart, that's your pain talking. You once said the same about allowing another man into your life, and yet, here I am. What happens when your heart begins to heal? I'll tell you what. You'll think back on this day and regret the decision you made."

"*Delta Airlines, Flight 91, now boarding at Gate A3. Rows 1-15.*"

"We don't have time for this. Let's go before we miss our flight." She pulled her hand away from his and reached for her bags.

Greg caught her by the shoulders and shook her slightly. "Gail, you're not listening to me. Stay here, marry Rashid, and be a mother to those babies."

Gail knocked his hands away and stood. "This is pointless. I'm not marrying Rashid. I'm going with you. End of story."

"No, you're not. I've changed my mind. I don't want to marry you."

Gail flinched and stared at him in shock. "You're lying," she said, her voice shaky.

"Delta Airlines, Flight 91, now boarding Rows 16 - 30."

He cupped her face with both hands. "You're right. I love you, and it's because I do that I'm doing this. This is not about the love we feel for each other, but about doing the right thing. I can't make you stay, and I won't lie and say I don't want you with me. But I know in my heart that if you walk away from your children now when it wasn't necessary, you'll never forgive yourself. You know that I'm right."

She looked at him with tears rolling down her face, her shoulders slumped in defeat. "I want you, but I want them too. I thought I'd protected myself, kept them from getting too close. I didn't expect leaving them to be so difficult, or to hurt so much. But how can I choose between the man who stole my heart and the children I carried beneath it?"

He kissed her and rested his forehead against hers. "You don't have to. I've already decided. Stay here, Gail, and do what's best for them."

"Delta Airlines, Flight 91, now boarding Rows 31-45."

"I've got to go. I'll make sure your things get to you. Go! Now! Tell Rashid he owes me big time for this. He'd better take good care of you. If you ever need me, I'm just a phone call away." He pulled her into his arms

214

for one last kiss and then took off running down the concourse.

"Last call for Delta Airlines, Flight 91."

Gail watched him run off, lost and confused. She didn't know what to do. Finally, she collected her things, turned, and walked away. Outside, she caught one of the many waiting cabs and had him take her home.

◆◆◆◆◆

Rashid shut himself in his study, unable to believe Gail was gone. He really thought she would change her mind, that the twins would be enough to hold her. Now that she was gone, he realized how very much he wanted her to stay. Today, he'd not only lost a friend and a mother for his children, he'd lost a piece of his heart.

He piddled around his office, hoping work would take his mind off her absence. When the phone rang, he ignored it. A few seconds after it stopped ringing, Carmelita knocked on the door. "Senor Rashid, it's Senor Richmont on the phone for you."

"I've got it, Carmelita. Thank you." He quickly picked up the extension in the office. "Greg? Has something happened to Gail?"

"In a way. I'm sending her back to you. As much as I love her and want her with me, I couldn't take her away from her children. She's cried almost the entire time since we left."

Rashid was stunned at this turn of events. "I don't know what to say."

"Tell me you'll take good care of her. That you want her for more than just the children's sake."

"I love her. I didn't realize how much until she walked out the door."

"Then love her for both of us. She isn't just coming back for the children. She wants you as well, though her conscience won't allow her to admit to it. In her mind, you're Crystal's husband, will always be Crystal's husband, and therefore off limits. Don't expect her to come to you or make it easy. She's returning, but only because I pushed her into it. Don't make me regret my decision."

"Thank you for what you're doing. If the situation were reversed, I can't say I'd do the same."

"This isn't about you. It's about her babies. If it were just you, I'd fight to the death before I let loose of my woman. You don't treat her right, I'll take you out, and they'll never prove it was me." He clicked off.

Rashid put the phone back in its cradle, a contemplative look on his face. Greg Richmont was a good man. Crazy as hell, but in a good way. What he'd told Greg was true. If Gail were his, he'd never let her go. When she got home he would do everything in his power to get her to marry him. Gail was his now. She just didn't know it.

When her cab pulled into the driveway, Rashid was already outside waiting.

"Is she all right? She's been crying like this the whole fare," the cabbie asked.

"She'll be fine in a minute." Rashid paid the driver and pulled Gail from the cab. He grabbed her things, tugged her up the steps, and into the house.

"Miguel! Take Ms. Gail's things to her room and call the airport to see what time her luggage will arrive. I believe the airline was Delta."

"Delta, Flight 91." Her voice was small and wobbly.

"We'll be in the den. I don't want to be disturbed, for any reason."

"Yes, sir. I'll make sure the others are aware. And may I say I'm glad you came back, Ms. Gail?"

She gave Miguel a watery smile. Rashid pulled her inside the den and into his arms. The minute they

216

closed around her, the dam broke and the silent trickle of tears became a noisy, gushing flood. She clutched his shirt tightly as her knees buckled.

With an oath, Rashid caught her up into his arms and carried her to the couch, sitting with her on his lap. She cried like her heart was broken, making him worry. Greg must have made a mistake. Would she be crying this hard if she wanted to be here with him and the twins? He didn't think so.

He had a better appreciation for Greg's dilemma. God knows he wanted this woman with him, but not if she was this upset about it. Her tears tore up his heart, making him want to do something, anything, as long as it made her happy.

When her crying calmed to the occasional hiccup, Rashid tried to set her on the couch so he could get tissues to wipe her face. She clung to him, refusing to let go. Her actions gave him hope. There was a box of tissues on the end table. It was a reach, but he managed to snag it and give it to Gail. He waited until her face was dry and she'd blown her nose before speaking.

"Greg called and told me to expect you."

"He sent me back." She took a shuddery breath and set the tissues to the side. "It was horrible. I wanted to go with him. Really I did, but I couldn't stop crying. The tears just kept rolling down my face. I didn't even realize it at first. He's such a wonderful man, and I love him dearly, but all I could think about were the twins. I should have been so excited. I was marrying the man I love. We were starting a new life together, and there I was, crying like my world was ending instead of beginning afresh. He deserves so much better than what he received from me."

Gail laid her cheek on his chest and wrapped her arms around his neck.

Rashid rubbed her back soothingly, offering what comfort he could. "He's not angry with you. He understands. Greg told me he sent you to me because he didn't want to be the cause of your losing another child. He knows you love him."

Gail pulled away and looked at him with more tears in her eyes. "Do I really? If I love him as much as I claim, wouldn't I have fought harder to stay with him? Why didn't I get on that plane and show him it was him I wanted, even though I was sad about leaving?"

"I can't answer that. You loved him enough to leave your family, friends, and everything you're familiar with on this coast to be with him. Maybe the answer is not that you loved him less, but simply that you love the children more."

She laid her head back on his chest and traced the design on his shirt. "I really thought I could do it, you know? Even though Mom warned me I couldn't. I thought I did a good job of protecting my heart. I told myself it was okay to love them a little. They're so precious, how could I not? But I was determined to control just how much of my heart I gave to them. I had it all figured out, only I was wrong, and now Greg is the one suffering for my arrogance."

"You aren't arrogant. You were just trying to protect yourself. Completely understandable, considering your history. And Greg's not suffering. He loves you enough to value your happiness above his own."

"That's what he said. Do you know what else he said?" She deepened her voice in an imitation of Greg's. "*Go home. Marry Rashid. Be a mother to those babies.*"

Rashid slid a finger under her chin and lifted her head until she was looking at him. "And are you?"

"Am I what?"

"You came home. Are you going to follow the rest of his instructions? Will you marry me and be a mother to our children?"

Gail nibbled her lower lip while she thought. "They were never supposed to be mine," she said quietly.

"But they are. What are you going to do about it?" He held his breath while he waited for her answer.

She was silent for a long time. "Marry you and claim what's mine."

Chapter Fourteen

Three weeks later, they stood before the minister on the pool veranda and exchanged vows, surrounded by family and a few close friends. Gail's parents, along with two of her brothers and their wives were present. Rashid's parents and one of his brothers also attended.

In a surprising feat, her mother talked Rashid into letting her take the twins to Alabama with them for a visit. She argued that Gail and Rashid needed time to get to know each other as husband and wife, and could do it better if they were alone. Gail was astonished when Rashid agreed.

Everyone had left and now the house was quiet. Gail nervously paced the floor of her room dressed in the satin, ruby-red, floor length nightgown she'd allowed Rachel to talk her into purchasing. Rashid wanted a "real" marriage. A real marriage meant sex, something she wasn't sure she was ready to handle. Rashid was in his study taking care of some last minute business, or so he said. She wasn't going in there to find out. He might think she was impatient to get their wedding night started and nothing could be further from the truth.

Her mind flashed back to her first wedding night with Jason. What a difference. Then, she'd been so excited, so euphoric over becoming Mrs. Jason Henderson, she couldn't stand it. She'd purchased the sexiest, sheerest nightgown she could find, lotioned down in his favorite body cream so she smelled good, and came out the bathroom to find Jason waiting with a glass of champagne and a dozen red roses he'd had delivered to their hotel suite. He'd been such a romantic.

She wiped sweaty palms on her gown and paced the room again. This, her second wedding night, was supposed to be for her and Greg, the man she was in love with, not Rashid, her husband who wasn't really hers. True, there was a wedding ring on her finger—a simple gold band she'd insisted on—and a signed marriage license, but in her mind, Rashid was Crystal's husband. Always was, and always would be, no matter that Rashid said otherwise.

Oh God, what the hell was she doing?

After crossing her room for about the thirtieth time, she couldn't take it anymore. She had to do something or she would scream. She changed into her bikini and went down to the pool. A couple of laps ought to calm her nerves.

Gail swam until she expended all of her nervous energy, then flipped onto her back and floated. It was quiet and peaceful here in the semi-darkness. The only lights on were the ones in the pool. She startled violently when a firm hand grabbed her ankle.

Rashid surfaced beside her with a grin. "Did I scare you?"

"No, I frequently jerk and spasm like someone having a seizure." She scowled at him and wiped the water from her face.

He laughed. "I'm sorry. I thought you heard me dive in. What are you doing out here?"

"It was too nerve racking, waiting in the room. I had to do something or risk going crazy."

His smiled disappeared. "Is the thought of sex with me that terrifying?"

Gail tilted her head back in the water and looked at the star-studded sky—anything to avoid eye contact. "It's not you specifically. Not all of it. I would be nervous right now no matter whom it was. I haven't been with a man since Jason."

"But I thought you and Greg..."

Gail shook her head. "In the beginning, I was pregnant and it just didn't feel right. Then he left. When he came home to pack up his apartment, the doctor still hadn't cleared me. This last time, there was simply too much to do. We'd waited this long. We decided we might as well wait until we got to Vegas and had a true wedding night. At least, that was the plan."

"You said, 'not all of it. ' What else are you nervous about?"

She glanced at him out the corner of her eyes. "I wouldn't say nervous. It's just strange. My head knows we're married, but my heart says you're my best friend's husband and off limits."

"I see." They both quietly tread water, each lost in their own thoughts. "Why don't we try taking things slow? Give both your head and your heart time to adjust."

A reprieve. Just like that, the tight knot of pressure lifted from off her shoulders. She smiled at Rashid. "That's sounds like a good idea."

Rashid pulled her close and with a few strong strokes, swam with her to the side of the pool.

"What are you doing?" She allowed him to tow her, his strange behavior arousing her curiosity.

"I want to kiss my bride."

"But I thought you said—"

"I said we'd take things slow. I didn't say I wouldn't touch you at all."

"Oh." She guessed she could handle a kiss, since he was being so understanding. He positioned her against the pool wall and boxed her in with his hands. Gail held on to the edge to keep afloat.

Rashid slowly leaned in and tentatively kissed her, as though afraid she'd spook. That he considered her so chicken-hearted pricked her pride, and she opened her mouth invitingly. He pressed a little closer but did nothing to deepen the kiss.

She pulled back, slightly irritated. "I thought you wanted to kiss me?"

Rashid smiled at her lazily. "I didn't want to give you more than you can handle."

His words sparked her temper and her pride. "I can handle anything you can dish out."

He slowly shook his head. "I'm not so sure about that, seeing how nervous you were about everything."

Gail saw red. "Handle this." She wrapped her arms around his neck, trusting him to keep her above water. She pressed her lips against his, licking at their seam, requesting entrance. When he wouldn't open his mouth, she nipped his bottom lip. When his mouth opened in reaction to the slight pain, she thrust her tongue inside.

As soon as she tasted him, she was lost. Passion rose and overwhelmed the prideful anger motivating her actions. Gail explored the interior of his mouth, trying to learn all its secrets. Rashid let her have her fun. Then he took control of the kiss.

Now this was the lover Crystal had bragged about.

He wrapped his arms around her and propelled them away from the side of the pool. Gail clung to him as they sank beneath the surface until the need for air drove them back to the top. She broke surface not too far from Rashid and treaded water, trying to catch her breath.

Rashid's intense stare caused her to look down to see what he was looking at. The top of her bikini was gone. She spun around in a circle, searching for it. She finally spotted it floating several yards away in the water.

When she glanced back at Rashid, he had a predatory look on his face. Some imp of mischief whispered in Gail's ear and with a provoking laugh, she challenged, "If you can catch me, you can have me." Then she dove deep.

Rashid was such a strong swimmer, he could have captured her immediately. Instead, he toyed with her, building the anticipation. She wondered if this was how prey felt. The chase heightened all of her senses. She focused completely on Rashid, aware of his every move.

A stroke of brilliance crossed her mind, and Gail lunged for the side of the pool, determined to change the playing field. In the water, Rashid had the advantage. On land, it fell to her. Rashid caught her against the side of the pool before she could climb out, trapping her with his aroused body.

"Gotcha! Turn around," he whispered into her ear.

Gail slowly turned until she faced him. His face was a tight mask of arousal, an expression she'd seen only once before. He lifted her until her breasts cleared the water. "Wrap your legs around my waist."

Gail immediately complied.

He cupped her breasts and rubbed her nipples with his thumbs. "I've dreamt about these, so many times. Every time I saw one of the twins nursing here," he squeezed her nipple for emphasis, "I wanted to nudge them aside and take their place." He dropped his mouth and latched onto her nipple.

Dear Lord, it hadn't been a fluke, she thought as fire streaked from her breast straight to her womb. She clutched the side of the pool, her body racked with sensation. He drew deeply, like he hunted for milk. He squeezed, tugged, and gently pulled on her other nipple, doubling the sensory overload racking her body.

"Rashid, please, I...argh!" Gail's back arched as she orgasmed. Then she felt him there, pressing into her core. When he'd removed her bottoms, she didn't know.

He pressed steadily into her. "You're so tight. Relax, you're fighting against me."

"Can't help it," she panted. Spasms still rocked her, causing her vagina to tighten and release around his shaft.

Rashid held her firmly by the hips while he pushed until deeply embedded. Once in place, he held absolutely still, his body as tense as a rock. He leaned forward and rested his forehead against hers. His move slid his shaft deeper, drawing a moan from both of them.

Several moments passed and he still hadn't moved. "Rashid, what are you waiting for?"

"I'm giving you time to adjust. You're so tight. I don't want to hurt you."

Gail tightened her inner muscles around his cock and moved her hips, stroking him with her sheath. "I've adjusted. Please! MOVE!"

He rocked into her, slow at first, then increasingly faster as she talked dirty to him, urging him on.

"Yes, just like that." She dropped her knees and dug her heels into the small of his back, opening her body for his possession.

"So good," he groaned into her ear. "I can't hold back. Trying to make it last," he panted. "Too tight. Your pussy is like a vise."

"Don't hold back. Let go."

His grip on her butt was bruising in its intensity. The water hampered his forceful movements, slowing them down. He drove deep and held, grinding against her as he came. His head dropped onto her shoulder as he panted for breath. "That did not go as planned. I intended to wow you with my prowess. Instead, I lost control like a teenager with his first girl."

She ran her fingers gently through his hair. "We have all night and the rest of our lives to get it right. I'd rather have honest passion than practiced expertise."

He leaned back and looked her in the face. "You mean that, don't you?"

"Yes. I don't expect sex between us to be perfect every time. It would be nice to orgasm each time we have sex. Multiple orgasms would be wonderful, but not realistic. Between hormonal fluctuations and life in

225

general, sometimes I will, and sometimes I won't reach climax. The important thing is that we both focus on giving each other maximum pleasure."

He cupped her cheek. "I make this promise to you: I'll always make every attempt to put your pleasure before mine."

"And I promise to do the same." She felt bereft when his softened penis slid from her body.

"And now, my lady wife, I suggest we head to our bedroom where the rest of our wedding night awaits."

"Gladly, Sir Knight." She laughingly followed him out of the pool and into the house.

◆◆◆◆◆

The rest of the week passed in a sensuous haze of pleasure. Rashid made good on his promise, and it became a competition to see who could bring more pleasure to the other. Rashid was a skillful, but serious lover. Gail made it her business to teach him how to play. Laughter rang out, as well as moans and groans of pleasure and completion when they retreated behind the closed doors of their bedroom, the study, the den or anywhere else the urge to make love hit them.

Only occasionally did the troublesome thought cross her mind that she was sleeping with another woman's husband. She pushed it aside to the best of her ability and didn't mention it to Rashid. She was happy, and that was all that mattered. She should have known it wouldn't last.

December—three months later

"A little to the left."

"That's where it was a minute ago."

226

"Just a little left this time. Last time you went too far."

Rashid moved the bare Christmas tree again and stood back from it.

Gail examined the tree, her head tilted to the side. "I don't know...what do you think?"

He frowned. "I think this is where I set it the first time."

"Maybe if you move it..."

"Gail..." he growled, casting an annoyed look in her direction.

She couldn't hold it in anymore. She fell back on the couch giggling. He was so gullible. For the last fifteen minutes, he'd been moving the tree into the same three positions.

"You imp! You're doing it on purpose." He dove onto the couch.

"Umph," she gasped as his weight landed on top of her.

"I ought to beat you."

She laughed in his face. "Oooh, hurt me baby."

"I have a much better idea." His hand snaked up her ribs and tickled.

She squirmed beneath him, shrieking hysterically. "Stop! Stop! I give. I give."

Gail twisted and turned, trying to avoid his marauding fingers. Then she bucked beneath him in an attempt to throw him off. When she was unsuccessful, she tickled him back.

"Oh, no you don't," he said, laughing.

He captured her hands and pinned them above her head. When he had her trapped beneath him, he grinned down into her giggling face. Lightening quick, their laughter turned to passion. Gail rose, meeting Rashid's descending mouth halfway. His lips were a breath away from hers when a high-pitched, singsong voice shattered the mood.

"Rashid! Babies! Mommy's home!"

Eyes opened wide, she stared at Rashid from inches away. She must be hearing things.

"Rashid! Carmelita! Where is everyone?"

A look of absolute fury crossed Rashid's face. He almost fell off the couch in his haste to confront Crystal.

"Senora Crystal?" Gail could hear the confusion in Carmelita's voice.

"Carmelita! There you are. Have Miguel get my things out of the car. I suppose my husband's at work? Where are my babies?"

The door to the den crashed against the wall.

"What the hell are you doing here?" Rashid stormed into the foyer as the door ricocheted off the wall and slammed shut behind him.

Gail shakily got off the couch and straightened the pillows. Rashid was yelling at the top of his lungs. Crystal's strident voice was a sharp counterpoint to his deeper tones. She hovered in the den. What to do? Their argument was not something she wanted to insert herself into.

This reckoning was a long time coming. Crystal had a lot to answer for. Rashid had every right to be furious. On the other hand, at this moment, she didn't doubt he was perfectly capable of killing Crystal. With visions of the police hauling her husband off to jail, Gail cautiously opened the door. She could have flung it open and they wouldn't have noticed.

"You leave, take off for a year and think you can just waltz in here, and pick up where you left off? Have you lost your mind?"

"It's only been eleven months and I had to leave. I wasn't well, but I've had treatment and I'm all better now. I'm ready to be a wife to you and a mother to our children," Crystal said tearfully.

He took a threatening step towards her. "If you think—"

"Rashid!"

Both their heads snapped in her direction.

"Gail? What are you doing here?"

"My wife lives here."

Crystal looked horribly confused.

"Rashid, we all have a lot to discuss. Bring Crystal into the den. Standing here yelling won't accomplish anything. Crystal, good to see you again. I was beginning to think you were dead." Too bad she wasn't, Gail thought to herself, then inwardly flinched at the uncharitable thought. Apparently, she was just as upset as Rashid, but someone had to be calm or things would escalate dangerously out of control.

She spotted Carmelita lurking in the doorway to the kitchen, a worried look on her face. "Carmelita, would you bring refreshments into the den?"

"Right away, Ms. Gail."

"Rashid. Crystal. After you." She held a hand out, indicating they should enter.

Rashid looked ready to argue. Gail narrowed her eyes in warning. With a snarl, he turned and stalked into the den.

"Gail, I don't understand. Did he say you two were married?"

"Come into the den. We can discuss it there, beginning with where you've been for the last year."

"Eleven months," Crystal corrected.

"Whatever." Gail turned and walked inside.

Rashid stood at the window, his hands gripping the sill so tight his knuckles showed white. Crystal came, sat at the other end of the couch, and looked around. "It looks different in here."

Gail sat in an arm chair. "Lots of things changed while you were gone. I'll tell you about them in a minute. But first, I want to know why you left and where you've been for all this time? Rashid hired a private detective to find you and came up empty."

229

Carmelita came into the room with a pitcher of tea and appetizers on a tray. "Thank you. Can you make sure we're not disturbed?"

"Si, Ms. Gail. It's nice to see you, Senora Crystal."

Crystal gave her a wan smile. "Thanks, Carmelita. It's good to see you too."

They were silent until she left the room, closing the door behind her.

"Rashid, would you like a glass of tea?" Gail asked.

"No."

Gail poured him one anyway and set it on the tray. "Crystal?"

"Yes. I am rather thirsty."

Gail poured two more glasses and handed one to Crystal. Then she sat back with her tea, projecting a calm she was far from feeling. She gave Crystal enough time to quench her thirst before prompting her again to explain.

"I've been in a private clinic just outside of Vegas, getting help with some emotional issues I couldn't deal with."

Gail glanced at Rashid who had his back still turned to the room. "What kind of issues?"

"I'm ashamed now to admit it, but I was so jealous of you. There you were, pregnant with the babies I begged you to have for me, and I hated you for it. I wanted a baby so bad." She threw a quick glance at Rashid's back. "I even tried to trick Rashid into getting me pregnant, but he wouldn't cooperate."

Gail swirled her glass, causing the ice to clink together. "That's why you checked into the clinic?"

Crystal nodded. "I really think I had some type of breakdown. I knew I needed help. There's no way I could have been a good mother to my babies the way I was."

"Why didn't you say anything? I'm your best friend, or I thought I was. Rashid was your husband.

You should have said something instead of just disappearing. Do you know how worried we were?"

"I was afraid if I told you how I felt, you wouldn't let us have the children. I didn't want that to happen. I could see how much Rashid wanted them. Why did you say Rashid "was" my husband?"

Gail looked to Rashid, waiting for him to jump into the conversation. He said nothing. He didn't even move. It was like he'd turned to stone. She sighed and began explaining. "You were gone for so long. Nobody could find you. We had no idea where you were or if you were even alive. Rashid divorced you."

"How? I haven't been gone a year."

Again, Gail glanced at Rashid, mentally willing him to say something. This time he glared at Crystal. Maybe his silence was a good thing. "He went to Guam and filed abandonment."

The glass in Crystal's hand shook. "But I was coming back. I wouldn't have left for good, not without saying anything."

Rashid's harshly muttered obscenities voiced his opinion of that statement as he turned back to the window.

Gail stared at her friend in stunned disbelief. "Crystal, how was he to know? You packed up everything, cleaned out your bank accounts, and left. What was he to think?"

Crystal reached forward, set her glass down, and took one of the napkins off the tray. "But I needed the money to pay the clinic. Insurance only covered so much."

She once again had tears in her eyes. Gail almost felt sorry for her. Almost, but not quite.

"Get out."

Gail looked at Rashid in surprise.

"But...I want to see my babies," Crystal protested.

231

"Get out!" Rashid never moved from the window, but his voice was so cold Gail shivered in response.

"But—"

"GET OUT!"

Rashid's expression scared Gail and it wasn't even directed to her. "Crystal, maybe you'd better leave. Give Rashid a chance to calm down."

Crystal looked from Gail to Rashid, and then back to Gail. "Maybe you're right."

Gail walked her to the front door.

At the threshold, Crystal paused. "I didn't get to see the babies."

Wanting nothing more than to get Crystal out of the house, Gail said, "I realize that, but right now, it's best you go. Give it a couple of days and then try again."

Crystal looked uncertain but resigned. "If you say so. Wow, you and Rashid? I never thought you'd be his type." With those words, she turned and walked out the door.

What the hell did that mean?

Gail wanted to hit something, preferably Crystal. First, she had an angry husband to soothe, if possible. Crystal would know how. The discouraging thought popped into her mind. Gail pushed it to the side. When she entered the den, Rashid was nowhere to be found.

◆◆◆◆◆

The twins roused from their nap, and she was busy for the rest of the day. Once they were tucked in for the night, she went into their newly remodeled bedroom suite for a much deserved shower. She hadn't seen Rashid since Crystal left. She was lying in bed, trying not to worry when Rashid came into the room. He went straight to the bathroom. Seconds later, she heard the shower cut on.

A short while later, he dropped his towel and climbed into bed beside her. They both lay there, staring at the ceiling, a tense silence between them. Somebody had to make the first move. Might as well be me, she thought, needing the reassurance of his body. She rolled to her side and laid a hand on his chest.

For a few tense moments, nothing happened. Gail wondered if she'd made a mistake. She went to withdraw her hand when Rashid exploded into motion. He grabbed her and pulled her into his arms. His kiss was frantic.

"I need you." He rolled her under him and penetrated her with one swift thrust. The ride was hard and fast, with an underlying desperate quality to it.

She held on and let him take her. This time was for him. Her husband needed her and she willingly gave of herself. When he finished, he rolled to the side and dragged her with him. "I'm sorry. I promised to always see to your pleasure first. Did I hurt you?"

"Don't worry about it. That was for you. This one's for me." She pushed him onto his back and went down on him, pleasuring him with her mouth until he was nice and hard again. Then she climbed on top and rode him.

"Touch me."

"Where?"

"My breasts."

He caressed her breasts and toyed with the nipples, just the way she liked. "Mmm, that feels good."

"Lean down so I can suck them."

She braced above him so her breasts hung in his face, keeping a steady rhythm with her hips. With Rashid, she could come just from having her breasts suckled. Having him buried inside her while he suckled? That was a pleasure explosion just waiting to happen.

She cried out as she came. Gail kept pumping her hips, trying to draw out every last drop of pleasure. Too weak to continue, she slumped on top of him. Rashid adroitly flipped her over onto her back.

"My turn again" He lifted her legs over his shoulders in her favorite position and rode her until she screamed. Only when she was totally satisfied did he allow himself to orgasm.

This time they lay together, their natural harmony restored. "Good thing we moved back into the master suite. All that screaming would have awakened the twins," he teased.

"Beast, you love it when I scream." Her head lay pillowed on his chest. His heartbeat was steady and relaxed. Gail waited. Then waited some more. Finally, she realized it was up to her to broach the subject.

"Want to talk about it?"

"No." His body stiffened beneath her.

"She's not going to go away."

"My lawyers will deal with her."

"I'm not sure that's the best approach to take in dealing with Crystal. I know you're angry. So am I. I just don't believe ending things on bad terms is in anyone's best interest."

"Things ended the minute she walked out the door. It's incomprehensible to me that she or anyone else could believe otherwise."

Gail wisely decided to let it go. There was no sense pushing the issue, especially since she couldn't fault him for feeling the way he did. Did she even want Rashid and Crystal at peace with each other? No, and the truth shamed her. His anger towards Crystal made her feel more secure in her marriage.

She was so pathetic.

Christmas morning...

Gail rushed to the kitchen. She was late. Breakfast should have been started an hour ago. At the door, she came to a screeching halt. Her mother stood at the stove and from the looks of things, had breakfast well underway.

"Mom! What are you doing? You're a guest. You're not supposed to cook."

Her mother glanced over her shoulder as she stirred a pot. "I'm not a guest. I'm your mother. Folks would starve waiting for you and Rashid to come out of that love nest of yours."

Gail flushed as her mind flashed back to the reason for her tardiness.

"Wake up, sleepyhead. Santa has an extra special present for you this morning."

"Yay, Santa," she groaned as Rashid's wickedly talented tongue returned to its place between her legs.

"It's not even nine yet. We like to sleep in whenever we get the chance."

"Un-huh, I was young and newly married myself once. I know what sleeping in really means. Still like to sleep in with your father from time to time myself."

Gail almost dropped the glass she just grabbed from the cabinet. "Mom, TMI!"

"Just because I'm getting up in age doesn't mean the heat has gone out of my fire. It only gets better as you get older. Your father bought one of those Kama Sutra books. If you and Rashid don't have one, you need to buy one. Lots of interesting positions."

"Mom, please. I do not want to hear about you and daddy's sex life."

"I'm just saying..."

"Enough! Do you need help in here? If not, I'll go help Rashid with the twins."

"All right, I'll change the subject. Don't go running off. I want to talk to you. Start cutting those sausages. Now, have you heard any more from Crystal?"

"No, and it's bothering me. It's not like Crystal to give up so easily."

Her mother turned and looked at her. "Was she really in a crazy house?"

"A private clinic," Gail corrected.

"A crazy house for people with money. Same difference. She said she'd been there getting treatment? Seems to me if she thought she could show up here and pick up where she left off, somebody let her out too soon."

"She probably thought she could talk Rashid around to her way of thinking. She always has in the past." Gail brought the knife down on the sausage with a bit of force.

Her mother pointed the cooking spoon at her. "You listen to me, missy. Don't matter what happened in the past. Every man has his breaking point. What she did, leaving Rashid without a word and two babies on the way...that was his. Don't matter what excuse she gives. He ain't gonna be forgiving or forgetting anytime too soon."

"That's what he said," Gail muttered.

"You don't sound too sure about that."

"He and Crystal were married for almost ten years. You never saw them together. He really loved her. I don't think a year is long enough for all of those feelings to go away."

Her mother left the stove and came over to the center island where Gail stood. "You're scared he'll go back to her."

Gail shrugged one shoulder. "He only married me because of the twins. With Crystal back, he doesn't need me."

"I don't know what cock and bull story Rashid fed you to get you to marry him, but that man loves you. Even a blind person can see it in the way he looks at you."

236

"That's just sex, but he and Crystal—"

Her mother leaned forward until her face was inches away. "Hush up and listen! You can't judge a marriage by what you see. Only a husband and wife know what goes on behind closed doors. Their marriage wasn't as perfect as it seemed. No one's is—" Her mother broke off abruptly, looking past her to the doorway.

Gail turned to see what caught her attention. Rashid stood at the entrance with Jamal in his arms. Her father was right behind him with Jamilah.

"Merry Christmas. Breakfast will be ready in a minute. Sit those young'uns down to the table. Gail, these grits are done. Feed your children."

"Merry Christmas, Daddy."

"Same to you, baby girl. Something sure smells good."

"Momma's preparing a feast. Should be done shortly."

"Somebody had to with folks staying in bed all morning," her mother threw over her shoulder.

"Nothing wrong with sleepin' in every now and again," her father said.

Gail groaned. "Please, daddy. Don't get her started."

Rashid mouthed, "What did I miss?"

She murmured her response, "Don't even go there."

Just then, the doorbell rang. "That must be Rachel and Frank Jr. Rashid, get the door," her mother ordered.

"Yes, ma'am." He grinned at Gail, amused at being ordered about by her mother in his own house.

Lord, give me strength. Her parents were staying the entire four-day weekend. They'd only arrived last night and already Gail had been reduced to praying. The next couple of days were going to be long.

For the next couple of hours, the place was a madhouse. Not only were Rachel and Frank at the door, but Deb and Tim surprised everyone by coming as well.

"We couldn't let y'all have all this fun without us," Deb answered when questioned.

After everyone ate, the women shooed the men and children from the kitchen while they cleaned and prepared dinner. The present exchange was scheduled for one. That gave the women two hours to get things done in the kitchen. With much laughter, they got busy.

"So, what's up with Crystal? You heard anything else?" Rachel pierced Gail with a concerned look from where she sat peeling potatoes.

"No. I don't like this silence." Gail brushed her bangs out of her face for the third time and continued loading the dishwasher.

"What reason would she have to keep in contact? Rashid divorced her," Rachel said.

"That means nothing to some women. I should know," Deb reminded Rachel from the sink where she was cleaning sweet potatoes.

Gail spoke into the silence that followed. "The twins."

"Humph, if she wanted them, she would have stuck around," her mother said.

Gail looked at her mother, then the rest of the women. "I know that's what we all believe, but it's just not that simple. Even though Rashid has custody, he can't legally deny her access to the children. Not in the state of Florida."

Deb asked, "How'd she take that whole divorce thing, anyway? You never did say."

"She was really surprised. I don't believe she thought he would divorce her, or act as fast as he did. She keep emphasizing that she hadn't been gone a year yet."

238

"Eleven months and one week. Big whooping deal. Any woman who abandons her family, especially right before Christmas, deserves to be divorced." Deb obviously felt no sympathy for Crystal.

"I wonder how much money Rashid gave her in the divorce settlement." An inquiring look at Gail accompanied the statement.

"Rachel, that's plain nosiness. Don't be prying into other people's financial affairs. And Gail, don't be telling your husband's business, not unless you really want to talk about it. Then, of course, we'll listen," her mother offered generously.

Gail bit back a grin at her mother's tactics. She was just as curious as Rachel, but didn't want to admit it. "I really don't know. I remember Crystal mentioning a prenup once, so it may not have been much."

"Now you girls know I don't like to get into y'all's business, but that's something you need to find out. Anything that affects you and the children, you need to know about."

Rachel, Deb, and Gail exchanged disbelieving looks at the blatant lie and burst into laughter. Her mother was in her children's business every chance she got. She didn't trust them to handle their lives on their own for fear they'd mess up.

"It's not important, Mom. I have plenty of money of my own."

"Must be nice," Deb muttered enviously.

"I'd give the money back in a heartbeat if it would bring Jason and Marcus back."

Deb was instantly contrite. "Oh Gail, honey, I forgot. As much as Tim gets on my nerves, I wouldn't trade him for all the money in the world."

"You think she wants him back?" Rachel voiced the question Gail was thinking.

"Ain't no man gonna take a woman back that walks out on him when he's doing all he knows how to keep her happy."

"I'm with Mom on this one. Besides, it doesn't matter what she wants. He's with Gail now." Rachel pointed at her. "You better fight for your man. Don't just hand him over. That Crystal always was a sneaky one. Watch out. When Rashid calms down, she may try to get him back."

Gail didn't want to discuss Crystal anymore. She initiated a change of discussion and heaved a sigh of relief when the conversation moved on to other things.

At one o'clock, they gathered in the den. Her father was designated Santa and he distributed the gifts under the tree. What followed was so loud and boisterous, she barely heard the doorbell when it rang. That no one else did was certain.

They'd given the staff time off for the holiday so she got up, picked her way over the mass of paper, boxes, and toys littering the floor and made her way to the door. Crystal stood on the other side. Gail forced herself to smile as she opened the door. "Merry Christmas. This is a surprise. Come in."

"I brought presents for the babies." Crystal beamed excitedly and held up the huge department store bags for Gail to see.

"Wow! Well, you're just in time. We're in the den opening our gifts now."

They walked in silence. The joyous racket coming from the den echoed all through the house. The minute they stepped through the door, a hush fell until only the Christmas carol playing softly in the background could be heard.

"Mom, Dad, you remember Crystal?"

"Hello." Their words were polite. Their expressions weren't.

"Merry Christmas, Mr. and Mrs. Jones."

"Crystal, I don't know if you remember them, but this is my sister-in-law, Rachel, and her husband, my brother Frank, Jr. Over there is my brother, Tim, and his wife, Deb. Y'all this is Crystal."

"Merry Christmas," they murmured, almost in unison.

"Rashid, Crystal brought presents for the twins. Isn't that nice?"

All eyes swung in his direction, awaiting his response. He looked up from his position on the floor where he was helping the twins open their gifts. Gail begged with her eyes. Please be nice.

"Yeah." And as an afterthought, "Merry Christmas."

She breathed a sigh of relief. Now if everyone would just behave, they might just get through this. Crystal picked her way across the room and sat on the loveseat Rashid was using as a backrest. Rachel glared at Gail and pointed her head in Crystal's direction. Gail gave a slight shake of her head. It was her seat but she wasn't going to make an issue of it. She sat on the couch with her parents instead.

"Look babies, I brought presents."

"They have names."

Gail kicked her mother. "Be nice," she hissed under her breath.

Crystal paused, looking disconcerted.

"Crystal, meet Jamilah Melek and Ahkeem Jamal," Gail said.

"Oh, what pretty names. Ahkeem, I have a present for you."

Jamal looked from the gaily wrapped box in Crystal's hands to his father, who was staring at Gail. She nodded at the present, indicating Rashid should take it. He did, but his reluctance was obvious.

The box contained a fancy toy fire truck, complete with bells and whistles. Rashid accidentally turned it on

241

when he set it on the floor. The flashing lights and siren scared Jamilah and she crawled for Gail as fast as her little legs would carry her. From the frightened look on his face and the way he gripped his father, Jamal wasn't too crazy about it either. Rashid turned it off.

"Why did you turn it off?" Crystal reached for the toy to turn it back on.

Deb remarked sharply, "Can't you see the noise is scaring them?"

Crystal glanced at Jamilah, who was huddled in Gail's arms, to Jamal, who was as far away from the toy as he could get and still be in his father's arms. "Oh, I see what you mean. I thought he would like it."

"When he's older, I'm sure he'll love it," Gail assured her.

Pacified, Crystal dismissed the issue and dug into the next bag. "I'm afraid I went a little overboard with little Jamie."

"Jamilah," Rachel corrected.

"Jamilah. Thank you. The dresses were all so pretty that I couldn't resist." She pulled out five or six frilly dresses that could only have been purchased from an expensive, children's boutique. "I also got her matching socks and hair bows. I know she can't play with the dresses, so I also got her this doll." She reached further into the bag and pulled out a baby doll that was almost as big as Jamilah. "Come see the pretty dresses, Jamilah."

Jamilah stuck her finger in her mouth and leaned back against Gail, watching the strange woman from the safety of her mother's arms. "Jamilah will have to warm to you," Gail informed Crystal.

"Yeah, she don't go to strangers," her mother added.

Gail glared at her mother. "What mom meant to say is that Jamilah doesn't go to very many people. Of the two, Jamal is the friendliest."

"I said just what I meant," her mother muttered.

Gail sent her another warning look. Then she noticed Jamilah rubbing her eyes. "What time is it? I'd better lay these two down for naps or there'll be no dealing with them later. Come on, Jamal. Let's go night-night." She held out her hand to him.

He left Rashid and stumbled towards her.

"I'll help you get them settled," Rachel volunteered as she scooped Jamal up into her arms and flipped him over her shoulder. His high-pitched giggles almost caused Gail to miss what happened next.

"Rashid, can I speak with you privately for a moment?"

Everyone froze. Heads swiveled toward Crystal and Rashid as they awaited his answer.

"I think—" her mother began.

"Mom! Why don't you go into the kitchen and prepare a snack for the twins. They'll sleep much better with something in their stomachs. Deb can help...*and hopefully keep her mother under control.*" The last whispered in an aside to Rachel.

"Come on, Mom. The babies look sleepy. They've had a busy morning. We don't want to keep them waiting," Rachel added.

Gail could see the protest forming on her mother's face. Her mouth opened and...

"Go to the kitchen, Martha, and check on dinner while you're in there. I'm getting hungry again."

Thank you, Gail mouthed to her father. He winked in return. Thwarted, her mother shot an angry look at her husband and rose gracefully to her feet. The three women standing in the doorway sighed in relief. Her mother might be pigheaded, but even she obeyed when Gail's father spoke.

"We can talk in the study." Rashid's quiet voice broke the tense silence, adding another layer to it.

"Come on, Rachel. Let's get these children into bed." She hustled the women out of the den before anything else happened.

As she climbed the stairs, she mentally forced herself not to watch as Rashid and Crystal entered the study. There were enough eyes on them already. Rachel tripped and almost fell because she was watching them instead of where she was going. Her mother lingered in the kitchen doorway until Deb reached out an arm and yanked her inside.

In the nursery, Gail set Jamilah on the changing table and braced herself for what she knew was coming.

Rachel wasted no time. "Why didn't you say something?"

"Like what?"

"I don't know. Something. Anything. Why'd you even let her in the door?"

"I told you. She has a legal right to see the twins. I don't like it but there's nothing I can do about it."

"That sucks. She didn't even know their names. And those toys...what was she thinking?"

"She likes kids, but she's not familiar with them. She has a lot to learn," Gail said, trying to be charitable.

"Why are you being so understanding about all of this?" Rachel groused.

"I don't know what kind of trouble Crystal can cause for Rashid, nor do I want to find out. It's just best not to antagonize her."

"I can go along with that, but why didn't you say something when she sat by your man?"

God, she was so sick of explaining herself. She threw the soiled diaper into the pail. "It's different for you. Frank married you because he loves you. Rashid married me to be a mother to these little ones right here." She swung Jamilah off the changing table and reached for Jamal.

"It doesn't matter why you said 'I do.' The fact is you did. That's your man now and you'd better start fighting for what's yours, or she'll steal him right from under your nose."

Gail closed her eyes and mentally counted to ten. "You don't understand."

"You're right. I don't. So enlighten me already. "

"One wrong move on my part and everything could blow up in my face. I don't want to lose everything that matters to me. Not again."

"Gail, look at me," Rachel demanded.

She finished changing Jamal and disposed of the diaper before obeying.

"Is it the babies you're afraid of losing...or Rashid?"

"Both," she whispered, afraid to say it too loudly.

"You love him."

"Yeah." Gail sat in the rocking chair and watched the twins playing on the floor with their blocks. "I wasn't supposed to," she continued. "This was about the babies. When Rashid said he wanted a real marriage, I didn't argue. After all, not only are we friends, but both of us are young, healthy adults who happen to be sexually attracted to each other. I thought, why not?"

Rachel stood with her arms crossed, leaning against a dresser. "But things changed."

"I think if we hadn't added sex to the mix, things would have gone on as before. But we did, and everything changed. It became...more."

"I don't remember who said it, but I heard that in women, where the body goes, the heart will follow. I guess for you it's true."

The nursery door opened and her mother and Deb entered with the twin's snacks.

"Put them on the table," Gail directed.

As soon as they saw the food, the twins rushed over to their activity table.

While she placed the food on the table, her mother said, "Gail, you should be in there with your husband. There's nothing she can say to him that you shouldn't be able to hear."

"This is something Rashid has to handle. If he wanted me present, he would have said so."

"I understand where she's coming from. I go through the same thing whenever Ashley comes around." Ashley was Tim's ex-wife. "She has to be very careful. Some things the men just don't want us involved in. Ex-wives are one."

"Well, I'm the mother-in-law. It's expected of me to meddle. I'm going back down there."

"Mom, please. Please don't interfere. Not in this. You'll only make things worse." Gail was close to tears.

Her mother visibly fought a battle within herself before nodding. "It goes against every protective instinct I have as a mother, but I'll leave it alone. I just don't want to see you hurt again."

"I know, Momma. Neither do I."

◆◆◆◆◆

Over an hour later, Gail knocked on the study door. "Rashid, it's me."

"Come in."

He sat at his desk, studying the papers spread all over the desktop. There was no sign of Crystal. "Where's Crystal?"

"She left."

"We're getting ready to eat. Are you coming?"

"Not right now."

"Oh." She waited for him to say something else. Finally, with her shoulders slumped and head held down, she turned and opened the door.

A hand appeared out of nowhere and pushed it closed. He leaned in until he pressed flush against her back, and spoke into her ear. "Stop worrying. Crystal is out of my life for good. I don't care what she says or does, that part of my life is over. Turn around."

If she turned, he'd see the fear she was too upset to hide. She shook her head.

"Wife, turn and look at me. I want to see your face when I say this."

Gail took a deep breath, braced herself and turned.

He cupped her face, lifting it to his. "I didn't marry you just to be a mother to the twins. My reasons were more selfish. I wanted you for myself. Your mother was right. Our friendship showed me what was missing in my marriage to Crystal. I made a vow to God and if she hadn't left, I'd be with her today. But she did, and every day that she was gone, I realized how much I didn't miss her. When you told me you were leaving, I was angry. I told myself it was on behalf of the children. Those three hours you were away were some of the worst in my life. You left and nothing mattered anymore. I realized then that I loved you. Do you hear me? I married you because I love you."

The tears at the corner of her eyes made a slow track down her cheek. "Why didn't you say so?"

"I knew how you felt about Greg. If I told you, it would have scared you away. I was willing to give you time to love me back."

"You're a very smart man." She rose up for a kiss.

Much later, she asked, "Well?"

"Well, what?" His mouth traveled from her ear to her neck, stringing a line of kisses.

"Aren't you going to ask if your plan worked?"

"Nope."

"Why not?" She leaned her head to the side, silently encouraging him to kiss this side as well.

"I already know." He paused to look at her.

"How?"

247

He nibbled on her left earlobe. "You talk in your sleep."

Gail pulled her ear away from his mouth and glared at him. "I do not!"

He grinned wickedly. "Yes, you do."

"You're lying."

"Honey, anything I want to know, all I have to do is wait until you're asleep and ask, and I do mean anything."

"I don't believe you."

"Oh, really?" He leaned in closer and whispered in her ear. "Your favorite fantasy is to be tied up and blindfolded while your lover takes you over and over."

"How...?" She jerked back so fast her head hit the door. "Oww!"

"Careful." He rubbed the sore spot on her head. "In the room, under the bed, is another present. A private one, purchased just for our enjoyment. When your family leaves, we'll try it out and see just how loudly I can make you scream."

Someone banged on the door. Gail jumped forward and bumped her face against Rashid's chin. "Y'all coming? Food's getting cold."

"We'd better go before Martha picks the lock and drags us out by our ears," Rashid murmured dryly.

"I heard that!"

They both laughed as they joined the others.

Chapter Fifteen

"Ms. Gail, you need to check on your husband." Carmelita met her at the door as soon as she entered the house.

"What's wrong, Carmelita?" She'd never seen the housekeeper so agitated. She was twisting the apron into tight knots.

"This man, he come to the door and ask for the senor. I get the senor for him. This man, he makes the senor sign and hand him a letter. The senor, he read the letter and turn red. He so furious, he go into the study and slam the door. I no see him since." Carmelita was so upset her English was slipping.

"How long ago was this?"

"An hour, maybe two."

Gail set her shopping bags on the table. She'd left to take advantage of the after Christmas clearance sales. "Will you have Miguel take these to our room when he gets a chance?"

"Si, si, you go check on the senor." She shooed her towards the study.

Gail lightly rapped on the door before sticking her head around the corner. "Rashid?"

"Look Lamont, just tell me how to proceed. You told me this divorce would stand in any court in America. How can she challenge it? I don't want to hear about unusual circumstances. I want answers. This is why I pay your firm's outrageous fees. Well, call me back when you do know something." He slammed the phone down.

Gail flinched, surprised the phone was still in one piece. The last time he was this angry was when Crystal arrived unannounced. "Rashid? What's going on?"

"This came while you were out. Read it."

Gail took the papers from his hand and began to read. As she did, her knees weakened and she slowly sank into the one of the armchairs in front of his desk. "This is a Declaration of Intent. She's challenging the divorce? On what grounds?"

"Keep reading. There's more."

Gail scanned the rest and sucked in a sharp breath. Crystal was suing for physical custody of the twins and requesting to be named custodial parent in the interim. She was accusing Rashid of breach of contract. According to the prenup, in case of divorce, Crystal would retain custody of any minor children. "Can she do this?"

"She's trying."

"What did your lawyer say?"

"I needed to hire a good divorce attorney who was familiar with the appellate process. Under normal circumstances, this case would never get beyond the petition but he's never heard of anything like this before. It just might intrigue the justice enough to allow it to be heard."

She looked up from the paperwork in her hand. "Did he recommend anyone?"

"Crystal already hired the best divorce attorney in town."

"She might have the best divorce lawyer in town, but I know the best one in the country."

"Greg."

"Yes."

"You think contacting him is wise, considering our history."

"There's no bad feeling between the two of you. He's the one that told me to marry you, remember? Besides, this is just the kind of case he likes to sink his teeth into." If anyone could keep them from losing the children, Greg could.

"Go ahead. Give him a call and see what he says."
She dialed his cell phone.

"Gail, twice in one week? Miss me, baby?"

"Always." It was the truth. She loved being with Rashid and the twins, but there was a piece of her heart with Greg's name on it.

"Does your husband know you're stalking me?"

"He's standing right here."

"Mmm, that's interesting. What's going on? I can hear from the tension in your voice that something's happened."

"Crystal hired a lawyer to overturn the divorce. She's also suing for custody of the twins."

"Who'd she get?"

"According to Rashid's lawyer, the best divorce attorney in town."

"Ronald Davis? He's good. I'm better."

"That's why I'm calling."

"Divorces obtained in Guam are legally sound. He won't have an easy time of it. What grounds is he basing his plea on?"

"Crystal's emotional instability."

"He's using an insanity plea?"

"Basically." She read him the Declaration.

"Damn, that's original. It might just work too. It's different enough to get the case heard, out of curiosity if nothing else."

"That's what the lawyer said." She nibbled on a fingernail.

"What is Rashid going to do?"

"His lawyer advised him to hire a good divorce lawyer. I reminded him that we knew the best one in the country."

"Flattery will get you everything. Hand Rashid the phone and go play with the babies or something. I want some privacy."

251

"Aye, aye, sir." She saluted, even though she knew he couldn't see her.

She handed Rashid the phone. "He told me to get lost. He wants to speak with you man-to-man."

His mouth smiled but his eyes were wary. "Don't go far."

She kissed him lightly on the cheek and left the room. Left to her own devices, she would only sit and brood. She went to the nursery and played with the twins until Rashid came and found her sometime later.

She followed him into their bedroom. "What did he say?"

"He'll do it if I let him have three nights with you alone."

"What?" Her eyes bugged out and her mouth dropped open.

"Is that because he asked, or because I agreed?"

Gail's mouth moved but nothing came out.

"Just kidding. His professional interest is peaked. He's going to talk to the Partners. He thinks he can persuade them to let him take the case."

"Did he say anything about the children? Will we have to give them to Crystal?"

"She can't touch the twins. They're ours."

"But you promised them to her in the prenup. Not only that, but courts usually favor the mother. If she gets a sympathetic enough judge, he may just give them to her, despite what she did."

He stared at her, the expression on his face revealing his indecision. Finally, he held out his hand. "Come with me."

He pulled her out of the room and back down to the study. "Sit."

He went to the wall and opened the safe hidden behind their family portrait. There he pulled out a folder and brought it to her. "Open it."

The file was labeled "Personal Documents." On the top was their marriage license. Underneath were two birth certificates belonging to the twins. "What am I looking for?"

"Read them. You'll know when you find it."

As she scanned the certificates, her eyes drew to the mother's name.

Gail Marie Henderson

She looked up at him with the documents gripped tightly in one hand. "I don't understand. This has me listed as their mother. The lawyers were supposed to fix this."

"You are their mother. Why change the truth?"

"Why didn't you tell me?"

"I did. More than once."

"I thought you meant biologically. You knew that. I didn't know you meant legally as well." She was trying to let this surprising turn of events sink in when an unsettling thought crossed her mind. "You mean I've been being nice to Crystal all this time and I didn't have to be?"

"Why is that?" He took the folder from her and placed it back into the safe.

She shrugged. "I didn't want her making trouble for you with the babies."

"Communication. So very important in a marriage." He tsked at her. "Next time, talk to me."

She was trying to come up with a zinger of a reply when Rashid sank to his knees in front of her and placed his hands on her thighs, distracting her. "I'm going to ask you a question, and I want total honesty," he stated.

"Sounds serious."

"It is."

She took a deep breath. "I'm ready. Lay it on me."

"Now that you know the children have always been yours, do you wish you would have made a different decision?"

"Are you asking if I regret marrying you? No. Why?" Where was this coming from?

"If Greg takes my case, he'll be around...a lot. It wasn't long ago that you were willing to give up everything for him. I need to know if I should be concerned about my wife spending time with her former fiancé."

She sat quietly for a moment before responding. "I love Greg. That hasn't changed, and I'm sure if I didn't have the twins I would be happily married to him right now." Then she cupped his face and leaned forward until their noses touched. "But, I wouldn't trade you for anything or anyone in the world. I'm glad I misunderstood about the children. It was the push I needed to do what I wanted to do anyway."

"Are you saying that if I had gotten to you first, you would have told Greg no?"

She pulled back. "No, that's not what I'm trying to say. When you were in Guam, my mother said I was using Greg as a buffer to keep you from getting too close. I scoffed at the time, but she may have been right. I was probably in love with you and didn't know it. All the signs were there, but I refused to see them. My mind just couldn't handle my being in love with my best friend's husband. It was difficult enough just admitting the attraction I felt for you. "

"Felt?" His hands slid up her thighs to the waistband of her pants, undid the button and pulled down the zipper.

"Feel?"

"I'm trying to." He peeled off her pants and underwear.

She grinned. "Well, you're not trying hard enough. I can't feel a thing."

He undid his jeans and pushed them down his thighs. "I'm just getting started."

"Have you always been such a slow starter?"

"I believe firmly that if I take my time, I'll do it right." He spread her legs and slid a finger inside her sex. It came away wet. He slid it back in. "Can you feel me now?"

"No."

He slid in two fingers. "Can you feel me now?"

Her grip on the arms of the chair tightened as she forced herself to remain still. "Not a thing."

He added a third finger. "What about now?"

"Umm, not really. Don't you have anything bigger?"

"Let me check and see." He felt around his pelvis. "Found something. Is this big enough?"

She tilted her head to the side and studied it. "I don't know. Looks kind of small."

He thrust into her. "Small? Does this feel small?"

"Must...have...been...the...angle," she gasped.

"So?"

"What?"

"Can you?"

"Can...I...what?"

"Can...you...feel...me...now?"

"ARRGH!!!!!"

"I'll take that as a yes."

◆ ◆ ◆ ◆ ◆

Two weeks later, Gail and Rashid stood in the crowded airport waiting for Greg to debark. Gail bobbed up and down, searching through the swarming mass for a glimpse of him. Rashid watched, a feeling of dread in his stomach. Suddenly, she lit up like a Christmas tree and a big, welcoming grin covered her face. She started to run forward then visibly checked herself.

255

"Go ahead."

She glanced at him, one eyebrow arched in inquiry while virtually bouncing in place.

"Go to him. You know you want to."

"You're sure?" Her gaze kept darting away, straining to keep track of Greg's position.

Hell no! "Yes, I'm sure."

She gave him a blindingly bright smile and then took off running. "Greg! Greg!"

Greg looked around, trying to home in on the voice calling his name. Rashid could tell the minute he spotted her. His expression changed and he began shoving his way past fellow travelers, intent on reaching his goal. When she was close enough, Gail launched herself into the air. Greg dropped his briefcase and caught her midair, spinning her around in a circle, and knocking several people aside before gathering her close in a bear hug.

Rashid looked away, hands clenched by his side. He would give them this moment. He owed Greg that much, but after this, Greg had better remember Gail was his wife and keep his hands off. When the happy reunion was finally over, they joined him where he stood off to the side out of the stream of traffic.

"Rashid." Greg nodded. His hands were too full for the traditional handshake greeting. One arm wrapped securely around Gail's waist. The other held his briefcase.

"Greg." He casually reached out and pulled his wife from Greg's side, hugging her securely against his own. "How was the flight?"

A mocking smile acknowledged Rashid's actions as he responded, "The food was lousy. I'm starving."

Gail made a sound that conveyed her sympathy. "We'll feed you once we get out of here. We can drop your luggage off at the hotel and then head to the restaurant. Where are you booked?"

"No hotel. Rashid's putting me up."

Gail stopped abruptly, causing Rashid to stumble. "At the house?" Disbelief echoed in her voice.

"No, the penthouse." He yanked, forcing her to walk or be carried.

Greg kept going.

"We have a penthouse?" Her attention completely focused on him and not on the congested walkway.

Rashid tugged her closer, out of the way of the stroller that rolled out in front of them. "No, the company does."

"Don't you own the company?"

He sighed and guided her around another obstacle. He could see Greg in the distance, headed toward the luggage carousal. "Yes, I own the company."

"Then we have a penthouse. Why haven't I heard about this before? All of those times you had me staying at the house, I could have been there instead. It's staffed, isn't it?"

"When someone's in residence. The rest of the time, it's maintained by a cleaning service."

"So?"

"What?"

She huffed in frustration. "Why didn't you let me stay in the penthouse?"

"The penthouse is for business purposes. Besides, I wanted you where I could keep an eye on you."

He brought them to a stop and stood off to the side, watching the luggage as it rolled out on the belt. He could feel Gail staring at him. When he looked down, she was watching him with an expression that didn't bode well for him. "Why are you looking at me like that?"

"You're very intelligent, crafty even."

"And?" He wondered where this was going.

"I'm just realizing how many times over the last year I've been maneuvered into doing what you want."

257

Busted! Play dumb or confess all? He caught sight of Greg reaching for his suitcase out of the corner of his eye. Confessions were out of the question. He'd deny it with his last, dying breath. "What are you talking about?" He knew his expression held just the right amount of bored curiosity. It was a look he'd perfected in the boardroom.

She gave him suspicious eyes. "I'm on to you now. You won't find me so easy to manipulate the next time."

"I would never try to manipulate you." Now that he had what he wanted, there was no reason. He turned as Greg joined them, hiding his grin.

"This is everything. Now all I need are some wheels. I'll head over to the rental section and catch up with you outside."

"You don't have to pay for a rental. Use mine and I'll use one of the other vehicles at the house."

"No offense, Gail, but no. I will not be seen driving the family station wagon." Greg shuddered. "Think of my reputation."

"It's not a station wagon. I drive a Santa Fe, an SUV."

"It's a station wagon pretending to be a SUV. SUV's are a hell of a lot bigger. That thing you drive is just...cute." His nose wrinkled in distaste.

"Watch it, buster. That's my pride and joy you're talking about."

"You can use the corporate car," Rashid interrupted. "It's an Impala. That should be manly enough to suite your image." He put a stop to things before the two of them could get going good. He knew they were just playing, but each teasing jab reminded him of how close he'd come to losing Gail to this man.

They piled into the Mercedes and headed for his Club where they could speak privately. Once they'd eaten and were ready to discuss business, Greg got things going.

"Are either of you familiar with the appellate process?"

Rashid shook his head. Before now, he hadn't had a reason to know.

"Not really. I've done research for appellate cases, but I'm not familiar with the actual presentation."

"That reminds me. Rashid, I need to borrow your wife while I'm here. There's a lot to be done and a short timeframe in which to do it. Gail, I need you to brush off your dusty paralegal skills and be my assistant on this."

His wife's eyes gleamed with suppressed excitement. Did she miss the legal work she used to do? Was she tired of being a full-time mother? This was something they needed to discuss later when they were alone, he decided. "That's no problem. Angelina is available to watch the children during the day. You realize that you can't charge me research fees if my wife is the one doing the research."

"Sure I can. All I have to do is pay Gail and bill you, after adding a little markup for myself, of course."

"I believe I'm already paying you enough. Why don't I just pay her myself and cut out the middle man?"

"You're not going to pay me—either of you. Rashid is my husband. This affects me as well. Anything I can do to help gives me less time to sit and worry."

"There's no reason for you to worry. Rashid has actually made my job easy. This should be nothing more than a formality."

"I'll remember that when I get the bill," Rashid commented.

"Quit complaining. I gave you a discount. I usually charge more for my services."

"Oh, joy."

Gail and Greg thought he was hilarious from the way they laughed.

When they quieted, Greg continued. "Here's how the process works. From now on, we're on a strict timetable. When Crystal received notification of the divorce, she only had so many days to request an appeal. The first step was her Declaration of Intent, which you received. Now her attorney has thirty days from the date of filing to submit a brief to the court explaining in detail the points of the divorce decree under protest, along with any supporting documentation he may have. Then it's our turn. We'll receive a copy of the brief, and have thirty days to submit our own, rebutting any claims made by the appellant along with any supporting documentation we have. The court will review both briefs."

He took a sip of water before continuing. "Sometimes they make a judgment based on the information presented in the briefs. If there's not enough justification for an appeal, the case will be dismissed. Or, the court may determine there's reason enough to warrant a hearing. At the hearing, both attorneys will have fifteen minutes to make a verbal plea to the justice. After which, judgment is made."

Gail looked puzzled. "We won't be called on to testify?"

"No. Any testimonies will be in document form and presented as written statements. Yet another reason why I need your help. I want you to type up all our witness depositions," Greg said.

"Where do we start?"

"I need copies of everything—the prenup, divorce decree, the surrogate agreement, the reports from the private detective service as well as receipts for the public notices that were posted in newspapers." Greg ticked the items off on his fingers.

"They're in the car in my briefcase." He'd been forewarned of what would be needed and was prepared.

"Good. I know Davis. I've opposed him many times and know how he operates. He's going to try to prove you violated the terms of the prenup to get custody of the children. Then he's going to try to use Florida law against you and render the grounds for your divorce invalid."

"But Florida accepted the divorce. If it hadn't, Rashid and I wouldn't be married right now."

"The Circuit Court accepted the judgment, even though Crystal hadn't been gone a full year. This is the State Supreme Court. They can reject it if they chose to do so, but I doubt that they will. It's very rare that they override a lower court's decision."

Rashid frowned. "Guam granted the divorce because I had sufficient documentation of my fruitless attempts to locate Crystal."

"And that's going to be the basis of our defense with this appeal. You went through a lot of trouble, time, and expense to locate Crystal. You took out weekly newspaper ads in every major newspaper in Florida and Nevada, first to find her, and then to notify her of the pending divorce. You hired a private detective to trace her and kept them searching for her right up to the day Crystal appeared on your doorstep. We'll formulate a more specific defense when we know the exact plea Davis is making. There's very little he can legally challenge: abandonment; lack of notification; and failure to comply with the terms of the prenup. That's it. Everything else is subjective and won't sway the court's opinion one way or the other."

"I still don't get the whole "emotional instability" angle mentioned in the Declaration," Gail confessed.

"It's just a means of grabbing the courts attention. If it were me, this is how I would play it. I would prove that my client's emotional instability made her not cognizant of her actions. Therefore, she didn't really abandon Rashid because abandonment requires a conscious decision to leave, of which she was clearly incapable. No abandonment. No grounds for divorce. I win. But fortunately for you, Davis isn't me."

Gail stared at Greg in awe. Hell, even he was impressed. He was glad he allowed Gail to persuade him to hire Greg. Finished for now, Rashid drove Greg to his office and took him to Security.

"Roger, this is Greg Richmont. He'll be using the corporate penthouse and car. Give him an I. D. badge and set up the necessary security clearances."

"Right away, Mr. Jabbar."

"You own all of this?" The "this" Greg referred to was a ten story building located on the river downtown.

"My company does. I'll show you around when we're done here."

He took them on a tour of the building. This was the first time Gail had seen it as well. Although she was aware of where it was located, she hadn't had the opportunity to visit before now. The first story contained retail shops, a bank, and a combination deli-café. The second and third floors consisted of leased office space. The fourth floor housed the company gym on one side and a cafeteria/lounge on the other. Rashid's corporate offices were located on floors five, six and seven. The remaining three floors divided into penthouses, all currently occupied with the exception of the company penthouse.

The tour ended at the penthouse. Gail explored while Rashid gave Greg the paperwork he requested. After setting a time for Gail to begin work with Greg the following morning, Rashid took his wife and headed home. On the drive home, Gail was full of "Greg this" and "Greg that." He wanted to gag her. Worse than the chatter were the dreamy silences. She would get this look of remembered pleasures in her eyes that had his hands clenching on the steering wheel.

Thoughts of gagging led to other thoughts, and soon he knew just how he was going to handle his wife. She needed a reminder of who she belonged to, and he knew just the way to do it. He waited until later that night to implement his plan.

When she came out of the bathroom, he was ready and waiting. He slipped up behind her and tied a blindfold over her eyes.

She laughed and her hands reached up to touch it. "What are you doing?"

He caught both her hands and brought them behind her back. "Do you trust me?"

"Of course."

"Then follow my lead." He waited for protests or questions. When none were forthcoming, he continued. "I'm going to lead you to the bed. When you feel it behind you, lie down and put your hands over your head."

"All right." Her response was a little breathy.

When she lay in the center of the bed on her back, hands above her head as instructed, he fastened one hand then the other to the restraints already in place. He waited until she'd finished testing her bonds before asking, "Comfortable?"

"Yes."

"Ready for the rest?"

"There's more?"

"Only if you want it."

"Give me what you've got."

"All of it?"

"Yes."

He shackled her ankles, one to each bottom post of the enormous four-posted bed, leaving her spread-eagle. Next, he grabbed the scissors. "You won't be needing this." He cut the nightgown straight up the middle.

"You do realize this was one of my favorites?"

"You can buy more." He pulled the gown and matching panties off and threw them to the side. Then he sat back and studied his wife's body.

After he was quiet for so long, her head lifted and she turned it, first to one side and then the other. "Rashid?"

"I'm here."

She zeroed in on the sound of his voice, turning her face in his direction. "What are you doing?" She shifted restlessly on the bed, as much as her bonds would allow.

"Waiting."

"On what?" Her voice held a slight edge to it.

"Shh, trust me."

Her head dropped back on the bed. He waited until he could see her muscles tensing, and she subtly began testing her bonds. Then he took an ostrich feather and stroked her all over her body—randomly—so she never knew where the next touch would land.

Her hands fisted and relaxed, over and over, and her toes curled. Goose bumps rose all over her body and her nipples puckered. When her skin was so sensitive that she began flinching away from contact with the feather, he laid it aside and switched to exploring her body with his hands and mouth.

"Rashid!"

"Yes, love?"

"Please."

"Please what?"

"I need…more."

"More?"

"Yes," she hissed.

"Like this?"

He slid two fingers inside her sheath and stroked her g-spot. She fell apart as an orgasm ripped through her body, but he didn't quit. He kept rubbing, driving her up and over the edge again before bringing her gently down. Then he aroused her all over again, starting at the beginning with a soft, fur flogger.

"Rashid!" *woosh*

264

"Come in me!" *woosh*

"No." *woosh*

"Why not?" *woosh*

"You're not ready." *woosh*

"Yes." *woosh* "I am." *woosh* "I...need" *woosh* "...you!"

"Not yet."

He threw the flogger aside and put his mouth right on the most sensitive part of her body. This was his. He owned it and before tonight was over, she'd never think of another man in connection with sex again.

She pleaded. She begged. She cried. She screamed, but most of all, she came—over and over again. When she lay docile beneath him and the slightest touch of his tongue caused her to flinch, he deemed her ready.

It amazed him that he'd resisted this long. Every time his body demanded he take her, every time his control wavered, he thought of Gail with Greg like this and it fired his determination to see this through to the end. He reached up and removed the mask. "Watch while I take you and know who I am."

With one forceful lunge, he embedded his penis balls deep inside of her. "Who am I?"

"Rashid."

He withdrew. She groaned and arched her hips, reaching for him the only way that she could. "Come back!"

"Wrong answer. Who am I?" He suckled her breast hard, the way that she liked.

She shrieked; then moaned. Her breasts were so sensitive, he was sure she felt a bite of pain mixed with the pleasure. "Who am I?" he demanded as he released her breast.

"Rashid DuPree Al Jabbar!"

"Wrong answer." He pinched her clit and her back arched off the bed. "That's my name. Now who am I?"

He released her and backed off a minute so she could think.

"My husband?"

"You don't sound too sure. Is that who I am?" He pinched both nipples hard then quickly released them, knowing she was so aroused that anything he did at this point would only increase her pleasure.

"Yes! God, yes. You're my husband."

"Right answer." He thrust back inside. Calling on all of his control, he rode her with shallow strokes, teasing her entrance. "And to whom do you belong?"

She arched her hips, trying to force him deeper.

"You didn't answer my question."

He pulled out again and she cursed him. "Rashid, quit playing. I need more."

He got right in her face. "I'm not playing," he said harshly. He willed her to see how serious he was about this. "This isn't a game. You're mine—body, heart, and soul. I won't share you with any other. Before tonight is over, you'll never think of being with another man again."

He stayed nose-to-nose with her until he could see comprehension dawn in her eyes. "Who do you belong to?"

She swallowed—hard. "You."

He drove into her. "Say it again."

"You."

"Louder!" The sounds of flesh smacking flesh filled the room.

"You!"

"Again!" The heavy bed began to rhythmically thump against the wall.

Her neck arched and her body went tight as a bow. "YOOOUUU!!!!" She screamed it. Her body jerked and convulsed beneath his.

Rashid held back his release. He wanted to come but couldn't. Her response wasn't enough. From now on, when she thought of pleasure, she would think of him and him only. No memories of Greg, or even of Jason, allowed.

He would be the only man on her mind, and in her heart!

Their sweat-slicked bodies glided against each other. Her hot, wet sheath made sucking noises as it tightened around his cock with each retreat, straining to keep it inside. Sweat dripped off his forehead and onto her and still it wasn't enough. He demanded more from his body and it gave, pulling on reserves he never knew he had. His cock swelled even more, causing the cock-ring he wore to tighten almost to the point of pain.

"Come! Now!"

"I can't. There's nothing...aargh!" She orgasmed again, her body convulsing. This one lasted longer than all the rest combined and was so intense, she blacked out.

Rashid lost the last of his rapidly fading control. He latched onto the skin of her neck with his teeth and suckled hard, drawing the skin into his mouth. Tomorrow, she'd wear his mark for Greg to see. A very visible, "hands-off" message the other man wouldn't fail to notice and recognize.

His muscles went rigid, beginning with his toes and worked its way up his legs to his balls, which drew up tight against his body. His fingers had a death grip on the sheets and his back bowed as an orgasm rose up from the depths of his soul. With a strangled cry, he came.

He shot endless streams of cum into her body. It felt like his body went into stores of semen unused for years and emptied them out, one jet stream at a time. After an eternity of bliss, he was finally empty.

Rashid collapsed on Gail, too drained to do anything else. He managed to lift his chest enough to allow her to breathe, but little else. He panted in her ear, moaning occasionally as aftershocks rocked her body, causing it to squeeze and release around his softening penis.

Finally, concern for his wife's well-being overcame his fatigue. He rolled off Gail and onto the bed. With one hand, he wearily reached up and undid the knot binding one wrist to the bed. She hissed as the blood began circulating. He stopped and gave the muscles a light massage before undoing the other.

"Better?"

"Much," she mumbled.

Rashid rolled off the bed, and undid the ankle cuffs. Once he finished massaging her calves, he hauled her to the end of the bed by her legs. "Up and at 'em."

He pulled her into a sitting position and then lifted her over his shoulder in a fireman's carry. She dangled like a boneless pile of mush. In the bathroom, he filled the deep tub with warm water and turned on the jets, then eased both of them into the churning water. She lay in his arms and allowed him to lather her, making no effort to assist.

When he was finished, he washed and rinsed them both. Then he climbed out, leaving her in it. "Don't fall asleep. I don't want you drowning."

"'Kay," she mumbled as she lounged against the back of the tub.

He went into the room and replaced the soiled linens with crisp, fresh ones. Then he went to gather his dozing wife from the bathroom. "I told you not to go to sleep."

"Not sleep," she mumbled on a yawn.

"You're doing a good imitation." He dried her body and laid her in bed naked before climbing in beside her.

She wrapped around him like a vine. "So good," she whispered. "Next time, I'm on top."

At the thought of her topping him, his cock twitched. "That sounds like fun."

"Mmm," she agreed before sliding back into sleep.

"We can do anything you want, baby. Just don't ever leave me," he whispered into her hair before allowing sleep to claim him.

Chapter Sixteen

"You're late. You were supposed to be here two hours ago."

Gail brushed past Greg into the penthouse, trying her hardest to walk as normal as possible. Her whole body was tired and stiff, even though she'd soaked last night and again this morning in hot, soothing water. "Sorry, I overslept. Long night."

He was instantly concerned. "One of the twins got sick?"

She flushed and turned away, not wanting him to see her expression. He'd ask questions and some things were just too personal to share, even with Greg.

"Whoa, what have we here?" He grabbed ahold of her chin and pulled the collar of her shirt away from her neck. "Damn! That's a hell of a passion mark. Somebody was feeling mighty possessive. This explains the walk."

Gail tugged her collar back in place. "Shouldn't we get started?"

He smirked. "I don't know. Can you sit? From the way you're walking, I'd say not."

"Yes, I can sit. I drove over here, didn't I? I'm not sore, just a little stiff." She did not want to have this discussion with him. Please, let it go, Gail begged mentally.

"Rode the hell out of you, didn't he?" He could barely keep the laughter out of his voice.

She glared at him, wishing she could smack him a good one. Then with a snarl, she turned and walked off. "Where do you have us set up? I brought my laptop."

"Hey, don't get mad at me. I'm not the one that went all Tarzan on your ass. What did you do to upset him?"

That stopped her in her tracks. She turned a puzzled face towards him. "Who said he was upset?"

"This does, darling." Greg flicked the love mark on her neck. "Rashid marked his territory. You must have done something to bring out his primitive nature. It sure as hell wasn't me. He was fine when he left here."

Greg didn't know what he was talking about.

But as Gail set up her workstation, she thought back over the previous evening. When they'd left the penthouse, Rashid had seemed quieter than normal, but otherwise fine. Had she done something to upset him?

On the drive home, he'd been preoccupied. Not that she'd noticed at the time. She'd jabbered the whole way home, receiving only grunts in return. What had she been blathering about? It took a bit for it to come to her. Greg! For forty-five minutes, she'd done nothing but sing his praises to Rashid. No wonder he'd reacted the way he did. Not that she was complaining. Last night was...indescribable. Definitely worth repeating, but this time for the right reason.

"Greg, I'll be back." She shut down her laptop.

He glanced up from his computer with a scowl. "You just got here."

"I know and I promise we'll get started as soon as I return. I need to go apologize to my husband." She was itching to get to Rashid and make things right.

Greg followed her to the door. "You really love him, don't you?"

She paused with her hand on the doorknob, and looked back over her shoulder. "Yeah. I didn't think I would, but I do." Even though they spoke with each other at least once a week, this was the first time she'd admitted to her feelings for Rashid.

"I'm glad."

She turned and leaned against the door. "You are?"

"Why the surprise? I knew when I sent you to him you were halfway in love with him. It didn't change my feelings for you then and it doesn't now. I still love you, enough to want what's best for you. Right now, that's Rashid. You're the reason I'm here. I'm doing this for you. But know this, if he ever messes up, if you ever decide to leave, you come straight to me, you hear? My arms will always be open." Greg spread his arms wide.

Gail stepped into them and hugged him tight. "I love you, too. That hasn't changed."

He wrapped his arms around her, held her close, and kissed the top of her head. "I know you do, and if Rashid and I were different men—less possessive, more willing to share—we might have made a threesome work."

She laughed and pushed him away. "You won't believe what he said. He told me your price for taking this case was three nights alone with me. Can you believe it? Mr. Possessive, willing to joke about something like that?"

Greg didn't laugh as expected. Instead, he caught her back into his arms until the entire front of her body pressed against his. "And if I had, would you have agreed?"

Two days ago, her body would have hummed with arousal, just from being this close to him. Today, she felt Greg and remembered Rashid's body pressing hers into the mattress last night. "I'm glad it's a decision I'll never have to make. I'll be back in a bit." She pushed until he released her and walked out the door, resisting the urge to look back.

She rode the elevator down to Rashid's office, her mind on the night before. Huge mistake. Her body moistened and her thighs became sticky with cream. What a time not to be wearing underwear, though she really hadn't had a choice. Her vulva and nipples were too sensitive to wear anything confining. She'd compensated by wearing a tank with a built-in shelf bra, and a long-sleeve blouse over a nice long broom skirt.

Ms. Brentman, Rashid's secretary, sent her right in when she arrived. "Go ahead. He's alone," she said as she reached for the phone to announce her.

"I'll announce myself. Thank you."

She walked into the office and locked the door behind her. Rashid looked up at her entrance and heat flared in his eyes.

She leaned back against the door with her hands still holding the knob. "I have a boo-boo. You need to kiss it and make it better."

A half-smile slid across his face at the mention of the game they played with the twins. "Really? And where might this boo-boo be?" He leaned back in his chair and rested his arms on the armrests.

She walked over to his desk and moved the paperwork out of the way. Backing against it, she eased carefully onto the desk in front of him and spread her legs. As she drew her skirt up to her waist, she pointed to her swollen nether lips. "Right here."

Rashid's eyes gleamed. "Poor baby. That's a big boo-boo. Lay back and let me kiss it. I promise I'll make it all better."

She lay back on the desk as he lowered his mouth to her slit. He French kissed her, sliding his tongue in and out of her opening until she was clutching his head with her fists. After the excesses of last night, it wasn't long before she was hovering on the edge. He stopped before she could fall over.

"You have anything else that needs kissing?"

He didn't give her a chance to answer, but leaned down until he was braced above her. His mouth claimed hers and he drank from her like a man in the desert who's finally found water after days of searching in vain.

Gail slid her hand between their bodies and undid the zipper on his pants. She reached in and stroked his rapidly hardening penis. "Take me," she whispered.

He groaned and his eyes closed in pleasure. His hips arched into her touch. "I thought you were sore."

"I lied."

He bit her earlobe. "Under normal circumstances, I'd be angry with you for lying to me, but in this instance, it can be forgiven." She positioned his rigid penis at her slick opening, and he entered her slowly. "You have to be quiet. No screaming. My secretary's right outside."

This man was turning her inside out, loosening all of her inhibitions. Why else would the thought of being heard excite her, taking her arousal to another level? She wanted sexy Ms. Brentman to hear and know what they were doing. In her own way, she was as possessive as Rashid. She wanted the woman to know this man belonged to her and no one else.

"Let her hear." She wrapped her legs around his waist. "It will keep her from getting any ideas about you."

At her words, a fierce look crossed his face. "As you wish."

God, she should have known better than to tempt Rashid. The man made her scream so loud it's a wonder security wasn't called. She was sure it sounded like he was killing her. Then again, maybe not. If she were dying, would she really have been screaming, "Yes! Yes! Oh God, just like that!"

Much, much later, Rashid escorted her out of the office and back to the penthouse. He was all smug male pride as they walked down the hall to the elevator. She, on the other hand, wavered and wobbled like someone who'd had one drink too many. The goofy grin wouldn't leave her face, no matter how hard she tried, and she caught herself humming tunelessly more than once.

Rashid hammered on the door and handed her over to Greg when the door opened. "I hope you have food in here. After she naps, she'll be hungry."

Greg looked her over from head-to-toe. "You walked her through your business looking like that?"

The wicked humor in Greg's voice penetrated her pleasurable buzz. "Like what?"

"Like you've just been thoroughly fucked," Greg informed her.

She sucked in a sharp breath. "I can't believe you just said that." Then she looked down. Her skirt was twisted and her shirt haphazardly buttoned. One touch let her know her hair stuck up all over her head. "Rashid!'

He tried looking innocent. "I think you look fine. You said you didn't care if she knew."

"Damn." Greg laughed. "That was some apology."

Rashid tipped her chin with his forefinger. "You came down to apologize?"

She twisted away. "I changed my mind. You don't deserve one now." She tugged at her skirt, trying to straighten it. Then she began to undo the buttons on her shirt.

Rashid reached forward to assist. "Here, let me help."

Greg knocked his hand away. "If you touch her again, I'll never get any work out of her today. Go! You've messed up my schedule enough for one day."

Rashid backed away. "I'll see you later at home." To Greg he said, "Don't work her too hard. She didn't get much sleep last night."

"So I gather. Don't worry. Message noted and understood. Now leave."

Gail's gaze bounced back and forth between the two men, wondering what Greg's cryptic words meant and the sudden tension between them. Whatever it was, Rashid understood. He nodded and left. Once he was gone, they finally managed to get some work accomplished.

◆◆◆◆◆

Four weeks later, Gail listened while Greg practiced his plea for what seemed like the tenth time that morning. Their brief had been prepared and filed two weeks ago, and now they were waiting to hear from the court.

"Gail!"

"Hmm?"

"Am I so boring that I'm putting you to sleep?"

She yawned and tried to appear more alert. "I'm sorry. It's just that I've been so sleepy lately. It's not you. Go ahead. I'm listening." She sat straighter on the couch and forced her eyes wide open.

He put the papers down, came and sat beside her. "Does Rashid know you're pregnant?"

"I'm not pregnant, just a little tired. My iron's probably low." She rubbed her eyes and shook her head, trying to wake.

Greg placed an arm on the back of the couch behind her, turning towards her. "Are you certain you're not pregnant? Cause this is just how you were when you were carrying the twins."

Gail glared at him. "Yes, I'm sure. Rashid had a vasectomy while he was still married to Crystal."

He arched his brow at her. "You do know pregnancy can still occur within the first six months after having the procedure done. Sometimes it takes as long as twelve months for all the live sperm to dissipate. Have you been using birth control?"

She shook her head. "No, there's no need."

"Did Rashid go back for his third and six month checkups to make sure the procedure was successful?"

276

All of these questions were making her nervous. "I don't know."

"Well, have you missed any periods?"

"I haven't had a period since before I was pregnant. My doctor said breastfeeding interrupted my cycle."

"I thought the babies were weaned now?"

"They are. I started weaning both of them at six months, but Jamilah took a little longer. I was still pumping milk for her until she was a little over seven months old."

He gave her his lawyer's face. "So they've been weaned for almost five months now and you still haven't had your period?"

She shrugged one shoulder. "I spotted once or twice, but that's about it. My GYN said that was normal."

"Put your shoes on." Greg stood and grabbed his wallet and keys.

"Are we going somewhere?"

"To the store to get you a pregnancy test."

Gail leaned further into the couch, refusing to budge. "For what? I told you that I'm not pregnant."

"Humor me."

She slowly rose to her feet and put on her shoes. "This is silly. You know that, don't you? I'll take the stupid test, but you're paying for it. I'm not wasting my money."

Four hours later, she looked at the little pee stick in horror. A plus sign signified she was pregnant. "Get me another one," she demanded of Greg, who leaned against the frame of the open bathroom door, arms crossed on his chest.

"I'm not going out and buying another test. You've taken four of the damn things, and all of them were different brands. You're pregnant. Face it."

She sank down onto the closed lid of the toilet and slumped over. "But I can't be. Rashid will never believe it's his. He'll think I cheated on him—with you."

He straightened. "Didn't you tell him I can't have children?"

"I don't know. I can't remember," she wailed. "This is terrible."

He shook his head. "I don't understand your reaction. You love the twins. I thought you'd be happy about this."

"Yes, I love them, but I never considered having more. Remember, I wasn't supposed to have them. I don't even know if Rashid wants more children. The subject's never come up." She put her face into her hands. "What am I going to do?"

"First, you're going to stop panicking and tell your husband the good news. He'll be happy. He loves children."

Gail lowered her hands and stared at him in horror. "Are you nuts? I can't tell him about this." She gestured to the four pregnancy tests lined up on the sink top, pausing to stare once again in disbelief at the results. When she looked back at Greg, he had an expression on his face that she knew boded ill for her. She sat up straight, hands gripping her knees. "Greg, don't you dare. Promise me you won't tell him."

"He needs to know."

"I'll tell him—eventually—just not until this appeal is over. I don't want to burden him. He's worried enough."

He put his hands on his hips and glared at her. "Rashid isn't the one worrying. You are. Tell him. He needs to know and if he finds out you knew and didn't say anything, he's going to be pissed. I would."

Gail ran agitated fingers through her hair. "I will, but not now. And you're right. It's me that's worried.

Can't you just let it wait until after the hearing? It can't be too much longer, right?" She begged with her eyes.

"I won't tell him on one condition—you go to the doctor. If you don't agree to start your prenatal care, I'll walk right down there and tell him now."

She sighed as the weight dropped off her shoulders. A reprieve. "Deal."

Gail held out her hand for him to shake.

He held out his phone to her instead.

She stared at it. "What's this for?"

"Call and make your appointment."

"Now? Don't you trust me?"

"No."

She snatched the phone out of his hand, and pushed past him out of the restroom. "Fine. I'll call."

When she got off the phone, he commented from behind, "I thought Dr. Hagan was your OBGYN?"

"No, he's Rashid's doctor. Mine is Dr. Jennings, and that's who I'm going to see."

He shook his head at her stubbornness. "You know Rashid will make you switch when he finds out. Why not just go to Dr. Hagan to begin with?"

Because he'll tell Rashid. Aloud she said, "I'll see any doctor he wants, after the hearing."

Greg crossed his arms over his chest and stood, eyes narrowed and feet braced apart. "You know, I'm beginning to detect a distinct lack of faith in my abilities. Listening to you, one would believe we were going to lose this appeal."

She went to him and placed a hand on his shoulder. "Greg, I have complete faith in your ability as an attorney. I recommended you, remember? However, I've learned not to place my absolute confidence in things. If I leave room for a little doubt, it won't hurt as much if things doesn't go as planned."

He brushed the hair off her forehead and tucked it behind her ear. "You're too young to be so cynical."

She shrugged. "Life lessons learned the hard way."

"There's no way this can go wrong. Between my brilliance and Rashid's meticulous planning, Davis doesn't have a legal leg to stand on. Stop being such a doubting Thomas and just believe. Like I said, this is just a formality. I told you they would throw out the custody issue and they did. Trust me on this, too."

"That's true, but they should have thrown out the whole thing."

Greg laid a reassuring hand on her shoulder. "I told you, this case is just interesting enough to spark the court's curiosity. How often does one like it come along? Why do you think the partners at my law firm agreed to my coming back here and taking this case? This is the kind that sets precedent. The prestige a successfully won case like this can bring to the firm is worth more than the fee Rashid's paying us."

She sighed. "Fine. I'll try not to worry. It's just that whenever things are going good, I've learned to watch out, 'cause that's when trouble comes knocking."

He squeezed her shoulder. "You've had enough of trouble. Relax. It will be fine. You can't afford to worry. Stress isn't good for the baby."

She groaned and put her hands over her face. "Did you have to remind me?"

◆◆◆◆◆

Her cell phone blared out a tune, pulling her from a sound sleep. Gail reached a hand out from under the covers and snagged it before it could wake Rashid. Who was calling at this time of night?

The caller's ID read "Private." No help there. Thinking it might be an emergency, she answered. "'Lo?" She cleared her throat and tried again. "Hello?"

"Gail, it's me, Crystal. Can we meet somewhere? I need to talk to you."

"Now?" The woman must be crazy. It was after midnight.

"Actually, I was thinking I could come over in the morning after Rashid left for work. Or maybe you could meet me for breakfast. My treat."

Gail caught herself, realizing she'd almost agreed out of habit. "There's nothing to discuss." She kept her voice low.

"There's plenty to talk about. You're married to my husband, living in my house, and raising my children," Crystal said, her voice strident.

Crystal's words sparked her dormant temper. Gail eased out of the bed and walked out of the room, closing the door softly behind her. "Those children belong to me. You weren't interested in them before they were born, nor were you around for the first year of their life, so don't go acting like I stole something from you. And if you wanted your husband, you should have thought of that sooner. Rashid's a good man and you just up and left. No explanation. No goodbye. Nothing. By your actions, you deserved to lose him and everything else you had with him. Goodbye, I'm going back to bed now with my husband."

"Wait! Please! You're right. What I did was wrong and I shouldn't have said what I did. Please don't hang up. You're my closest friend. Please, just give me a few minutes of your time, a chance to make things right."

Gail's mouth dropped open. "Your closest friend? That's not saying much, is it? Do you even know what friendship is? A friend wouldn't ask someone who'd recently lost their only child to have a baby for them. And if for some crazy reason she did, and the friend stupidly agreed like I did, they damn sure wouldn't go off and abandon them. Besides, this is about more than your leaving. You swore to me you would stick with me

281

through every step of my pregnancy. That it would be the two of us together doing this, and you didn't. Rashid was the one with me at every doctor's appointment. He was my coach during childbirth classes. He watched over me and made sure I ate and exercised like instructed, and he was the one there in the delivery room with me when it was time for them to be born. When Jamilah got sick and we were so afraid we were going to lose her, it was the two of us in that emergency room while you were off getting your head straight. And you think a few minutes of conversation is going to make things right? I don't think so. Frankly, I'm not interested in anything you have to say because there is nothing you can say to justify what you did." All the crazy, conflicted feelings Gail had towards Crystal were gone now and in its place was pure, unadulterated anger.

"Everything you just said is true. I know I messed up in so many ways. That's what this appeal is about. I'm trying to fix the mistakes I made with you and with Rashid. Everything that's happened is my fault. You and Rashid are together now because I gave you no choice. He stepped in to fill the void I left when I didn't do as I promised, and I know the only reason the two of you married was because of the babies. They needed a mother and I wasn't there. I wasn't ready then, but I'm ready now. Ready to be a mother to them and a better wife to Rashid. I just need you to give me another chance."

Gail walked further into the hallway, away from the bedroom door. If Rashid should awaken, she didn't want him to overhear her end of the conversation. "Another chance," she echoed, her voice flat. "And exactly how do you expect me to accomplish this?"

"When the judge overturns the divorce, let me and Rashid have the babies. My lawyer says if you're willing, we can still do a step-parent adoption, making me the babies' legal mother. Then Rashid and I can raise them as originally planned."

"You're crazy as hell! I'm not giving you my children. Hell, I wouldn't even leave you alone in the room with them for a minute, let alone adopt them. I'd let the State take them before I signed them over to you." She wasn't a cussing woman but Crystal was taking her there. Give her my children? Over my dead body.

"GAIL! How could you say something so cruel? I'd be a good mother to them, I swear. Just give me a chance to prove it." She could hear the tears in Crystal's voice.

"Forget it. You had your chance and you blew it. Besides, why should I trust you? You as good as admitted that you never wanted the twins to begin with. You were just using my surrogacy in another one of your psycho attempts to carry a pregnancy to term." Gail paced the hallway and landing in long, angry strides.

Crystal sniffed, openly sobbing now. "I know and I'm sorry, so sorry. I've accepted that I'll never have a child of my own. I know I said all of this before, but this time I really mean it. The counselor helped me to see the damage I was doing to myself mentally and physically, as well as to the people I love because I wouldn't accept the truth. Please, please, I'm begging you. Don't take my babies away from me. They're all I have."

"Then you have nothing. I'm not giving them up. This whole conversation is a waste of time and effort, just like this appeal."

"This appeal is not a waste. Rashid loves me. I know he does, and once we're remarried, he'll forgive me and things will go back to the way they were. He just needs a chance to calm down. You even said it yourself. Once he's no longer angry, everything will be fine."

The confidence in her voice grated on Gail's nerves, pushing her anger up a notch. "Don't bet on it.

283

Not this time." She ended the call and set her cell phone on one of the hall tables. Too angry to return to bed, she walked around aimlessly before heading into the nursery to watch her children sleep.

"I fought against loving you in the beginning, too afraid to claim you the way that I wanted to from the time I felt your first movement, but now I'll die before I let anyone take you or your father away from me."

She straightened their covers and kissed them gently on the head before leaving the nursery. From there, she wandered out onto the balcony overlooking the pool. It was cold, and what she had on was flimsy. The heat from the open door didn't reach where she stood at the railing, but she couldn't go back inside, not just yet.

She was angry on so many levels. Angry with Crystal for thinking she would give up her kids, just because she asked. Angry at the betrayal of their friendship and angry at the guilt she felt because the words Crystal spoke were true. Gail was living in her house, married to her husband, and raising her children. It didn't matter that she'd planned none of it, or that Crystal had brought it all on herself with her scheming. Friendship, betrayal, guilt—all these feelings warred inside Gail in a confusing blend. Over fifteen years of close friendship didn't come undone in less than a year.

Strong arms wrapped around her from behind and pulled her back into a solid chest. "You are going to freeze. What are you doing out here?"

"Did the air wake you? I'm sorry." She snuggled into the warmth of his embrace.

He nuzzled the skin behind her ear. "I always wake when you're not beside me. Why are you out here instead of in bed with me, where you belong?"

Gail leaned her head to the side, granting him greater access. "The phone rang and afterwards, I couldn't go back to sleep."

"Who was it?"

"Crystal." Her voice still held a tinge of anger.

His arms tensed when he heard the name and his voice hardened. "What did she want?"

Gail turned until she faced him and looped her arms around his neck. "It's not important. She's not important."

Rashid stared at her. She knew he was trying to read her expression. He knew her well by now and probably guessed she wasn't as unaffected as she pretended to be. "What did she say to you?"

She rose up on her toes and kissed him. "Shh, I don't want to talk about her. We have better things to do." She rubbed invitingly against him. "You can help me get back to sleep."

She could tell from his stiffness he didn't want to let it go, but she eased around him and lowered the straps of her gown, letting it drop to the floor. Underneath, she wore only a thong.

"Coming?" Gail tossed the question over her shoulder as she sauntered for the bedroom, making sure there was plenty of sway in her hips. At the doorway she struck a sexy poise. One hand stroked her left nipple while the other dipping lightly inside her panties to tease her clit.

He closed the balcony doors and scooped her gown off the floor before following her into the room. "We both will be soon," he promised.

◆◆◆◆◆

"Wait for me! I'm coming. " Gail ran down the stairs, shoes in hand.

"No, you're not. Let's go, Greg." Rashid kept striding towards the door, glancing over his shoulder briefly to see if his wife was finally listening.

"This affects me as much as it does you," she argued as she stopped to put on her shoes.

He sighed and turned around. "We discussed this last night, and again earlier this morning. You're not coming. Stay home with the children."

She turned to Greg in an obvious attempt to get him to intercede on her behalf. He'd deal with that later when he had more time. "Greg, tell him to let me go. I should be there."

"Don't look at me. I'm not getting in the middle of this," Greg told her.

Smart man.

His wife turned back to him, ready to argue her case. He cut her off. "You're not going. This whole thing is making you sick enough as it is. You're barely eating and when you do eat, you can't keep it down. You've lost weight. Your nerves are so bad that you jump at the least little thing. Stay home. If you're here, I don't have to worry about what the stress of this whole affair is doing to you and can concentrate on the appeal."

"Yes, Gail. You don't want to chance getting sick while there, do you? You know how stressed out you get. Imagine if you passed out and we had to call 911. We wouldn't want that happening, now would we?" Greg's tone was heavy with meaning.

She glared at Greg. Rashid ignored the byplay between the two, intent on bending his wife to his will. "There's no sense in your being there. You can't come into the courtroom with us. You'd have to sit outside and wait."

"But at least I'd know what was going on. And I could sit with you while we waited for the case to be called."

"No, you won't know what's going on, not unless one of us came out and told you. We don't even know where we are on the docket. It could be the last case of the day. Stay home where you'll be more comfortable. At least this way, if you get sick again you can lie down," Rashid stated firmly.

"Yes, Gail, stay home," Greg added. "It will look bad to the Justice if Rashid is stressed and distracted, worried about you. Your being there will ruin my concentration as well, knowing at any moment you could become sick."

Rashid sighed impatiently and checked his watch. His keys were jingling in his hands. He didn't have time for this. "We need to go. I'll call when we arrive." He turned on his heel and headed for the door.

"Call me the minute you know something." She was on their heels as they walked outside.

"No need. We already know the outcome," Greg told her.

"Call me anyway."

"All right." Rashid threw his hand up in the air. "If it will make you happy, I'll call. Can we go now? It's a two-hour drive to Tallahassee and we can't be late."

Gail hugged herself, and stepped from foot to foot. "Be careful. Drive safe and don't speed. You know the Troopers patrol heavily on I-10. Greg, you show that Davis guy up, you hear?"

"Yes, ma'am." Greg gave her a sharp salute and then got in the car. Rashid already had the engine started.

He pulled out of the drive, watching as Gail slowly turned and walked back into the house, her shoulders slumped dejectedly. "You have everything?"

"Yes."

"Everything?" he stressed.

"Boy, you're as bad as your wife. Yes, I have it but it won't be necessary."

"This is the future of my family we're talking about. I can't afford to take any chances. In my shoes, what would you do?" Rashid took his eyes off the road long enough to emphasize his point.

"Probably the same," Greg acknowledged. He patted his briefcase. "It's here, if we need it."

Satisfied, Rashid turned his attention to getting them to court on time. He would have loved to have his wife by his side, but this sickness of hers concerned him. The way she kept throwing up reminded him of when she was pregnant with the twins. She hadn't been able to keep anything down then either.

Gail swore it was nerves. She was certainly twitchy enough. This appeal was obviously bothering her. She lay beside him in bed at night but he doubted she slept. The strain showed. There were dark circles under her eyes and her appearance was wan. He was glad this was almost over. Any longer and he'd have dragged her to the doctor despite her objections.

The two-hour drive was over in minutes to his overly active mind. They signed in and had to wait until their case was called. Crystal arrived with her lawyer, Davis. Greg told him that although the Justice had agreed to allow the two of them to view the proceedings, only the lawyers could speak.

The Bailiff called their case number and they filed into the small courtroom. Justice Thomas Mason presided. He sat at the front of the courtroom, the large State of Florida Seal over his head. To his immediate left was the court reporter, a middle-aged black woman with graying hair. The Bailiff took his position to the right of the bench. Both lawyers went to their designated seats and the session was called to order.

Since Davis represented the appellant, he presented his plea first. He was extremely eloquent in his delivery, using most of his allotted time to sway the Justice to his way of thinking. Then it was Greg's turn.

Greg took each of Davis's points and knocked them down, one by one. He presented hard evidence to substantiate his case. Then cited a well-established precedent that supported and upheld the lower court's decision to recognize the Dissolution of Marriage decree obtained in Guam. Ten minutes into his plea, he was finished. Then it was time for the Justice to make his ruling.

"Mr. Davis. Mr. Richmont. I have reviewed the evidence set before me and listened to your pleas. Based upon the briefs, I've already denied Mrs. Jabbar custody of the children. She was never established as the legal mother, and therefore, by law, they cannot be considered children of the marriage. Mr. Jabbar was well within his rights not to petition for or establish custody of the minor children in the Dissolution of Marriage decree."

The Justice gave Crystal a hard stare before continuing. "As to the plea of Emotional Instability on the part of the appellant, unless Mr. Davis has legal documentation proving that Mrs. Jabbar was declared incompetent by a court or court appointed doctor, she is deemed fully cognizant of her actions and legally responsible."

"Now to the last and final plea, the question of abandonment." Justice Mason leaned forward with an intent look on his face and planted his forearms on the bench, one hand on top of the other. "Florida law states that a spouse must be absent for a period of twelve months or more before a divorce can be legally obtained on the Grounds of Abandonment. Of this, I'm sure Mr. Jabbar was fully aware, having been advised by his legal counsel. It sickens this court when U. S. citizens seek to circumvent the law by going outside of the country to obtain what they want. Mr. Jabbar was not abandoned—despite all of the documents presented to the contrary as proof—as evidenced by the return of his spouse within the twelve-month timeframe. I rule for the appellant. This Dissolution of Marriage is nullified and any subsequent marriage is annulled. Mr. Jabbar, I highly suggest that the next time you file for divorce, you do it the legal way. Case closed." He banged his gavel on the bench.

The Bailiff called out, "All rise."

They stood as the Justice exited the courtroom.

Rashid sank back into his seat in stunned silence, while across the room, Crystal whooped and hollered, babbling excitedly to her lawyer, Davis. He'd never actually believed they'd lose, though he made preparations for it, just in case.

Davis crossed over to Greg, hand held out and a smug look on his face. Crystal brushed past her lawyer, headed directly for where he sat. "Rashid! Honey! Now we can be together and everything can go back to normal."

He stopped her in her tracks with a look. "Give her the papers."

Greg reached into his briefcase, pulled out a manila folder, and handed it to Davis. "Here's a copy of the divorce papers we'll be filing as soon as we get back to town. There's a copy for you and one for your client. Oh, and Ms. Jabbar is not to set foot on the property where Mr. Jabbar resides."

Davis sputtered, "You can't do that. That property is the marital residence. You can't deny the wife access."

"We can and we will as long as Mr. Jabbar's minor children are in residence," Greg said.

"But...I would never hurt the babies," Crystal interjected. "I want to be their mother. Why do I have to stay away?"

Greg ignored her. "In addition, the property may have been the primary marital residence, but it was obtained before the marriage, thereby falling under the provisions of the prenuptial agreement, of which I'm sure you have a copy, making it the property of my client alone. He is well within his rights to deny access. You have twenty days to respond to the petition or we'll file No Fault. Have a good day." He gathered his papers, placed them back into his briefcase, and turned to leave—a clear dismissal. Rashid was right behind him.

"Wait! Rashid, you can't do this. Davis, tell him he can't do this." She rushed behind them. "I love you. We're supposed to be together. I know you're angry, but give me a chance to fix what I did. I can make it up to you, just give me time." She laid her hand on his back.

He turned suddenly, knocking her hand to the side. "Get this through your head. I don't love you. Nor do I want you. The sooner you're out of my life, the better. Now excuse me. I need to get home to my wife and children." He turned his back on her and walked off.

"But I'm your wife," she wailed, running after him and clutching at his arm.

He snatched it away. "Not for long." With one last contemptuous look, he walked through the door Greg was holding open.

"Twenty days, Davis. I'll be waiting." Greg followed Rashid out of the courtroom.

Outside, Greg asked, "Are you going to call Gail?"

Rashid shot him a look that questioned his sanity. "I am not a fool."

"She's not going to handle this well at all."

"You think?" He got in the car and slammed the door. The minute Greg's door closed, he gunned the engine and shot out of the parking lot. "I fear her reaction."

"Something about this whole thing's not right. Davis was too cocky, too smug. He didn't seem surprised by the verdict at all."

"Never mind that. How long until I'm free of this marriage?" He wasn't interested in Greg's analysis. They'd lost. That was all that mattered, that and fixing this as soon as possible.

"Shouldn't take too long. It's a straightforward, no fault divorce. There's no property to argue about, and no dependent children to slow things down. I'd say as short as six months, depending on how soon we can get on the docket."

Rashid banged his hand on the dash. "Damn it, that's not soon enough. Gail won't wait that long. Is there nothing you can do to push this through faster?"

"I still have a few contacts. I'll see if I can pull some strings."

"I can't lose her." He gripped the steering wheel until his knuckles turned white. "She means everything to me. I'm sure you understand." He turned tortured eyes and allowed Greg to see his fear before turning back to the road.

"Yes, I do," was Greg's soft reply.

Chapter Seventeen

The heavy front door closed with a bang that resounded through the house. Gail jerked to a sitting position on the couch where she'd fallen asleep after fighting off yet another bout of morning sickness. The phone lay by her hand. That better be a burglar and not her husband. The same husband who had promised to call as soon as the trial was over.

She rushed as fast as her unsettled digestive system would allow into the foyer. Damn, not a burglar. "Rashid, you were supposed to call. You promised. I've been waiting by the phone all day."

Then she got a good look at the grim expression on both men's faces, and her knees lost their strength. The blood left her head in a rush and black spots swam before her eyes. She dimly heard one of the men say, "Shit!" Two pairs of hands reached for her, each seeking to catch her sagging body before her head hit the marbled floor.

Rashid snarled, "I've got her."

He lifted her into his arms, carried her back into the den where she'd been and laid her gently on the couch. He sat beside her on its edge. When she tried to sit up, he pushed her back down. "Lie there."

"Rashid, I'm fine now. Just got a little light-headed. Crystal won, didn't she?" She looked back and forth between Rashid and Greg, who stood at the end of the couch, a concerned expression on his face.

"This is just a temporary setback. We've already served her with divorce papers and filed a copy at the courthouse once we arrived in town." Rashid brushed her hair off her forehead. His eyes drilled into hers, willing her to believe him.

Gail sat up and looked around the room. "I'll have to move," she said, half to herself.

"You're not going anywhere." Rashid's stern tone brought her attention back to him.

"Rashid, I can't stay here. What if she refuses to sign? My living here looks bad. She can use it against you."

"It doesn't matter if she won't sign. Florida is a No-fault state, so he can divorce her without her agreement. We filed on grounds of Irreconcilable Differences. Her refusal to sign the papers would simply be proof of their differences." Greg's expression became puzzled. "I still can't believe I lost to Davis. Based on the evidence alone, he should have lost. Something's not right about this. I can feel it."

"It doesn't matter why we lost," Rashid snapped impatiently. "Let's just focus on doing what needs to be done so that we can get on with our lives."

"I still need to move. What if she moves back in? I can't live with her in this house." The very thought of it boggled her mind.

"That won't happen. I made it very clear she wasn't welcome here. This is our home. You are my wife. I don't care what the court says," Rashid said.

"But this is the home she shared with you. Isn't Crystal legally entitled to stay here if that's what she wants to do?" Gail directed her question to Greg.

"If this was Rashid's house, she could make a legal issue of it. But it's not. He signed it over to you," Greg said.

She fell back onto her elbows on the couch as shock temporarily robbed her of her ability to speak. "What! When?" The eyes she raised to meet Rashid's were dazed.

"After we married. I offered to buy you a house and you chose to remain here. So I put this one in your name. This way, if anything ever happened to me, I'll know you and the children have a roof over your heads."

The surprises were getting to be too much. She unconsciously pressed her hand in a protective gesture against her stomach as she rested unsteadily on one elbow. When she looked up, Greg's attention focused on her belly. She snatched it away.

"Tell him."

She shook her head. "Not now."

"Tell me what?" Rashid asked.

"You do it or I will. It's after the hearing. Now tell him."

"But we lost. We weren't supposed to lose, remember?"

"What is it I need to know?" From his tone, Rashid was becoming irritated.

Greg's tone offered no quarter. "We had an agreement. You said after the hearing. I kept my end, now you keep yours."

"But—"

"She's pregnant." Greg's words seemed to echo.

"How far along?" Rashid demanded.

"See? I told you he would think it was yours," she accused Greg.

"At least two months." Greg spoke over her, his attention focused upon Rashid.

Rashid glared at her. "I know damn well it's my child you're carrying. What I want to know is why wasn't I informed sooner? No wonder you've been so sick. What does Dr. Hagan have to say about your weight?"

Greg glared at her as he continued to tattle. "He doesn't know. She's using her old doctor."

Rashid's eyes narrowed and a small vein at the corner of his eye began to pulse.

"Greg! Enough! I can tell him the rest." She didn't like the look in her husband's eye, and Greg was only adding fuel to the fire.

"I told you to tell him when you first found out. He deserves to be pissed."

"How long has she known about this?"

Gail opened her mouth, but Greg beat her to the punch. "At least three weeks now. Maybe more."

"And she told you, but not me? Her husband and the father of her unborn child?" Rashid's voice was dangerously quiet. Gail subtly began scooting back on the couch, away from her furious spouse.

"I only know because I forced her to take a pregnancy test. She's extremely stubborn. Argued me down that she wasn't pregnant, even though all the signs were staring her in the face. She had to take four of the damn things before she would finally admit it."

Gail pulled her legs to her chest and tried to roll off the couch. "You two carry on. Obviously, I'm not needed here."

Rashid's hand clamped down on her thigh in an unbreakable grip. "You're not going anywhere."

"Well now, that's my cue to leave. I have some things I want to check into. You two have fun." Greg waved and left the room, leaving behind a tense silence.

"Get your doctor on the phone. I want to talk with him."

Inwardly, Gail flinched at the icy command in his voice. Outwardly, she tried not to show she was affected. "Dr. Jennings is a female and I'm sure she's gone home by now."

"Get her on the phone. NOW!"

Gail scrambled to comply. Rashid had never raised his voice at her. She called the practice, figuring she'd get the after-hours phone service. Instead, Dr. Jennings answered. Figures. If Gail had wanted to speak with the doctor, she would have been unavailable, but because it was Rashid, she was still in the office.

She handed Rashid the phone then listened in horror as he drilled the doctor on her medical credentials, her experience, and demanded a detailed summary of Gail's condition. Her mouth dropped open when he high-handedly commanded that the doctor transfer Gail's file to Dr. Hagan, their "family" doctor, who would be handling Gail's prenatal care from now on.

"Rashid! I can't believe you just did that." She dropped her face into her hands. "I'll never be able to face her again. I'll be lucky if she agrees to keep me as a patient. She probably thinks my baby's father is a dictator." She sighed mournfully. Dr. Jennings had been her doctor for over ten years, and good doctors were so hard to find. Now she'd have to switch.

"You think that bothers me? You are my wife, the woman that I love. I'll take no chances with your wellbeing."

She lowered her hands and looked him square in the face. "I'm not your wife, Rashid, and according to the courts, I never was." Her voice was quiet.

He cupped her chin and used it to pull her closer. "I don't care what the judge said. You're my wife. The mother of my children. We're a family, and I won't let you go. I'd kill anyone who tried to take you away from me." The look in his eye was deadly.

She tried to draw back but couldn't. He wouldn't let go. His assertion scared the crap out of her. "Let go, Rashid." She pressed against his chest, straining backwards.

"No, not until you understand how I feel. I love you more than I've ever loved anyone in my life. The children are just an extension of that love. I won't let you go." He swallowed so hard she saw his Adam's apple bob. "I can't let you go. Losing you would kill me."

What she saw in his face caused her to stop pushing against him and wrap her arms around his neck. He dragged her closer and clutched her tightly against his body. Gail hid her face against him, still unnerved by his intensity. Rashid walked that fine line between ultra-possessive and killer-crazy. Thank God, his protective instinct was as strong as the possessive gene he'd inherited from his culture, if not stronger.

In a lightning fast move, he flipped her over his knee.

Whack! "That's for not telling me you're pregnant."

"Ouch, Rashid. Stop. That stings." She wriggled and tried to roll away, but he held her fast.

Whack! "That's for not taking better care of yourself, even though you know you're carrying my child."

"Hey!"

Whack!

"Ouch! This isn't funny."

Whack! "That's for worrying me."

Gail twisted and squirmed, trying to get off his lap. She could feel his hand hovering over her behind. "If you keep spanking me, you're going to have to kiss my butt and make it all better," she warned breathlessly.

Whack! Whack! Whack! Whack! Whack! "Don't ever keep something like this from me again. If it's important, I want to know as soon as you do."

He helped her off his lap, and she stood rubbing her wounded posterior. "I promise. The next time I find myself unexpectedly pregnant, I'll tell you immediately," she muttered sarcastically.

His eyes narrowed in warning and he reached for her, his intent clear. Gail jumped back, hands held out in front of her to hold him off. "Okay, okay, okay. Important stuff. Tell you immediately. Got it."

Rashid rose to his feet, looming dark and dangerous, and unbuckled his belt. "Go to our room."

"Why?" She took a cautious step back, eyes on the belt in his hand.

He tossed it onto the couch and reached for his tie. "So I can kiss it and make it better." His tie joined the belt. "Did you not say I would need to do so?"

She gave him a sexy grin as comprehension dawned. Gail backed towards the door, unbuttoning her shirt, her eyes on the expanse of chest slowly being revealed as Rashid rapidly unbuttoned his. When her hands reached for the front catch on her bra, he stopped what he was doing to watch. She played with the catch before releasing it, and then spun around. "Race you! First one in the room gets to be on top." Then she ran out of the door, laughing like a lunatic as she raced up the stairs.

Rashid swore and chased after her.

◆ ◆ ◆ ◆ ◆

"I can't believe that bitch won," her sister-in-law said.

"Neither can I." Gail twirled the phone cord around her fingers.

"What did Rashid say? I bet he's pissed."

She rolled her eyes. "Rashid doesn't waste time getting angry. He was prepared. As soon as the judge gave his verdict, he had Greg serve Crystal with new divorce papers, right there in the courtroom."

"Have you told Mom yet?"

Gail pulled the phone away from her ear and stared at it in disbelief. "Rachel, have you lost your mind? Tell mom my marriage was annulled, and Rashid and I are currently living in sin? No, ma'am. You know how she is. This time the divorce will stick, and it won't take long. Then he and I will have a quiet ceremony somewhere with a Justice of the Peace. Rashid's not even calling it a wedding. He says we're renewing our vows. As far as he's concerned, we're still married."

"I can understand you not telling her about this, but does she know you're pregnant again?"

"No, and don't you tell her." Gail flopped back on the bed and glanced behind her once more to make sure the bedroom door was closed.

"Did you finally tell Rashid?"

"Yeah, he knows." She rubbed her hip lightly.

"Did he react like you expected?"

"No. Not only did he know the baby was his, he was pissed I thought he'd think otherwise."

"Told you, but I will admit that under the circumstances, it was a reasonable assumption on your part. I mean, come on. The man had a vasectomy. Most husbands would be screaming "adulterer" and headed for the nearest divorce attorney."

"I know. That's what I was afraid of."

"All right, we've talked about everybody but you. How do you feel about all of this?"

Gail reached for the remote and lowered the volume on the television. The News at Lunch was just coming on. This was the moment she'd been waiting for, the reason why she called Rachel to begin with.

"I'm mad. No, I'm beyond mad. I'm pissed. Thanks to Crystal and some judge, my marriage and the last six to seven months of my life mean nothing. All that we went through adjusting to each other, and poof, with one swipe of the pen, it was all undone. Now we're right back where we started, only this time, I know the twins are mine."

"I'm sorry, but I don't see it that way. You're making it sound like the last year of your life was a waste, and it wasn't. You have a man who loves you, two beautiful babies, and another one on the way. I agree with Rashid. This is just a minor setback. He'll get the divorce. You two will remarry and things will continue as before with none the wiser. How long before the divorce is final?"

"I don't know. If Crystal doesn't contest it, it could be as little as six to eight weeks. But if she decides to fight..." Her voice trailed off as a picture of Rashid flashed on news. She reached for the remote and turned up the volume.

"You got your divorce and that's the end of it, right? Think again. Local, wealthy businessman, Rashid Al Jabbar discovered that earlier this week when the Florida State Supreme Court ruled his divorce was illegal and overturned it. What makes this case so interesting is Mr. Jabbar had already remarried."

"Angela, why would one Florida court grant him a divorce then another one overturn it?"

"John, that's part of the problem. Mr. Jabbar flew to Guam to obtain his settlement, something many Americans do. Usually, because Guam is a US Territory, the divorce is upheld, which is why Mr. Jabbar was able to obtain a marriage license in Florida to remarry."

"What was different about this case?"

"According to Florida law, a spouse has to be absent for twelve months before a divorce can be obtained on grounds of abandonment. Justice Thomas Mason accused Mr. Jabbar of leaving the country to circumvent state law and ruled against him."

"Gail?"

"Shhh."

"Didn't you say he obtained his marriage license in Florida?"

"Yes, and that's what makes this case so unusual. The Supreme Court rarely goes against the lower court's ruling. Before Mr. Jabbar could be issued a wedding license, the court had to first recognize his divorce. And get this, the new wife—or would that be former wife?—is listed as the mother of Mr. Jabbar's two children, which makes this case all the more intriguing."

"Gail, if you don't start talking right now, I'm going to hang up. What's going on?"

"Oh God, Rachel. It's on the news."

"What's on the news?"

"The appeal, our marriage. They even mentioned the babies. How on earth did they find out about all of this?"

"You know those news hounds. They go through public records looking for this kind of stuff. It must be a slow week. What did they say?"

"They were discussing how the divorce was overturned as being illegal even though Rashid had obtained it in Guam and had since remarried."

"That's not so bad. This isn't even the main newscast. I'll bet this story is just a filler. Watch and see. Something more interesting will happen and this will all blow over."

What it did was blow up, like a big mushroom cloud. The Associated Press picked up the story, which attracted the attention of the national news networks. Someone got the bright idea to interview Rashid and Crystal, to see what their reactions were to the appeal results. Rashid referred the media to his lawyers, who issued an official statement on his behalf.

Crystal, on the other hand, agreed to the interview, which only made the situation worse. Gail couldn't accuse her of lying to make the story more sensational, but Crystal lacked any kind of discretion. She blurted out the whole sorry tale: their friendship, the surrogacy agreement, her jealousy that led to her retreat to a private medical clinic, and the subsequent marriage between Gail and Rashid.

The media went crazy. This story was juicier than expected. Everyone wanted to know more. The news media, tabloids, talk shows and radio programs—

everyone was calling, trying to get them to appear on their show. The phone rang off the hook until Rashid changed it to an unlisted number.

Nothing was private. In their quest for knowledge, reporters dug into everything. Crystal and Gail's friendship was speculated upon. The death of Gail's husband and child was brought out for review. Then the media somehow found out about Gail's current pregnancy. That was the final straw.

She became a prisoner in her own home. Anytime she went outside the gates of their community, the paparazzi were all over her. Her blood pressure soared under the strain of it all, and the doctor put her on bed rest.

Rashid was livid.

Their continued silence only increased speculation. Who was at fault? Opinions divided. Some blamed Crystal for creating the situation and running away when she could no longer deal with it. Others blamed Gail. To many, Gail was a heroine who'd made the best of a bad situation. To others, she was the scheming hussy who saw her opportunity and stole her best friend's rich, attractive husband. The only person not considered by public opinion to be at fault was Rashid. Who could blame him for doing whatever it took to provide his children with a mother?

In the midst of all of this media frenzy, Gail's mother swooped in like an avenging angel. She came into their home issuing commands like a drill sergeant. "Gail, pack your bags. I'm taking you home."

"My wife is not going anywhere. This is her home."

Her mother turned on Rashid. "And you! You've got this big fancy home and all this money. Do something about this. Put a stop to it. I know you can. What I don't understand is why you haven't. While you're ending this mess, my daughter and grandbabies will be with me in Alabama."

That vein started pulsing above his eye again. Gail began to pray. This was not going to be good. She held her breath as Rashid opened his mouth to respond. "With all due respect, madam, I refuse to let you come into our home and take my wife and children from me."

"Rashid, Mom..." Gail began hesitantly.

"Rashid, son. Let's go into the den and have a talk. Martha, you go and pack supplies for the twins, enough to last a few weeks. Gail, do as your mother instructed."

She looked at her father, shocked at his interference. "But Daddy, I—"

"Gail." That's all he said. That's all that was necessary. She looked helplessly at Rashid before turning to go do as told. While she didn't want to leave Rashid, part of her would be happy to get away from the media circus surrounding their home.

She wasn't told what her father said to Rashid, but whatever it was, it was effective. In the middle of that same night, around three in the morning, she and the twins rode off in her parent's car, headed for Alabama. Rashid's last words echoed in her mind. "I'll put a stop to this and bring you home as soon as possible. Take care of yourself and my children."

In Alabama, Gail's mother imposed a media blackout. She wasn't allowed to watch television or read the newspaper. Her mother even forbade her to go on the internet. All calls screened and no one was allowed to discuss what was going on in the outside world with her.

Slowly, Gail began to relax. Her blood pressure came down. Her appetite returned and she once more slept peacefully at night. Her mother took over the care of the twins and allowed Gail to do nothing more strenuous than move from one room to another. Her job, she was told, was to relax and take care of herself and her unborn child. Surrounded by the love and support of her family, Gail blossomed.

◆◆◆◆◆

Gail lay relaxing on the sun porch at the back of the house, enjoying the late afternoon air. Her mother was in the kitchen cooking and entertaining the twins. The soft sounds of cool jazz and childish chatter floated in the air.

She awakened to the slow glide of her wedding band being removed from her finger. "Rashid! How did you get here? When did you arrive, and what are you doing with my ring?"

"I'm taking it off so that I can replace it with this." This was a three-carat diamond and gold eternity band, which he placed on her finger before sliding her simple wedding band back on. Then he leaned forward and kissed her.

Gail wrapped her arms around him, and pulled him down with her until they lay on the wide couch with Rashid on top of her. It had been a long three weeks. She was hungry for him, so very hungry. When they finally came up for air, she told him, "I missed you."

He grinned, a flash of strong white teeth. "I've missed you, too. That's why I'm here. To collect my wife and children and bring them home where they belong."

She groaned, imagining her mother's reaction to this announcement. "Any news on the divorce?"

He pulled back from nibbling on her neck. "Haven't you been watching the news?"

"No. Mom wouldn't let me. Claimed it wasn't good for my health. Turns out, she was right. What have I missed?"

"The news broke this morning. Justice Thomas Mason has been suspended from the Florida State

Supreme Court, pending a grand jury investigation on allegations of his accepting bribes from lawyers."

Her brow furrowed. "Thomas Mason? Isn't that the justice who presided over our case?"

"Yes, and all the cases he presided over have been reopened by the head Justice."

"How did they find out? What made them suspicious?"

"Crystal."

"Crystal?" She pushed him off her and struggled to sit up. Rashid reached out and helped.

"You heard right. Davis confronted her about all of the media attention. Apparently, he somehow let it slip he'd bribed the judge, and that was why they'd won the appeal. Crystal went straight to the District Attorney. The D. A. leaned on Davis and he caved. He sold Mason for a lighter sentence."

"But it's Davis word against Mason's. Why would they believe Davis when he'd already plead guilty?"

"Because he had proof. He taped a couple of their conversations and kept records of their financial transactions."

"So what does this mean for us? Are they scheduling another hearing with a different justice?"

"No, they've already ruled in our favor. Seems Greg was right. We should have won. Would have won if not for Davis and Mason." He slid his hand up her thighs under her skirt, and grabbed her underwear. "Lift up."

She did, her mind more on their conversation than his actions. "So, we're still married?"

"Yes." He reached for the zipper on his pants.

"And we no longer have to worry about Crystal?"

He freed himself from his pants and lifted Gail onto his lap. "Crystal's history. She called and apologized for all the trouble she'd caused. Asked me to convey to you how sorry she was for everything and that she hopes you two can still be friends. Last I heard she was headed back to Vegas to that clinic."

He fingered her, testing her readiness, then he shifted her until he embedded inside.

"Rashid," she hissed. "We can't do this here. My parents are right inside."

"I'm not waiting another moment. You'll just have to be really quiet."

She bit back a moan as he spread her skirt to cover their actions. Planting his feet further apart, he punched up with his hips in short, sharp jabs that hit all the right spots inside. Suddenly, he stopped. When Gail tried to move, he clamped a hand down on her hips and shook his head.

A moment later, her mother appeared in the doorway. "Gail, did Rashid tell you the news?"

"Just now." God, she hoped she wasn't blushing. She'd never been able to successfully hide anything from her mother.

Rashid stroked her back in a manner that appeared soothing to the casual observer, but inside he was flexing his shaft, making it bounce around and drive her crazy. The expression on his face was one of utter peace and contentment. Gail wanted to slug him.

Her mother smiled. "That's good. I'm sure you two have a lot to discuss. Rashid, are you staying the night?"

"No, we're leaving. I chartered a plane and it has to be back tonight."

The wretch! Even his voice sounded normal, giving no clue as to what was going on beneath her mother's watchful gaze.

Gail bit her lip. Her orgasm was getting close. She absolutely refused to have one in front of her mother. She dug her nails into his shoulders, signaling him to get rid of her.

Her mother's face fell into lines of disappointment. "You'll be staying for dinner at least, won't you? The children need to eat."

"We have a few hours before we need to depart. There's plenty enough time for dinner. Besides, Gail needs to feed this little one, as well." He used one hand to cup her rounding stomach.

Satisfied, her mother turned to leave. Rashid stopped her. "Has my wife been eating well? Has she been taking care of herself?"

"I've been making her eat. For the last three weeks, she's done nothing but eat and sleep. Finally put back on some of the weight she lost."

"I can tell." He grabbed Gail by the hips and bounced her a few times on his lap, careful to keep her skirt in place. Gail's eyes tried to roll back into her head as she bounced up and down on his cock. "She's heavier. Whatever you're feeding her, it's doing the trick."

Her mother beamed at the compliment. "Let me get back to the kitchen before I burn dinner. Food will be ready in ten minutes," she said as she headed for the door.

The minute her back was turned, Rashid reached down and pinched Gail's clit, startling a shriek out of her that she quickly muffled against his chest.

"Did you say something, Gail?" her mother asked, turning back to face them.

"No, ma'am."

"I must be hearing things." Her mother shook her head and left the porch, for good this time.

Gail bit Rashid on the chest, hard.

He wrapped his hand in her hair and pulled her head away from his pectoral muscle. His mouth crushed hers as his arm wrapped around her waist, locking her to him. He pumped furiously into her until they both came.

She lay panting against his chest. "You...are...so...evil. I can't believe you did that."

A wicked laugh was his only response.

Five years later...

"Watch me, Godma!" He gave a mighty Tarzan yell that ended with a huge splash.

"Jamal! No more cannonballs. You almost landed on your sister's head."

"But Mom, I had to show Godma Crystal what I could do."

"Yeah, Mom. He had to show Crystal what he could do," came the laughing comment from behind her.

"Uncle Greg! Uncle Greg!" The ringing chorus came from the three children frolicking in the pool.

"Greg! You made it." Gail leaned to the side to see behind him. "Did you bring her?"

"Yes, I brought her. She's in the room, getting changed."

"Uncle Greg! Watch me do a cannonball." Jamal tugged on Greg's pants leg until he gained his attention.

Greg crouched down to his level. "Okay, but try not to hit your sisters. I actually like them."

"Yeah, they're okay for girls."

Greg ruffled his water slick hair. "Show me what you got, slick."

"Watch out below!" Jamal jumped into the pool, leaving his sisters scrambling to get out of the way.

"Rashid, do something about your son," she commanded as he dropped into the seat beside hers.

"He executed a perfectly brilliant cannonball. He doesn't need any help from me," Rashid said.

"Oooo! You know what I mean." Gail tried to hit him, but he caught her hand and brought it to his mouth, kissing her fingers. Then he opened her hand and slowly licked her palm, eyes at half-mast.

Gail gasped and then moaned. Though they'd been married for over five years, he still could get her wet with just a look from those sultry, dark eyes.

"Hey, none of that! There are children present," Greg shouted, breaking the sexual tension between Gail and Rashid.

Rashid grinned, showing all of his teeth. "You, my friend, are jealous. Where's this woman we've heard so much about? It's about time you got your own and stop lusting after mine."

"You're just mad because you know she wants me in return," Greg teased.

Gail laughed. The two men had become great friends over the last few years. They frequently spent time with Greg in California, and he stayed with them whenever he was in town visiting. He'd been present at the birth of their last child, Angel, and as her godfather, had been given the privilege of naming her.

John Singleton dropped into the chair beside Crystal. "The meat's almost done. When I take the ribs off the grill, I'll lower the flame and you can bring out the chicken."

"Oh, good. I'm starving," Crystal told him.

John was Crystal's husband, a minister she met in Nevada. The two had been married for over a year and were expecting their first child. So far, so good. Crystal was in her sixth month and having no complications. The doctors didn't expect any, either. Gail was so happy for her.

"I'll get the chicken." She rose to her feet.

"I'll help." Rashid followed.

"Man, we'll never get it, now. I'm warning you, if you're in there too long, I'm coming in after you," Greg informed them.

Laughing, Gail turned and almost plowed into a pretty brunette. "Oh, I'm so sorry. You must be Leslie. Greg's told us so much about you."

Greg came over and stood by his fiancé. "Sweetheart, this is Gail and the brute standing beside her is her husband, Rashid. The pregnant lady is Gail's friend, Crystal, and the man next to her is her husband, John."

A blur flew out of the pool and attached itself to his leg. "And this little beauty is my goddaughter, Angel. Angel, say hi to Ms. Leslie."

Large brown eyes peeped out from behind his leg. "Hi, Ms. Lelly."

"Oh, what a precious angel," Leslie said.

Rashid snorted. "More like a—"

Gail slapped a hand over his mouth. "Ear's listening." She nodded at Angel.

He licked her palm and she snatched her hand away. "Nice meeting you, Leslie. Have a seat. Make yourself at home. We don't stand on formalities here. Excuse us. We're on our way to get the chicken for the grill."

She stepped around the couple and towed Rashid with her to the kitchen. He immediately backed her into the counter and lowered his head for a kiss. Gail wrapped her arms around his neck and poured all of her love into it. When they broke apart, they were both panting.

Gail leaned her forehead against his chest. "Are you sure you're okay with Crystal being here?" She knew the answer but needed to hear it again to be sure.

Rashid tipped up her chin so she could look him in the eye. "I was okay with it when you asked, and I'm fine with it now. She means nothing to me, but if having her here makes you happy then it makes me happy as well."

311

It had taken time, but she and Crystal had managed to work out their differences. Some would call her a fool for allowing this woman back into her life, but how could she not? Because of Crystal, she was married to a wonderful man and had three beautiful children.

The friendship they had now was much stronger than the previous one, now that there weren't any lies and jealousy getting in the way. Crystal had received the help she needed and met a wonderful man in the process. She'd confessed that being with John had taught her what true love is. Best of all, Crystal had matured over the last few years and was a much more caring individual, not as self-centered as she used to be.

"You know, I've been thinking. We should have another baby."

"What! No. Absolutely not." She pushed away from him and went to the fridge.

"But we make such pretty ones and we can certainly afford it," he said.

"No, Rashid." She grabbed the pan of chicken and used her hip to close the refrigerator before setting the pan on the counter top.

"Think about it. We'll discuss it later."

Gail reached up into the cabinet and pulled down an extra roll of foil and the extra pan she'd purchased for the cooked chicken. "There's nothing to discuss. I said no, and that's final."

She walked out of the kitchen with the items and didn't see the gleam in his eyes.

◆ ◆ ◆ ◆ ◆

Later that night, she lay spread eagle, tied to the bed, panting. "Rashid, let me come. You're killing me."

He glanced up from his position between her thighs. "Not until you agree to another pregnancy."

"Rashid! I can't believe you're...ahhh! Do that again!"

His mouth hovered over her clit. Her body trembled and shuddered beneath him. "Will you give me another baby if I do?"

"Yes, yes. Anything you say. Just don't stop what you're doing."

He grinned. "I thought you'd see things my way," he said, and lowered his head.

A long time later, before drifting off to sleep, she told him, "This is absolutely the last one."

He smiled in the dark. "We'll see."

About the Author

Zena Wynn is a multi-published author of erotic and sensual romance in various romance subgenres: Interracial, Contemporary, Paranormal, Sci-Fi/Fantasy, and Inspirational. She writes the type of stories she loves to read—stories with great characters who, through love and determination, overcome all the challenges that come their way. Her heroes and heroines are passionately, lovingly, devoted to each other. Zena wants her characters to stick with readers long after "The End."

To learn more about Zena Wynn, visit her website: www.zenawynn.com. Connect with her on Facebook: https://www.facebook.com/zenawynn. Or contact her by email: zenawynn@yahoo.com.

Beyond the Breaking Point
© 2013

Breaking point. Everyone has one. For Dr. Cassidy Brannon it was discovering her husband, Phillip, in a compromising position with his best friend Max's almost fiancée, Amber, while vacationing with the other couple. Angry and heartbroken, she and Max indulge in a night of drunken, vindictive sex. The next day, Cassidy returns home with one goal in mind— divorce.

However, nothing goes as planned. Phillip, hell bent on fixing their marriage, won't agree to a divorce. What was only meant to be one, never to be spoken of again, night with Max is evolving into something much more complicated. Then Cassidy discovers she's pregnant. With both Max and Phillip adamantly claiming to be the father, how much more can Cassidy take before she's pushed beyond the breaking point?

Broken
© 2014

Max Desalvo is a broken man. Two years ago he gave his heart, soul and body to another man's wife, Cassidy Brannon. And, he'd thought, his child. They'd made promises, vows. One year. One year for Cassidy to secure her freedom, so they could be together. Unable to be in the same city with Cassidy and not see her, hear her voice, or touch her, Max left. While gone he waited, waited, and waited for the call that never came.

Now he's returned to Philly, his home. Running into Cassidy was inevitable, but she isn't the woman he remembers. If he's broken, she's shattered. And Phillip, her husband is dead. Why hadn't Cassidy contacted him once she was free? And why does she gaze at him with eyes full of hurt and mistrust, as though he were the one to break her heart?

Max has a choice. Discover the truth of what happened and reclaim the love he's lost or forever remain...broken.

To Jon, With Love
© 2014

How does a young wife save her marriage when her husband's half a world away?

When Evie signed on to be Mrs. Lieutenant Jonathan McCoy, she knew his military career and imminent deployment came with the package. Then Jon left, the months passed, and Evie discovered being a soldier's wife is a lot more difficult than she'd believed. She and her husband communicate, but nothing much is being said. Unwilling to burden her husband with her fears for their marriage and with no one else she can talk to, Evie's at her wits end.

Then her mother forcefully suggests Evie attend one of the military wives' support meetings. Reluctantly, Evie goes and the advice they give her shocks Evie with its simplicity—write Jon a letter. Can a handwritten letter really save her marriage? And if it works, will she be able to hold it together until her soldier comes home?

Naughty Seductions: The Naughty Student
© 2014

When Serena Smith uses a creative writing assignment to needle her straight-laced, uptight English professor, she knows she's playing with fire. Can she handle the consequences her naughty actions inspire?

Nina Chronicles 1: Nina's Dilemma
© 2014

Nina Wallace is your typical American woman. A divorced mother of two, she draws strength from her faith in God. Fellowship with her church family keeps loneliness at bay. If, sometimes in the deepest dark of night, she wished a pair of strong, male arms held her tight, she suppresses the desire. Nina has been there, done that, and still bore the scars from her last disastrous relationship. As a result, she's more than content to wait on God to send love her way.

Suddenly, Nina has three men vying for her attention: Roberto, Ronald, and Timothy. Which one will Nina choose? More importantly, which man is God's choice for her? Faith, like love, is a matter of the heart. But what's a woman to do when she no longer trusts her heart?

Nina Chronicles 2: Worth Fighting For?
© 2014

Just because Nina has finally let go of the past doesn't mean the past has let go of her. Love doesn't come easy and sometimes you have to fight for what you want. Will Nina determine that the love and happiness she's found with Roberto is Worth Fighting For?

Books by Zena Wynn

True Mates
Mary and the Bear
Nikolai's Wolf
Tameka's Smile
Carol's Mate
Claiming Shayla
Rome's Pride

Nina Chronicles 1: Nina's Dilemma
Nina Chronicles 2: Worth Fighting For?

Beyond the Breaking Point
Broken

Fantasy Island: Mya's Werewolf
Fantasy Island: Cyn's Dragon
Fantasy Island: Fantasy Man

To Jon, With Love
The Contract
Illicit Attraction
A Matter of Trust
The Question
Seduced by a Wolf
Reclaiming Angelica
Naughty Seductions: The Naughty Student
Reyna's Vampyr

Made in the USA
Las Vegas, NV
03 August 2021